MW01491017

Wild Bill Rides Again

Jim Antonini

Copyright © 2023 Jim Antonini

All rights reserved. No part of this book may be reproduced or transmitted in any form or by any means, electronic or mechanical, including photocopying, recording or by any information storage and retrieval system without permission in writing from the publisher.

Pump Fake Press — Morgantown, WV
Paperback ISBN: 979-8-218-24055-4
eBook ISBN: 979-8-218-24056-1
Library of Congress Control Number: 2023915860
Title: *Wild Bill Rides Again*
Author: Jim Antonini
Digital distribution | 2023
Paperback | 2023
Book front cover painting by Chris Antonini.

This is a work of fiction. The characters, names, incidents, places, and dialogue are products of the author's imagination, and are not to be construed as real.

Dedication

I would like to thank Chris Antonini for the artwork and Geoffrey C. Fuller for the editorial and writing advice.

Chapter 1
Pennsylvania

Day One. Thursday, April 27. 6:04 AM

The day started like all the rest. It was early, a Thursday morning in late April. As his wife slept, Bill Moreland dressed in the dark, like he had for the past twenty-eight years. He thought of nothing. His mind was empty, on life support. He was spent. An hour-long, always boring and sometimes frustrating, commute to his job at New Citizens Bank in Pittsburgh awaited him. He could never understand how it took an hour to travel twenty-five miles in the morning but an hour and a half to travel the same route back in the evening. On that morning, his fiftieth birthday, as he waited for the coffee to brew, he estimated that he commuted about two and a half hours a day, five days a week, for twenty-eight years, or roughly seven-hundred-fifty days. Knowing he had wasted that much time of his life commuting to a job that drained his soul was a heavy pill to swallow.

It's not that Bill wasn't successful. He'd taken a job at the bank soon after graduating college. It was the only place he'd ever worked. He started out as a teller before becoming a loan officer, then loan manager. He was quickly promoted to vice president of investments. By the time he turned forty-five, he was bank president, the second highest ranking official. He rose quickly because he did good work, but also because he was humble, loyal, and well-liked by everybody from the janitors to the receptionists to the bank's investors. He was quiet and known to be naïve, mostly keeping to himself and staying out of the workplace drama. Most importantly, he was intelligent,

1

especially when it came to finance and investments. He'd made himself and the bank's investors a great deal of money through the years.

From the start, though, a lavish lifestyle was never important to Bill. He would have been perfectly happy in the country, living in a modest house, driving a reasonably priced, fuel-efficient car and sending his kids to public schools. But his wife, Rita, and his two kids, Susie and Tommy, felt differently. They needed the biggest house in the best and most exclusive neighborhood, the newest luxury cars, and the most elite private schools. Bill always felt invisible at his family's social events, usually ignored by their friends and acquaintances. With few friends of his own, he often walked his cavernous home alone late or very early as if he were a ghost, having died years before. He found it harder to keep friends as he got older. His one-time close buddies were still around, but most had become more strangers than friends.

xxx

The first thirty minutes of Bill's commute that morning was a blur. Like most days, he hadn't remembered much to that point in the drive. It had become all too familiar. He was on auto-pilot. He'd just turned onto Interstate 279, a bypass highway that led directly into downtown Pittsburgh. There he would usually first encounter the heavy morning traffic. He eased into a slow-moving line of commuters and delivery trucks. Car horns blared. Both lanes were gridlocked. An oversized electronic sign blinked a warning that read, "Bridge work, heavy traffic, long delays expected." Bill sighed and glanced into the rearview mirror. He reached for his phone and dialed his administrative assistant. His most important meeting of the year was scheduled that morning.

"Sandy, can you re-schedule the investor meeting this morning? I'm going to be late."

"How late? Some of the investors are already here."

2

"The interstate's backed up. There's construction on one of the bridges. It could be an hour."

"But the meeting is about the bank merger."

"I know what the meeting's about."

"They have other offers."

"I know. I know. There's nothing I can do."

"The investors want to get this done this morning. You know how impatient they can be."

"Can Alex sit in for me?"

"He's out."

"Out?"

"On vacation."

"He's always on vacation."

"Can you do the meeting from your phone?"

"I don't have the quarterly reports or the other bank's portfolio with me."

"What do you want me to tell them?"

"Can you stall them?"

Bill turned off his phone and slammed it on the seat. He gazed out the front windshield. Nothing moved. He glanced in the rearview. Traffic was backed up for miles. He squeezed the steering wheel and rested his head on it. Suddenly, his car engine loudly belched, the engine coughed and sputtered. He checked the gas gauge. The tank was full. White smoked poured from the front of the hood.

Bill shut off the engine and hopped out of the car, leaving the door open. The cars and trucks stuck in traffic behind him pounded their horns as the traffic ahead started to move. He lifted the hood. A thick cloud of smoke poured from the radiator. He glanced up and peered in each direction. The car and truck horns bellowed louder. He searched for relief, but no one offered to help.

He ripped off his sport coat and hurled it into the front seat before popping the gear shift into neutral. The driver's door propped open, he held the steering wheel, leaned his body into car, and struggled to push the disabled vehicle to the side of the

3

road. Drivers yelled obscenities and flipped their middle fingers as they slowly passed.

"Go on," he yelled, flipping his middle finger. "Go on, you assholes! Go! Nothing at the end of this highway! Nothing! I've been there! I gave up an entire life for it!"

Bill threw himself back into the car and whipped the door shut. He gritted his teeth and raised his arms as if ready to slam the steering wheel. Instead, he took a deep breath and slowly lowered his arms, grabbed the steering wheel. Smoke poured from the engine. Remaining silent, he violently shook the steering wheel until his ringing phone stopped him. He stared at it a moment before finally answering it. It was his wife, Rita.

"Hey," she said without allowing him a chance to respond. "If you have time today, can you log onto Pitt's website and print out an application for Susie. You know she won't do it herself. I would, but I'm busy. And my wine order should arrive sometime later this afternoon. It'll be at the UPS store. You have to go there and pick it up. Because it's wine, they won't deliver it to our house. They need a signature. They're open 'til six. You need to get it today or they send it back to the winery, and I'll still get billed for it. All right, see you tonight."

Bill didn't say a word.

"Oh, and happy birthday," she said. "Maybe we can get something to eat later."

He turned off the phone, chucked it aside, and buried his head in his folded arms.

xxx

Tommy Moreland drove his recently leased Mercedes Benz coup through Pittsburgh morning traffic. It had been given to Tommy in the fall by his father who promised to buy it if Tommy maintained a 3.0 GPA through his freshman year. But Tommy was barely passing. He knew the car was going back to the dealer at the end of the semester. He and Albert, his best friend and fellow fraternity brother, were coming off an all-

4

night bender. Tommy had just turned 21; he and his father shared the same birthday. Tommy and Albert were still drunk and high from an all-nighter.

A can of beer between his legs, Tommy zipped in and out of traffic, impatiently changing from one backed-up lane to another. He loudly revved the engine each time he punched the accelerator, only to slam the brakes when he pulled too close behind another car. He turned up the volume on the car's top-of-the-line sound system and lifted the beer from his lap and chugged the rest of it. He crushed the empty beer can and tossed it in the back seat with the other remains of the night. As a lane of traffic opened, Tommy gunned the car into the clear. He glanced to Albert, whose red glassy eyes were but slits. He looked back to the road. A slow-moving car had suddenly pulled in front of the Mercedes.

"Shit!"

Tommy slammed the brakes and jerked the steering wheel to the right to avoid a collision. The Mercedes veered off the road, roughly bounced onto a sidewalk, and clipped a telephone pole, shearing it in half. The broken end of the pole perilously hung, tangled by wires, over the busy highway. The front end of the Mercedes dipped forward as it flipped over an embankment and soared sideways into a car dealership, striking multiple shiny new Cadillacs. The Mercedes violently landed on its roof, flinging glass and plastic before spinning to a stop.

Dangling upside down, Tommy and Albert hung from their seat belts. The smell of burning rubber filled the air. Shattered glass and leaking engine fluids surrounded the smoking car. Tommy's face was cut and nicked but he didn't feel severely injured. Brushing small pieces of windshield glass from his hair, Tommy looked to his sobbing friend. His face pale, drained of blood, he had pissed himself. His pants and shirt were soaked.

"You all right?" Tommy asked. Albert only nodded silently. "Don't tell my father."

Sirens howled as a pair of police cars squealed into the lot. Blue and red lights flashed. Upside-down and still hanging from the seat belts, Tommy and Albert watched a pair of black leather police boots approach. A single empty beer car dropped from the back seat and rolled out one of the smashed windows. The cop knelt and glared into the window just when several other empty cans suddenly rattled into the parking lot.

xxx

With large sweat marks under his armpits and oil stains on the front of his dress shirt, Bill scowled out the window of his office near downtown Pittsburgh. The sky was a spectacular blue without a cloud in sight. In the bustling city park below, new mothers sipped gourmet coffees and pushed babies in strollers. Fit college students jogged the paths around the park. The dogwoods and cherry trees were draped in white and pink blossoms. The lilies and daffodils, the robins and cardinals, were back after a nearly forgotten winter.

Bill scanned his cramped office. The outdated panel on the walls was dreary, covered with numerous framed certificates nobody cared about and discount department store portraits of forgettable landscapes. He turned back to the window. A radio in the office was tuned to the financial-planning station that provided background to all his mornings. Two almost lifelike men droned the business news of the day in monotone voices. Bill's administrative assistant entered and stared at Bill, a stack of color-coded folders in her hand. He didn't turn or acknowledge her, even though he knew she was there.

"I've been trying to reschedule the meeting, but. . ." Her voice trailed off. Bill didn't respond or turn. "I have the quarterlies and the employee evaluations."

Bill still didn't turn. Instead, he talked into the window.

"I sleep in a box. I drive a box. It brings me to this bigger box where I stare into that box." He motioned to the computer on his cluttered desk. "That all-consuming, life-draining son-of-a-bitch of a box. Every day. All day. That's all I ever do. That's what we *all* ever do. Is that all there is?"

He glanced to her. She showed him no expression.

"I need out of the box."

"We lost the merger," she said.

"I heard." He turned back to the window.

"Alex called. He isn't too happy."

"How do I get out of the box?"

xxx

Bill's commute home was uneventful. The leaky radiator hose had been fixed while he was at work. As he approached his neighborhood, the sun nearly set, darkness was falling fast. Nothing was more depressing than leaving for work in the dark and returning home in the dark. Paralyzed by routine and numb to life, the daily grind no longer tired him. The miles had not only mounted on the dashboard of his car but on his spirit.

He drove into the driveway, looking for Rita's car. He wanted to take her out for dinner to celebrate his birthday, but no car, no Rita. He needed a beer, maybe several of them. His daughter's car was out of the garage, which meant her boyfriend was likely inside the house. Susie rarely left home unless it was to pick up her boyfriend, Chuck. Susie had just turned twenty that winter, and Chuck was six years older. Chuck didn't drive. Bill didn't like Chuck much, felt Chuck smothered his daughter. She wouldn't do anything without him and that included getting a job or going to school. Chuck spent half of his time drunk, and the other half stoned. Other than being tall and somewhat handsome, he was an empty change of clothes with little personality, no energy, and few prospects. He wasn't even interesting.

Carrying a large cardboard box filled with high-end bottles of wine, Bill entered the house. Susie and Chuck were snuggled on the living room couch, watching a movie. Dirty ashtrays and empty beer cans littered the coffee table. The volume on the TV was excessively loud. Bill could barely hear himself think. Neither Susie nor Chuck acknowledged his presence. Bill set down the case of wine, grabbed the television remote, and paused the movie.

"Hey," Susie moaned as Bill moved two full cans of beers from the polished wood surface of an imported coffee table onto drink coasters. "Mom needs a ride."

"She has her car," Bill said, pushing Chuck's extended legs off the table.

"She just called."

"Where is she?"

"Where do you think?"

"Again?"

"You're never home."

"Yeah, it's called a job. You ought to try it sometime." Bill tossed an application packet on the couch beside her.

"What's this?" She reached for the packet.

"It's an application for college. You still have time to submit it for the fall semester. You have no excuse now."

Susie held out her hand for the remote control. Bill hesitated before giving it back. As she restarted the movie, Bill walked into the messy kitchen. Soiled dishes were piled high on each side of the sink. Dirty drink glasses and empty beer cans were scattered everywhere. The trash can overflowed. Bill opened the refrigerator, searching for a snack. It was mostly empty except for an expired carton of milk, a couple of Chinese take-out containers, and an assortment of condiments in the door. He slammed the door shut.

xxx

Bill stood in the corridor outside the entrance to the country club bar. Before entering, he watched his wife sip from an oversized martini glass. Although a long-time member of the club, he rarely visited. Years before he would take his wife and kids to the pool or play golf or tennis with a friend or colleague.

But recently, Rita was the only one in the family who regularly took advantage of the club's amenities. She enjoyed the daily happy hour as well as the parties exclusively held for the club's members throughout the year. Over the past few months, she had become friends with several regulars of the happy hour crowd who hung out there multiple days each week. Bill's visits to the club now were mostly limited to picking her up as she was often too inebriated to drive. It usually took him an hour and a couple more drinks before he could get her out of there.

Bill lingered at the bar entrance. He watched Rita giggle and with a young married couple, Brent and Ashley Spence. They were twenty years younger than she was. The young man flirted with her, even with his attractive wife by his side. Rita openly flirted back, occasionally touching his knee that practically rested in her lap or tapping his arm that was stretched out on the bar beside her. She loved the attention. And the regulars and bartenders loved her. She was well-known for buying multiple rounds of drinks over the course of a visit and leaving large tips at the end of the night.

As Bill hesitantly stepped into the bar to retrieve his wife, his phone rang. He checked the number as he backed out of the bar and into the lobby. The number was local but unfamiliar. His initial thought was to not answer it, but he did, sensing it may be important. The call was brief. It was the Pittsburgh city police. Rita would not be the only family member who needed to be retrieved that night.

After ending the call, Bill stomped into the bar. When Rita and her two friends spotted him approaching, their conversation abruptly stopped as if they were talking about him or about something he wasn't supposed to hear. The silence grew awkward as Bill joined them at the bar. Rita glanced to Bill before turning away and reaching for her drink.

"Rita, we need to go."

"Settle down." She deliberately sipped the last of her martini. "Get a drink. Relax a minute."

"We need to go. Now."

"I'm not ready." She nodded to the bartender and pushed her empty glass towards him.

"We really have to leave," he said, motioning to the bartender not to make the drink.

"Come on, Bill," Brent spoke up. "Get a drink. This one's on me."

"Thanks, but we really have to go." He looked at the bartender and shook his head before turning to Rita. "Can I speak with you in private?"

Rita first glanced to the bartender, then looked to the young couple beside her.

"I'll be right back," she said, adding in a voice loud enough for the bartender to hear. "And, I'm having that martini."

Bill helped her off the barstool. She was a little unsteady on her feet as she reluctantly followed him to the lobby.

"How many drinks have you had?" he asked.

"What is it? My friends are waiting."

"Tommy got arrested. It's more serious this time. We need bail him out."

She stared at him a moment, wordlessly, before she turned away and stepped back into the bar.

"Rita," he called out, following her. "We need to go."

"Not until I have one more drink," she said, not turning as he chased after her.

As Rita chugged her last large vodka martini of the night in two large gulps, Bill paid her tab. He then helped her out of the bar. She was noticeably drunk, leaning into him as he held her tightly so she wouldn't fall. He practically dragged her across the parking lot to his Buick. He opened the passenger side door for her and eased her into the seat, lifting her legs and rotating her body so she faced the front windshield before closing the door. He turned out of the parking lot, heading towards downtown Pittsburgh, away from their home. Rita sat up and squinted.

"Where are you going?"

"To pick up Tommy."

"Take me home."

"You're coming with me."

"Take me home first."

"But that's over twenty-five miles out of the way."

"Take me home. I'm not feeling well."

"No, you're coming with me."

"Take me home!" she hollered but he didn't respond. "Stop the car!"

"I'm not stopping the car. You're coming with me."

"I need you to stop the car!" she shouted, reaching for the door handle. "Stop the goddamn car, Bill!"

He glanced to her. The color had drained from her face. She placed her hand on her belly. Sweat beaded on her forehead. She swallowed hard several times as if trying to keep something down. She repeatedly smacked her lips.

"Bill! Stop the car! Now!"

He eased the car off the road as she swung the passenger side door open. Before the Buick came to a full stop, she flopped out of the car and onto her hands and knees on the gravel and violently vomited for several minutes.

"Happy birthday to me," he mumbled and got out of the car to collect his wife, who was still collapsed on the ground.

xxx

Bill parked near his garage door, got out and hurried to the passenger side door. He helped his wobbly wife out of the car, and she leaned against the car while he darted ahead to open the front door of the house. He could hear the TV blasting from the living room, where his daughter and her worthless boyfriend probably hadn't moved since he left. As he held the door, Rita awkwardly staggered towards him, her purse dangling from one hand and her shoes in the other. The palms of her hands were dirty, and her knees were cut and scraped. Finally, inside the house, she tossed her shoes down the hallway and their banging against the wall drew Susie's and Chuck's attention.

"What's wrong with Mom?" Susie asked without getting off the couch.

Bill didn't respond as Rita tromped unsteadily up the stairs, tightly gripping the banister, oblivious to the world. Once she safely topped the stairs, Bill turned to the front door.

"Where you going now?" Susie asked.

Bill turned and stared at her and Chuck. "There's more to the world than that couch and those crummy movies, you know. I heard the city can be a lot of fun on a Thursday night."

"We know, Dad," she said with a shrug, "but where you going?"

"Tommy got arrested."

"He fall off the frat house roof drunk again?"

"I wish that's all it was."

xxx

Bill rarely raised his voice. His kids had only seen him angry a handful of times. It was Rita who often disciplined Susie and Tommy when they were out of line. But Tommy knew he was in big trouble, and he was expecting the worst possible reaction from his dad as he had been warned multiple times about his excessive drinking, dangerous driving, and poor decision making. If Tommy had a choice, he'd rather have spent the night in jail with a group of hardened criminals than get bailed out by his father.

Tommy's prediction was correct. Bill was furious, so furious that he didn't speak or acknowledge Tommy the entire time it took to process and bail him out of jail. Once Tommy was free to go, he nearly had to sprint to keep up with his father, who briskly walked away. After about fifteen minutes of silence, Bill finally spoke—and he didn't stop talking for the rest of the drive home.

"They've taken your license away, and you're never getting another car from me! And as of tonight, you're out of the fraternity house and coming back home. And you better not

12

ever set foot in that shithole place again."

"What about my things?"

"Screw your things! You're not going back there."

"But I need my clothes, my textbooks, my—"

"You're not going back there," Bill yelled, interrupting him. "So, figure out a way to get them. *You are not going back there!*"

"How will I get to class?"

"That's another thing you'll need to figure out. Your mother's home. Your sister's home. There's also Chuck. He ain't got anything going on. I don't know. There's a local bus that goes in and out of the city from our neighborhood every day. Take the goddamn bus! I don't freakin' know. That's your problem."

"But—"

"*Don't say a word.* Got that? Not another goddamn word. There's nothing I want to hear from you now." Bill grabbed a sheet of paper from the dashboard that listed the many charges that were filed against Tommy. "What in the hell were you thinking?" Bill looked back and forth to the road and the charges on the list. "Reckless driving. Destruction of property. Driving under the influence. Possession of a controlled substance. And it goes on and on!"

Bill angrily wadded the rap sheet and tossed it at his son.

"You're lucky you didn't kill someone. Or yourself. *Jesus Christ!*"

"Dad, let m—"

"Don't say another *damn* word! You just turned twenty-one, dude. You're on your own now. I will never bail you out of jail or anything else ever again. You got that? Do you? *Do you?*"

At first reluctant, Tommy finally nodded sheepishly before looking away.

"So, don't even think about calling me ever again when you're in trouble. *You got that?*"

xxx

Bill turned off the overhead light and quietly tiptoed into the master bedroom. Rita lightly snored. He stared at her a moment before untangling the bedsheets and blankets wrapped around her legs and body and re-covering her. Because it was unseasonably warm that night, he opened the windows to allow the fresh spring air to blow away the stale air that had built up after the long winter.

At the dresser, he pulled open the top drawer and retrieved a sealed box of Cuban cigars, a recent gift from one of the bank's biggest investors. From another drawer, he lifted an unopened bottle of rare, high-end bourbon, also a gift but from one of the bank's board of directors. He'd hidden the bottle in the dresser because Tommy surely would have taken it if he knew it was in the house.

A framed family photograph from years before caught his attention. He studied the photo for many minutes, slowly running his index finger over Rita's smiling face, over the happy faces of his two children. With a sigh, he turned to his sleeping wife and again stared at her. Moving to the bed, he softly patted her on the head and gently brushed his lips across hers before leaving the room with the cigars, whiskey, and photograph.

Remembering it was his fiftieth birthday, he dragged a lawn chair from the garage into the middle of his rarely used backyard to enjoy the rest of the beautiful evening. The framed photograph under his folded arm, he carried the cigars and whiskey. Until that night, he'd had little reason or time—at least he thought—to enjoy them. He unfolded the lawn chair and set the photo on the ground beside him. He cracked the seals on both the bourbon and the box of cigars.

The other houses in the neighborhood were blacked out and quiet except for his. The peacefulness of the evening was disrupted by his own family. The annoying soundtrack of the cheesy movie his daughter and her boyfriend watched blared from the living room. His son, who had yet to show any remorse for his unlawful transgressions from earlier, had locked himself in his bedroom, playing a violent video game;

explosions and repetitive machine gun fire echoed from the house.

Unable to appreciate the solitude and serenity of the moment, Bill took a deep breath before placing the box of cigars in the lawn chair and resting the bottle of whiskey in the grass, wet from the evening's dew. Without much thought, he quietly slipped through the darkness and entered a side door that led to the garage and down a flight of stairs to the basement. At the fuse box, he didn't hesitate as he hit a breaker and shut off the power to the entire house. A collective shout rang out in unison after the house immediately went dark and silent.

Impassive, Bill quickly retreated to the lawn chair that stood alone in the manicured yard and reached for the cigars and the bourbon. A balmy breeze blowing from the south tickled his face. He savored the honey-sweet scent of tulips, daffodils, and lilac that hung in the spring night air. He nearly filled a pint glass full of whiskey and lit a cigar. Taking several deep and satisfying puffs off the cigar, he leaned back in the chair and stared to the heavens. He never noticed the stars from his backyard before. They appeared as diamonds in the sky, close enough to touch. Sitting below them, looking up, he felt a sense of smallness and insignificance. He wondered, as he often did, if his life to that point was a waste. But unlike those other times, a feeling of calm overcame him. It was a calm he hadn't experienced since he was a much younger man. He didn't let the frustrated and helpless chants of his kids, or the horrible and embarrassing events of the day, distract his suddenly uncluttered mind as he enjoyed the bold cigar and the heavy pour of bourbon.

"*Dad! Dad!*" he heard his kids calling from inside the house, over and over. "*Dad? Where are you?*"

After losing himself to the monotony of everyday life for the past few decades, Bill knew he had to make a change before it was too late. He had no idea what he needed to do, but he had to do something, and he had to do it soon. He still had a little soul left, and because there was so very little, he didn't have time to waste.

xxx

Day 2. Friday, April 28. 5:10 PM

With the framed family photograph that he took from his bedroom the night before prominently displayed on his desk, Bill smoked one of the Cuban cigars in his office. He knew it was against the bank's 'No Smoking Policy,' but he figured no one would say anything as most of the employees had left for the day. The bank's main office had just closed for the weekend. His assistant, Sandy, suddenly entered the office.

"I thought I smelled something burning," she said. "I didn't know you smoked."

"I'm just happy it's Friday, I guess," Bill said and stubbed out the cigar in an ashtray he'd brought with him to work that morning.

"Any plans?"

"I'm not sure yet. I'm thinking of going for a long drive somewhere."

"Where to?"

"Don't know. How 'bout you?"

"Roy and I are going to try that new tapas restaurant in Squirrel Hill."

"I heard it's great."

"Yeah, and I guess, authentic. We've never had real Spanish food before."

"You'll have to tell me how it is."

She nodded and stared at him a moment.

"You okay, Bill?" she asked. "You haven't seemed yourself the past few days."

"I'm fine. Just a little tired. A drive away from here will do me good."

Sandy turned, but before she could leave, he called out: "Thanks for everything."

16

"Huh?" She turned, puzzled.

"I couldn't have done this job without you. You're the best."

"Is this about the merger?" she asked, continuing to study him. "Don't sweat it. I know Alex is upset. He'll get over it. There'll be more opportunities."

"It's not that."

"I'll see you Monday morning, Bill."

"Yeah, sure."

After Sandy left the building, Bill glanced to the clock on his desk. It read 5:30. He was alone in the bank. As bank president, he was responsible for closing the building each evening. This included ensuring the bank was empty of people, securing all the cash on the premises, locking the building's access doors and vault, and importantly, activating the after-hours security system. Bill had done this just about every night for the last ten years.

He slowly walked the quiet hallways of the bank's office area, checking to make sure all the office doors were closed and locked. He grabbed his paycheck from his employee mailbox and stuffed it in his pocket. He was the only employee who received a check as opposed to receiving his pay by direct deposit. It gave him a sense of achievement to physically hold the check and appreciate the amount of money the bank was paying him to work there. Leaving the mail area, he entered the bank vault and stared at trays filled with over a million dollars in cash that were stacked to the ceiling. The bank had an unusually large deposit that day from a new business account.

Like every other night, he stepped out of the vault and began to push the heavy, reinforced-steel door closed. But he stopped. He glanced over his shoulder before hurrying to another part of the bank, leaving the vault door open. He weaved through the corridors of the bank's two floors, turning off the lights in each hallway. He backtracked through the same halls but under the cover of darkness. He knew the blind spots of the security cameras from years of experience and carefully stayed out of their roving eyes. He finally entered the security control room.

He shut off two switches: The first controlled the entire security system, including cameras and alarms, and the second, only known to him and the bank's director of security, served as backup in case of a malfunction or a power outage. It was wired to a separate power source.

After disabling the security system, Bill rushed back to the vault like a shadow at midnight and grabbed several trays filled with bundled stacks of cash. With the trays, he dashed to his office where he opened a closet and retrieved two garment travel bags that contained changes of clothes he kept at the bank. He dumped out one of the garment bags—its contents mostly workout clothes he wore to the gym—and filled it with the cash. Without emptying the second garment bag, he filled it with the rest of the money. He then fired up his computer and accessed his personal bank accounts. He made a few transactions before aggressively swiping the computer, its monitor and keyboard, and everything else off the desk. The computer crashed to the floor, cracking the monitor's screen. As he retrieved the empty trays that once held the cash, he stomped on the computer keyboard and smashed it into pieces. He violently slammed one of the plastic trays on the top of his desk. Chips of desktop wood and plastic tray flew. He chucked the tray aside and ripped open the top drawer of his desk and rummaged through it until he found a letter opener, a very dull letter opener.

Closing his eyes, he plunged the pointed end into the fleshy part of his right hand. He let out a wall-melting scream as blood gushed from the jagged gash and dripped on his desk. Feeling like he may pass out from the pain, he took several deep gasps. After regaining his composure, he gathered the empty trays and hustled back to the vault, leaving a trail of blood on the floor. At the vault, he tossed the blood-stained trays inside. He quickly returned to his office, collected the garment bags, grabbed the cigars, and headed for the door. But before leaving the room, he glanced back to the rubble of items from his desk on the floor and reached for the photograph of his family. The frame's glass had been cracked. Taking the photo with him, he rushed down a flight of stairs to a parking garage, making sure to run his bloody hand down the railing.

With his body hunched over and hiding his face between the garment bags, he slinked through the parking lot and slipped into his car. He propped the garment bags up in the passenger seat and placed a Pittsburgh Pirates ball cap on the headrest to make it look as if someone was riding with him. He made sure to squeal his tires as he sped out of the garage and into the busy rush hour streets of downtown Pittsburgh.

xxx

A filthy taxicab appeared out of place as it rounded one of the many cul-de-sacs in the exclusive neighborhood in which the Moreland family lived. Rita got out of the back and slammed the door. She shuffled to the front porch of her palatial home, turned, and scanned the quiet neighborhood. It was nearly eleven o'clock. Nothing stirred. Several of the homes were dark as most of the neighbors had already turned in for the evening. A lone dog could be heard barking in the distance. Bill's Buick was nowhere in sight.

Rita unlocked the front door and entered. Tommy, his body nearly engulfed in the cushiony sectional sofa of the living room, stared trance-like at the large screen of the TV as he played a car-racing video game. The volume of the game was blisteringly loud. The sound of squealing tires and revving engines blared throughout the house. A nearly empty two-liter bottle of cola sat on the table in front of him. The skunky smell of marijuana smoke lingered. He didn't acknowledge his mother.

"Have you seen your father?" she called over the noise, but he didn't respond.

She wandered to the large picture window in the living room and studied the front yard and driveway. She peered out for many minutes.

19

"This is not like him." She shook her head. "He always answers his phone."

Suddenly, a car approached the cul-de-sac and appeared in the driveway. Rita sighed, looking relieved, and rushed to the front door. But it wasn't Bill. It was Susie.

"The strangest thing just happened," Susie said, entering the house. "I went to use my credit card to pay for dinner with Chuck, and it was denied."

"Denied? The one your father gave you?"

"We tried to take out cash with my debit card. It didn't work either."

"Your father didn't come home," Rita said, moving back to the living room window and staring out. "I'm worried. If I don't hear from him in the next hour or so, I'm calling the police."

"He's fine, Mother," Susie said, joining her at the window. "He likely stopped for a drink or a bite to eat. He's done that before. You know how stressed he's been."

"He always answers his phone."

"Maybe he forgot it at work. He's done that before, too."

"No. This feels different." She turned to her daughter.

"It'll be all right, Mom."

"Bring me my purse," Rita said. "I need my phone. I'm calling the police."

xxx

Bill knew he had about a 12-hour head start before Rita would realize he wasn't coming home. She'd likely notify the authorities. His goal was to reach Florida by daybreak. Leaving the city via the Fort Pitt tunnel, his hands noticeably shook as he tightly grasped the steering wheel. He kept checking the rear-view mirror and glancing over his shoulder. Sweat poured from his forehead. No one followed. As he merged onto I-79 and headed south, he struggled to keep himself calm enough to maintain the posted speed limits. He couldn't afford to get pulled over, or his journey would end before it got started. The cut from the self-inflicted gash continued to bleed, soaking the cuff and sleeve of the right arm of his shirt. Some of the blood had dripped onto his lap. He continually took deep breaths as he tried to remain calm. The traffic thinned the further he traveled away from downtown Pittsburgh. He constantly scanned each side of the highway for state troopers.

After an hour's white-knuckled ride from Pittsburgh, he spotted the state of West Virginia welcome sign in the distance. It felt as if a two-ton boulder had been lifted off his shoulders. He loudly exhaled, draining all the air from his lungs. Juiced from the sudden release of adrenaline into his bloodstream once he crossed the Pennsylvania line into West Virginia, he let out a scream that made his ears ring. He chased the evening sun as it set over the lush verdant hills of West Virginia. He rolled down the windows, filling the car with a blast of cooling mountain air.

xxx

Bill pulled the Buick off the highway at a scenic overlook near the small West Virginia town of Weston, high in the winding hills. He took in a deep breath—then suddenly burst into dance, around and around the car, pumping his arms in the air and laughing uncontrollably. Passing truckers honked in salute. Finally, he stopped and gazed one last time over the peaks of the purple mountains in the distance to the glowing orange sky at dusk. He never felt bigger. He was a giant. He was finally free. He intended to find out what was behind those hills.

Back on the road, the bleeding from his hand stopped somewhere near Summersville on U.S. Route 19 south. Blood stained the steering wheel, the car seat, his shirt, and the lap of his pants. He looked as if he had just finished a long shift at a slaughterhouse. He wasn't tired but felt reborn. He pushed through the night over the fog-covered rugged hills of southern West Virginia, to the Big Walker Mountain tunnel and into a short stretch of Virginia and through the East River Mountain tunnel. He didn't slow down until he traveled through North Carolina to South Carolina and stopped in a small town off I-77 called Riverview.

There he tossed his phone in a dumpster next to the gas station. He also took time to clean the cut on his hand and change clothes, leaving the blood-stained ones behind in a different dumpster. He soon found himself back on the highway on an empty stretch of I-26, cruising east through the center of the rural South Carolina landscape until merging onto I-95 south.

A bright, nearly full moon lit the roadway that traveled along the Atlantic shoreline as he sped through the marshlands of Georgia, following a small convoy of trucks. It wasn't until he approached the Florida state line that he noticed the first hint of morning. Low hanging stratus clouds appeared to the east in the morning light, hugging the horizon and splintering the orange glow of the slow rising sun. His suddenly heavy eyes squinted in the early morning haze as he crossed the St. Mary's River into Florida.

xxx

Day 3. Saturday, April 29. 6:35 AM

The sun had just come up. The neighborhood was draped in fog. Rita sat alone in the early morning shadows on the back deck of her house, holding a coffee in one hand and a cigarette in the other. Her eyes and nose were red. She'd been crying most of the night. There had been no word from Bill.

She had slipped out the back unnoticed to escape her house cluttered with strangers. The living room was filled with local police and other authorities from both the state police and sheriff's offices. The driveway and cul-de-sac in front corralled their fleet of vehicles. She'd been interviewed for what seemed like hours by different detectives who asked the same questions, again and again. *What was Bill's current state of mind? Have you noticed any peculiar behavior from him in recent days?* She had nothing for them. Tommy and Susie had retired to their bedrooms sometime in the middle of the night. They too were subjected to the same questions. They also couldn't provide any useful information for the detectives. In the days and weeks leading up to his disappearance, Bill seemed his usual stressed and distant self.

As the neighborhood woke up, curious neighbors, either out for an early morning jog or to walk their dogs, began to assemble in the streets around the Moreland house as multiple police cars shuttled in and out of the driveway, some with their lights flashing. Word had trickled out to the local media and the first television trucks from different news outlets arrived. As Rita huddled by herself in the back trying to hide from the attention and chaos that was building in the neighborhood, Detective Eric Banner who was leading the investigation, a young deputy named Andrew Morton from the sheriff's office, and Alexander Medford, Bill's boss and the CEO at the bank, joined her on the deck. Upon seeing Mr. Medford, she immediately stubbed out a cigarette and stood, greeting him with tight hug before weeping uncontrollably in his arms.

"I'm so sorry, Rita," he said, rubbing her back.

"What happened, Alex?" She pulled away.

"There's no sign of him."

"And his car?"

"No sign of it, either."

"Since we last spoke, Ma'am," Detective Banner said as Rita turned, "we have some more information."

"Is Bill all right?" she asked.

"Are you sure you hadn't noticed any unusual activity or behavior from your husband recently?"

"As I have said over and over again to you all, I haven't noticed anything different."

"No red flags—money issues or the sudden presence of strangers?"

"I said, *no*," she exclaimed. "If you have new information about Bill, I want you to tell me right now!"

"Over a million dollars is missing from the bank," Alex said.

"A million dollars?" She glanced to Alex with a puzzled look.

"And all your accounts at the bank have been mostly emptied."

"Emptied?" She turned to Detective Banner. "And you think Bill took the money?"

Banner and Deputy Morgan shrugged.

"You know Bill," she said to Alex. "He'd never steal from anyone. He's a good man. If he has a fault, he's too honest. *Painfully* honest."

"I know, Rita," Alex said. "That's why this is all so baffling. I've never known a more loyal employee."

Susie appeared on the back deck wearing only a long tee-shirt that did little to cover her shapely body. Both Deputy Morton and Detective Banner stared.

"What about the security cameras?"

"We're actively checking them now, Mrs. Moreland." Morton glanced at Rita, then back to Susie. "We should have more later today."

"Will Dad be all right?" Susie asked, embracing her mother as Rita sobbed in her arms. "And our money's gone?"

"We're using all the resources we have to search for your husband, Mrs. Moreland," Banner said. "Also, I'm letting you know that the FBI has been called and will be helping in the investigation. The lead agent is on his way here as we speak."

"The FBI?" Rita mumbled.

"Now, who'll pay for my cigarettes?" Susie asked as Deputy Morton glanced around before reaching into to his shirt pocket, pulling a cigarette from a pack, and handing it to her.

Chapter 2
Florida

Day 3. Saturday, April 29. 9:52 AM

Having been awake for over twenty-four hours, Bill felt the fatigue starting to set in. He didn't want to rest yet; first, he had to ditch his car. Next, he needed to find another one. He hadn't figured that part out yet, but he did have a bag full of cash and knew money had a way of solving problems. When he exited I-95 and drove into Jacksonville, Florida, it didn't take him long to find a garage that offered long-term parking. He chose one based on its location in a busy retail district with numerous car dealerships in the adjoining blocks. At the gate of the garage's entrance, he was greeted by the attendant.

"Can I help you, sir?"

"I need a long-term parking permit."

"We sell 'em by the month, three months, six months, nine months."

"How much?"

"Two-hundred dollars a month."

"I'll take a three-month permit."

"That'll be six-hundred dollars plus tax," the attendant said, pressing some buttons on a cash register that spit out a thin cardboard permit. He exchanged the permit with Bill for the cash. "Put this in the window when parked here. Use it to lift the gate when you enter and exit."

Bill took the permit before entering the dimly lit five-story garage. The parking spaces on the bottom levels, most likely short-term spots, were filled. More spaces were available as Bill traveled up to the top levels. Many of the cars on the top levels had backed into the parking spots and were even covered by tarps for long-term storage. Finding what he thought to be the perfect spot on the fourth floor, he backed his Buick into an open space between two covered cars. He wanted to hide the back license plate as best he could. He also thought by parking between two cars that likely were being stored would limit the foot traffic around his car. After shutting off the engine, he studied the parking permit and jotted down the garage's address and his car's parking space number on a scrap of paper he slipped into his wallet. He also wrapped a few strips of fresh masking tape around the fleshy wound of his right hand.

He grabbed the garment bags that contained the money, the photograph of his family, and a box of Cuban cigars from the front seat and moved to the back where he opened the trunk. He threw one of the garment bags into the trunk along with the cigars and photograph. He kept the bag that contained both money and a few changes of clothes. He reached for several of the cigars and stared a moment at the family portrait before slamming the trunk closed. He glanced around the empty garage a few times, knelt and hid a set of car keys on a small ledge underneath the back bumper. He popped up and rushed toward the elevator but stopped and looked back. It likely would be the last time he ever saw the Buick.

Bill stepped out of the cool garage and into the hot morning sun. The air was heavier and more humid than what he'd left behind in Pennsylvania. He slung the twenty-five pound garment bag with cash over his shoulder and pulled the Pittsburgh Pirates ball cap low over his eyes to shield his face from the bright sun. He waited for a traffic light to change before crossing a busy four-lane highway to a used car dealership that appeared to be opening for the day. The lot displayed over sixty used cars. The owner watched from the showroom window as Bill methodically walked each aisle of the available cars. The owner remained in the building until Bill stopped and glanced to the showroom, obviously in need of help. In a flash, the owner hurried outside and enthusiastically greeted Bill.

"Can I help you, buddy?" The owner reached out his right hand and noticed Bill's bandaged hand. "I'm Louis Sanders, the owner."

"I need a car," Bill said without looking him in the eyes or shaking his hand.

"Anything in particular?" Mr. Sanders asked, his hand still extended. "We got all the models. We're runnin' some good trade-in deals and financing pla—"

"I need a car immediately," Bill interrupted. Mr. Sanders lowered his hand. "I'll be paying in cash."

"See anything you like?" Mr. Sanders asked, guiding Bill into the aisle of his most expensive models.

"This may seem like a strange question." Bill lowered his voice, still not looking Mr. Sanders in the eye. "Do you have anything in stock you've been wanting to get rid of? Say, something that doesn't quite have all its paperwork."

At first, Mr. Sanders didn't reply. He glanced over his shoulder then studied Bill and his injured hand.

"I don't have a driver's license or insurance," Bill said. His voice cracked and as he nervously fidgeted.

Mr. Sanders stepped closer to Bill, so close Bill could smell the morning coffee on his breath. He glared directly into Bill's eyes. Bill finally looked up and returned the glare, neither blinking nor glancing away from Mr. Sanders.

"I could lose my business license if I—"

"You'll never see me again," Bill interrupted. He continued to hold Mr. Sanders' gaze.

"I should call the cops. Why should I trust you?"

"I'm buying a car today," Bill said. His voice shook, but he was trying to sound confident. "And I know there's someone on this strip who will sell me one for the right price."

Mr. Sanders stepped back from Bill and looked to his showroom, stroking his chin.

"Will you help me? I'll be out of Jacksonville within the

hour."

"I have a highly successful thing goin' here, sir," Mr. Sanders said, shaking his head. "And I'd like to keep it that way."

"You're saving my life, Mr. Sanders. I will make it worth your trouble."

"This may be a mistake, but. . ." he whispered, not looking at Bill. "In the garage, we have a Chevy Equinox. Eight years old. Somewhere around fifty-thousand miles. We got it some time ago at an auction. It must've been stolen or a repo. It has no title, and the VIN number has been removed."

"There's no history on it at all?"

"No history."

"How does it run?"

"It runs fine."

"Can I see it?" Bill intensively studied Mr. Sanders. "Like I said, you'll never see me again."

After some hesitation, Mr. Sanders led Bill to the garage behind the showroom. He pointed at a dusty, black SUV in the corner.

"An Equinox? What'd you pay for it?" Bill asked. Mr. Sanders shrugged, seemingly not wanting to reveal that piece of information as he negotiated a price. "Come on. I want to give you a good deal. What'd you pay for it?"

"Because we got it without a title," he said. He paused. "We paid six-hundred-fifty dollars for the car."

"Sounds like quite a deal."

"Yes, a very good deal."

"I'll give you ten thousand for the car and six-fifty for a temporary tag." Bill started to dig into the garment bag with jittery hands.

Mr. Sanders tried to play it cool, but he couldn't hide the excitement in his eyes.

"This could be one of the best deals you ever made, Mr. Sanders." Bill reached out the stack of money.

With a slight nod, Mr. Sanders took the money and walked to a key display on the garage wall. He plucked a set of keys off a nail and bent down to pull a temporary cardboard license plate from a trash can. Cardboard temp in hand, he strode to the Equinox. He started it and let it run as he attached the temporary plate to the back bumper. At the rear of the garage, he hit a red button on the wall, opening a large automatic door to the lot. He motioned for Bill to come get the car.

"I never want to see you again," he said as Bill slid into the driver's seat. "And you've never been here before. Got it?"

"Have a good day, Mr. Sanders."

"I think I already did."

His hands shaking a little from the risky transaction with Mr. Sanders, Bill put the car in gear and pulled out of the lot into traffic. A celebratory scream, loud enough to be heard as far away as Miami, burst out of him. He had passed his first test. He had a new car. But not allowing himself time to celebrate — or rest or even eat — he'd stayed focused. He drove the Equinox a few blocks before parking in the lot of a big box chain retailer. With the garment bag over his shoulder, he scurried inside to buy a new phone, figuring he would need one for his travels, particularly one that would be hard to track. After checking out several different models, he purchased three prepaid, no-contract phones with cash. He planned to use multiple phones to possibly confuse the authorities who undoubtedly would be searching for him. They may have already started.

Anxious to get back on the road, he followed signs that directed him to I-10 through the downtown streets of the Brooklyn district of Jacksonville. He decided to take the interstate west and head to Texas before making any definitive plans. He might stay a night in New Orleans on the way. That was one place he'd always wanted to visit, but Rita would never allow it as she had been there once before on a work trip. She found the city to be, in her words, "filthy, dangerous, impoverished, and insufferably hot and humid." He'd heard only good things about the city from others and wanted to find out for himself.

As he approached a junction for I-10, the arrow on the sign

pointing in the opposite direction of the interstate was labeled Jacksonville Beach as the destination. Without a second thought, Bill changed course and wheeled the car into the other lane and headed for the beach. He found himself driving east on U.S. Route 90. As he neared the ocean, he scrambled to open the sunroof and all the windows like a giddy little kid, trying to get his first whiff of the healing salty sea air. He first passed a series of inlets and marinas before crossing the Intracoastal Waterway by way of the McCormick Bridge. He continued to follow Route 90, which became Beach Boulevard, for another mile until turning north on State Highway A1A that ran along the Atlantic. After another half mile, he drove past the city pier before spotting what looked to be a diner that advertised an all-day breakfast. Not having eaten since lunch the day before, he pulled into the lot of the eatery, a short walk from the beach.

As he entered, the comforting smells of frying bacon and brewing coffee stopped him in his tracks. Waiting to be seated, he salivated as he scanned the bustling eatery, his stomach growling like an angry dog. The diner's small footprint was divided by a long counter and stools with a continuous series of small booths that lined two side walls, with a plate glass window in the front. An overcommitted waitress got his attention and pointed to the counter as she waited on a young family of four. Bill worked his way through the narrow space crammed with hungry patrons and busy servers and busboys. He squeezed into the last available stool at one end of the counter between the wall and a three-hundred-pound cab driver. He lifted the garment bag over his head and positioned it between his knees to give himself more room at the counter. He made sure to slip one of his legs through the strap as to not forget the bag later. The waitress working the counter hustled over to him with a glass of ice water and a menu.

"Anything else to drink?" she asked, not really looking at him as she checked the other diners at the counter she'd been waiting on.

"Your largest coffee."

Bill had not been this excited to eat in a long time. The waitress quickly returned with a coffee along with creamer and different sweeteners. He studied the menu before glancing up and watching the lone short-order cook work the grill like a maestro, his spatula a conductor's baton. One side of the grill was covered with bacon strips, small cuts of sirloin, and sausage, both links and patties. Mounds of frying cubed potatoes with onions and peppers, some piled as high as four inches, were next to the grilling meats. Bill was mesmerized by the cook's effortless motions as he simultaneously attended to multiple orders of omelets and fried eggs on the other side of the grill.

As Bill waited to order, he fixated on the scores of bacon strips that sizzled and popped with each explosion of grease. The anticipation of his new journey waned a bit, the cooking bacon a reminder of family breakfasts with Rita and the kids. When they were younger, he would cook large—which he considered *legendary*—bacon breakfasts on the weekends. It was a family tradition, particularly on Sunday mornings. For many minutes, his sleepy mind drifted to memories of happier times. With a sunny grin and his eyes closed, he quietly sat at the counter waiting for the server to return. But the chaos of the hectic diner quickly brought him bought back to reality. He couldn't escape his present situation. He was tired, hungry, and suddenly alone. His seat at the diner felt a million miles from home, and even further from those happier days with his family. For the first time since leaving, he wondered if he would ever see them again.

"What are you havin'?" the waitress asked, snapping him out of thought.

"The classic breakfast."

"How'd you like your eggs?"

"Fried. Over easy."

"Grits or home fries?"

"Home fries."

"Toast or a biscuit?"

"Biscuit."

"Sausage or bacon?"

"Sausage. No bacon."

xxx

With a full belly and nearly overwhelmed with exhaustion, Bill staggered to an empty area on the beach, drunk on food. He kicked off his shoes and socks and rolled up his khakis to his knees. Carrying the shoes and garment bag but leaving the socks behind, he settled on a spot of dry sand about twenty feet from the edge of the ocean's rolling waves. He unfolded the garment bag and positioned it like a lounge chair, leaning back on it and lowering the ball cap over his eyes. Within minutes, he fell deeply asleep to the sounds of the pounding waves and the constant call of gulls overhead. His goal was to take a much-needed nap before returning to the road. Even though he had the different car, he knew he couldn't get complacent. He needed to keep moving. He couldn't risk staying in one place for too long.

He probably would have napped all afternoon, but the encroaching waves with the incoming tide gently lapped against his bare feet. The warm water rolled across the dampened sand, and each new wave soaked the lining of his pants. He fell out of his deep sleep and transitioned from light sleep to full wakefulness. But even as the water puddled around him, he didn't open his eyes. His first thoughts were dreamlike — taking the money, leaving his family, and running off to Florida had never really happened. He expected to wake in the comfort of his own bed with Rita by his side, and everything would be normal.

But as his pant legs filled with seawater and the scorching rays of the midday Florida sun burned his exposed skin, he was eased back to reality, gradually waking from the dreamy haze as if lost in a drunken stupor. Somewhat confused, he glanced around a now-crowded beach, trying to figure out where he

32

was. The gawking of seagulls echoed loudly in his head. He twisted his body and spotted the recently purchased Chevy Equinox parked in the nearby lot of the diner where he had breakfast. He recognized the garment bag behind his back. With his bandaged hand, he reached for his beloved Pirates ball cap, which had fallen off to the sand as he slumbered. This was far from a dream; he was a fugitive. A felon, wanted by the state of Pennsylvania. Knowing he had to return to the road, he quickly gathered his things and scampered to his car, wishing instead the dream were true.

xxx

Wanting a full tank of gas to limit stops once he returned to the road, Bill pulled into a convenience store and gas station at the last exit before I-10 and parked by one of the gas pumps. Using his employee credit card that belonged to the bank, he paid for the gas and attached the pump to the opening of the Equinox's tank. As the car filled with fuel, Bill leaned against the back bumper and dialed his wife's cell number using one of the prepaid phones. The call was two-fold. First, he hoped it would be a signal to Rita that he was all right. She had to be worried, even though she likely wished him dead for robbing the family's bank accounts. Second, he planned to leave the phone behind in Jacksonville to throw off law enforcement who may be searching for him.

As the phone rang, a group of rowdy teenagers zoomed up in a tricked-out red Honda Civic with the bass speakers loudly bumping. The Honda parked at the pump next to Bill. There were five guys in the car: two black, two white, and one Latino.

"Hello? Hello?" Rita's tinny voice came from the phone. It sounded as if she had been crying. "Hello? Bill? Bill? Is this you?"

Bill slowly lowered the phone and stared at it a moment before shutting it off. He felt entirely different after hearing Rita's distressed voice and thinking about what he had done to his family. He wanted to erase the previous day and all the damage he had caused the bank and, most importantly, Rita and the kids. He wanted to go home. But before he could dwell too long on the remorse he felt, one of the teenagers who was pumping gas into the Honda shouted to him.

"What's in the purse?" he yelled, referring to the garment bag that hung from Bill's shoulder.

Trying to ignore him, Bill didn't respond as a second kid, bigger and more intimidating, got out of the car and approached.

"What's in the purse?" the second kid asked. "Must be somethin' special to be wearin' it like that."

Bill flipped the phone to the approaching kid. He caught the phone and studied it, appearing confused by Bill's action.

"There's a lotta minutes left," Bill said. "Use 'em up."

The clip on the handle of the gas hose filling Bill's car popped. After reattaching the hose to the pump, Bill flung the bank credit card to the kid filling the Honda like a small frisbee. The card spun by him and fell to the ground.

"Keep it," Bill said. "Max it out."

"What's the catch?" the kid asked, kneeling for the card. "You a cop?"

"Nah, I'm the Easter Bunny, and you just hit the jackpot. The PIN number is 1-2-1-2. Spend away."

Before the two young men could react, Bill hopped in his car and sped out of the lot.

xxx

Traffic was heavy for most of the first hour until he reached the outskirts of Osceola National Forest. He was tired and didn't have the same positive energy as he had on his all-night jaunt from Pennsylvania. His bandaged right hand throbbed. He was hot, uncomfortable, and cranky. The air conditioning in the Equinox didn't work. With the sunroof and all the windows open, the sticky air roared in his ears. He pulled the Pirates cap on tight to protect his bald head from the hot afternoon sun. He had overeaten at breakfast, and the greasy meal weighed heavy on his belly. Acid from a leaky valve in his stomach seeped back into his esophagus, making it feel as if he had a burning brick stuck in the middle of his chest. He was cranky because he had barely slept in over thirty hours, except for the brief nap on the beach. Every other driver on the road not only irritated him but became his enemy. Normally a defensive driver, Bill uncharacteristically cursed and yelled out loud in the solitude of his car when another driver appeared to be in the wrong lane, drove too slowly, or cut in front of him. He even angrily stared down a young girl who watched him from the back seat of her family's passing car.

"What are you looking at, Sunshine?" Bill screamed. "Huh? You have a problem? Do you? Huh?"

xxx

Through a small opening between the mostly closed curtains of the living room picture window, Rita spied on an even larger crowd of media trucks and bystanders in front of her house. Some of the accumulating law enforcement vehicles were forced to park on parts of her perfectly manicured lawn. A few deputy sheriffs were stationed there to either relay updated information to Rita or monitor the phones should Bill possibly call. Tommy had barricaded himself in his bedroom to play video games; Susie wanted to meet with her boyfriend but was not permitted to leave the house. Instead, she flirted with the young deputies who crowded the living room and kitchen. Rita had been comforted all day by a close friend who was staying with her.

As Rita dragged hard on a cigarette, she glared through the slit while a black, government-issued luxury SUV appeared and drove onto the lawn to park near the front door. FBI agent Julius Stack had arrived. He was a tall, distinguished gentleman in his middle fifties with thick dark hair peppered with gray. He hustled out of the vehicle with several FBI colleagues and Detective Banner, who had overseen the investigation to that point. They entered the house without knocking.

Agent Stack led the group into the living room. He stood out, lighting up the room like the brightest star in the sky. He would never be described as a wallflower. Agent Stack was a man of presence who oozed confidence and commanded attention from those he met for the first time. Whenever he entered a room, he assumed — as did most of the others present — that he was the most important person on the scene.

"Did you find my husband?" Rita coldly asked Detective Banner, stubbing out her cigarette in an ashtray overflowing with lipstick-stained cigarette butts and standing. "And what about the strange phone call I received earlier? I know it was Bill. He's in trouble, isn't he?"

"The call may have come from Florida."

"Florida? That's a long way from here," she said staring at Agent Stack.

"Yes, it is," Banner said as he and Stack awkwardly stood across from Rita who paced the floor. "We have tracked your husband's phone to a small town in South Carolina off of I-77."

"South Carolina?"

"We have deputies from the local sheriff's department there searching for it as we speak. And the bank's credit card that is registered in your husband's name is currently being used in the Jacksonville, Florida, area. That's also where we think the unlisted call you received this morning came from. He likely drove through the night to Florida."

"It may not be Bill, right?" she asked. "It could be someone else, couldn't it?"

"Yes, it could be, Ma'am, but—"

"And what about the security cameras?" she asked, interrupting the detective.

"Unfortunately, there is no video. All the security cameras at the bank had been disabled minutes before the alleged incident occurred."

"Disabled? How?"

"Probably by your husband, Mrs. Moreland. He was the bank's president and, as you obviously know, had the authority to do so," Agent Stack said as he leaned forward, extending his hand out to Rita for her to shake. "I'm Special Agent Julius Stack of the FBI. I'm taking over the investigation. The FBI believes your husband is the likely thief."

"With all due respect, Mr. Stack, please be mindful of what you say," she said, pulling her hand away. "This is my house. You are a guest here. So, please be respectful. You don't even know my husband. He is a good man. He'd never steal from anyone."

"Perhaps, Mrs. Moreland."

"Please sit," she said as Stack and Banner took seats on the couch.

"We envision two scenarios," Banner said. "The first, based on the evidence of a struggle at the scene."

"Struggle?" Rita asked. "At the bank?"

"Yes, Ma'am," Banner nodded. "Your husband may have been assaulted or forced against his will to steal the money. It then is possible that he is currently being held as a hosta—"

"Or he is at the bottom of the Allegheny River," Stack interrupted.

"Agent Stack," Banner scolded him, "Come on. Please."

"Or the second," Stack said, "and most likely scenario, your husband took the money himself. He turned the cameras off and staged the scuffle."

"You do not know Bill, Mr. Stack. He is *not* a criminal."

"If your husband was attacked, why was he not left behind? Why have we not heard from the abductors? They have the money. There is no need to hold him for a ransom. Like I said, if he was attacked as you want to believe, he is likely at the bottom of one of those three ugly brown rivers downtown. There would be no need for him at this point."

"I know my husband! He wouldn't steal from anyone! He's

not a thief!"

"I would advise you, Ma'am," Banner said, "with all the media gathering outside, to not comment or answer any questions concerning the details of the investigation. I also would limit your trips outside your house. And that goes for your kids as well. I suggest having a friend or neighbor run your errands if you need something."

"Has your husband suffered any financial setbacks recently?" Stack asked.

"For the hundredth time, *no!*"

"What about gambling?" Stack continued to press her. "Did he have a thing for slot machines? High stakes poker games? Did he bet on sports?"

"No. Absolutely not."

"What about girlfriends, Mrs. Moreland?" Stack taunted her. Rita's face flushed red with anger as she stopped pacing and stood over him. "Has your husband ever had an extramarital affair? Someone he would want to keep quiet. You know, someone younger, with a little more energy. More carefree. A trophy, as rich male executives call them."

Without hesitation, warning, or worries about the consequences, Rita viciously slapped Agent Stack with her open hand across the face, nearly knocking him off the couch. Turning his head, he grimaced and gently rubbed at his reddened cheek before glancing to Detective Banner and his FBI partners. They all shook their heads. Banner scowled, showing him an unsympathetic and disappointed expression. Stack knew he perhaps went too far. He also knew he deserved the slap and probably more. But he was only making sure that Rita was telling the truth. Based on her reaction, he believed every word.

"Get the hell out of my house!" she yelled, pointing to the front door. Banner and the FBI agents in the living room and foyer looked at each other. "All of you! Out! Get the hell out!"

"I know these cases, Mrs. Moreland," Stack said before leaving as the others exited the house looking like a lost herd of confused cattle. "Your husband is on the run. He is running away from an empty life that no longer satisfied him. And I will find him, Mrs. Moreland. I always do."

Rita nearly pushed Agent Stack out of the house, violently slamming the door behind him. Bawling, she leaned back against the door before sliding down to the floor. As hard as it was for her to hear Agent Stack say it out loud, she knew he was right. Bill was gone, likely forever, and it probably was her fault.

xxx

As Bill traveled further west across the rural swamplands of northern Florida, the traffic lightened as he entered the least populated portion of the state. His mood also changed from agitated to anxious. An unsettled feeling overwhelmed him as the drive dragged on. He came to the stark realization that he had perhaps irreparably harmed his family, both emotionally and financially. It was despicable enough that he stole nearly a million dollars from the bank, but he had selfishly taken nearly all the family's lifesavings as well. His initial intention was to teach Rita and the kids a hard lesson. He wanted to prove to them his importance and show them that he was not an impotent middle-aged man but someone they couldn't exist without. But what he failed to appreciate in those fleeting moments was the love he had for them, despite the many years of trouble. He also knew he likely had overstepped his intentions, wondering if it wasn't too late to make it right and turn himself in.

His flustered mind raced, bleak, as heavy storm clouds rolled in from the west, blocking out the sun and cooling the afternoon. He battled with the voices in his head for most of the gloomy ride through the northern panhandle of Florida. Turning himself in to the authorities was probably his best option. He had over a million dollars on him but no plan for it. He likely would never be able to enjoy it as most of the money would be spent on trying to avoid the authorities.

He also wondered how long he would remain free. He was not an experienced criminal. He didn't know what he was doing, and he was the first to admit it. He'd probably get caught sooner than later. He couldn't be on the run forever, and he'd have to take his new journey alone. He doubted he could reveal his secret to a travel companion without getting robbed or turned in. Nothing seemed sadder and more desperate than life on the road alone without anyone to spend the money with or to share the experience. Stealing the money had no consequential purpose, other than destroying his family. And with no productive purpose, he was left with little choice but to give himself up.

xxx

The storm had passed without rain as Bill squinted into the setting sun. He'd been driving for a little more than five hours and needed to stop for gas and stretch his legs. After crossing the Apalachicola River somewhere not far from Pensacola, he exited the interstate and drove a few miles into a mostly deserted center of a small town that he didn't catch the name of. He found a quiet convenience store and gas station and parked next to one of the six unoccupied gas pumps. Slowly unfolding his cramped body, he lifted himself out of the car and did a few stretching exercises and deep knee bends before walking into the store. With the garment bag draped over his shoulder, he loaded his arms with a collection of snacks and soft drinks and paid for everything with cash, including the yet-to-be-filled tank of gas.

At the pump, he threw the bag of snacks into the passenger seat and attached the gas nozzle to the Equinox. He leaned against the car and studied one of the prepaid phones he had purchased. During the last hour of his trek, he had convinced himself to call Rita to tell her he was coming home. He started to enter her number but stopped when the nozzle clicked, indicating the car was filled with fuel. He glanced to the pump and noticed a plain block building across the street—a Boys and Girls Club in disrepair and badly in need of a fresh coat of paint.

The lights were on inside the building, and he could see in the front window a group of giggling young kids playing ping-pong. Overgrown weeds had taken over much of the playground behind the facility. Playground equipment like swings, jungle gyms, and sliding boards were rusted and damaged, appearing unusable. Basketball hoops at each end of a cracked concrete court were bent forward with both nets missing. He turned off the phone and stuffed it in his pocket. After returning the gas nozzle to the pump, he reached into the car and emptied the plastic bag of snacks and drinks into the seat. He took out a bundle of cash in the amount of ten thousand dollars and wrapped the money in the bag. Leaving his car at the pump, he hustled across the empty two-lane street to the club.

He entered the club, which looked like an outdated banquet hall inside. The walls were paneled with dark faux wood, and scores of plastic folding tables and chairs were stacked on top of each other at one end of the hall. Party streamers hung from the white fiberglass drop ceiling. The one ping-pong table had been pushed into the middle of the hall. Four kids playfully chased the bouncing ping-pong balls across the floor, and one adult, a black gentleman who looked to be in his forties, turned to approach Bill.

"Can I help you?"

Without saying a word, Bill extended the plastic bag of money to the man, who accepted it with a puzzled look. The kids had retrieved all the bouncing balls from the floor and intently watched.

"It's for the club and the kids," Bill said.

The guy slowly unwrapped the bag. His face lit up as he pulled out the bundle of cash and showed the kids. All four of them began to squeal and hop up and down upon realizing the generous gift. The man then scanned the club for Bill, but he was gone. The man scrambled outside, the kids following, and spotted Bill as he neared the gas pump across the street.

"Thank you!" the man called out.

Bill nodded as he ducked into his car. A warm feeling he had never experienced before overcame him. His heart pounded. The palms of his shaking hands were sweaty. He suddenly felt like the most important man in the world. He loudly revved the tired engine of the old Equinox a few times before driving into the deserted street. The black man from the club smiled and held up the cash as the four kids wildly waved their arms and continued to jump up and down. Bill grinned and waved back, speeding by them. He couldn't wait to return to the interstate. He'd finally found a reason to stay on the road.

Chapter 3
New Orleans

Day 4. Sunday, April 30. 12:01 AM

Not long after crossing the Florida state line into Alabama, Bill felt the immediate need to piss. He found a rest area off I-10 outside Seminole, Alabama, not far from Mobile. After taking care of business, he decided to take a much-needed nap, not longer than an hour or so. He planned to arrive in New Orleans before daybreak under the cover of darkness. He moved his car to the most remote area of the rest stop's parking lot and backed into a spot. He wanted to face the rest area building, with a clear view of the facility grounds, so no one could sneak up behind him.

He reclined the driver's seat and quickly fell asleep, rubbing absently at the still painful cut on his hand. Instead of a short nap, he slept hard through the night. The next thing he knew, he was roused by the dawn chatter of mockingbirds that had gathered in nearby trees. Rubbing his red swollen eyes, he shifted his cramped body as he returned the driver's seat to its upright position. A sharp pain shot up his aching back as he tried to get comfortable. Wiping condensation from the inside of the windows, he stared into the early morning fog. He needed to get out and stretch his stiff muscles. The parking lot was much livelier than it had been when he pulled in the night before. Travelers walked dogs or milled around as they smoked cigarettes and sipped at fresh cups of coffee. He wanted to go inside and get a coffee himself, but he noticed an unoccupied Alabama State Police cruiser parked near the entrance of the rest stop's busy building. The coffee would have to wait. Time to move on. He faced about a two-hour drive to New Orleans.

The remaining hour-long drive through Alabama was blurred by fatigue and the foggy morning driving conditions. He soon found himself crossing into Mississippi. With little traffic at that time of the morning, he pushed the Equinox to the max, maintaining a consistent eighty miles per hour as he raced towards New Orleans. He first crossed a short causeway that extended over the Escatawpa River near Moss Point and entered the Pascagula Wetlands. Continuing through the Magnolia State, he passed over the many small rivers and creeks that spidered the miles of swamplands before crossing a much longer causeway that extended over the West Pascagula River.

Glancing to the GPS system on his phone, he noticed a sign for U.S. Highway 90 that ran parallel just south of I-10 along the gulf coast. Bill had never been to that part of the country nor seen the Gulf of Mexico, and he wanted a more scenic drive off the main road. He turned onto a cut-off road that led him to U.S. Route 90 not far from Ocean Springs. On 90, his speed slowed, but the scenery improved. The fog had been replaced by a golden morning sky filled with high hanging clouds in the distance. He drove for miles along low-lying white sandy beaches with breathtaking views of the gulf. The deep blue waves were calm and light, the beaches mostly empty except for a few early morning hikers.

The other side of the road reminded him of the antebellum era as he drove past what was left of old plantations and mansions, many of which had been replaced after the devastation caused by Hurricane Katrina. He sped by miles of giant oaks, the branches of some covered in Spanish moss. As he traveled further west, many of the homes had been rebuilt and appeared more modern. Ancient oaks that once lined the road or marked the different properties had been reduced to stumps, obvious reminders of the high winds and ocean surge caused by different hurricanes through the years. Along each side of Highway 90, he also passed family steak and seafood restaurants, waffle and pancake houses, occasional resorts and beach motels, many painted in art deco blues and pinks. As he neared Biloxi he passed a historic lighthouse and gazed at numerous boats trawling for shrimp not far from the shore. Newly built, multistoried luxury casinos prominently lined portions of the Biloxi coast.

Bill wanted to stop and walk the beaches. He wanted to wade in the warm gulf coast waters. He desperately needed coffee. He craved a large southern breakfast. But something inside him wouldn't let him stop. He pressed on toward New Orleans, passing through Gulfport, one of the larger cities in Mississippi. In no time, he sped across Bay St. Louis into Pass Christian via an impressive two-mile bridge rebuilt after Katrina. As he continued west on Route 90, he eventually returned to I-10 and found himself only twenty miles from the Mississippi-Louisiana border.

After entering Louisiana, I-10 veered south to loop around Lake Pontchartrain and directly pass through the greater New Orleans metropolitan area. Not having any idea where he was heading, Bill took the exit labeled Orleans Avenue toward Vieux Carre once he entered the city limits — remembering from his one year of high school French that 'Vieux Carre' translated to 'French Quarter'. At the end of the exit ramp, he turned left onto Orleans before taking another left onto Conti, a narrow, one-way side street in the French Quarter. He found an open parking spot on Conti and nearly stumbled out of the Equinox with excitement. He'd grabbed the heavy garment bag, hung it over his shoulder, and walked away from the car.

The morning sky was overcast and hazy. The smell of brewed coffee and toasted baguettes filled the air. It looked as if he might be only a few blocks from the infamous Bourbon Street. Conti was especially active despite it being early. Two garbage trucks, both overfilled with plastic trash bags and leaking a foul-smelling gray liquid, crisscrossed at the intersection of Dauphine and Conti. Business owners hosed off the sidewalks and entrances in front of their establishments, attempting to wash away the Saturday night's spilled beer and spent cigarette butts. Residents in apartments with balconies above the businesses enjoyed their Sunday morning coffee and watered lush arrangements of azalea, phlox, and hibiscus, all beautifully displayed in different shades of red, pink, and white.

To avoid a stalled street cleaner that splashed sudsy water on each side of Conti, Bill turned on Dauphine Street. He still had no plan and walked without any destination. He just walked. As he hiked down Dauphine, he passed Irish pubs and gay bars, still lively and raucous from the night before. Their jukeboxes provided the soundtrack to the morning. He crossed paths with young revelers who should have turned in hours earlier. The stench of urine hung strong in the hot morning air. The busted brick sidewalks were littered with broken bottles and human waste, leftovers from a night of too much living. He stopped at a small Baptist church with a line of homeless men and women on the sidewalk. Some were passed out. Others asked for spare change. Bill checked the front door. It was locked. The Sunday morning sermon and free meal service were to start later that morning. He made note of the church's street address, intending to come back.

Reaching St. Ann, he noticed a massive arched metal sign lighted by several large white flashing bulbs that read "Armstrong," marking the entrance to Louis Armstrong Park. He turned on St. Ann and headed toward the park, crossing the four-lanes of a quiet North Rampart Street. Bill entered the park under the arched sign and spent the better part of the next hour studying the statues and placards of early New Orleans jazz legends before resting by a small pond. He walked through Congo Square, the first space where enslaved blacks and others of color were free to meet centuries before. He passed camps of more homeless folks. Evidence of recent drug use scattered the ground. He encountered more Saturday night refugees, not ready to leave the weekend behind, their necks draped with gaudy beads; they shared cans of cheap beer and fruity alcoholic beverages in large plastic containers shaped like aliens, footballs, or hand grenades.

Bill continued through the park and found himself on Dumaine Street. He walked by the manicured grounds and the fountains of the Mahalia Jackson Theater for the Performing Arts and into the adjoining Treme neighborhood, famous for its jazz clubs and soul food joints. Across Dumaine stood a white brick building with a green metal roof and siding—a neighborhood community center. As he neared the entrance, he fished a ten-thousand-dollar stack of cash out of the garment bag and rolled it into a plastic bag he had in his pocket. He yanked at the front door of the building, but it was locked. He pressed his face against the front door window glass and peered inside. Most of the lights were off, but Bill could see a shadow moving about the lobby, so he started to pound on the front door. Suddenly, a frail and elderly black man with a wrinkled but distinguished face appeared.

"We closed on Sundays," he shouted through the locked door, a mop in one hand.

"I have a delivery!"

"What delivery? They ain't no deliveries on Sunday."

Bill held up the bag and showed the man. The man shrugged and unlocked the door, opening it but a crack. Bill slid the bag of money to the man through the opening.

"Give that to your boss. It's a donation for the center."

"What donation?"

"Just make sure your boss gets it."

The man studied Bill before slowly unrolling the bag and delicately pulling out the stack of hundred-dollar bills. He glanced up, but Bill was gone.

xxx

Weary, worn, and hungry from the road, Bill stood outside the community center for many minutes, soaking in solitude and his anonymity. He appreciated the early vibe of New Orleans.

Vibe was a word he never used or fully understood. But for the first time, he felt it. He had only been there for a short time, but New Orleans had a vibe all its own. It was unlike any place he had ever been, more exotic and mysterious. It felt as if he had entered another country or world.

Everything about New Orleans was different. The sky looked different. The early haze of the Sunday morning had lifted, and the sky was a color of blue he had never seen before. The morning sounded different. The bells from a nearby church rang loud enough to wake the dead and stir the living into song. A choir could be heard singing with more energy and more feeling than he was used to from the churches back home. Their collective voice sounded more honest, legitimate, real. He recognized the tune as he hummed along, quietly singing the chorus under his breath, "I'll fly away, oh glory, I'll fly away." The morning even smelled different, the humid air filled with a boiling blend of Cajun spices, pork, and seafood, like a soup simmering.

Hungry, Bill walked towards the smell, hoping a popular local restaurant was at the end of his jaunt, prepping for lunch. For most of his trek, the neighborhood streets were eerily quiet. Many of the houses were abandoned, appearing haunted. As Bill turned a corner, he encountered three middle-aged black men seated in folding chairs in the street around a large bubbling pot propped over a blue propane flame. Bill had found his pot at the end of the rainbow, but unfortunately, it was not a restaurant. He had stumbled on a group of gentlemen enjoying the friendship of a classic Louisiana seafood boil. The pot of 'gold' overflowed with pounds of crawfish, gulf shrimp, andouille sausage, corn cobs, and potatoes seasoned with bulbs of garlic and onions and a blend of cayenne pepper, paprika, and oregano. It smelled like heaven.

"You lost, son?" one of the men, Oscar, asked as Bill stared at the steaming pot.

"I was," Bill said, "but not now. This was what I was searching for. I smelled your soup from blocks away. I was looking for a spot to eat lunch."

"You ain't from around here, are you?" Oscar asked. "That ain't soup."

"No, sir. I'm from Pennsylvania."

"Mus' be your first time here?"

"Yes, it is."

"This is what you call a crawfish boil."

"Grab you'self a bowl," Darryl, one of the other men, said. "It's jus' about ready."

"No. No. I don't want to intrude."

"Grab a bowl," Oscar said. "There's plenty. "

"What's your name, son?" Darryl asked.

"Bill."

"Get a bowl, Mr. Bill, and pull one of those chairs over here."

"You sure?"

"Of course, we're sure," Oscar said, looking to the one fellow who had yet to speak. "Ain't that right, Sleepy Boy?"

"Yeah, you right," Sleepy Boy answered as he got up from his chair and stood over the boil.

Bill followed their orders and stepped to a small table near the steaming pot and reached for a bowl, plastic fork, and a handful of napkins.

"You'll need more than that," Darryl said.

"Plenty of ice-cold beers in that cooler, Mr. Bill. Help you'self."

Bill pulled a bottle of Dixie beer from the cooler, and Sleepy Boy moved to a second table and covered it with a long sheet of white cooking paper. He put on oven mitts and reached through the billowing steam for the handles of the metal strainer full of food in the boiling pot. He slowly lifted the strainer up, allowing the hot water to drain into the pot. He shook the strainer several times—up and down, up and down—to drip out the last of the water and dumped the heavily spiced seafood, sausage, and vegetables onto the paper-covered table. Steam rolled off the glorious mound of bright red crawfish, the largest shrimp he'd ever seen, and chunks of blistered andouille sausage that sizzled and popped on the table as if it were alive.

"Looks good, Sleepy Boy," Oscar said.

"Yeah, you right."

"You have the honor, Mr. Bill," Darryl said. "Enjoy!"

With a ladle, Bill scooped up several servings and loaded his bowl, filling it with plenty of crawfish, shrimp, and sausage. He returned to his folding chair and plucked the largest crawfish from the bowl for a closer look, studying what appeared to be a miniature lobster.

"Never eaten a crawfish, have you?" Oscar asked.

"No. No, I haven't."

"Come over here," he said, grabbing a crawfish off the table and holding it up. "See this? Pinch and twist the head, like this, and pull off the tail."

Oscar separated the head and tail of the crawfish.

"The meat's all up in the tail here," he said. "But before you go for the meat, you need to suck out the head, like this."

The man put the dismembered crustacean's head to his lip and slowly sucked like taking his last living breath, removing the buttery organ and the spiced juices from inside the head.

"Best part in my opinion," Oscar said, wiping his lips with his sleeve. "Ain't that right, Sleepy Boy?"

"Yeah, you right," Sleepy Boy said, his lips stained red with spices as he devoured the 'mudbugs' like a competitive eater.

"Now for the tail," Oscar said who was demonstrating how to eat a crawfish to Bill. "I'm sure you've eaten a lobster before."

"Yessir."

"Same thing, jus' smaller," he said, peeling away the meat in the tail from the shell and holding it up. "Simple as that."

At first, Bill struggled to peel the shells from the crawfish with his bandaged hand.

"What you go an' do to your hand there, Mr. Bill?" Darryl asked.

Bill glanced to the bandage that was stained an orangish-red color from the Cajun spices.

"Just a little clumsy."

Bill continued to awkwardly grapple with the crawfish until he snapped it in half. He sucked hard on the head, causing him to instantly cough and nearly choke on the spray of spicy juices that hit the back of his throat.

"Here," Oscar said, handing Bill another head to taste. "Take a long, slow suck. Let them flavors hang around on the back of your tongue before you swallow."

Bill tried again, sucking slow and long, looking to his three new friends and grinning with an enthusiastic nod. He then stripped away the shell from the tail and popped the morsel of meat into his mouth. He was hooked as he devoured the crawfish from his bowl as if their zesty tails of meat were kernels of popcorn. After only a few minutes, beads of sweat began to form on his forehead and the back of his neck. His tongue and lips started to tingle.

"Woah," he said, wiping at his forehead and lips with a napkin and taking a deep breath. "I'm feeling the heat. These suckers are spicy."

"I always like to say," Oscar said. "It you ain't sweatin', then you ain't eatin'. Ain't that right, Sleepy Boy?"

"Yeah, you right."

xxx

After several beers and a couple more bowls of the delectably zingy seafood boil, Bill lingered, happily chatting away the afternoon with his three new friends. He practically melted in his chair, his belly and mind both completely satisfied. Despite the heat and sticky air, there was nowhere else he would rather be. If there were clouds in the sky, he didn't notice them. His world, his universe, finally were perfect. New Orleans—it felt like home.

"Can I ask you what's in the bag, Mr. Bill?" Darryl asked.

"Everything I own is in that bag."

"What brings you 'round here?"

"Business."

"Business? Ain't no business happenin' here. Less of course, you plan to bulldoze these homes and put up condos."

"I made a donation."

"Donation?"

"To the neighborhood community center."

"You drove all the way from Pennsylvania to do that?"

"Yep."

"Damn, Mr. Bill," Darryl said, shaking his head and looking at Sleepy Boy. "That's something, ain't it, Sleepy Boy?"

"Yeah, you right," Sleepy Boy answered.

"Why here?" Darryl asked.

"It seemed like the place to come. It felt right."

"How long you been in New Orleans?"

"A few hours," Bill said. "It's not like any other place I've been. It's feels different."

"'Cause it is different."

"But everyone—the mayor, police, developers, and even the governor..." Darryl wandered to the cooler to get another beer. "Everyone wants to change it."

"We jus' tryin' to save its soul."

"How long you stayin', Mr. Bill?" Darryl asked as Bill stood to leave.

"Likely just passing through."

"Where you headin'?"

"Not sure yet."

"Not sure yet?"

"I'm not so different from you guys." Bill turned and walked away. "But I need to keep moving. I'm trying to save what little soul I have left."

Before Bill could get too far down the street, Darryl noticed a bundle of cash on the food table. He reached for it and flipped through the brick of hundred-dollar bills: ten thousand dollars.

"Jesus Christ!"

The other guys glanced up as he raised the money to show them what Bill had left.

"We can't keep that," Oscar said. "Ain't that right, Sleepy Boy?"

"No, sir."

"Hey, Mr. Bill!" Darryl called out to Bill. "Come back and get your money."

"That's not my money!" Bill yelled before he turned a corner and disappeared.

xxx

Bill followed the same route back to retrieve his car, returning to the French Quarter by way of St. Ann Street. He turned onto Dauphine and revisited the small Baptist church he had stopped by earlier in the morning. He gazed in the window. The Sunday morning service was over. Several of the church's members tidied up the small chapel as Bill entered. A younger gentleman with a long, wispy beard approached; he appeared to be the pastor. Before he could say a word, Bill extended a paper bag. It contained ten thousand dollars.

"For the church," Bill said as the pastor took the bag. "I've heard from a few locals nothing but fantastic things about the good deeds you're doing here."

"We try," the pastor said, reaching into the bag and pulling out the stack of cash. "Oh, my goodness!"

"Keep up the good work."

"Wait, my brother. Please wait. Can I get your name? I want to let the others in the congregation and community know about your generosity. We are extremely limited. Our operation is modest, and our facility is small. You don't know how much this helps us and the less fortunate we serve here. You were sent from heaven."

Bill didn't initially respond.

"Please, sir," the pastor pressed him, extending his hand.

"Bill from Pennsylvania." He shook the pastor's hand.

"Bill from Pennsylvania? That's it?"

"That's it."

"God bless you, my son. Bless you."

xxx

Bill cautiously drove the narrow, congested streets of the French Quarter to a guest house on St. Peter that was recommended by one of the men at the seafood boil. He maneuvered around parked taxi cabs, beer trucks, and curious and drunken tourists lined along Bourbon and St. Peter Streets. He found the guest house and parked in a temporary spot as he checked in. As luck would have it, he got the last available room. He moved his car into a secluded courtyard under the second-floor room he'd reserved. He gathered the garment bag and climbed a set of rickety wooden stairs to enter the room.

It was a simple, no-frills room with bed, television, dresser, closet, and bathroom. The room's balcony overlooked St. Peter Street. He opened the double doors and propped them open, allowing the musty-smelling room to fill with the fresh but humid air from outside. Bill stepped onto the balcony and leaned against a cast iron metal railing to watch the lively streets below. He intended to spend the rest of the afternoon in a lounge chair on the balcony. Instead, after a long and much-needed beer piss, he flopped onto the bed with the strap of the garment bag still draped over his shoulder and neck. Too tired to move, he immediately fell asleep.

xxx

Day 4. Sunday, April 30. 3:21 PM

The sky cracked open with a loud blast of thunder, startling Bill as he walked. Heavy rain flooded the low-lying French Quarter streets. Getting soaked, Bill took shelter in a dark but lively dive bar on Conti Street: The Rose. Shaking the water from his arms and head, he stepped inside the cozy joint. The jukebox roared as shots of whiskey were poured and passed around. His nap

54

had rested and revived him, and he took a seat at the bar near an open window. A warm glow of neon lit the place. As he watched the storm from the safety of a barstool, an attractive bartender named Kat approached. She was a tall brunette with an athletic build, long hair, dark eyes, and elaborate tattoos that ran the length of each arm.

"What'll it be, stranger?"

"A margarita. On the rocks."

She reached for a bottle of tequila in a basin under the bar.

"Nah, better get me the good stuff."

She pulled another bottle off the shelf behind her, fixed the drink, and slid it over to him. He chugged the drink in one big gulp.

"I'll take another."

"Slow down, stranger. I'm here all night," she said, fixing the drink. "What happened to your hand?"

"I cut myself shaving." He glanced at his bandaged right hand.

"You must use an awfully big razor."

"Something like that."

"You from around here?" she asked. "I haven't seen you before."

"First time here."

"You in town for business?"

"Just passing through."

"Where you headed?" she asked, setting the second margarita in front of him.

"West."

"West? Can you be a little more specific?"

"Probably Texas. Maybe Arizona or New Mexico. I'm not sure yet."

"I think about getting out of here all the time."

"What's stopping you?"

"This job. A dog. A boyfriend."

"Now might be the time — you know, before it's too late."

"Too late?"

"There's no worse feeling than when you discover your life

has passed you by. Believe me, I know that feeling." He paused. "Do you have a house payment?"

"No."

"A car payment?"

"No."

"Kids?"

"No."

Bill finished the second drink.

"You're awful thirsty, stranger."

"You can't imagine how thirsty."

xxx

Rita's eyes and nose were red from crying. As she had for the good part of the past few days, she stared out the living room's large picture window. Her normally immaculate lawn and driveway had been rutted by police squad cars and media trucks. Reporters and curious strangers milled about in the street in front. A frenzy of activity took place behind her inside the house. Detectives worked their phones. Friends and family paced the crowded house. Concerned neighbors continually showed up at the front door with assorted casseroles and other baked goods.

Rita was confident Bill would return.

"Something had to have happened to him," she muttered. "He doesn't have it in him to leave me and the kids."

xxx

Bill stared at his phone and dragged hard on a cigar, wanting to call home. Several empty margarita glasses were lined up on the bar in front him. He felt awful every time he thought of Rita and the kids. He'd never turned his back on them before. He'd always been there when needed. He slid the phone into his pocket and peeked at his bar tab before shooting a look to Kat, who flirted with a customer. He stubbed out the cigar and peeled several twenties from a thick wad of cash to pay his bar

56

bill. He glanced to Kat one last time, studied her a moment, and tossed an extra hundred-dollar bill on the bar for her tip.

Bill quietly stepped out of the bar into the orange and purple glow of dusk. On the sidewalk in front, he felt tipsy and alone. The storm had passed, leaving damp and heavy air. Bill studied Conti Street in each direction. The French Quarter streets were abuzz, much busier than when he was out earlier. The festive sounds of a brass band filled the night. A river of people, mostly tourists holding cocktails and oversized beers, flowed on Bourbon Street in the direction from Canal to Esplanade. Wishing to be lost within the Sunday night crowd and needing to be anonymous, Bill turned for Bourbon. But before he could get too far, Kat sprinted after him, holding the garment bag and the hundred-dollar bill he left on the bar.

"Hey! Hey! Wait a minute! You forgot this!" she called out, reaching out the bag.

Bill stopped and turned, quickly grabbing the bag.

"Shit!" he exclaimed, hurriedly throwing the strap of the bag over his head. "Thank you. Thank you! Everything I own is in this bag."

"And your money on the bar," she said, holding the hundred-dollar bill.

"No, no, that's yours."

"I can't take this. It's too much."

"Buy your boyfriend and dog a steak. Take it. Have some fun."

She glanced to the money, then to Bill.

"Thank you for the good service," he said.

She smiled and nodded.

"Come back and see me again, Stranger. I'm Kat. The next drink's on me."

He nodded as she disappeared back toward the bar.

xxx

Kat approached her apartment in the Marigny neighborhood.

She could hear the Foo Fighters blaring from more than two blocks away. Foo Fighters was the favorite band of Ken Mercury, her currently unemployed boyfriend; the music was coming from her apartment. She also could hear what sounded like the loud talking and laughing of Ken's two best friends. She audibly sighed, having just worked a double shift at the bar. It had been a long fourteen hours on her feet. She was exhausted. All she wanted was a quiet place to disappear with her beagle, Tito.

At the front door of the apartment, she sighed again and closed her eyes. She liked the Foo Fighters but not every single night. She pushed the front door open and gazed inside before entering. A raucous poker game was taking place at the cluttered kitchen table. Empty cans of local beer were scattered throughout the place. A half-empty handle of cheap Irish whiskey was prominently displayed in the middle of the kitchen table. By the looks of the small stack of poker chips in front of Ken, it appeared he had lost nearly all his money, most of which he stole from a drawer where Kat kept her tips for the week.

Kat entered a thick haze of cigarette and marijuana smoke that hung in the air. She glared at Ken. He was a strikingly handsome young man in his middle twenties. He was tall and slender with bright blue eyes. On the outside, he looked to be the whole package, and he could be quite charming. But on that night, like most nights, he was noticeably shitfaced—both stoned and drunk. His face was flushed, his eyes bloodshot, his eyelids but slivers. His lush blonde hair was tousled. Kat was immediately greeted by Tito enthusiastically leaping into her arms. She turned down the volume of the stereo system and walked through the living room, holding Tito.

"Hey!" a chorus of voices called out from the kitchen.

"I could hear you all the way on Esplanade."

"You're late," Ken said as she stepped into the kitchen.

"I was busy at the bar."

"Grab, your things, Babe. We're going out."

"I'm going to bed."

"Come on," he pleaded. "Half-off drinks at the Alibi tonight."

"You don't look in shape to go anywhere."

"It's service industry night. And because you work in the service indust—"

"I know several bars and restaurants looking for help," she interrupted, glancing to each of his friends. "Get a job and you wouldn't need me for the discount."

"Come on, Babe."

"I'm going to bed. I have to be back at the bar early tomorrow."

"Jus' for an hour, so we can get a few cheap drinks."

"I'll see you in the morning." She turned away and disappeared into the bathroom.

Ken looked to his friends and shook his head. The sound of running water came from the shower as he reached into Kat's purse and dug out the hundred-dollar bill that Bill had given her as a tip. Ken glanced to the closed bathroom door, held up the bill, and grinned to his friends before stuffing it in his pocket. They clumsily headed for the door. Before leaving, Ken turned the volume back up on the stereo.

xxx

Bill found himself back in the room of the guest house. He'd visited a few of the famous French Quarter bars and sampled gin fizzes and Sazeracs, two local favorites, before retiring for the evening. He wasn't in the mood to celebrate. The many alcoholic beverages he had consumed had not lightened his spirit but soured it. Instead of losing himself to the festive atmosphere of New Orleans, he'd become claustrophobic among the overly energetic and imposing crowds that gradually grew as evening fell. He'd also become paranoid, as if everyone around him knew who he was.

He shut the lights off to the lonely guest room, closed the

balcony door, and pulled the heavy plastic curtains over the windows. He crawled under the comforting covers and wondered whether it was time to go home and turn himself in. Even in the darkness, he could not escape the revelry in the French Quarter streets. Bands in nearby St. Peter Street clubs played all night long, and the conversations and laughter outside the balcony door never stopped. He thought of Kat, the friendly bartender he'd met earlier that night. Although he desperately needed rest, he tossed and turned for hours until finally passing out sometime after four in the morning. Regardless of where he was headed next, home or the highway west, he knew he had to get an early start.

But the early start never happened. Bill awoke at seven o'clock to a ringing alarm next to the bed. He stared at the clock and scanned the guest room, trying to figure out where he was and how he got there. Upon realizing he was in New Orleans, he slammed off the alarm and rolled over in bed. He convinced himself that another day in New Orleans couldn't hurt. He easily fell back to sleep and didn't move for over five hours as if his body was paralyzed. It was the best he had slept in years.

xxx

Day 5. Monday, May 1. 1:17 PM

A hot afternoon sun greeted Bill as he stepped out of the guest house to clear his pounding head. He turned towards Esplanade and explored the more residential side of the French Quarter. The brick walls that lined the narrow streets were covered in Spanish ivy that had yellow and white jasmine grown over it. Wrought iron lattice fencing of the porches and balcony railings decorated the brightly painted creole cottages on both sides of the streets. Mostly hidden lavish courtyards of the homes offered a glimpse into the secret lives of the residents. The fragrant scent of the blooming jasmine mixed with the skunky smell of burning reefer that wafted from the balconies above. The calliope of a steamboat anchored on the banks of the Mississippi whistled a familiar "Let Me Call You Sweetheart." Bill hummed the song to himself for the rest of the afternoon, unable to get it out of his head.

Feeling somewhat better, he lit a cigar and strolled back and forth from each end of the French Quarter, from Esplanade to Canal Street, from North Rampart to the Mississippi River. The streets were busy with tourists, artists, and street performers. He found lunch at a little take-out market that was enthusiastically recommended by a local at one end of Royal Street. On an open spot of thick grass in the middle of bustling Jackson Square, he sat and devoured a tasty fried shrimp and oyster po-boy, the Peacemaker they called it, and a 24-ounce can of Miller High-Life. He lingered in the square to digest lunch. He studied the Lucky Dog vendors as well as the many tarot card readers lined up in rows at small tables on the stone walkway that separated St. Louis Cathedral and the square's park. He considered having his fortune read but didn't—afraid of what the future had in store for him. Multiple brass bands entertained the crowds with jazz unique to New Orleans. On each corner of the square, different men were painted gold or silver and performed for tips. A long line had formed on Decatur Street at one end of the square outside Café Du Monde, the famous eatery known for chicory coffee and a sugary doughnut-like pastry called a beignet.

As the afternoon slipped away, distant storm clouds started to form over the city. Not wanting to get caught in a downpour, he quickly gathered himself and returned to The Rose, the Conti Street bar he had visited the night before. If he were to be invisible, that bar seemed like a good place to hide. The wind had picked up, and a steady rain started to fall. He pulled open the front door, hoping that Kat would be working. He couldn't lie to himself. She was the real reason he stayed another day in New Orleans.

Kat smiled once Bill entered and motioned to a bottle of tequila. He nodded and took a seat at the bar by the open window, watching the storm roll in as she prepared a margarita. The place was mostly empty. The jukebox played but at a much lower level than the night before.

"How long will you be in town?" she asked, placing the drink in front of him.

"I was supposed to leave this morning."

"What kept you here?"

"A friendly bar," he said, lighting a cigar.

"How's the drink?"

"Wonderful," he said, after taking a big sip. "But I gotta be out of here first thing in the morning."

"Yeah?"

"I have to keep moving."

"What are you running away from?" she asked as lightning flashed outside. A crash of thunder followed, shaking the barstools and liquor bottles on the shelf behind the bar. The lights flickered.

"Jesus!" Bill said, ducking and briefly covering his head with his arms.

They both glanced out the window as the pouring sheets of rain swirled with the wind.

"But what are you running from?"

"Running from?"

"I see your type in here all the time."

"My type?" he asked, shaking his head.

"A middle-aged man bored with his life comes alone to New Orleans for the weekend."

"Nah, my situation's different."

"How so?"

"I can't say."

"What'd you do, Stranger?"

A young man walked into the bar before Bill could answer.

"Excuse me," Kat said, walking away to wait on the customer.

Bill finished the drink and pulled out his phone, wanting to send Rita a text. He stared at the phone a moment, then studied

Kat, who was fixing him another margarita. He slid the phone back into his pocket.

"Tell me about your boyfriend," Bill said as she returned.

"My boyfriend?"

"What's he like?"

"It was love at first sight. My better judgement told me it was a mistake. But the little devil on my shoulder told me to go for it. I figured we'd have some fun for three or four weeks, and then I'd move on."

"And now?"

"It's been two years and counting. Some days I can't stand seeing his face."

"But you won't leave?"

"I have, but I've always come back. I don't know why. We've been together so long I've forgotten who I was without him." She paused a moment. "You know what I mean?"

"I do. Believe me, I do."

"I figure we'll always be together. We have our good times and some bad—too much drama, it seems. Living in New Orleans, there's always a party. We've gotten caught up in the lifestyle here, you know. We drink more than we should. But the alcohol chases the boredom away and mostly makes the sex fun. He needs to get a job."

"It's the opposite in my world," Bill said with a laugh. "Alcohol mostly puts me and my wife to sleep."

"So, you have a wife?" she asked. He stopped grinning and briefly glanced away, awkwardly covering his wedding band. "What'd you do to her, Stranger?"

Before Bill could answer, a group of young fellows, obviously locals, entered the bar. They greeted Kat with hearty salutations. Envious, and maybe a little jealous, Bill stared as each of them hugged and pecked her on the cheek. They took seats at the bar as he intently studied them. Kat placed a shot glass in front of each of them. She slid one glass over to Bill before filling the shot glasses with tequila. The three regulars immediately drained the shots. Bill grabbed his and the

63

smoldering cigar and wandered over to a refurbished and almost obsolete CD jukebox.

It was an older jukebox—one filled with scores of CDs as opposed to the more popular digital internet jukeboxes. Instead of having access to almost any song ever recorded, Bill was limited to selecting songs only from specific discs. He liked this type of jukebox better. Each turn of the jukebox tiles brought a new surprise, revealing solo artists and bands he hadn't thought about since he was a much younger: The Ramones, Cheap Trick, Bo Diddly, The Rolling Stones, Hank Williams, The Pogues, Tom Waits, Waylon Jennings, The Who, Elvis Costello, and his all-time favorite, Patsy Cline. He slid a few bucks in the money slot, knocked back the shot of tequila, and made several selections.

Bill returned to his barstool as the Stones' song "Fool to Cry" started to play. Kat refilled his empty shot glass.

"What'd you do to your wife?" she asked again.

"Can you turn the jukebox up a little?"

"Tell me, Stranger," she pressed him, turning a knob behind the bar to increase the volume.

"I should've been home, like, a thousand hours ago."

"You're in trouble, aren't you?" Kat studied him as he relighted the cigar.

"There's nowhere else I'd rather be." He turned to the jukebox. "I own hundreds of records and never listen to any of them. I'd forgotten the feeling a great song gives me. Ever since I got to New Orleans, everything feels right."

He held up the shot glass.

"I had forgotten what a good drink tasted like. And before, a good cigar made a shitty day bearable, but now. . ." He puffed on the cigar. "I've made one horrible mistake in my life. I stood still for too long. I wish that I'd moved way more than I did. I wasted the best years of my life."

"What's your name, Stranger?"

"William Runner," he lied without hesitation. "You can call me Bill. Bill from Pennsylvania."

She reached out her hand. He took it and held it firmly.

"You're wild, Bill, you know that? Bill from Pennsylvania."

He held onto her hand and studied her, before finally letting go. His next jukebox selection started to play. It was "Crazy" by Patsy Cline. He turned in his barstool and stared at the jukebox with the most contented look, his face flush and warm. He couldn't help but wonder how he ended up in that exact spot at that exact time with all that he had done the past few days. The feeling from earlier at the crawfish boil had returned. He finally felt at peace with all things. This was where he was supposed to be. He'd finally found it.

Maybe taking the money was worth it after all, he thought, *just to be in this moment.*

He drained the shot of tequila. Kat returned to fill the empty glass. He watched her, before speaking up with a courage he thought had long left him.

"Do a shot of tequila with me, Kat."

"No, no, no, Bill. I'm working."

"Don't take this the wrong way," he said, hesitating a moment. "But you look like what a Patsy Cline song sounds like."

She showed him a funny expression as he motioned to the jukebox.

"A beautiful song, a beautiful voice," he said, turning back to her, "and a beautiful young woman. I love Patsy Cline."

She smiled, blushed a little, and hesitated before responding.

"That's the nicest thing anyone's ever said to me."

"I mean it."

"I know you do."

"Come on, do a shot of tequila. I'll be gone tomorrow."

She reached for another shot glass behind the bar and filled it.

"To you and your travels, Wild Bill."

They raised their glasses and knocked back the tequila.

She studied him and briefly grinned before walking away to wait on another group of patrons who had just entered the bar.

Bill glanced out the window. The rain poured harder. He dragged on the cigar.

"Let it rain," he mumbled to himself. "Let it rain all spring. I could come here every day until they catch me, or the money runs out. I don't care."

xxx

Rita glared at Agent Stack, who was hunched over in a chair in the kitchen with a phone against his ear. He had been that way for most of the afternoon. Her house was filled with numerous local detectives as well as several FBI agents. Hundreds of people had gathered in the street outside her house. More media outlets had arrived, many from outside the Pittsburgh area. Rita stepped towards Agent Stack and continued to stare her frustration at him until he glanced up to her.

"What are you still doing here?" she asked. "Shouldn't you be out looking for my husband?"

"I am leaving for Florida in a few hours."

"Shouldn't you already be there?"

"I am doing everything I can, Ma'am," he looked away from her. "My men are in Jacksonville now. You have to trust me."

"Did you see anything from the cameras inside and outside the bank?"

"No," he answered without looking up.

"How 'bout the garage where Bill parked?"

"No."

"What about the video from downtown? Detective Banner said you were analyzing tape from different cameras at stoplights and at the tunnel."

"We got nothing," he said, still not looking up.

"Did you see his car?"

"Yes."

"*Yes*? Was Bill driving?"

"Yes."

"*Was he alone?*"

66

"Maybe, probably."

"You need to start talking, Stack. What is the hell is going on?"

"He was driving," Stack said, finally glancing up. "Looked like there was something in the passenger seat beside him. We have not been able to figure it out yet. We do not think it was another person, but we are not a hundred percent sure."

"What do you mean you're not sure? It might have been the gunman who was trying to hide. Bill's probably being tortured right now!"

"He ain't kidnapped," Stack said with a smirk and a shake of his head. He stood. "He ran away like all of them—a coward."

"I gave you another chance, Mr. Stack, and allowed you back into my home," Rita said, calmly but sternly. She was trying her best to maintain her composure as the loud and chaotic house immediately went silent. "Bill and I may have our problems, but he's not like all of them. He's a good man. A very good man. And because you're rude and lack professional decorum, I don't want you to ever set foot in my house again. You got that!"

xxx

Just like the day before, several empty glasses were gathered on the bar in front of Bill as he watched Kat joke with the other customers. He was clearly intoxicated and needed to get back to his room at the guest house. She glanced over to him as he fumbled with his money. She quickly appeared with two shot glasses filled with tequila.

"I thought about what you said yesterday. Maybe you're right. Maybe I do need to get away. Keep moving you know. But. . ."

They knocked back the shots, and both grimaced. As the afternoon had faded into evening, the shots had gotten progressively harder for Bill to stomach.

"But what?"

"I'm listening to a middle-aged man in an obvious mid-life crisis. You'll get your kicks, and when reality sinks in, you'll run back to your wife and the safety of your old life."

"No, no, you're wrong."

"And your wife will gladly take you back."

"I can never go back."

He stood on shaky legs. "Really nice to meet you, Kat. You're my first real friend on this new journey."

Her initial smile turned serious as Bill clumsily reached for the bar's front door.

"Bill, wait," she called out.

He stopped at the door and turned. They stared at each other.

"I wanna go," she said.

"What?"

"I wanna go with you."

"Where?"

"Wherever you're going next?"

xxx

Day 6. Tuesday, May 2. 7:10 AM

In a local deputy office in Jacksonville, Florida, the five teenagers who Bill gave the bank credit card and mobile phone to were seated around a table in a crowded interrogation room. They each were eighteen years old and had all dropped out of high school. They were handcuffed and wore orange jumpsuits. For some reason known only to him, Agent Stack wanted them to be interrogated together. Multiple deputies guarded the door both inside and outside the locked room. Stacks of boxes that contained expensive sneakers and assorted electronics, such as new phones, car stereo equipment, and video game consoles, were piled high on the table. Teams of local detectives and one FBI agent were questioning the five delinquents when Agent Stack arrived. The room went silent as he entered. He slammed the door behind him as if inconvenienced to get the attention of the teenagers. He wasted no time in starting the interrogation.

"How did you get the credit card?" Stack leaned in close to the face of the black kid who appeared to be in charge.

"Like I told them," the kid said, motioning to the other officers in the room, "someone gave it to us."

Before asking another question, Stack pounded his fist on the table, startling the young men and causing them to jerk up straight in their seats.

"I do not have the time or the patience for you little shits to fuck with me. How did you get the goddamn credit card?"

"Someone gave it to us," the black kid said as the others nodded. "That's the truth."

"Someone just doesn't give someone, especially you dipshits, a credit card."

"Well, someone did."

"Who?"

"I don't know. I never saw 'em before."

"I am not asking you again. Who the fuck gave you the card?"

"We didn't know 'em."

Stack tossed a photo of Bill onto the table.

"Is this the guy?" he asked, tapping on the picture.

The five teenagers each studied the photo, glanced at each other, and shrugged.

"Well? Is this the fucking guy who gave you the card?"

"It could be," the black kid who was in charge said with shrug.

"What do you mean, it could be?"

"I'm not sure," he said staring at the photo, before looking up to Stack.

"Not sure?"

"All you crackers look alike."

"Jesus Christ!" Stack yelled, obviously frustrated. "Is this the guy? I am not asking again!"

"I don't know."

"So, you are telling me," Stack said to the black kid, before pausing and glaring at the others, "that a stranger you have never seen before or can identify hands you a bank credit card and gives you the PIN number?"

"Yeah, I swear! I thought he was a cop, tryin' to set us up."

"It looks like he did, kid. It looks like he did."

"Seems like we ain't the only ones who've been set up," the kid mocked Stack, glancing around the room crowded with other law enforcement officials.

Stack and the kid stared. After a few moments, Stack turned away from him and headed for the door.

"Lock 'em back up! I do not want to see their faces again!" Stack barked out as he left the room. "Also note that they were uncooperative and hostile."

xxx

Badly hungover and nauseous, Bill slowly packed his bags in the guest room. He thought about staying another day and sleeping off the hangover, but he knew he couldn't stay in one place for too long. He had absolutely no idea where he was going next. Suddenly, there was a knock on the door. It startled him. Thinking the party was over and the authorities had found him, he tiptoed to the door and peered through the peephole. He sighed and gently pulled the door open. Kat stood before him with a knapsack hanging from her shoulder. They stared a moment, before Bill turned and walked back into the room. She stepped into the room behind him but hesitated at the door.

"I didn't think you'd show up. Shut the door."

She closed the door as he dumped out the garment bag full of money onto the bed.

"Holy shit!"

"Have you seen a million dollars before?"

She picked up a bundle of cash.

"That's ten thousand dollars."

"Jesus Christ, Bill! Where in the hell did you get this?"

70

He quickly started shoving the money back into the bag.
"I stole it."
"What?"
Bill slung the bag over his back.
"If you come with me, you'll be an accomplice to a pretty serious felony. So as you can see, this is much more than a mid-life crisis."
Neither of them moved.
"Well? Are you coming?"
"I'll go," she answered after a short pause.
"Damn girl, you got balls."

xxx

Bill and Kat were about five miles out of the French Quarter heading west towards Texas. She had kicked off her shoes and rested her bare feet on the dashboard in front of her. He had the radio tuned to an AM classic country music station. With the car windows rolled down, Kat loudly and playfully sang along to a Hank Williams, Sr.: "Settin' the Woods on Fire." Bill glanced to her and smiled. She leaned into him and tried to get him to join her in singing the song. Grinning, he shrugged and shook his head. As they drove away from the city, she poked her head out the window. Her long hair flew with wind as she waved goodbye with both hands to New Orleans.

Noticing the exceptionally heavy morning rush hour traffic heading into downtown New Orleans, Bill suddenly stopped the Equinox on an empty overpass that crossed above a busy highway that led into and out of the city. On the expressway below, there were two lanes of stalled traffic, backed up for miles, as far as they could see. Bill showed Kat a sneaky grin as she stared back with a puzzled look. He pulled off the road, shut off the engine, and reached into the garment bag, digging out two stacks of cash. He handed one of the bundles of money to Kat.

"What's this for?" she asked, still studying Bill.

He got out of the car without answering and headed for the sidewalk on one side of the overpass. Kat followed as Bill peeled off the tab of paper that held the hundred-dollar bills together in the stack. They both leaned over the concrete wall and stared to the traffic below.

"Look at those sorry sons of bitches down there," he said. "That used to be me."

Kat glanced to Bill who flipped a single hundred-dollar bill off the bridge with a flick of his wrist. The bill lazily floated with the warm morning breeze, before landing on the hood of one of the cars below. He flipped several more of the bills into the air. Eventually, people started to get out of their cars and look up to the overpass, before retrieving the free money. Kat held onto her stack of money and watched Bill as he continued to toss the money off the bridge, a single bill at a time. Car horns started to honk as even more people got out of their cars to gather the money.

"Make it rain, Kat," Bill said as she ripped the tab of paper off her stack of money and tossed the entire ten thousand dollars into the air.

A green cloud of hundred-dollar bills rained from the sky. Bill tossed what was left of his stack of money as well. They both smiled as the giggling crowd below, briefly distracted from their monotonous commute to work, chased the money as it fluttered in the wind. Many folks walked the line of congested cars and shared some of the money with others in neighboring cars stalled in traffic. Drivers in cars further back in the line of traffic who couldn't see what was happening blared their horns louder and more continuously. A siren could be heard in the distance.

"It's time to go," Bill said to Kat. They dashed for the car.

"Is this what you've been doing?" she asked as they hopped in the car. He didn't answer. "What a nice thing. What a really beautiful thing, Bill."

"And fun, too." He was grinning at her as they drove away.

"You're the best, Wild Bill!"

Chapter 4
Texas

A black Cadillac Escalade with government plates was parked in the bustling lot of the big box store in Jacksonville where Bill had purchased the three mobile phones. Agent Stack sat in the driver's seat. Spread on the dashboard and front passenger seat were piles of paperwork that included store receipts and phone records. He held a phone to his ear in one hand and a coffee in the other. He peered at the store's entrance as the phone continued to ring. Finally, the call was answered.

"Any news, Boss?" the voice of an agent on the other line asked.

"I tracked down the credit card and all the purchases," Stack answered. "Everything ended here in Jacksonville. I got nothing."

"What about the phone call from Florida?"

"A pre-paid phone. There's no name associated with the account or phone plan."

"You think he's still there?"

"Nah. He's long gone. He's on the run. He was stalling us."

"What's the plan now?"

"I'm not sure yet. Been wondering about that all morning."

"Are you sticking around?"

"For one more night," Stack said. "Think I will head back to the room. File the report on what I have so far."

"We'll keep our eyes out in Florida for his car?"

"He will screw up," Stack said. "They always do."

"It seems he had a well-thought-out plan."

"Maybe."

"And he appears to be organized."

"We will catch him. Don't worry. This one may take a little time. I get the feeling we are chasing a cautious, calculating, and highly intelligent individual."

Day 6. Tuesday, May 2. 3:40 PM

It was a quiet ride for the rest of the drive through the swamplands of western Louisiana. The morning was overcast and dreary with periods of light drizzle. For much of the drive, Bill and Kat hadn't talked much. As they raced towards Texas, they passed south of Baton Rouge, crossed the Atchafalaya National Wildlife Refuge, and drove just north of Lake Charles. Kat napped into the early afternoon as they drove on, not intending to stop until one of them needed a bathroom break or the Equinox was out of gas. In no time, they crossed the Sabine River and entered Texas. Bill had planned to stay on I-10 and head west. Instead, he changed his mind for no specific reason as they neared Houston, taking I-45 north. Kat finally awoke and stared out to the busy highway for many miles without saying a word. Bill kept glancing to her, but she never looked back. He wondered if she was having second thoughts about joining him.

"You, all right?" he finally asked.

"I'm bored, Bill. We haven't stopped for hours. Let's do something."

"Like what?"

"Let's make a donation. Get a drink. I don't know."

"Where?"

"Take the next exit. We'll find someplace."

Bill followed Kat's orders and left the interstate. They soon found themselves in a sparsely populated part of Texas on State Highway 21. Somewhere between Midway and Austonio, Bill reached into the garment bag and pulled out a stack of hundred-dollar bills. He handed her the cash and stopped at a lone mailbox on the side of the highway. Her face suddenly lighted up as she excitedly exited the car and slid a hundred-dollar bill into the box. This continued for miles. Bill stopped at each mailbox they approached, and Kat gifted every single one of them with cash.

On a dusty backroad, they came upon an elderly man sitting on a porch of a rusty mobile home. Kat hopped out of the Equinox and trotted towards him, waving her arm. He greeted her at the top step of the porch as she handed him five-hundred dollars. He happily clapped after counting the money as they pulled away. After another mile or so, they drove up to a refurbished, Adobe-style house that had a large painted sign in front.

"What did that say?" Bill pointed to the sign as he pulled the car into a parking lot.

"A sober living shelter for men and women."

Grinning, Bill handed her a ten-thousand-dollar stack of cash. She took the money and started to walk towards the entrance of the shelter.

"Kat, wait," Bill called.

She stopped and returned to the car as Bill handed her the pair of sunglasses he'd been wearing.

"You better put these on. We need to be careful."

She slipped the sunglasses over her eyes. "You know, you'll be famous when this is all over."

xxx

Still wearing a black suit, Agent Stack was alone in a swanky hotel suite. He lounged in a recliner watching cable news and sipping a glass of bourbon. Its bottle, nearly empty, was on the table next to him. He stared with open contempt at Bill's picture that stretched across the entire television screen.

"Authorities describe the investigation of the runaway banker from Pennsylvania, William Moreland, as at a standstill," the news anchor reported. "Sources at the FBI have been mum to this point. They are, however, asking for the public's help. If anyone has any information related to the case or to the whereabouts of Mr. Moreland, they are asked to call the number on the bottom of the screen."

Stack drained the rest of the bourbon in the glass as the news anchor transitioned to the next story.

"In another, just-as-mysterious case," the news anchor said as Stack poured the last of the bourbon from the bottle into the glass, "anonymous donations of thousands of dollars to assorted charities in Florida continue across the southern United States."

"Florida?" Stack said, slowly sitting up and leaning forward in his chair.

"Authorities have no information on the identity of the person or persons responsible for these charitable acts. It's been estimated that well over forty-thousand dollars have been donated to date."

There was a knock at the door. He didn't acknowledge it for a moment, still studying the television screen.

"The last reported donation occurred at a sober living facility in Texas as recently as today," the newscaster said, concluding the report.

"Texas?" Stack mumbled, easing himself out of the chair.

There was a second knock. Stack walked to the door without taking his eyes off the television screen. He opened the door to an attractive, formally dressed middle-aged woman. He waved her into the room and pecked her cheek.

"As always, you look wonderful, my dear," Stack said, looking back to the television. "But can you excuse me? I need to make one quick phone call. Then I belong to you."

The woman nodded and took a seat on the couch as Stack dialed his phone and paced the floor as he talked.

"Hey, Boss," the agent on the other end of the line said. "What's up?"

"I finally figured out his game."

"The banker?"

"He is giving the money away. I guess the good life all those

76

years has him feeling guilty."

"How do you know?"

"I know. Trust me on this one."

"What's the plan?"

"He is in Texas. I am taking the first flight in the morning," he said, glancing to his lady friend who smiled at him from across the room. "I am somewhat occupied right now."

"Anything we can do?"

"Let the boys in Houston know I am on my way. Make sure there are a couple of cars and agents ready to go when I get there."

"All right, Boss. Give me a call when you land."

"I will have the banker by the weekend."

Stack hung up the phone and looked to the woman on the couch.

"Do you want to go out for dinner or stay in?" he asked. "We could get room service and a bottle of wine."

"Let's stay in," she said. "Sounds more fun."

"Yeah," Stack said, grinning and joining her on the couch. "I do not want to see anyone else tonight."

xxx

It was a clear and warm Texas night. The air was still. After a long day on the road, Bill and Kat had checked into a locally owned, nondescript motel called the Sleep Inn off I-35 not far from Fort Worth. After checking in, they shared take-out from a nearby diner. They were quite hungry. They each sat on one of the two double beds in the room, feasting on fresh garden salads and baskets of French fries and onion rings.

"Do you have family?"

"My mom's in Chicago."

"Is that where you're from?"

"Yes." She nodded. "I was a mistake by two people who should've never been together."

"Do you talk with your mother much?"

"All the time. I have so many great memories with her. But sadly, she's never been happy, always searching for something. She's done it all. Men. Drugs. Religion. Seemed like she had a new boyfriend every few months when I was young. Mostly creeps. When I was old enough, I had to get out of there. It was hard watching someone you love destroy themself."

There followed an extended silence as they ate their food. Bill studied her, wanting to ask more questions about her past. But he sensed she was uncomfortable talking about it.

"What'd you tell your boyfriend?" he said, breaking the silence.

"About what?"

"About this?" he answered, motioning to the motel room and the garment bag of money that hung from a closet door. "And coming along with me."

"I didn't."

"What?"

"I packed up and left without saying anything. He understood. I was tired of trying to make it work. I'm sure he figured I needed another break away from him."

"Have you talked with him since you left?"

"No, but I'm sure I will. Like I told you, I always go running back."

Bill bagged up his empty food containers and got up from the bed to toss them away.

"What was it like when your kids were young?" Kat asked as she slowly picked at the fries.

"What do you mean?"

"Did you go on family trips, vacations?"

"Of course."

"Where?"

"Huh?"

"Where did you go?"

"We'd go to the beaches in the Carolinas. Disney several times. We—"

"I never did any of that stuff," she interrupted. "My mom

was always working. I never really knew my father. He disappeared when I was young."

"That's a tough break."

"For a little girl. Yes, it was."

"Come on," Bill said, reaching out his bandaged hand and pulling her up from the bed. "Let me buy you a drink somewhere."

xxx

It was late. Rita had hardly slept since Bill disappeared. She sat alone in her darkened living room, staring blankly at the local eleven o'clock news on the television. Although the first fifteen minutes of the newscast was dedicated to the story of Bill and the missing money, they didn't have anything new to report; neither did the police or the FBI when she'd spoken with them earlier. For the first time in her life, she had been abandoned. She never felt more alone or helpless as she waited for news, good or bad, regarding Bill's whereabouts. As she dragged hard on a cigarette, car headlights suddenly flashed inside the room and danced across the wall. A car had pulled into the driveway. She quickly stubbed out the cigarette and took a deep breath before hurrying to the window to check who was there.

Maybe Bill has come home, she hoped.

At the window, she studied the car: a deputy's car from the local office.

They must have something important, she thought, eagerly waiting for the deputy. *They would've have called at this hour. Maybe they found Bill or know where he is.*

She recognized Deputy Morton as he got out of the car. He was working this case. As she headed for the front door to greet him, Susie came bounding down the stairs. She was not dressed for bedtime as Rita expected; she was dolled up as if she were headed to a party or dance club. Her hair was washed and curled. Her make-up was fresh and perfect. She wore a short leather cocktail skirt and a designer jean jacket with a tight sparkling top.

"Where are you going?" Rita asked. "I thought we agreed not to leave the house."

"I have a date."

"With Chuck?"

Susie shrugged but didn't answer as the doorbell rang. Rita frowned and retreated to the living room, staring to the floor. Susie excitedly pulled the door open and greeted the handsome deputy with a hug and a quick kiss on the cheek.

"You smell great!" he said as she pulled away from him. "And you look even better."

Susie tried to whisk him away, but he stepped inside and politely removed his hat.

"Is your mother awake?" he asked.

After a brief hesitation, Susie motioned to the living room. Holding his hat over his chest, the Deputy Morton quietly stepped into the room. Rita stared out the picture window but didn't turn to him.

"Ma'am?"

She didn't respond, lighting a cigarette.

"I have nothing new to report."

She still didn't turn or acknowledge him.

"We've been doin' all we—"

"Please have Susie home at a respectful hour," Rita said.

"Yes, Ma'am."

The young deputy waited a few moments for Rita to turn to face him. She never did ands Susie eventually led him out of the house.

xxx

Across the highway from the motel where Bill and Kat were staying, they found a sprawling country-and-western roadhouse bar called the Woodshed in a strip of retail shops and restaurants. The place was basically an enormous faux

80

wooden barn that could hold hundreds of people. As they approached on foot, they noticed the parking lot was full, which seemed peculiar because it was a weeknight. Mostly new, high-end pickup trucks and SUVs continually circled the lot, searching for open parking spaces. Fortunately, or unfortunately depending on who you asked, it was karaoke night at the bar. Kat was thrilled, but Bill not so much. As they would come to find out, the Woodshed was popular on karaoke night—and every other night.

After paying a cover, Bill and Kat fought their way through a young and sweaty crowd of wannabe cowboys and cowgirls, who were mostly fraternity and sorority members from the local colleges dressed in cowboy hats and boots. They luckily found a couple open stools at the spacious horseshoe bar at the back of the place opposite a large, elevated stage in front. They were waited on by cute blonde with short hair and decked out in a cowboy hat, boots, and denim shorts—obviously the club's official employee uniform. Bill and Kat started drinking what were called Mega-Margaritas that came frozen in 32-ounce glass mugs. After they each had a couple, they felt bloated and changed their drink of choice, wanting to avoid the mixers, sours, and ice used in the margarita and go straight to the business end of the drink. They moved on tequila shots—lots of them. They even got the bartender, Janie, to join them.

It wasn't long before all three were somewhat tipsy. They laughed, booed, and cheered the different bar patrons in their amateur attempts to sing such classic songs as Johnny Cash's "Folsom Prison Blues," Sade's "Smooth Operator," and Black Sabbath's "Iron Man."

"Y'all goin' sing one for us tonight?" Janie asked Bill in a pronounced Texas twang as she refilled his empty shot glass with tequila.

"No way!"

"Come on, Bill. It'd be fun," Kat said.

"Absolutely not!"

"No one here knows you," Kat said. "What are you afraid of?

We're a long way from Pennsylvania."

"It doesn't matter. You'll never get me up there."

"How 'bout you, Kat?" Janie asked. "You gonna do a song?"

"I will need a lot more of these," she said, pointing to the shot glass.

Janie filled Kat's shot glass and one for herself. Kat held up her shot of tequila. Bill and Janie followed as all three knocked back the shots. Janie reached for a large cowbell behind the bar and started to ring it, interrupting the host of the karaoke night.

"Oh!" The host spoke into the microphone from the stage. "It sounds like we may have a participant at the bar!"

Janie pointed at Kat as a cheer rang out and, like Moses' parting of the Red Sea, a path in the throng of people between the bar and the stage opened. After shaking her head with initial hesitation, Kat stood up to a rousing ovation. She worked her way to the stage and was helped up by the evening's host. After selecting a song from an extensive catalogue, she approached the microphone.

"I'm Kat from New Orleans," she announced as the crowd cheered again. "This is for my friend, Bill, sitting back there at the bar."

Sounding nervous at first, she started to sing the Patsy Cline hit, "Walking After Midnight." After the first verse and a few appreciative "Woo-hoo!"s from the audience, her voice got stronger and louder to impressively delivered the country classic. To Bill's and Janie's surprise, Kat had a lovely singing voice. She ended the song to a roar from the drunken crowd. At first, it appeared as if she wanted to stay there and perform another song, but instead, she peered into the bright lights and scanned the bar area.

"Is my friend, Bill, back there?" she asked over the microphone.

Janie pointed to Bill and rang the cowbell several times as Bill demonstrably shook his head and waved his hands.

"Let's get Bill up here," Kat called into the microphone.

Bill kept shaking his head but the crowd loudly chanted,

"*Bill! Bill! Bill!*"

Shrugging, Bill finally stood from his barstool. The crowd exploded in applause as he worked his way on unsteady feet through the crowd to the stage. Kat and the host helped Bill up as the crowd continued to chant, "*Bill! Bill! Bill!*"

Kat hugged Bill and hopped off the stage to return to the bar as he quickly selected a song, like he had one in mind. It was the George Strait country standard, "All My Ex's Live in Texas."

Almost immediately after the music to the song started, Bill discovered that he didn't have to worry about how poorly he sounded as practically the entire crowd sang along with him. Extra emphasis was given to the song's chorus as Bill directed the crowd with waving arms like a conductor of a choir, "All my ex's live in Texas! *That's why I hang my hat in Tennessee!*"

It sounded glorious. It was epic. Like a superhero, Bill stood on that stage bigger than life — the center of everyone's attention. For the first time, he was king for a night. And it felt good.

At the bar, Janie slid Kat another shot of tequila and asked, "Are you with him?"

"Not in the way you're thinking. What do they say? It's complicated. He rescued me from a situation that had gone bad. I'm just along for the ride."

"Y'all from around here?"

"Just passing through," Kat said, shaking her head. "We're staying at the Sleep Inn across the highway."

The song Bill was singing finally ended, first to a loud cheer, then to more chants of "*Bill! Bill! Bill!*"

"Is there a liquor store nearby?" Kat asked Janie.

"What do you need? I may be able to help."

xxx

Giggling, Kat and Janie playfully chased a highly intoxicated Bill from the bar to the motel. Kat carried a liter of tequila. Janie held a bag of lemons. They ran after Bill across a four-lane highway and through the motel's parking lot as he darted around each of the cars parked there. Briefly losing the two ladies, he scrambled to the door of the motel room and rushed to unlock it. Nearly out of breath, he dashed inside the room, slammed the door behind him as the ladies, laughing loudly, quickly followed him. Inside, Bill stopped at one of the room's beds and turned. The ladies busted through the unlocked door and tackled him, knocking him onto the bed. The three of them wrestled for many minutes as they rolled around. Like a drunken turtle stuck upside down, Bill struggled to sit up as Kat lifted Janie to her feet. The two of them started to hop up and down. Bill's limp, inebriated body bounced on the bed for several minutes before finally being tossed into the air. He landed hard on the floor in a tight space between the wall and the rocking bed.

All the jarring made Bill nauseous. His body suddenly cold and clammy, he began to sweat. The tequila that filled his belly felt as if it had moved to his throat. As the ladies jumped, danced, and sang with each other on the bed, Bill quickly and awkwardly crawled to the bathroom. He reached the toilet, flipped the seat up while on his stomach, and pulled himself up to the bowl. He briefly rested his chin on the edge of it until he couldn't hold his stomach any longer and violently vomited into the toilet. His empty belly cramped with dry heaves for many minutes until he rolled onto his back where he would remain. The room spinning, he heard Kat and Janie loudly singing the classic Camper Van Beethoven song, "Where the Hell is Bill?" The song's repetitive phrase "Where, where the hell is Bill?" echoed through the room. Before passing out, he couldn't help but wonder the exact same thing.

xxx

Day 7. Wednesday, May 3. 8:33 AM

A sliver of light cut through a break in the curtains, waking Bill, who was nearly paralytic under a layer of blankets. His head

84

ached as if a spike had been driven through it. His stomach burned. The bandage on his right hand had fallen off, exposing the red and swollen stab mark across it. He struggled to open his eyes and smacked his dry, sour mouth. It took him several minutes to remember where he was and how he got there. It was the worst hangover he'd ever experienced in his life.

With a deep breath, he strained to lift his body into a sitting position. Slumped over, he swung his legs out from under the covers. Rubbing at his sleepy eyes, he glanced down and noticed he was completely naked below his waist—no pants, no underwear, no socks, no shoes. To the best of his recollection, he was fully clothed when he was last awake. He frantically searched the recesses of his clouded mind about what might have happened just as the bed suddenly moved. He shot a look over his shoulder. Kat, who was sleeping beside him in the middle of the small bed, rolled over. Beside Kat, Janie slept on the other side of the bed. Neither appeared to be wearing much. The motion of the spinning ceiling fan caught his eye, and he spotted his boxer shorts hanging from the fan.

"Oh, shit," he mumbled, grabbing the two pillows beside him to cover his private parts. *What in the hell did I do?*

He slid off the bed and picked his boxers from the fan, before dragging himself to bathroom. Doubled over, he stepped into the boxer shorts leaning against the sink for support. He remained bent over for several minutes to allow a sudden wave of stomach queasiness to pass. Leaning his head under the faucet, he flipped it on and took a couple sips of the metal-heavy water to wet his dry mouth. He breathed deeply and dropped on the closed toilet lid until he regained enough composure to leave the bathroom without puking.

Remembering that the motel provided free coffee, he slipped on a robe he found in a closet, stepped into a pair of shoes, and left the room. Bill's closing of the door woke both Kat and Janie. They both sat up and stretched. As the previous night's escapades slowly returned, they looked at each other and giggled, before falling back onto the bed, laughing.

Bill entered the lobby and walked directly to the coffee pot, trying not to make eye contact with the motel manager at the reception desk. He passed a muted television set tuned to cable news without noticing; the reporter was live in Pittsburgh in front of Bill's house.

As Bill reached for three Styrofoam cups, the manager said loudly, "We're out of cream."

"Huh?" Bill asked, not turning.

"We're out of cream. For the coffee."

"It's not the cream I'm here for." Bill filled three large cups with steaming black coffee. He headed for the door with the coffees.

"Are you in room 127? We had a lot of complaints about you last night."

"So?"

"So, I didn't bother you. I saw the two young women you came in with. I wasn't going to be the one who spoiled your fun."

Bill didn't respond as he reached for the door.

"I was wishin' I was you last night."

"The way I feel this morning, I'm wishing I was you right now."

Carrying the coffees, Bill entered the room. Kat sat alone on the bed, her legs crossed. She wore nothing but a tight tank top and a skimpy, lacey white thong. Bill immediately turned his head.

"Jesus Christ. Put your damn clothes on. *Goddammit!*"

Smiling as Bill kept his back turned, Kat wrapped a blanket from the bed over her head and body.

"I brought you both coffees," he said and set the cups on the nightstand. "They were out of cream." He scanned the dark, stuffy room.

"Where's our bartender friend?"

"She split."

"Split?"

"She had to work."

Bill took a seat on the still-made bed.

"I wasn't wearing any underwear when I woke up." He avoided eye contact with Kat. "I don't remember a thing. I didn't. . . We didn't. . ."

"You pissed yourself. I didn't want you to sleep in wet pants."

"So, you saw my —"

"It's no big deal, Bill," she interrupted. "I've seen a man's penis before."

"But not mine."

"Trust me. Most, not all, but most of them are all the same."

xxx

Puffing a Cuban cigar and hiding behind a pair of oval sunglasses with thick, white frames, Bill lounged at the pool of the roadside motel. He bought the gaudy sunglasses in the lobby. They were woman's sunglasses — the only style they had. Still badly hungover, he and Kat skipped on their plans of making more donations and stayed at the motel all day. They both felt too ill to leave. Bill looked ragged with a scraggily beard. The khakis he wore had been hacked into shorts. His tee-shirt was stained, the weathered Pirates cap on his head. He sipped at a can of Lone Star beer to cure his hangover while Kat took a swim.

Bill watched her effortlessly swim laps around the pool. The kick of her legs and the backstroke of her arms were fluid, easy, and flawless. She freely glided from one end of the pool to the other with barely a ripple on the surface of the water. Bill couldn't take his eyes off her. He stared, mesmerized by the clean straight lines of her slender body as she sliced through the water. She was everything he was not — confident, graceful, free. She was fearless and without inhibition. There wasn't a risk she wouldn't take.

Finally, she easily rolled onto her belly like a playful dolphin, breaching the water as she reached for the wall on one side of the pool and lifted herself out. Water poured off her as she bent over in front of Bill and grabbed a towel. She readjusted both pieces of her dripping bikini. He continued to stare as she spread out the towel on a lounger next to him less than a foot away. She looked to him, knowing he had been watching.

"I used to swim in high school," she claimed. "All-state."

He nodded with the most contented smile. A light breeze had been blowing most of the afternoon. As her wet and glistening body dried in the warm Texas sun, goosebumps formed on her bare legs, arms, and stomach. Bill continued to stare at her, trying his best, but not having much luck, to look away. He hoped the dark sunglasses hid his roaming eyes.

"What are you looking at?"

"Your tattoos," he answered as he scanned every inch of her nearly perfect body.

"Do you like them?"

"Yeah. Yeah, I do. I think they're sexy."

"Do you have one?"

"Nah. Nah," he said, shaking his head. "It was different back in my day. I was led to believe you'd never get a job if you had a tattoo, particularly one that was openly visible. Only sailors, convicts, and construction workers had tattoos."

"Would you get one now?"

"I'm not sure." He shrugged. "There's been nothing I've seen so far that I'd want permanently stamped on my body."

"Everyone I know has a tattoo."

"It's a generational thing, I guess. You do have to admit there's a lot of bad tattoos running around. We're a country of bad tattoos. Especially in Pennsylvania. I know. I've been to the public pools." He took a swig of beer, still spying her drying body. "Do each of your tattoos have meaning?"

"Of course."

"How 'bout that one?" He pointed to a three-dimensional horseshoe on the outside of her left bicep.

"I've been lucky," she said, twisting her left arm and studying the tattoo. "It's a reminder of how lucky I've been. It could've all gone wrong for me. I had a challenging upbringing. But I'm healthy. I have some self-awareness. I think I know who I am. I try to see the big picture in everything and not get weighed down by the small shit. Except when it comes to my asshole boyfriend, I hope I'm a pretty good judge of character. Like when you came into the bar."

"Me? In New Orleans?"

"You obviously weren't a local. But after talking with you, I found you different, not the typical out-of-towner or tourist. You weren't in New Orleans to get wasted for a weekend It seemed you had a greater purpose. It also seemed you did something naughty."

"Naughty?"

"And you were almost proud of it. I was intrigued. I had to find out more about you. I wanted to know what secret you were hiding."

"Nobody's ever found me intriguing before."

"Maybe you hadn't done anything interesting or dangerous until you robbed the bank," she paused. He continued to stare. "What'd you think of me?"

"You were the reason I stayed another night in New Orleans," he said, before motioning to the pool and her outstretched bikini-clad body next to him. "It might have been the best decision I ever made."

"Yeah. It's been fun so far."

"And of course, I found you attractive. Exotic. You're not from my bland, dull world. And friendly. You were so welcoming. I was a stranger."

"I mostly work for tips, Bill. I have to be welcoming."

"But you were sincere. Don't take this the wrong way, but I find you to be somewhat maternal, motherly. Even though I'm old enough to be your father."

"Maternal? I can understand welcoming and friendly, but *maternal*?"

"And I still feel that way. Like you're watching over me. Protecting me. Keeping me safe. I need that."

"You always know what to say to make me feel good about myself. No one has ever told me things like you do."

"I wish I could talk to my daughter this way."

"I bet you haven't tried."

"No. I've tried, but her interests and experiences are so limited. And it's my fault."

"It's not your fault. I didn't have a father. We are who we are."

"You were never sheltered. I smothered my kids," he said, before finishing the can of beer. "Even though you are close to my daughter's age, you seem much older, more worldly. And certainly, wiser. You have an old soul, Kat."

Bill reached into the small Styrofoam cooler of beer.

"Can I have one of those?" she asked. He pulled out two cans of Lone Star.

"What's the meaning of that one?" Bill asked, handing her the beer, and pointing to a multicolored cartoon-like chicken leg on her left shoulder.

"I got that one the last time I ate meat. A whole bucket of spicy wings. About three years ago. I'll probably never eat meat again."

"And what about that one?" Bill asked, pointing to a fleur-de-lis on the inside of her left forearm. "An obvious reference to New Orleans."

"New Orleans saved me."

He pointed at an exceptionally well-done portrait tattoo of what looked like a young woman on her right shoulder. "Who's that?".

"That's my mother's high school yearbook photo."

"She's beautiful." He stared at the tattoo a few moments before looking up. "I see where you get your good looks."

"As beautiful on the inside as the outside. She's just been dealt a bad hand. And she's a poor judge of character, especially with men. Much more than I am."

"And the vine?" Bill pointed out a vivid green vine and leaves that started on the bottom of her right shoulder and wrapped around her bicep several times until stopping at her elbow. "And what is that in the vine there?"

"This?" she said, rubbing the red and blue Chicago Cub baseball team logo, featuring a cartoon blue bear inside a red 'C'. "Go, Cubbies."

"Go, Pirates!" He doffed the Pirates cap that protected his balding head. "Is that the ivy from the wall of Wrigley Field?"

"My mother worked the concessions at Wrigley Field when I was growing up. She'd sneak me into afternoon games in the summer when I was kid. It wasn't a problem because the Cubs weren't very good back then and there were always plenty of empty seats. I would sit in the last row in right field where she could keep an eye on me from the concession stand she worked." Her grin widened. "I came of age at Wrigley. I had my first kiss there. My first cigarette. My first beer. I was probably fourteen and a cute boy who had to be nineteen bought it for me. All behind the Old Style beer tent under the outfield bleachers and out of sight from my mother."

"Those must be nice memories. You're glowing."

"I can't help but smile when I think back to those days. An overly curious teenage girl could get in a lot of trouble at a Cubs baseball game. Good trouble. And it was fun, too."

"Your short life and stories are better and more colorful than mine, and I've lived three more decades than you."

Enjoying the moment, they lifted their beer cans and tapped them, before chugging what was left. Bill reached in the cooler and grabbed a couple more.

"Any other tattoos?" he asked, handing her the beer as he scanned her body.

"I have one more," she said without expression, not taking her eyes from his.

Bill lifted the sunglasses and rested them on his forehead. She teasingly fingered the waistband of her bikini bottom, slowly running her index finger back and forth underneath the band. As he glanced to her stomach, she eventually pulled the left side of the waistband down an inch or so, exposing much of the bare skin of her upper thigh. He fixated less on the small tattoo stamped there than he did on the definitive tan line that separated her golden-brown belly from the much lighter and softer naked skin just left of her pubic area.

"Do you know what it is?" she asked, pulling the bikini bottom further down and exposing more of the bare skin.

"Ahhh," he mumbled, still ogling the normally forbidden area where the tattoo was located.

"A compass," she said.

Bill squinted and leaned up from his chair for a closer look. Obsessed with what Kat was showing him, he suddenly felt an intensity he hadn't experienced since a teenager. Hoping Kat didn't notice, he nonchalantly covered his groin area, which had been mostly dormant for years.

"If you're ever down there," she said as he looked up into her serious, gazing eyes. "It's so you don't get lost."

Glancing back to the tattoo, he unintentionally squeezed the can he was holding, causing beer to explode out the top like an erupting volcano. She let go of the waistband of the bikini bottom as it snapped back into place.

"I got that tattoo when I turned fifteen," she said. "It was my first one."

"Any reason why?"

"What do you mean?"

"Why that specific area?"

"I just lost my virginity."

"A boyfriend?"

"An older kid down the street from where I lived."

"Can I ask? How was it?"

"The kid was in way over his head."

They briefly stared at one another, before finishing the beers. Bill felt exactly as that older kid down that street must have. After setting down the empty beer can, Kat wrapped the edges of the towel she was lounging on around her shoulders and arms.

"I'm ready to go inside."

"We've haven't eaten yet today," Bill said. "I'm finally starting to feel better. Are you hungry?"

"Starving."

"Let me take you someplace nice."

"Wouldn't that be risky?"

"They don't know we're in Texas yet. We have the money. Let's spend it before they come and take it back."

xxx

As the sun was setting, Bill parked outside a fine steak and seafood restaurant in a strip mall not far from the motel. He circled the lot a couple times, before finding a spot near a back entrance. The tables and bar inside appeared to be full. He led Kat to the front door, opening it for her and following her inside the lobby. The place was a little more upscale than he expected. The ornate bar top and bar back were trimmed in mahogany. A decorative crown molding in the same wood trimmed the ceilings. Vibrant watercolor portraits adorned the walls. White tablecloths covered the tables. The dining room was lighted with long-stemmed candles. All the diners were formally attired. Some men sported jackets and ties, and their lady guests wore sparkling evening gowns.

Waiting for the restaurant's host to acknowledge them, Bill glanced to Kat. Her hair was still wet from her afternoon swim. She wore cut-off denim shorts, a tank top, and leather sandals. Bill looked down at himself. His clothes were tattered and smudged. He wanted to eat at someplace nice but also busy, hoping to blend in with the other diners. Instead, the two of them stuck out like a wart on the nose of a pretty face.

"You sure about a steakhouse?" he asked her.

"I'll find something. I still eat fish and shrimp."

Lifting the sweat-stained ball cap from his head, Bill slowly shuffled up to the host, displaying a peace sign with his two forefingers. The host ignored them.

"A table for two," Bill said.

93

"Um. . ." The host looked from Bill to Kat; his cold stare seemed to condemn their relaxed attire. "This is a formal place. Collared shirt for men. No shorts." He pretended to scan a seating chart while he spoke. "This isn't the Golden Corral."

Bill slid a hundred-dollar bill from his pocket to the palm of his hand.

"And besides," the host said, looking up from the chart, "I don't see a single open table at the moment."

"I think you need to study that chart a little closer," Bill said, uncupping his palm and flashing the hundred-dollar bill long enough for the host to see it.

The host studied Bill a moment, before glancing into the bustling dining room. "Well, actually, I think I may see something in the back."

Bill and Kat followed the host into the buzz of the obviously popular restaurant. Bill stared to the ground, avoiding eye contact with the other diners. He didn't want to be recognized as the fugitive banker, and he also was embarrassed of how he looked. The host led them to a small, dimly lighted table in the back not far from the swinging door entrance to the kitchen. The host scrambled over to Kat as she reached for one of the two seats at the table, pulling it out for her. He motioned for Bill to sit and lighted the candle in the middle of the table.

"Our finest and most romantic table, sir."

"Thank you." Bill slipped the hundred-dollar bill into the host's hand.

"The server will be with you two in a moment. Enjoy!"

"Before you run off," Bill said, "please bring us a bottle of your finest Bordeaux."

"Certainly. Certainly, sir!"

"I think they're trying to hide us back here," Bill whispered.

"This place smells amazing," Kat said, scanning the dining area.

"You sure this is all right," Bill said, studying the menu. "Looks like mostly steak, chicken, and pork."

The host promptly returned, holding a dusty bottle of red

wine and two glasses. He held out the bottle and showed Bill the label.

"A Bourdeaux. 2015. Produced by Chateau Contenac Brown. Highly rated. Highly recommended."

"Great," Bill said. "Fine. Fine."

The host reached for a wine key in his back pocket and delicately pulled the cork from the bottle with a quiet pop. He set the cork down on the table and motioned to Bill's glass, offering him a taste.

Bill shook his head and pointed to the wine glasses. "Fill 'em both up. We trust you."

"As you wish, sir," the host said, filling both wine glasses. "Enjoy! The server will be over momentarily."

"You wouldn't mind waiting on us, would you? I think we're ready to order," Bill asked, looking to Kat who nodded. "We'll make it worth your trouble."

"No problem, sir," the host agreed. "I'll be back in a minute. I need to find someone to work the host's stand in front."

The host rushed off as Bill and Kat raised the glasses of wine and clinked them together.

"Here's to another day of freedom," Bill said, before they each took rather large gulps of the four-hundred-dollar bottle of wine.

"What do you think?" he asked.

"Pretty delicious. But I've had better."

"Me, too, girl."

"What are you ordering?" she asked.

"I'm thinking the 20-ounce ribeye. How about you?"

"I am leaning towards the stuffed shrimp. . ."

Before she could fully respond, a server walked by their table, carrying a tray covered with plates of sizzling and buttery chargrilled steaks. Kat sat up in her seat and examined the tray as it passed. Many of the steaks on the tray were so large they extended over the edges of the plates. None of them looked less than four inches thick and must have weighed at least sixteen ounces. Mounds of loaded baked potatoes accompanied each of them.

"Fuck it," she said, leaning back into her seat. "I'm getting the prime rib."

"What about the vegetarian thing?"

"It's been a good run."

xxx

Soiled plates and bowls and empty glasses in different sizes littered the small dining table. The candle had long burned out. The tab for the epic meal had been paid. Bill and Kat were the last two people in the restaurant. They were nearly done with their third bottle of wine. Each bottle was more reasonably priced and just as tasty than the one before it. Neither had trouble finishing the thick and succulent steaks that practically melted in their mouths. Not much was said between them as the marathon meal was ending. Both were tired; they needed sleep. Holding a wine glass, Kat leaned back, her chair pushed away from the table a bit. Bill stared at her, finishing the last of his wine.

"What was it about New Orleans?"

"New Orleans chose me."

"Chose you?"

"Yes. New Orleans chose me. You just don't move there and stay. New Orleans has to choose you."

"I don't understand."

"I went there for Mardi Gras with my first serious boyfriend a few years ago. I was supposed to stay a week."

"What happened?"

"I couldn't get myself to leave. I felt this overwhelming urge to stay. An urge I can't explain to anyone other than those who have ended up there. I fell in love with the place, got an apartment, a job, and started bartending."

"What about your boyfriend?"

"He tried living there with me. He really wanted to stay, but in the first week, he got mugged, his car was stolen, and he tripped on the sidewalk late one night, shattering his wrist and elbow."

"Where is he now?"

"Back in Chicago. New Orleans didn't choose him. He didn't belong. Almost everyone I know there who came from somewhere else has a similar story."

The restaurant host who had waited on them appeared at their table, carrying a dessert tray of several delectable-looking treats that included different cheesecakes, a chocolate torte, crème brûlée, and homemade apple pie with a scoop of ice cream.

"You were too generous," he said to Bill, then glanced to Kat. "Please pick a dessert. It's on me."

"I don't think I have any more room," Bill said. He motioned to Kat with a wave of his hand. "What do you think?"

"Sorry. I'm too full."

"How about a cocktail or digestif?" the host offered. "Please, on me."

"We need to go," Bill said. "But thank you."

"I feel awful about earlier when you two first arrived. I need t—"

"No worries," Bill interrupted him. "Thank you for the good service. We'll be out of your hair in a few minutes."

"No, no, take your time," he said. "Thank you all so much."

"What was the damage on the meal?" Kat whispered after the host had left.

"It was over a thousand."

"Shit, Bill!"

"Including the hundred-dollar bill I gave for the table. I gave him five hundred more."

"Why so much?"

"I'm sure he has to deal with a bunch of assholes in a place like this. I could see it in his face. Believe me, I know. I had deal with some of the worst people on earth for the last thirty years."

"I need to go to sleep, Bill."

"Did you enjoy your meal?"

"Maybe the best meal I've ever had," she said, smiling. "Thank you."

"We deserved it, I think. But no more like this after tonight. The rest of that money is for charity and to keep us free."

xxx

Staring at himself in the motel bathroom mirror, Bill lathered his sunbaked face with shaving cream. The television blared from the other room, tuned to a cable news station. The network was reporting about a series of anonymous donations to assorted charities across the southern United States. Not paying attention to the news report, Kat sat on the edge of one of the twin beds in the room, wearing only a tight tee-shirt and the bikini bottoms she swam in earlier in the day. Her legs were tight against her chest as she meticulously painted her toenails. Distracted by the loudness of the television, Bill stomped into the room in search of the remote control, oblivious to the fact that the report was about his donations. In his search, he noticed Kat and what little clothes she wore.

"Jesus!" he exclaimed, turning his head. "What did I tell you? Put some clothes on! And turn that down or find another station!"

As Kat reached for the remote control, the news story changed as a picture of Bill, his employee identification photo from bank, flashed on the screen. The caption under the photo read: "William Moreland, Missing PA Banker, $1,000,000 Gone."

Bill and Kat stared. His face turned white as snow as if he'd just seen a ghost. For the first time on his journey, the situation felt real, and not like a dream or some silly game. His face and name and what he had done were plastered on the national news for all the world to see. He was a criminal. A wanted man.

"I wouldn't shave if I were you," Kat said.

Speechless, Bill looked to Kat and then back to the television as the reporter provided what few details of the news story were known: "Initial evidence uncovered by the FBI indicates that the missing banker was recently in Florida."

"FBI?" Bill said. "Shit."

"You told me your last name was Runner," she laughed as he sheepishly shrugged "What are we going to do now?"

"We get up early. Make the donations as planned. Then move on."

Bill washed off the shaving cream and got into one of the beds. Kat crawled under the covers of the other bed, clicking off the television. Bill turned off the lamp between the two beds that lighted the room. For nearly twenty minutes, they both tossed and turned, trying their best to sleep even though the news story was still fresh in their minds. Finally, Kat spoke in the dark.

"Tell me more about your daughter."

"Huh?"

"What is she like? Do you miss her?"

"Sure, I do."

"Would she be having as much fun as I am?"

"Ha! She's sees me in a little bit different light than you do."

"What? The misunderstanding dad?"

"No, the world's greatest bore."

"Come on," Kat said, sitting up and glancing towards him. "Look at you! You're wanted by the FBI. You're Wild Bill. The missing banker from Pennsylvania!"

"I miss my son, too," he said, not feeling amused by her enthusiasm. "I failed as a father. There's nothing about my kids that's extraordinary. They've just coasted along, only doing enough to get by. They never had jobs. They were never given responsibility. I never pressed them."

"What about your wife?"

"I miss Rita the most."

"Rita?"

"She's a completely different person now compared to when I first fell in love with her. My first and only true love. And I really loved her."

"Loved?"

"She was so beautiful and kind and humble and fun-loving. What the hell happens to people? I'm sure I've changed as well."

"It's natural, Bill. People evolve as they get older, and sometimes two people grow apart."

"I remember when my wife and I started dating. We were skinny-dipping in a lake not far from the campus where we lived."

"You, Bill? Skinny-dipping? I can't picture that."

"I used to be pretty fun sometimes," he said. He sat up and looked in her direction as she intently studied him in the dark. "So anyway, the sheriff pulled up on us. We scrambled for the car, leaving our clothes, shoes, everything. We drove off with nothing on, dripping wet. We drove that way for miles. I'll never forget it. We laughed and laughed the whole way home."

"You need to call you wife and let her know you're all right."

"I wish I could go back to that exact night, thirty years ago," he said, "and try this thing called life all over again."

"But you can't, Bill. You know that."

"I got maybe a week or so to try, if I don't get caught first."

"Everything will work out, won't it?"

"Maybe in books and movies," he said, before pausing. "I don't know about real life."

"Oh, no!" Kat screamed out, doubling over in pain. "Oh, boy!"

"What? What is it?"

"Jesus Christ! My stomach!"

"Your stomach?"

"It feels like a butcher knife has suddenly been thrust into my gut," she moaned, holding her stomach. "Oh, shit!"

"The steak?"

Before she could answer, she ripped the covers off the bed and dashed to the bathroom with a cramping stomach that nearly took her breath away. Slamming the door behind her, she collapsed to her knees and hurled the contents of her gut into the toilet bowl for most of the next fifteen minutes. She spent another twenty minutes on the floor next to the toilet until the pain in her belly subsided. Concerned, Bill stood outside the bathroom door, waiting for her to emerge.

"Yep, the steak," she said, stepping out of the bathroom, the color from her face gone, her hair messed. "A 16-ounce, seventy-five-dollar, flame-grilled Texas Black Angus, perfectly cooked medium rare prime rib to be exact."

"Three years is a long time without meat."

"Yes, it is," she said, taking a deep breath and throwing herself on the bed.

"We'll eat lighter and healthier tomorrow. I promise."

"Bullshit, Bill. I've been craving a pepperoni pizza for two years now. We're having pizza covered in meat tomorrow. I'm back."

xxx

Day 8. Thursday, May 4. 10:31 AM

Despite what they had planned, Bill and Kat slept in late the next morning. Kat was still somewhat nauseous from the steak dinner. They didn't have much to say to each other as they got ready in the room or on their drive to a nearby toy store. They intended to make a donation, grab a pizza and bring it back to the motel room to eat. Then they'd check out. It was Kat's idea to buy a truckload of bikes and then have them delivered to a local orphanage.

Carrying nearly twenty-thousand dollars, Kat entered the store. She wore the white-framed sunglasses Bill had bought at the motel to hide her identity. Bill waited in the car. After about twenty-five minutes, she exited the store with the manager. The store's delivery truck suddenly appeared from a parking lot in back. It already had been loaded with everything Kat had purchased. She'd used the entire amount of money and bought hundreds of bikes, scooters, and skateboards. She bought every single one they had. As the store manager climbed into the passenger side of the truck, Kat trotted over to Bill's car. He rolled down the window.

"I'm riding with them," she said. "You can follow."

"Riding with them? Follow? We need to get back to the room and check out."

"I want to help them pass out the bikes."

"We've been here too long. We need to get out of town."

"No, not yet. I want to see the kids' reactions to our gifts. Don't you? Isn't that what it's all about?"

"No, that's not what it's about. It's not about us. It's all about them. Nobody needs to know what we're doing."

"Come on, Bill."

"Where's the orphanage?" he asked.

"Not far from here," she said. "They wanted to do some publicity. Call the local televisions station."

"No, absolutely not!"

"That's what I told 'em. And I wouldn't give 'em our names," she said, before pausing. "It'll be all right. I'll keep my distance. No one needs to see me. I promise."

xxx

Before leaving town, Bill and Kat stopped for lunch at a local pizzeria. Carrying two boxes containing large pizzas, they approached a pair of homeless men who sat on the sidewalk about a block away from the pizza shop. Bill had noticed them earlier when the two men were digging through a dumpster behind the shop. They were obviously searching for something to eat.

"Got any spare change?" one of the men called out as Bill and Kat walked towards them. "Anything? For this guy's sake." The homeless man pointed to his sleeping friend stretched out on the sidewalk beside him. "If I don't get somethin' to eat soon, my buddy here's in trouble. Big trouble. I'm so damn hungry. I may carve 'em up and eat 'em right here, right now."

Without hesitating, Bill handed the man one of the pizzas. The man looked dubious before opening the box to a still steaming 20-inch pizza covered in pepperoni and sausage. His face lit up, his grin widened at the sight of the glorious pie.

His expression got serious. "What's wrong with it?" He obviously didn't trust Bill and Kat.

"What?" Bill shrugged.

"What'd you do to it?"

"We didn't do anything to it."

"Take a bite. Both of you."

"What?" Bill asked.

"We saw you in the dumpster," Kat said. "We thought we'd get you two something to eat."

"Take a bite," he said again, extending the pizza out to them.

"So, you were going to eat something out of the trash but not this?" Kat asked.

"That piece," the man said, pointing at one of the slices.

"Jesus," Kat mumbled, before pulling a piece of pizza from the box. "Technically, I'm still a vegetarian, but I'm not afraid."

She took a big bite, then a second one, and wiped tomato sauce from her face.

"Are you happy?" she asked.

"And here's a little something else for your troubles," Bill said, handing the guy a hundred-dollar bill. "Buy your friend something nice."

The homeless man looked puzzled, holding the cash in one hand and the open pizza box in the other. After Bill and Kat disappeared down the street, he kicked his sleeping friend.

"Clean yourself up, boy. We're goin' dancin'."

As Bill and Kat approached the Equinox, they noticed a police car parked across the street. The two policemen in the car intently watched.

"Oh, shit," Bill mumbled, motioning with his head in the direction of the police car.

"I see 'em," Kat quietly said. "Stay calm. Don't do anything unusual."

"Unusual? We're nothing but unusual."

"Relax, Bill. It'll be all right. We haven't done anything wrong here."

As they reached the Equinox, one of the policemen, the heavier and older one of the two, got out of the car and approached. Bill and Kat quickly got into their car.

"They can't find out who you are," Kat whispered.

"Excuse me, you two," the cop called out. He peered into the driver's side window.

"Is there a problem, sir?" Bill asked nervously.

The second cop had gotten out of the car and stood several yards away, providing backup.

"We were wonderin' what you were discussin' with those gentlemen back there?"

"Uh, um, uh," Bill glanced from Kat to the officer.

"Can you two please get out of the car?"

"But. . . But, your officer, um. . ." Bill stammered.

"Get out of the car!"

After an initial hesitation, Bill opened the car door as Kat leaned over the steering wheel from the passenger side.

"My father and I are here trying to reconnect," she lied. "We've been separated a long time."

"Get out of the car, please. Now."

Bill awkwardly got out. Kat slid across the front seat and followed him out the driver's side. The cop studied the inside of the car. The garment bag full of money was hidden under the passenger side seat.

"Have you been drinkin'?" the officer asked Bill.

"No, no, your officer."

"What's your business with those two fellows back there?" The cop looked first to Bill, then to Kat. "They're infamous around here. You know, two little fish in the big pond at the bottom of the weed-and-pill supply chain. Folks come to them with their problems."

"My father was homeless at one time," Kat again lied. "We were just trying to help out a couple homeless brothers with a hot meal."

"If our eyes weren't playin' tricks on us, me and my partner could've sworn that we seen money exchanged."

"We gave them money," Kat said. "Don't people do that around here? But we didn't buy anything. We mean no harm."

The cop continued to study Bill who nodded. His hands shook and he tried to hide them. His legs were wobbly and weak. He felt as if he were about to pass out.

"Empty your pockets," the cop ordered as his partner stepped closer. "Both of you. On the hood. I want to see everything."

The color had drained from Bill's face; Kat shook her head slightly.

"Isn't this illegal?" she asked.

"Do you got a witness? Come on, now! Everything out!"

"Don't do it, Bill."

"If you have nothin' unusual, we'll let you go. Come on! On the hood!"

Bill deliberately reached into his front pocket and pulled out the motel key and some loose change. He set it all on the hood of the Equinox. Kat again shook her head.

"Is that everything?"

Bill didn't answer.

"Where's your wallet?

Bill again glanced to Kat.

"I'm pretty sure we don't have to do this," she said.

"Where's your goddamn wallet?"

The cop glared at Kat, before stepping within inches of Bill and reaching for the wallet that bulged from Bill's back pocket. Without warning, Kat suddenly dashed away, headed for a wooded area off the side of the road. Instinctively, both police officers gave chase.

"Sleep Inn!" Kat screamed out, before disappearing into the woods.

Once the cops were out of sight, Bill hopped inside the Equinox and peeled away. His heart raced as he white-knuckled the steering wheel. The parked police squad car became but a speck in his rear-view mirror as he sped off. Taking several deep breaths, he tried his best to calm himself as he raced back to the motel. He reached under his seat. The garment bag was still there. He checked his back pocket. He still had his wallet. After about twenty minutes, he made it safely back to the motel and pulled into the lot.

"Shit!" He slammed his hands on the steering wheel. "The motel key!"

Without slowing, he wheeled the Equinox around the parking lot, recklessly driving over the sidewalk as he pulled into two lanes of oncoming traffic. He sped back to the site near the pizza joint where he and Kat had been held. His initial thought was to forget about the key and get a new one, but he quickly became worried the police would find it. The key directly connected him to room 127 at the Sleep Inn. He couldn't give up his location, especially after Kat had called out Sleep Inn when she ran away.

As Bill returned to the scene, the lone police squad car fortunately was still parked there empty. He scanned the area. No sign of the two cops. Bill skidded to a stop, kicking up a cloud of dust and gravel. Leaving the car running, he whipped open the door and stumbled out. He dropped to his hands and knees and searched frantically for the motel key. After seconds that seemed like hours, Bill found some pennies, a nickel — and the key. He sat back into the dust with cuts and dirt stains on his bare knees. He again scanned the area for the policemen before lifting the key to his face and kissing it repeatedly.

xxx

Bill's car was safely parked around the back of the motel where it couldn't be seen from the main road. He hunkered down by the front window of the darkened room and peeked out one side of the heavy plastic curtains, waiting. Hours passed. There was no sign of Kat. He waited for the local police or FBI, expecting them to storm into the motel's lot at any moment to arrest him. He had no plan if they did. He prayed Kat had not been captured and hoped for her safe return to the room.

As the evening ticked towards midnight, Bill tried not to lose hope. But the longer Kat remained missing, the more likely she'd been arrested. He stopped himself several times from leaving the motel to go in search of her, knowing it would be too risky. He had to be patient. He had to trust her. She wanted him to stay there and wait. He knew she was doing everything in her power to get back there. He decided not to leave the room until morning. If she didn't return by then, he would have to make the difficult decision of going into town to look for her or leaving her behind.

The parking lot was relatively quiet for most of the night as Bill kept a close watch from his room. Sometime close to three o'clock in the morning, he spotted a lone figure on foot race across the main road that ran parallel to the motel entrance. He wiped his eyes to make sure he wasn't imagining things before standing and pressing his face against the window glass. The figure appeared to be female, and she seemed to be jogging in the direction of his room. Finally, recognizing Kat, Bill rushed to the door and whipped it open as she ran towards him, falling into his arms. He smothered her body in a tight embrace, dragging her inside and closing the door. He had never felt more relieved in his life. He was overjoyed. After he released her, Kat staggered to one of the beds and collapsed. Bill returned to the window to check to see if she had been followed. Not seeing anyone, Bill clicked on a lamp. Her face and bare legs were covered in scratches and deep cuts. Her elbows and knees were badly scraped and bleeding.

"Oh my God, Kat? What the hell happened? I was so freaking worried!"

"Not only was I a swimmer in high school, I also ran cross country."

"Jesus Christ!" Bill exclaimed, grabbing a bottle of water from the coffee table, and handing it her. "Here's some water."

"I bet I ran twenty miles," she said, grimacing in pain as she sat up and took a drink. "A lot of it through brambles and thicket. I fell four or five times."

"What were you thinking?"

"I knew if they found out who you were, we were going to jail." She drained the water bottle with one long chug. "As you reached for your wallet, I sized up the two cops and looked for an escape route. I figured I could overrun them. And I knew they'd chase me."

"Where've you been all this time?"

"Once I got away from them, I hid until the sun went down. After that, I tried to make it back here. Then got lost."

"Jesus, Kat. That was crazy."

"We're still free." She was still huffing and puffing, nearly out of breath. "That's all that matters."

"Are you hungry? I can get some snacks from the vending machine or run out and grab something from a drive through."

"No, no, Bill. I can't eat. Not now. I feel sick. I haven't felt right since eating the prime rib."

"Clean yourself up and get some sleep. We need to get out of here early in morning."

xxx

After showering and cleaning her many wounds, Kat crashed onto the bed. She could barely move her battered body and buried herself in a pile of covers. Bill had fallen asleep in the bed beside her, loudly snoring. The TV was on, tuned to cable news with the volume low. Kat glanced to the screen as the newsreader began an update on Bill's story. His picture was on the screen with a new caption that read, "Missing Banker, Reward Posted." Kat tried to watch but was unable to fight off exhaustion. She fell deeply asleep to the newscaster's soothing voice. Even Bill's thunderous snoring couldn't keep her awake.

"There are no new leads in the case of the missing Pennsylvania banker. A reward of fifty-thousand dollars is being offered for any information that leads to his capture."

xxx

Day 9. Friday, May 5. 6:56 AM

The first light of the new day seeped into the musty motel room, waking Kat. She was too tired and too sore to move. Bill continued to snore in the other bed. The television was still on from the night before. She watched the news for the rest of the morning, drifting in and out of sleep. Bill didn't wake except to roll over a few times. A legal call-in talk show came on in the early afternoon. A loud and opinionated legal expert named Cassandra Stevens hosted the show. The morning topic was Bill, the "missing banker." Kat watched with one eye open, letting Bill sleep a little longer.

"A wealthy banker steals a million dollars!" Ms. Stevens bellowed. "When is enough enough for the rich in this country?"

"He left his wife and children," the show's co-host, Milton Shears, a former lawyer to celebrities, said. "Unfortunately, this man appears to have no respect for human dignity."

"This is all speculation," a guest on the show challenged them. "We don't know the whole story. There are reports that he was kidnapped."

Laughter rang out around the set.

"There was blood and evidence of a struggle at the crime—" the guest said defensively.

"*Puh-leze*," Ms. Stevens interrupted. "All easily staged. Where were the surveillance videos? The cameras had all been turned off. How *convenient*." She stared into the camera. "We have a caller. Linda from Toledo. You're on The Law Today."

"I am just appalled at the behavior of corporate executives in this day and age," Linda said. "I feel for that poor family. When did families become disposable?"

"When they catch Mr. Moreland," Ms. Stevens responded as Kat sat up in bed, watching from the motel room, "he should

109

be made an example of. The courts need to come down on him swiftly and harshly."

"You're all wrong," Kat said out loud.

"A man's first honor is to his family," Ms. Stevens said.

Kat reached for the phone next to the bed as she checked the number on the television screen. She dialed it.

"Hello," Kat said to the show's screener. "I'm with the banker right now. You can call me Katherine."

Ms. Stevens glanced away from the camera. A puzzled expression grew on her face.

"What's this? Is that right? Are you sure?" Ms. Stevens asked, before looking back to the camera. "I am told we have a Katherine on the line who supposedly is with the missing banker right now. Ma'am? Katherine?"

"Yes," Kat quietly answered.

"Can you hear me?" Ms. Stevens asked.

"Yes."

"Where are you?" After a short pause, she asked, "Are you with Mr. Moreland right now?"

Kat still didn't answer.

"Katherine, are you still with us?"

"I wanted to clear some things up," Kat said. "Everything you've been saying about Bill is completely inaccurate."

"How so?" Ms. Stevens asked. "It doesn't sound like he's kidnapped. It appears he's alive and well."

"Bill's a good person."

"What is your relationship with him?" Ms. Stevens paused, but Kat didn't answer. "Katherine, are you still with us?"

"Bill is sick about leaving his family. He loves and misses them very much, but he feels the need to do something bigger. To give back to the less fortunate and hope that others follow his example."

Ms. Stevens glanced to the show's producer who swirled his hand around in a circle, wanting her to keep Kat on the line.

"Please explain."

"I'm sure you've been following the story about the mystery donor."

"What are you trying to say?"

Bill suddenly shot up in bed, looked to Kat and then glanced to the television. Realizing what was happening, he angrily grabbed the phone cord that ran behind the nightstand and ripped it out of the wall.

"You are all wrong about Bill, Lady!" Kat hollered, but the phone was dead.

"What in the hell are you doing?" Bill yelled, jumping from the bed and pacing the room.

"Katherine? Katherine? Ma'am? Are you still there?" Ms. Stevens' voice filled the room.

"Now, we got ourselves a juicy story," Mr. Shears said.

"It seems we lost the connection," Ms. Stevens said, staring at the producer who showed a 'throat-slash' gesture.

"Get your things!" Bill screamed, yanking the plug on the television.

"You wouldn't believe what they were saying about you," Kat said without getting off the bed.

"Get your goddamn things!" Bill shouted louder as he scrambled around the room, gathering his belongings.

Kat didn't move.

"Get up, goddamit! We need to get out of here! Come on!"

Kat still didn't budge. Bill stopped picking up his things and stared at her.

"Come on, Kat! It's time to go!"

"Don't you ever talk to me like that again," she said sternly but calmly. "You got that. Do you?"

They stared for a few moments.

"I'm sorry," he said, "but this isn't a game."

"I know it's not a fucking game, Bill! If it wasn't for me, you'd be in jail this morning!"

"We have to go, Kat. Please."

xxx

Bill hastily exited the motel room, Kat behind him. At the car, he opened the trunk and tossed the garment bag of money inside it. She scanned the parking lot full of cars. Checking over her shoulder, she reached for an emergency repair kit in the trunk before Bill could close it and retrieved a screwdriver. He studied her as she kneeled behind the car next to his and unscrewed the Texas license plate. She continually checked over her shoulder to see if anyone was around.

"Go back to the room, take the beer cans from the trash, and look for some string or rope," she ordered.

"We have to get out of here. *Let's go.*"

"Get in the room. No one needs to see you right now. I'll be there in the minute."

Flashing her a dirty look, he reluctantly retreated to the motel room door as she exchanged the temporary Florida plate on Bill's car with the Texas plate she had just removed. She flipped the screwdriver into the trunk and shut it. She again scanned the parking lot before hustling back to the room. Bill had stacked six empty beer cans on a table.

"Did you find some string?" she said, hustling around the room and opening the closet and different dresser drawers.

"Uh, no."

"Start poking holes in those cans," she ordered as Bill shrugged. "Do it."

She tossed him a can opener that had been attached to a mini refrigerator by a magnet. "Here, use this!"

As he poked holes in the cans, she scrambled to the window and yanked all the curtain cords from the wall. She grabbed her knapsack from the floor beside the door.

"You made a big mistake calling that show, Kat. What were you thinking? You're smarter than that."

Ignoring him, she pulled out a manicure set from a pocket in the front of the bag and retrieved a small set of scissors. She immediately cut the curtain cords in six pieces about three feet long, before hurrying over to the empty beer cans.

"Get the soap from the bathroom," she said.

"Kat, we need to go. I'm sure the FBI and Texas State Police are on their way."

"*Get the soap.*"

As Bill stomped into the bathroom, Kat tied each of the six beer cans to a separate cord.

"What are you doing?" He came out with two bars of soap. "We need to go. Right now."

"Get your things, Bill."

They rushed out of the room with all their belongings, the dangling cans clanging in Kat hands. She hurried to the back of the car and began to tie the cans across the back bumper. Bill watched, holding the bars of soap.

"Now, write Just Married on the windows," she said, not looking up as she continued to tie the cans to the bumper.

"Just married?"

"We need a cover. Do it."

"We have to go. The cops will be here any minute."

"Do it."

"With what?"

"The soap."

He looked at the soap in his hands.

"*Do it.*"

He leaned over the trunk and wrote 'Just Married' in large, loopy letters across the back window.

"Put it on thick," she ordered, tying the last beer can to the bumper. "And the side windows, too. Write Bill and Kat if you want."

He hesitated and turned to her, "Bill and Kat?"

"Just do it. We need to get going."

xxx

Wiping the sweat from his forehead, Bill drove the empty stretch of Texas Highway 81, trying not to speed. He wore the white-framed woman's sunglasses. The empty beer cans rattled behind the car. Kat was slumped low in the passenger seat and studied Bill, who continually checked the rearview mirror. He took several deep breaths before putting his hand over his mouth, appearing as if he were ready to vomit. He constantly squinted his eyes and shook his head. He hadn't said a word for forty-five miles.

"You, all right?" she asked, but he refused to look at her. "Talk to me, Bill. I said I was sorry about the phone call. It was a dumb move."

He just stared to the deserted road.

"Please, don't be mad at me. I thought I was helping."

Suddenly, a police car appeared ahead, moving in the opposite direction, and zoomed by them with its lights flashing and siren blaring.

"That's the fourth state trooper we've seen," Bill finally said, but still didn't look at her.

"I'm sorry, Bill."

He drove on without acknowledging her, wiping at the perspiration that had formed on his bald head. She reached over and touched his hand as if an offering of peace. He immediately pulled his hand away and rolled down the window, partially sticking his head out. A helicopter appeared overhead; sirens could be heard in the distance. Bill slowed the car.

"What are you doing?" she asked, turning in her seat and checking the empty roadway behind them.

He jerked the car to the side of the road and screeched to a stop. He pulled the keys from the ignition, scrambled out the driver's seat, and rushed to the trunk. Kat followed.

"Bill, speak to me!"

His feet tangled in the dented and scuffed beer cans, nearly tripping. He opened the trunk and handed her the car keys before crawling in.

"Bill?"

"No matter what happens, don't let me out until Oklahoma."

As he nestled in the belly of the trunk, he took several deep breaths. His face ashen, sweat rolled from his head and dripped off his nose. He swallowed hard a few times and again covered his mouth with a fist.

"It'll be all right, Bill," she tried to reassure him.

"I hope so."

"I won't let you down." She slammed the trunk.

xxx

Kat drove at a steady pace for over an hour, trying her best to maintain the posted speed limits. Traffic was sparse as the sun set over the Texas plains to the west. At the beginning of the drive, she was continually distracted by the rattling beer cans and loud thumping noises in the back as Bill fidgeted in the trunk. She hoped he had enough air to breathe. She hadn't heard anything for the last several miles. She wanted to stop and check on him but kept driving.

She was making surprisingly good time. The Oklahoma state line was less than thirty miles away. She had not told Bill, because she knew what his reaction would be, but she had booked them a room at a cheap motel in Norman. She also didn't tell him who she was meeting there: her boyfriend, Ken Mercury. As she pressed on, she noticed more flashing red and blue lights ahead. She slowed the car as she approached what appeared to be a roadblock. Her first thought was to turn around and run, but she knew the police would catch her. Her second thought was of Bill in the trunk. No matter what was about to happen, she couldn't let anyone open it. A tall, young Texas highway patrolman with a weightlifter's build waved her to a stop where multiple police cars were parked in such way as to block most of the highway in each direction.

"What's up, Officer?" she asked, rolling down the window.

The highway patrolman aimed a flashlight in the front and back of the car.

"We're lookin' for a bad guy," he said.

"Bad guy?" she asked with a mischievous smile. "How bad?"

He shined the flashlight into Kat face and smiled as he checked her out, directing the beam of the light across her chest and then slowly down her long, bare legs.

"Bad enough," he said.

"What'd he do?"

"Robbed a bank."

"That doesn't sound so bad."

"What's your business tonight, Ma'am?"

"Oh, I'm just a lonesome Texas cowgirl who's lost her way."

"Do you need some help in findin' it, Ma'am?"

"Are you flirting with me, Officer?"

"Why no, Ma'am," he said with a slight grin. "I'm on duty."

"That's too bad."

"Where you headed?"

"Oklahoma."

"What's in Oklahoma?" The cop asked as he flashed the light on the smudged words written in soap on the windows of the car.

"It's a secret," she whispered.

"A secret," he said, smiling. "You can tell me."

"My new husband," she said with a frown.

"Bill?" the cop asked, reading the name on the window.

"He goes to school in Norman."

"And you must be Kat?"

"We just got married."

"I see," the officer said, checking out the crunched beer cans hanging from the back bumper. "I'm sorry."

"Sorry? About what?"

"Sorry to hear you have a husband."

"I thought you weren't flirting with me."

"No, Ma'am," he said, shaking his head.

"Will you let me go, Officer?" she asked. "My husband is waiting up for me. He can be impatient and grumpy. It's our honeymoon."

Grinning, she winked as the highway patrolman hesitated a moment.

"Have a good evening, Ma'am," the cop said, before waving the state police car blocking the roadway to move aside. "Congratulations on your wedding! Bill is a lucky man!"

116

Chapter 5
Oklahoma

Day 9. Friday, May 5. 8:01 PM

As darkness fell, Kat found herself leaving Texas and crossing the Red River into Oklahoma on Highway 81. She guessed that she had about a two-hour drive to Norman. She turned off the headlights and eased the car to the side of the road, parking underneath the Oklahoma state welcome sign. Before getting out, she checked the highway in each direction. The road was empty. She exited the car and went to the back, accidentally kicking at the tangled and dented beer cans that hung from the bumper as she opened the trunk. Because of the darkness and the light bulb in the trunk having burnt out, she couldn't see much inside. The trunk was silent, and nothing moved.

"Bill?" she whispered. "Bill? Bill! Are you okay?"

After a moment of silence, he appeared from the depths of the trunk and crawled awkwardly out. He held a flashlight. He clicked it on and shined it at Kat's face. She smiled. He then shined the light on himself. One of his pant legs was completely soaked from the crotch to the knee.

"Ah, Bill."

"I was fine 'til you got stopped."

"I told you I wouldn't let you down."

"When I first heard that trooper's voice, the flood gates opened. There was nothing I could do to hold it back. I'm just glad I didn't shit myself."

"Let's get you changed."

"What's the use?" he mumbled, walking to the passenger

side of the car. "You don't mind driving, do you?"

"No, no," she said as he climbed into the passenger seat and closed the door with his head down.

xxx

As they drove deeper into Oklahoma, little was said between the two of them. Bill kept checking the passenger side rearview mirror. Nobody followed. They had made it out of Texas unnoticed and mostly unscathed. Initially, the traffic on Highway 81 was relatively light. As they got closer to Norman, it had started to pick up some. They were about eighty miles away when Kat finally informed Bill of the plans she had made for them.

"Now, don't get mad," she said, handing him a slip of paper.

He glared at her a moment, before glancing to an address of a motel that was scribbled on the piece of paper.

"I booked us a room in Norman for the night."

"Without asking me first?"

"Yes, without asking you first."

"In your name?"

"No."

"In my name?"

"Of course not." She paused. "We're meeting a friend of mine."

"A friend? A good friend?"

"Yeah, a good friend."

"Can we trust her?"

"*He* doesn't know I'm with you."

"*He*?"

"Yes, *he*!"

"So, he's a *good* friend."

"Yes, he's a good friend."

"How good of friend?"

"It'll be fine, Bill."

"I don't like it this. I don't like it at all."

118

He checked the motel name and address again, shaking his head.

"I knew you'd be mad."

"Nobody else needs to know who I am. We're not staying there."

"You can do what you want, Bill," she said, "but I am."

Before Bill could respond, the car engine belched and sputtered a couple of times before shutting off. Kat was able to coast the dead car and maneuver it to the side of the road off the highway. They both shot a glance to the road behind them then to the dashboard. The car had run out of gas.

They got out and walked behind it. Bill looked panicked as Kat scanned the surroundings of the mostly desolate highway. They were stranded in the middle of nowhere. She again surveyed the empty plains that ran along each side of the road, before glancing to the trunk. She opened it and looked to Bill. He studied her before staring at the inside of the trunk.

"I need to get gas," she said, motioning with her head to the trunk.

"Yeah."

"And you'll need to get back in there."

"I can't."

"Look around, Bill," she said, again scanning the landscape. "There's nowhere else to go."

"I'm not getting back in there."

"You need to stay here with the money and the car. What will we do without a car?"

"I'm not getting back in there. I'm sorry."

Oncoming lights appeared in the distance behind them and quickly approached.

"Get in there, Bill," she ordered as he hesitated. "Get in the trunk!"

Nearly tripping on the beer cans tied to the back bumper, Bill stumbled in as Kat slammed the trunk closed. A late model Plymouth slowed as she flagged it down, wildly waving her arms. The car stopped. The passenger window rolled down, and an elderly couple greeted her.

"I've run out of gas."

"Did you jus' get married?" the older woman asked, noticing the soaped windows and beer cans at the back of the car.

"Yes."

"What happened to the groom?" the old woman asked, craning her neck in search of Kat's companion.

"In Norman. Can you help me?"

"Sure. Get in."

xxx

Curled up inside the trunk on his side with his knees to his chest and his arms around them, Bill could initially hear Kat's voice outside. He also heard a car door shut, then silence. After listening intently for a moment, he couldn't tell if the car had driven away or not. He continued to listen closely but still didn't hear a sound.

"Kat?" he called out not much louder than a whisper. "Kat? Are you still there?"

Believing the car had left, he changed the position of his body and lounged back in the trunk, trying his best to relax as he waited for Kat to return. Anxious about the situation and unable to get comfortable, Bill instead tossed his body around in different positions before beginning to hyperventilate. He tried to calm himself by taking several deep breaths. He had no way of seeing what was happening outside the car, and more importantly, what or who approached. He also had no idea how long he'd be stuck in the trunk, but he knew he needed to relax, or he was doomed.

After only a few minutes, he heard what sounded like a truck pull next to the car. His heart nearly jumped out of his chest as he heard footsteps circle the car and stop behind the trunk. He inhaled a deep gasp of the stale, humid air and held it, trying not to make a noise. He said a prayer under his breath as it sounded as if the footsteps walked away from the car. He exhaled only to hear what then sounded like heavy chains being dragged across the asphalt to the front of the car. Suddenly, Bill felt the car rock and slightly lift off the ground as the chains were being attached to the front wheels. It was at that point he realized the car was getting towed.

He nearly shit himself when the sound of an industrial-size hydraulic jack hummed to life. As the front end of the car was hitched to the tow truck and lifted off the ground, Bill's body rolled across the trunk. The beer cans tied to the back bumper began to rattle. He had lost all control of the situation. With little air and becoming claustrophobic, the beat of his heart quickened, and his body grew warm as sweat formed from the top of his head to the palms of his hands. He started to hyperventilate again but more violently. He pulled his shirt over his mouth and nose and took several deep, slow breaths. There was no one there to help him. He would have to save himself.

Bill's body violently jerked to the other side of the trunk as the driver gunned the tow trunk, dragging the dead car over the berm and onto the main road. Bill's mind raced as he fidgeted in the darkness, trying to formulate a plan. It was mostly a smooth ride for the first fifteen miles or so. He convinced himself not to do anything desperate at that point. He kept as quiet and still as possible, believing the best time to escape would be at the impound yard or garage after the car was dropped off. He wouldn't make a move until the driver left to go home.

The driver must go home, right? he thought. *He can't stay there all night, could he? Unless, unless, he's the night shift guy.*

Before Bill could ponder any longer, the tow truck and car he was trapped inside slowed and seemed to turn east, distracting him. The new road was more uneven for the next several miles as the tow truck moved at a greatly reduced speed. Bill guessed that they were getting close to the impound yard. He took another series of deep breaths, trying to calm himself.

At a convenience store and gas station, Kat set a two-gallon plastic container on the ground and filled it with gasoline, before placing it through the open back window of the elderly couple's Plymouth. She rushed into the convenience store and grabbed bottles of cold water, candy bars, and bags of potato chips. In the waiting line at the register, Kat dug out some cash from her back pocket and checked over her shoulder for the elderly couple, who stood at a magazine rack. The couple flipped through the pages of a local trading post bulletin that listed assorted items for sale or trade. After paying for the gas and snacks, Kat walked by the couple.

"I'll be in the car."

She hurried outside and opened the back door, expecting the couple to follow. Kat glanced into the store, still holding the car door open. The couple casually studied the odds and ends in the bulletin, even tapping at specific entries on different pages. After waiting a few minutes, Kat slammed the car door shut and returned to the store.

"Come on! Come on!"

The elderly man pointed to the bulletin and shrugged.

"If you're buying it," Kat said, "buy it! Let's go!"

The elderly man looked to his wife and shrugged again before putting the newspaper bulletin back onto the rack.

xxx

Dragging Bill's car, the tow truck drove into the impound yard and parked. The driver pushed a button on a remote that hung from the truck's sun visor, locking the gate. The impound yard was completely encased in a six-foot chain-link fence. Above that was two more feet of razor-sharp barbed wire. The yard was filled with an assortment of over thirty old cars in different conditions. Many had weeds or small trees growing through their rusted-out bodies. Within minutes, the driver had removed the chains from the front of Bill's car. Bill's cramped body bounced in the trunk as the car was dropped into its final resting position. Bill held his breath and remained motionless, listening to what was happening outside. It sounded like the driver had entered some type of building as a door opened and loudly slammed shut. What Bill didn't expect was that the owner released a barking, seventy-five-pound German shepherd into the yard. As it approached Bill's car, the dog stopped barking and began to curiously sniff around the outside of the trunk. Bill continued to hold his body as still as possible. The dog was so close he could hear it breathing.

Inside the office, the tow truck driver filled out some paperwork regarding Bill's car and reached for a scrap of paper with a phone number on it. He entered the number in his mobile phone.

"Agent Stack?" the driver spoke into the phone. "Yeah, this ABC Towing off 81 in Oklahoma. I picked up the last of the disabled cars the sheriff called about."

"I'll try to get an agent up there within the next hour to check it out."

"It ain't goin' nowhere. I'll be here all night."

xxx

As the dog milled about the yard, Bill rolled over onto his stomach and stretched his arms, running a search along the bottom of the trunk. He eventually found the screwdriver Kat had used to exchange the license plates. He also found the flashlight he used earlier, turning it on and shining it at the leather back of the back seat. With no time to waste, he urgently stabbed at the seat numerous times with the screwdriver, leaving gaping holes in the leather upholstery. With both hands, he ripped at the tears in the back seat, peeling off large strips of leather. Behind the leather covering, he dug out large chunks of padding and foam from the pillow-like cushions. Using the screwdriver like a crowbar, he frantically jerked,

123

tugged, and bent a series of wire springs within the cushions. Bill's face was red as the temperature quickly spiked in the confined trunk. Breathing heavily, he continually wiped at his eyes as perspiration poured from him.

After hollowing out a small tunnel in the back seat, he paused and intently listened for any noise outside the car. Not hearing a sound, he sucked in his belly, grabbed the garment bag of money, and slowly slithered and fought his way through the tight space. Once in the back seat, he cautiously raised his head and peeked out a window of the car. He immediately noted the locked gate, the chain-link fence, the barbed wire. He scanned the property for the dog, who was stretched out on its stomach in the middle of the yard, gnawing on what appeared to be a rawhide bone. He glanced to the tow office. He could see the driver sitting at a desk and scrolling through a phone with his thumb.

Bill noticed a slice of cold pepperoni and sausage pizza left over from the night before on the front seat. He again looked to the dog before reaching for the pizza slice. Not allowing himself any time to get scared, he gently opened the backdoor of the car as quietly as he could. The dog immediately lifted its head and shot a piercing glance towards the car. Bill slid his body out and softly closed the door, before flipping the piece of pizza over his head with a basketball hook shot in the direction of the dog, who chased after it.

As the dog attacked the pizza, Bill dashed in a full-out sprint. As he neared one corner of the yard, he heaved the garment bag over the fence and leaped into the air, grasping onto its chain-links. After wolfing down the scraps of pizza, the German shepherd turned and began to wildly bark, galloping towards Bill. Desperately hanging onto the fence with a sweaty death grip, Bill checked over his shoulder. The angry dog closed in; Bill frantically attempted to scale the fence. As he reached for the top of it just under the barbed wire, the dog lunged and latched onto one foot. A sharp pain radiated through his entire body as the dog sank it sharp teeth into the sole of his right foot.

Too frightened to let go of the fence or succumb to the pain, he yanked at his right leg, and the dog fell away with one of Bill's leather shoes in its mouth.

Distracted, the dog angrily growled and ripped at the shoe as Bill shimmied to the top of the fence. Without hesitation or fear for pain, he grabbed onto the barbed wire with both hands and rolled his body over the top. He plunged eight feet to the ground, landing awkwardly on his left side with a thud that sounded like someone hitting a watermelon with a wooden baseball bat. A piece of Bill's sports jacket ripped and hung from the barbed wire at the top of the fence. Upon hearing the constant barking, the tow truck driver appeared at the door of the office and gazed out.

The fall briefly knocked the wind out of Bill. After a few terrified breathless moments, he finally was able to take a breath and searched the ground around him in a panic for the garment bag of money. The German shepherd aggressively and repeatedly vaulted its muscular body against the fence and barked louder and more savagely. Finding the bag and ignoring the pain, Bill sprinted into the darkness of the wide open plain, carrying the bag of money under his right arm like a halfback in football.

"Sampson!" the tow driver called to the triggered dog, walking into the yard. "Sampson! What is it? Sammy! What d'ya got, boy?"

The dog dropped the gnarled and slobbered shoe at the feet of his owner who picked it up and studied it a moment, before staring at the car. He then glanced to the fence that surrounded his property and spotted the piece of Bill's coat fluttering in the warm wind.

xxx

Bill ran as if being chased by a pack of wild dogs. Despite only wearing one shoe, he had never run that fast in his life, ever. And he kept running without stopping or even slowing for well

125

over a mile, until he collapsed and fell face first onto the dusty ground. He gagged multiple times in between deep gasps for air, trying his hardest to catch his breath. Both of his hands were splotched with bleeding sores. It felt as if a sharp spear had been rammed deep into the ribs on his left side. He rolled onto his back, his sweaty face and forehead caked with a thick coating of dirt. He spit the dry dust from his lips and stared at the sky. The moon was full and hung low in a background of a million stars. After his breathing finally slowed, he took one especially large breath of the fresh air, feeling free for the first time in hours.

"I might lay here all night," he said out loud, before cringing in pain. "I may have no choice."

The serenity of the moment and his newfound freedom were short-lived. He could hear the faint barks of the tow yard German shepherd — and a siren in the distance. With a bit of a struggle, Bill lifted his battered body into a sitting position. He couldn't move more than that for many minutes. He looked to his scarred hands, both bloody and swollen. His filthy, blistered right foot was barely covered by a torn and frayed sock. His ribs on the left side ached with each breath. But he had to press on. He squinted into the dark night at the desolate landscape. There appeared to be a light to the north.

xxx

Holding the shredded remnant of Bill's coat and the gnawed shoe, the tow truck driver walked back into his office. The German shepherd curled upon a blanket near the desk. The driver pushed at a pile of papers until he found the scrap of paper with a phone number he needed. He studied the piece of cloth for a moment before calling the number.

"Agent Stack? This is Vic at ABC Towing. You may want to get someone here sooner. I think I got somethin' you may be interested in."

The sweet and pungent smell of gasoline filled the Plymouth. The elderly lady in the passenger seat held her nose. With the plastic container of gasoline on her lap, Kat slumped in the back seat of the couple's car. She studied the landscape along the highway as it zipped by. A knot filled her gut. She was nervous, not for herself, but for Bill. She had to get him out of the trunk as soon as possible. She also needed to get him some of the water. He had to be dehydrated.

Kat fidgeted in the back seat. The ride back to Bill's car was going much slower than she wanted. She checked the speedometer. The elderly man was driving ten miles below the speed limit. Kat leaned forward between the couple.

"I don't mean to be rude," she said, "but can you speed up a little?"

The elderly man glanced at Kat in the rearview. He didn't change speeds. He always drove that fast on that section of 81.

"Please!"

"What's the rush?" the woman asked, still holding her nose.

"Please! Can you hurry?"

"Do you have something important in the car?"

"Everything I own is in that car."

"Do you go to school in Norman?"

"No."

"No?"

"I just need to get there, and fast. My new husband's waiting."

The car slowed. Kat scanned the surroundings. The berm next to the highway was empty as the man pulled the Plymouth off the main road.

"Why are you stopping?" Kat asked. "What are you doing?"

"I brought you back."

"Brought me where? I need to go to my car!"

"Yes. This is where we picked you up."

"No! I need to be taken to my car!"

"Yes, this is the place," he said.

"But where's my car?"

Kat pushed the backdoor open and hopped out. She scoped the area. "Are you sure this is it? Where's the car?"

She knelt and picked up a scuffed and crumpled beer can. "Oh, no. Bill. Oh, Bill."

Standing, she studied the dark highway in each direction, still holding the full container of gasoline.

"Do you need us to drive you to Norman?" the elderly lady asked. "We don't mind."

Kat didn't initially respond but stared at them blankly. The pit in her stomach now seemed the size of the Grand Canyon.

xxx

Like a lost dog missing a leg, Bill hobbled with an exaggerated limp in the direction of the light, holding the garment bag against his chest with folded arms. His intended destination was further than he initially estimated, but he pushed on, his wounded foot dragging for well over a mile. Another quarter mile to go, it looked like. He didn't let the pain stop him, only occasionally slowing just long enough to listen for the barking dog or an approaching siren.

As he neared the light, he came upon a boundary of wooden fences, the outskirts of a farm. He checked over his shoulder before gently easing his aching body through the middle slats of the fence. The grassy field housed scores of cattle. A barn sat a few hundred yards away, the source of the light that inspired his trek. The light was attached to the top of the barn and illuminated a transport farm truck with its engine running. Through a gate on the back of the truck, there was ramp where a parade of 200-pound hogs were being led by a single farmer.

Under the cover of darkness, Bill sneaked closer and hid behind a fence post. The truck's bed was enclosed by rows of metal rails six inches apart, the top open. He needed to get onto the bed of the truck. He crept closer and crouched behind a collection of water and food troughs.

Once all the hogs are in, he thought, *I won't be stopped.*

Bill stood for a better look. The hogs were finally loaded, and the farmer closed a heavy padlock that secured the back gate of the bed. He packed a chaw of Redman tobacco in his palm, before stuffing it in one of his cheeks. The farmer walked towards the driver's side, and as soon as he reached for the door, Bill dashed from his hiding place and heaved his precious bag of money over the passenger side rail into the bed with the passel of pigs. He leaped and latched onto the outside metal rail, hoping to be in the farmer's blind spot.

Bill hunkered down as low and as close to the rails as possible and didn't move until the truck was out in the open. As the farmer pulled onto a dirt road and picked up speed, Bill lifted himself up to the top rail and flopped over it, falling into the bed. His fall was broken by a pair of plump but champion hogs. As his bruised body slid off the pigs, he discovered the floor of the bed held a three-inch slurry of mud, piss, and manure. The stench was overwhelming. Bill gagged then hurled the contents of his cramping gut. After a series of dry heaves, he caught his breath and located the soiled garment bag in the muck. His spirit nearly broken, Bill crawled to the end of the truck's bed closest to the cab and tried his best to hide as a few of the larger pigs nipped at his one bare foot and rooted at his crotch.

xxx

Because of the urgency Stack sensed in the tow truck driver's voice, he visited the impound yard himself with multiple agents and a canine unit. The gate to the yard was open as several vehicles with Stack and his agents pulled in and parked. The tow truck driver greeted them and pointed to Bill's car. Stack and two agents slowly walked around the car a few times, studying the car and its interior without opening any doors yet.

"I haven't touched it since I dropped it here."

"What's up with these beer cans tied to the back?" one of the

FBI agents asked.

"The banker must have crashed a wedding," Stack said.

"And stole the married couple's car?"

Another agent put on gloves and checked the driver's side front door. It was locked — as was the back door on that side and the passenger's side front door. The passenger side back door was unlocked. Stack shined a flashlight inside the car as the agent gently pulled the door open and discovered the large hole carved out of the back seat.

"Any keys?" Stack asked.

"No, sir," said the tow truck driver.

"Climb in there," Stack ordered the agent, "and see if you can unlock the other doors."

A camera flashed as another agent snapped a picture of the hollowed-out back seat before his partner crawled into the car. He reached to the front and hit the button that unlocked the other doors and the trunk. With a handkerchief, Stack carefully opened the trunk and studied its contents. He reached in and grasped the screwdriver Bill used to free himself. Holding the screwdriver with the handkerchief, Stack dropped it into a plastic evidence bag held out by one of the agents.

"Any idea why this car was parked on the side of the highway?"

"I believe it ran out of gas," the tow truck driver said.

Stack nodded and continued to study the inside of the trunk. The agent inside the car backed out of the passenger's side front seat and held up a soda cup with a straw sticking out of it. Lipstick stained the top of the straw. The agent also held up a pair of white-framed woman's sunglasses.

"The banker was not alone. Explains the eyewitness reports in Texas."

"Fingerprints?" one of the agents asked.

"Yeah, everything, inside and out," Stack said.

"So, what happened here?" one of the agents asked.

"The banker and his accomplice ran out of gas," Stack answered. "The female subject went for gas while the banker hid in the trunk. Our friend here found him before she got back."

Stack glanced at the tow truck driver. "Please give us the location where you found the car. We need to get someone there as soon as possible. The female subject may still return or be searching for the banker there."

The tow truck driver nodded as Stack turned and motioned to the fence.

"Where did you find the piece of coat?"

The driver handed the shred of fabric to Stack and pointed to the area of the barbed wire where Bill had climbed over. Stack walked to the fence and peered into the dark distance. He could see a single light.

"What is out there?"

"A farm," the driver answered.

"Farm? What farm?"

"A farm with hundreds of acres. Cattle. Poultry. Hogs. Everything. You name it."

Stack handed the agent in charge of the canine unit the piece of Bill's coat.

"Get the hounds and take them to the farm, starting right there," he said, pointing to a spot outside the fence. "He can't be too far on foot. If he takes the main road, we will get him at a roadblock."

xxx

It was bumpy ride for Bill for several miles until the farm truck reached the main road. Bill assumed it was Route 81 but wasn't certain. It was actually Highway 77. Crouching among the hogs, he couldn't see much. He did notice the flashing lights that suddenly appeared ahead, reflecting off the pavement of the highway. The truck slowed, and he slid deeper into the muck, trying to disappear.

The truck was directed to stop at the roadblock by Oklahoma state troopers. The farmer rolled down his window and was greeted by two troopers—one who walked to the back of the truck and the other who approached the farmer.

"What ya' haulin'?" the cop at the front asked.

"About four tons of hogs."

"Where ya' takin' 'em?"

The farmer glanced over his shoulder and cupped his mouth with one hand, like he was about to tell a secret.

"To slaughter," he whispered. "The pigs know, somehow. But cows don't. I got to get 'em there by mornin'."

The trooper showed the farmer a photograph of Bill.

"Have you seen this man?"

"No, sir," the farmer said, shaking his head. "I ain't seen no one in days. Been too busy getting' these hogs ready."

"Can we search the back?" the cop asked. Another trooper in back was inspecting underneath the truck with a flashlight.

"Sure, but. . ." The farmer trailed off.

"But what?"

"It's not a pretty sight."

"Goddang!" the trooper in back called out, covering his nose with the inside of his bent elbow.

"See?" the farmer said, nodding.

"What's back here?" the trooper asked, hopping up onto the back bumper and looking over the railing of the truck's bed. "I've only smelled one thing worse."

With the flashlight, the trooper surveyed the bed, crowded with bobbing and squealing pigs huddled against each other. Bill had pulled the garment bag under his head and curled himself into the fetal position under a group of muddy porkers who rooted at the torn jacket on his back. It both hurt and tickled. Although nearly buried in the slop, he was too petrified to move or make a sound.

"What do ya' got?" the trooper from the front asked.

"I can't believe we eat these things," the other cop said, sweeping the beam from the flashlight across the crowded truck bed multiple times.

"Anything unusual?"

"No normal human could stand this and hide back here for too long," he said, hopping off the back bumper. "I got nothing. All clear."

xxx

Day 9. Friday, May 5. 11:15 PM

The elderly couple's old Plymouth parked in a temporary spot in front of the Slumberland Motel off Highway 77. It had taken them a little more than fifty minutes to reach the motel. They were fortunate not to have encountered any of the many roadblocks that had been set up in the area. Having a keen knowledge of the local highways, the elderly man had used a series of backroads that he believed to be the quickest route.

The Slumberland was a roadside inn with a retro, art deco look. The freshly painted white stucco walls gave it a relatively clean appearance. Across the lot from the lobby, there was a small pool and two levels of guest rooms in a separate L-shaped building—ten rooms on the bottom floor and ten more on the top. The motel's private laundry room and a vending area were located at the "elbow" of the ground floor. In the same building, connected to the lobby, there was a small lounge that offered food and drinks until midnight. The lounge also provided room service for the motel's guests.

"Thank you all so much," Kat said to the elderly couple.

"You're very welcome," the elderly man said with a genuine smile and enthusiastic nod.

"Please let me pay you for your time and trouble."

"No, no," the man said. "Glad we could help."

"I hope you find your car," his wife said. "And your husband."

"Thanks again," Kat said. "God bless you two."

Slinging her knapsack over her right shoulder, she got out of the car holding the container of gasoline. She glanced around the motel's parking lot as if searching for someone. She set

133

down the gas can outside the lobby's entrance and disappeared inside. She checked in and was given room 12, the last one available for that night. After leaving the lobby, she walked across the parking lot. It was getting late.

The strong, almost irritating, smell of chlorine from the small pool near her room filled the air. She felt helpless, worried about Bill, and couldn't help but wonder if she'd ever see him again. She had no means to communicate with him and knew the odds were low that he'd find or even remember the name of the place. Maybe he still had the slip of paper with the Slumberland's address on it—or maybe not. Lighting a cigarette, she stood by the door of her room and waited. Suddenly, a familiar, mid-size American model pickup truck drove into the lot. She waved to the driver who parked near the entrance to room 12. It was Ken Mercury, her boyfriend from New Orleans.

"Your hair?" she called out, immediately noticing his freshly cropped head. "What'd you do to your beautiful hair? Your golden locks are gone."

"You know how hot New Orleans can be at this time of year."

Kat excitedly greeted Ken with an all-encompassing embrace, nearly squeezing the life from him. Despite her fun on the road with Bill, she had missed Ken. After a brief exchange of pleasantries, she unlocked the door to the room and grabbed Ken by the hand, leading him in. She glanced outside, hoping to see Bill, and closed the door.

She practically attacked Ken, hopping into his arms and locking lips. With their bodies entangled, they backpedaled through the narrow motel room into the bedroom, undressing each other along the way. They fell back onto the bed. Ken flipped Kat over and rolled on top, kissing her neck aggressively and digging his hand deep between her bare legs. Any thoughts Kat had of Bill were far away.

After a zesty, two-hour sex romp that started in the bed, moved to the floor, and ended in the shower, Kat emerged from room 12 for a much needed and very satisfying cigarette smoke as Ken rested. She puffed hard as thoughts of Bill and the concern for his safety returned. There still was no sign of him.

xxx

Covered in pig slop and smelling worse than a sewer, Bill sat, partially hidden, in the shrubs and flowers against the side of a convenience store and gas station building. Shivering and sneezing constantly, he was too damaged and defeated to move, feeling as if he'd been violated by the curious pigs. It had taken the last of his energy to leap off the farm truck when it had stopped for a fill-up. He wondered if he was at the end of the road. He had no plans as he pondered his next move. He knew he couldn't stay there. He was sure the store employees would call the authorities if they spotted him.

He studied the parking lot as a rusted and gray 1990s model Ford Escort pulled into a spot not far from where he was sitting. Sensing an opportunity, Bill used the side of the building for support as he hoisted himself up and limped towards the Escort as a young man in his early twenties got out.

"Hey, kid?" Bill called. "I'll give you a thousand bucks for that car."

"Huh?"

"I'll give you a thousand bucks for the car." He pulled a grimy handful of hundred-dollar bills from his pocket.

"It's not for sale."

"Two thousand."

"But I need it. How will I get to work?"

"Four thousand." Bill pulled more money from the soiled garment bag.

"For this thing?" the kid asked. "Do you need the title? I can run home and get it."

"No."

The kid hesitated a moment then reached for the cash and gave Bill the car key.

"Are you in some kind of trouble?" The kid studied Bill's

desperate demeanor and filthy appearance.

"Can you do me one last thing?" Bill handed the kid another hundred dollars. "I noticed some souvenir tee-shirts and shorts inside. Can you grab me one of each? Large. And a pair of flip-flops. You can keep the change."

The kid nodded and turned for the store.

"One other thing! What town am I in?"

"You're about twenty-five miles northeast of Norman."

After collecting the items the kid had purchased, Bill found a hose that was connected to a spigot on the side of the store. He unattached a sprinkler from the other end of the hose and turned on the water to let it pour over his head. The water was refreshing but a tad bit cold. He did his best to cleanse his stained body: he scrubbed at the top of his head, over his face, behind his ears, and down his arms and legs. Shivering and wiping at his runny nose, he kicked off his one shoe and sock and rinsed his blistered and scarred feet and each hand.

Dripping, barefooted, he scurried to the men's restroom behind the store and locked himself inside. He ripped off his pants and underwear to dry his legs, feet, hands, and head as best he could with wads of paper towels. With a deep breath, he lifted his arms and screamed from the pain in his left side as if he were freefalling from an airplane, struggling to peel his shirt off his wet, sticky torso. Eventually, he got the shirt off with one last blood curdling howl that resulted in a knock on the bathroom door.

"Hello?"

"I'll be out in a minute," Bill called.

He leaned against the moldy bathroom sink for a few minutes to catch his breath. As he waited for the pain in his ribs to subside, he caught a reflection of his withered naked body in the mirror. He saw for the first time the horrifying black and red bruise that stretched from his arm pit to his butt cheek on his left side. He assumed he'd broken a rib or four. His hands were covered in oozing pockmarks; he wondered if his grand joyride was worth it.

There was another knock at the door. Mainly using his right hand, Bill pulled on the clean tee-shirt and shorts, slid his wet feet into the flip-flops, and pulled the weathered Pirates ball cap from the garment bag, placing it on his scratched bald head. He tossed the badly soiled clothes into a trashcan, grabbed the garment bag, and exited the restroom.

"You, okay?" the guy who was waiting asked.

"Kidney stone," Bill lied, hurrying by the man, not allowing him to get a good look at his face.

"Christ, buddy. I feel your pain."

Bill rushed to his newly purchased car and started it up. He turned the heat to high and let the warm air blow across the bare cold skin of his shivering arms and legs for many minutes. Digging through the car's glove compartment, Bill found a map of Oklahoma. After unfolding it and studying it a moment, he pulled a slip of paper from his wallet with the address to the Slumberland Motel on it. He was destined for Norman, but he would take the back way.

xxx

After Ken had rested from his long drive and the exhausting but fun frolic with Kat, they ducked into the motel's bar, The Stagecoach Lounge. Besides the bartender, they were the only two people there. The place was more of a-shot-and-a-beer dive bar than a typical motel lounge. It mostly served the motel guests but was popular with some nearby locals who enjoyed the above-average bar food that was served late every night of the week. The interior was nothing special, the décor drab and outdated, the walls covered by dinged dark wood paneling and decorated with faded paintings of stagecoaches. An actual wagon wheel, its white paint chipped and peeling, hung behind the bar from the water-stained drop-ceiling.

The bartender that night was a cheery chap named Jack Lilliard. He was a bald and bloated middle-aged man with a flushed red face who sipped all night from a tumbler filled with rum and coke. He was known for his quick wit, tasteless jokes, and the gaudy short-sleeve bowling shirts that clung to his thick barrel chest and hard fat belly. Jack strictly worked from a limited drink menu, serving only domestic beers and simple cocktails that could be made with gin, vodka, rum, or whiskey and a single mixer.

Kat and Ken ordered bottles of beer and two shots of cheap Irish whiskey and wandered over to an outdated jukebox filled mostly with bland and forgettable 1990s era CDs of country music artists, such as Garth Brooks, Randy Travis, Clint Black, and Alan Jackson. Kat inserted a five-dollar bill and picked country standards from legends like George Jones, Conway Twitty, Johnny Cash, and Dolly Parton. As the Willie Nelson song "Angel Flying Too Close to the Ground" began to play, Kat and Ken knocked back the whiskey shots and leaned into each other for a slow dance. Watching from the bar, Jack reached for a knob that controlled the jukebox and turned up the volume. With a contented smile, Kat rested her head on Ken's chest as they slowly swayed to the music. He nibbled her ear.

"You didn't need to run off," Ken whispered. "We could've talked."

"Things have to change."

"I know. I'll change. I promise."

"You've said that before."

"It's different this time." He leaned away from her, searching for eye contact. "I know what it's like to lose you."

She smiled, grinding her body into his and rubbing her knee between his legs.

"Goddamn, girl," he whispered, glancing to Jack who watched from the bar. "What's gotten into you?"

"Being on the road changed me," she said as he leaned into her arms. "Not being attached to anything."

"Where you been?"

"No one place. Just kind of moving around."

"Alone?"

"No, with this neat guy named Bill."

"Bill?"

"I met him at the bar in New Orleans."

"And you ran off with him?"

"I was at a low place, Ken. You know that. You were part of it. But I've really missed you."

"Have you and Bill been doing the—"

"*No.*"

"So where's Bill now?"

"Sadly, I don't know. We got separated. There's a chance he may meet us here."

"Meet us?"

"Yeah, he's sharing the room with us."

"So what happens after tonight?" The song on the jukebox ended, and he pulled away. "Are you leaving with Bill?"

"I want to stay with you." She paused. "But I can't go back to New Orleans."

"I'll follow you anywhere."

"Let's move around a little and see the country."

"But what will we do for money? We're broke."

"Yeah, that's one thing I haven't figured out yet."

"You want another drink?"

"Same thing. I'm going out for a smoke."

xxx

Day 10. Saturday, May 6. 12:31 AM

Kat leaned against the front brick wall of the lounge and puffed a cigarette. A rusty Ford Escort rumbled into the lot in a cloud of white smoke, its muffler barely hanging on, only attached by duct tape and wire clothes hangers. Bill parked and scanned the lot. The distressed condition of the Escort piqued Kat's interest as she tossed away the cigarette she was smoking. She squinted in the low lighting of the lot and tried to get a clear glimpse of the driver. As Bill turned and studied the entrance to the lounge, their eyes met. With outstretched arms, Kat sprinted towards him as if welcoming home a celebrated war hero. Wiping at his runny nose, Bill hadn't fully lifted his aching body out of the car when she nearly tackled him in full stride, bouncing him off the side of the Escort.

"Oh, my God! Bill! Bill! You made it!"

She embraced him in a smothering bear hug.

"Easy, easy, easy," he moaned, pulling his arms in against his body to protect his sore ribs.

"Oh, Bill! I thought you were gone forever," she squealed in excitement. She kissed his cheeks and quickly cringed away. "Woah! Good God! What is that smell?"

"Can a man catch the swine flu from a pig?" he asked as she cupped her hand over her nose. "I may have been violated."

"Are you okay?"

"I think I have a fever." He wiped at his dripping nose.

"What happened?"

"I spent over an hour buried deep in shit in the back of a truck hauling pigs."

"Oh, Bill."

"Before that, I fell eight feet from a chain-link fence after getting tangled in barbed wire." He showed her the scabs and inflamed sores on his hands. "I think I broke my ribs. I can barely take a full breath."

He winced as she lifted his shirt and gently ran her warm fingers over the blood-pocked bruise that covered the left half of his torso.

"And before that," he said, pointing to his swollen and scarred right foot, "a nasty German shepherd the size of a horse tried to eat my foot for dinner. Luckily, he only got my shoe."

"Jesus Christ, Bill," she said, grinning. "I can't even imagine—"

"And if you remember," he said, interrupting her, "I'd already pissed myself two times earlier in the day."

"What's up with the clothes you're wearing?"

"I paid a kid four-thousand dollars for this piece of junk," he said, pounding on the roof of the Escort, "and this outfit he found in the gift shop of a convenience store."

Kat was speechless, eyeing Bill and shaking her head.

"Where's our room? I need a hot shower and to lay down a minute. I am exhausted, running on empty. I'm pretty sure I have a cold."

"It's over there, room 12," she said, pointing across the motel's parking lot. "But I have to check with Ken first to find out if you can use it."

"Ken who?"

"My friend I told you about. The room's in his name."

"You mean to tell me after every goddamn thing I survived through today I have to get permission from a guy named *Ken* to take a shower!"

"Calm down, Bill."

"*Calm down*?"

"Let me go in the bar and ask him. I'm sure it'll be all right."

"I'm getting my own room," he said, turning for the lobby.

"You can't."

"What do you mean, I can't?"

"There's no more available."

xxx

With the garment bag draped over one shoulder, a grumpy Bill pouted, waiting for Kat. She quickly reappeared. Ken reluctantly followed her, not taking his eyes off Bill who glared back. Ken stepped a few short feet of Bill and stared him down like a confident boxer who had just entered the ring. But Bill didn't blink nor look intimidated; he took a step closer.

"Ken," Kat said. "This is Bill."

"I didn't know what to expect before I came out here," Ken said, not extending his hand. "I expected a harder man. A chiseled piece of iron, maybe."

"Can I take a shower in the room?"

"Instead, I find a daisy. A wisp of what's left of a fifty-year-

141

old man, well past his prime."

"Can I take a shower or not?"

"Who smells as if he's been fuckin' a donkey."

"Let him take a shower, Ken!"

"I'll be quick," Bill said. "Then I'm gone."

Ken looked from Kat to Bill and pulled the room key from his pocket. Bill reached for the key, but Ken tossed it over his head. It landed several feet away.

"Jesus Christ, Ken! *Grow up.*" Kat retrieved the key and handed it to Bill. "We'll be in the bar, Bill. Come meet us when you're done."

"I may need some help, Kat," he said, not looking away from Ken.

"You have to bathe the little baby as well?" Ken asked, smirking.

"Go in the bar, Ken. Order me a beer. I'll join you shortly."

"I'm not going anywhere without you."

"Just give me a minute with Bill."

Ken stepped closer to Bill, their scowling faces inches apart. Neither said a word. Neither blinked.

"Ken! In the bar!"

Ken glanced to Kat and turned from Bill as if walking away but dipped his shoulder and forcefully drove it into Bill's chest. Without hesitating, Bill shoved him back. Ken angrily spun around, raising his clenched fists. He stepped closer to Bill. Their chests touched. Bill's heart pounded harder.

"Jesus, Ken!" Kat snapped, squeezing her body in between them and pushing them apart. "Go inside!"

After an initial resistance, Ken disappeared into the bar.

"He seems nice," Bill said.

"He can be a real ass sometimes."

"Help me, Kat. I can barely walk," he said as she took his hand and led him to the motel room. "I'll need help getting my shirt off."

"Don't worry. I got you, Bill."

"We should be moving on."

"Let's stay the night."

"I don't think it's a good idea."

"Wait until morning."

"It may be too late by then."

"You need some rest."

As they neared the motel room, Bill stopped and asked, "Are you leaving here with me?"

"When I first got here, I was thinking of staying with Ken," she said, before pausing. "But now, I'm not so sure."

"What do you see in that guy?"

"We have a long history together. We're still working some stuff out."

"I don't like him."

xxx

Kat stayed in the room with Bill for a few minutes. She first helped pull his shirt over his head as he couldn't extend and lift his left arm high enough to do it himself. The two of them stared a moment at his bruised and grimy body in the bathroom mirror. He closed his eyes, trying to erase the image from his mind. Kat found him a bottle of over-the-counter analgesics in her purse to treat his multiple aches and pains, and promised to apply first-aid cream to his cuts and bruises after he showered.

She left the motel room to rejoin Ken at the bar, and Bill turned the shower on as hot as he could stand it. He stepped into the steamy, pulsating jet of water, letting it rain over him. With his head down, he watched the water at his feet turn dirty brown before disappearing down the drain. His legs, sore from too much activity and weak from little food, could no longer support him. He eased his battered body down to sit on the bottom of the tub. He hoped the hot water would soothe his aching muscles and bones. With a fresh bar of soap, he scrubbed every inch of his body, and even after repeatedly scouring, he couldn't get the stink off. No matter how many times he washed himself.

It would be nearly an hour before he could drag himself out of the tub, dry off, change back into the tee-shirt and shorts, and join Kat and Ken at the bar.

xxx

Feeling somewhat rejuvenated and needing a drink to treat his bruised psyche and body, Bill limped to the lounge and pushed open its heavy wooden door. The country music classic by Merle Haggard "Silver Wings" blared from the jukebox. Kat and Ken were locked in an intimate embrace, not unlike a teenage couple slow-dancing for the first time at a high school prom. Her head resting against his chest, they swayed at their own pace, disconnected from the actual rhythm of the tune and oblivious to their surroundings. They didn't notice Bill as he purposely walked close on his way to the bar.

"Handsome couple," Jack said as Bill winced climbing onto the barstool. "You know 'em?"

"Yeah, I know them," Bill unenthusiastically grumbled.

"Ah, to be that young again," Jack said, still staring at the couple, before looking back to Bill. "What it'll be, friend?"

"A margarita."

"I ain't got the right stuff to make ya' a good one," Jack said, shaking his head. "Will a tequila shot do?"

"Sounds good," Bill said as Jack placed two shot glasses in front of Bill and filled them.

"That kid's balls must be blue and screamin'," Jack said, grabbing one of the tequila shots and pushing the other one to Bill. "Those two have been like that for almost an hour."

Bill and Jack sucked down the shots as Kat and Ken gently rocked their entangled bodies from side to side even though the music had ended. Bill set his empty shot glass on the bar. Jack quickly refilled it.

"These are on me," he said, refilling his empty shot glass as well. "By the looks of those fresh bumps and bruises on your face and hands, I'd guess you had a pretty tough day."

They both choked down the tequila. Wiping at his runny nose, Bill swiveled on the barstool and stared at the dancing couple. Kat leaned away from Ken and grinned. After releasing her, he took her by the hand and led her to the door. Before leaving, she glanced back to the bar and spotted Bill watching her. They stared a moment. She looked almost mournful. Bill glared back desperately, as if he would never see her again.

"Another shot of tequila." Bill studied the closed door to the lounge through which Kat left. "And I'll take care of their tab?"

"They told me to charge it to their room," Jack said, refilling the shot glasses.

"Don't worry about it," Bill said, turning to Jack as an odd-looking fellow who appeared to be in his middle to late twenties entered from the corridor that connected the lounge with the motel's lobby.

"I'm tired of playin' the odd job, random task handyman around here," the man loudly announced, showing the palms of his blistered and calloused hands. "I've done so much diggin' today, my hands are fallin' off. The ants have moved on. And the worms have been exposed for what they are."

"And one for him, too," Bill said as the man hopped on the stool next to Bill.

"That's mighty kind, stranger. I'm Leo Malcom Jeffries."

"Nice to meet you. I'm Bill."

"Bill? Bill, what?"

"Bill. . ." He tried to remember the name he'd given to Kat earlier on the trip. "Uh, Bill Runner."

"Nice to fuckin' meet you, Bill Runner," Leo said, enthusiastically and aggressively shaking Bill's hand so hard it hurt. Jack slid him a tequila shot. "Thanks for the drink, Bill Runner!"

The three of them lifted their shot glasses — tequila slopping on the bar — acknowledged each other, and swallowed hard on the tequila. Dropping their heads, Leo and Bill both closed their eyes and grimaced.

"Damn, Bill," Leo said with a sneer. "God, I hate tequila."

Leo was a wiry pale man with stringy, sandy brown hair and a patchy beard. Each of his arms were decorated with a series of uncomplicated tattoos that looked as if he'd done them himself at his kitchen table. Like Bill, he wore an Oklahoma University tee-shirt along with a pair of hacked-off jeans and mud-caked work boots with the laces untied.

"How come there's never any women in here, Jack?" Leo asked, scanning the dark empty bar.

"Because you and all your fabulous freak brothers have scared 'em away."

"So, check this. I get paged," Leo said, beginning a story, before glancing to Bill. "And get me and Bill a bottle of PBR."

"Thank you, Leo," Bill said as Jack placed the beers in front of them.

"So I get paged. It seems the men's room pisser in the lobby don't flush."

"You guys smoke?" an obviously inebriated Bill held out three Cuban cigars.

"Who don't?" Leo said, snatching one of the cigars.

"Lock the door, Leo," Jack said, reaching for a cigar. "It's late enough. Let's close the bar and smoke these suckers now."

After Leo locked the front door to the lounge and shut off the "Open" sign in the window, he returned to the bar, and Bill lighted the cigars. They each were silent for several minutes, puffing hard on the fine cigars. The closed bar quickly filled with a thick haze of gray smoke.

"I like you, Bill," Leo spoke up, admiring the smoldering cigar in his forefingers. "Damn, my friend! Smooth!"

"So, what happened in the lobby bathroom?" Jack asked.

"Two shots of Crown, Jack!" Leo called out. "For me and my buddy, Bill!"

"So, what happened?" Bill asked as Jack poured the whiskey shots.

Before Leo could continue the story, his phone, secured in a holder attached to his belt, rang. He checked the number as he

146

reached for the shot of whiskey.

"My friends from Stillwater are thorns in my side." He shook his head, holding up the shot glass and not answering the phone. "But whiskey, here's a true friend."

Leo and Bill drank the shots. Bill swallowed hard and shook his head, squinting in search of the beer to chase the whiskey.

"*Jesus.*" Bill grunted. "Let's take it easy on the shots. That one nearly came back up."

"So, what happened, Leo?" Jack asked. "In the lobby?"

"I get paged about the pisser in the lobby. A dude is waitin' for me. I test the urinal. Yep, it don't flush. But it drains."

"So, what's the emergency?" Jack asked.

"Dude says he has to flush it before he can use it."

"Huh?" Jack asked.

"Why the need for the pre-flush?" Bill asked.

"Maybe a disinfection task. I don't know." Leo shrugged. "I read that viruses are protein-coated. They're tough to kill. I guess you never know when one of 'em will jump up and bite you on the dick, I guess."

"Or does the sound of the flush make it easier to go?" Jack wondered.

"Or maybe the flushing man knows something the rest of us don't?" Bill said.

"Good point, Bill," Leo said, sliding the empty beer bottle away from him. "I'll take another, Jack. How 'bout you, Bill?"

"No. No. I need to slow down a bit."

"Sure is quiet in here," Leo observed, putting the cold bottle of beer to his lips, and nearly draining it in one gulp.

"Please don't play the jukebox, Leo," Jack said, handing him the remote control to the television. "God, I hate country. All country music. That's the worst goddamn jukebox in Oklahoma. I can't listen to that shit anymore!"

"What do you wannna watch?" Leo asked, aiming the remote control at the television behind the bar.

"I'll stay another half-hour, Leo," Jack said. "Then I'm shuttin' this place down for the night."

It had been over an hour, and Bill and Leo were still at the motel lounge. The wide-screen television over the bar was tuned to a public broadcasting station. Leo had the volume cranked up high to compensate for the hearing he'd lost from attending too many heavy metal concerts. Bill and Leo were smashed. They couldn't stop giggling. At some point, they each draped their arms over the other's shoulder. Even Jack, who was well-known for his strong constitution and quenchless thirst for alcohol, was openly intoxicated and unsteady on his feet. All three shouted, interrupting and talking over each other, and competing with the loudness of the television.

"Look at those crazy sons of bitches in Venice," Leo said, motioning to the television screen. "Blowin' glass and drinkin' beer. Looks like fun. I really need to travel and see the world, you know. Get out of Oklahoma."

Jack switched the channel with the remote control and stopped on a fishing show.

"God, I used to love to fish, but the carp have taken over the rivers here," Leo said, staring at the television screen. "Carp eat crap off the river bottom. They have specially formed mouth parts to make that an easy task. Did you know new sewage systems take advantage of the special capabilities of carp?"

"What the hell?" Jack mumbled, shaking his head.

"I used to take a lot of crap, Leo," Bill said. "But I never ate it. I don't know shit about carp."

All three started to laugh. Leo leaned over and fell into Bill's arms.

"Of course, a carp is not a person, at least not as it is reincarnated," Leo joked, barely able to talk in between the giggles. "A fellow would have to rack up a lot of bad karma to be reincarnated as a carp."

They roared in laughter. With the remote control, Leo channel-surfed, until stopping on a travel show that appeared to be set in Florida.

"We got to get out of here, boys," Jack said.

"One more shot?" Leo asked.

"This is it," Jack answered, pouring them shots of whiskey. Leo and Bill became distracted by the blaring television.

"Who'd ever want to live in Florida?" Leo said, reaching for the shot glass. "It ain't nothin' but Mickey Mouse, sinkholes, early bird specials, a need for deciduous trees."

"Drink your shot," Jack snapped. "We got to go."

"The real estate developers ran off the poor Sioux and poisoned the reef," Leo continued. "What a circus."

"Drink up! Drink up!"

"You watch a lot of cable, don't you?" Bill asked Leo, wiping at his nose, which wouldn't stop running.

"But I hear the sex is easy to come by in Florida," Leo went on. "Did you know because of Viagra, the VD is on the rise in seniors livin' in retirement communities there?"

"Leo!" Jack shouted. "Time to go!"

Bill and Leo raised their shot glasses and saluted each other, before tossing them back in one final burning gulp. Leo held onto Bill who nearly fell off his barstool. After steadying himself, Bill reached into his pocket and threw five hundred-dollar bills onto the bar.

"I got everything," Bill said. "And whatever's left, you can keep, Jack."

"That's way too much, Bill."

"No. No."

"I can't take yo—" Jack started but Leo interrupted him: "We'll take that bottle of Crown then."

Jack grabbed the two-thirds full bottle of Crown Royal and handed it to Leo. "That sounds fair. Now, get the hell out of here, you two."

"Where we goin' next, Bill?" Leo asked.

"I need to go to bed."

"Come to my room for a nightcap."

Arm in arm, Bill and Leo staggered out of the blacked-out lounge singing the classic Irish folk song by Lonnie Donegan, "It Takes a Worried Man" quietly, so not to wake anyone. Creeping across the motel's parking lot, Leo swung the hand that carried the whiskey bottle like a conductor leading an orchestra. Twice they had to stop so Leo could support Bill, who slowly limped. As they neared the motel's second building, they began to sing louder. Leo's room was not far from the room that Kat and Ken shared. Once they reached room 12, Bill signaled for Leo to halt. They sang the old-time tune even louder, almost to the point of shouting: "It takes a worried man, to sing a worried song. Yeah, it takes a worried man, yeah to sing a worried song. I might be worried now, but I won't be worried long. . ."

The door to room 12 slowly cracked open. Wearing nothing but a man's button-down shirt, Kat peeked out.

"What are you doing, Bill?"

"Nothing," he answered, grinning drunkenly like a child caught misbehaving. "What are *you* doing?"

She didn't respond as the door opened wider. With a perturbed look, Ken glanced first to Bill then to Leo, making note of their closely matching Oklahoma Sooner shirts.

"Who are you two supposed to be? The Boomer Twins?"

"Did we wake you?" Leo asked.

"No, you interrupted us."

Bill studied Kat, eyeing her barely clothed body. She looked away, trying to avoid eye contact.

"We wanted to see if y'all would like to party?" Leo held the bottle of whiskey.

Bill continued to stare at Kat; she wouldn't look at him.

"We got our own party going on here," Ken said as he started to close the door. "We don't need you two dipshits."

The door slammed in their faces. They didn't move for a moment until Leo reached over and locked arms with Bill. As

150

if on cue, they both started singing the folk song at the exact same moment.

"Yeah, it takes a worried man, yeah to sing a worried song. I might be worried now, but I won't be worried long. . ."

Carrying the bottle of whiskey, Leo led Bill to his motel room. Leo lived full-time in the room. It was part of his payment for serving as the Slumberland's maintenance man, and most importantly, it also ensured his twenty-four-hour availability if there ever was a problem at the place. His room was no different from any of the other twenty that were rented out nightly in that it had a single bathroom, kitchenette, and larger room with a bed, television, and desk. Unlike the other rooms, however, Leo's was cluttered, nearly filled to the ceiling with junk, a hoarder's paradise. There were hundreds of record albums in crates everywhere, even in the bathroom. Overflowing cardboard boxes of assorted plumbing accessories, car parts, different tools, and other odds and ends were crammed into the kitchen. Heaps of clothing piled high on the bed. A narrow path through the clutter on the well-worn carpet connected the rooms. A black and white television near the bed was on but with the volume muted.

Bill sat at a chair by the desk as Leo fumbled with a record album he was trying to put on a turntable. It was the Jonathan Livingston Seagull soundtrack performed by Neil Diamond. Once the music started to play, Leo opened a drawer in a dresser and pulled out what looked to be a bag of marijuana, a small pipe, and a lighter and stumbled to a seat on an open space on the floor. He waved to Bill.

"Come join me on the floor," he said, motioning to Bill. "Get the whiskey."

Feeling dizzy, Bill grabbed the bottle of whiskey before gingerly easing his wounded body next to Leo on the limited open space of the floor. Leo packed the bowl with weed and fired it up. He hit the pipe hard and inhaled a large puff of smoke, holding it in his lungs as long as he could. He reached the smoldering pipe to Bill who shook his head.

"I didn't think people listened to records anymore?" Bill said as Leo exhaled the smoke from his lungs in a large cloud that lingered between the two of them. "Isn't it all digital now?"

"I get 'em at yard sales," Leo croaked, trying not to cough. "I love yard sales. They're the closest thing we got to time travelin'."

"I can see," Bill said, studying Leo's many treasures. He swallowed a large swig of whiskey as Leo took several quick hits off the pipe.

"You remember Jonathan Livingston Seagull, don't you?"

"My kids had to read the book in school."

"This Jonathan Livingston Seagull stuff makes me think about where I'm headed," Leo said, blowing out a long stream of smoke, "and how I need to get on the stick with things."

He reached the pipe to Bill who shook his head.

"We're not killin' anyone, Bill."

Bill reluctantly took the pipe and stared at it a moment. Leo handed him the lighter. Bill put the pipe to his lips.

"It's been a long time, Leo," he said, before lighting the weed in the bowl and cautiously inhaling the smoke.

"Where you headed, Bill?"

Bill slowly exhaled; the smoke hung around him. He couldn't hold back a short fit of coughing. Leo drank from the whiskey bottle.

"I don't know, Leo," he said in between coughs. "I'm just driving until I get past all the bullshit or run out of highway. Whatever comes first. There's got to be someplace, somewhere real. I need a place to hide."

"You'll be drivin' forever, my friend," Leo said, trading the whiskey for the pipe. "Nothing's real these days. It's all fake, man. The internet. The TV. Reality shows. Smart phones. Smart cars. Pop stars. Tits. Presidents. . ."

He hit the pipe and held it out to Bill, who took it without hesitation.

"Damn. I'm fucked up," Leo confessed. "I'm sure Jonathan Livingston Seagull never acted like this."

Bill deeply inhaled the smoke into his lungs.

"I'm almost thirty, and I ain't done shit," Leo said, chugging on the whiskey. "I need a purpose to my life."

Bill coughed a few times then grinned, staring at the bowl.

"It feels good, don't it, Bill?"

Bill nodded; his smile grew as if he was lost in thought. He played with his wedding ring.

"What's your story, Bill Runner?"

"No story," he said, looking down.

"I meet people from all over the world that pass through here. Everyone has a story."

Bill took a quick drag off the pipe and passed it back to Leo.

"Come on, Bill. Tell me. What's your story?"

Bill sat quiet for a moment before slowly exhaling the smoke from his lungs.

"You want the truth?" he asked, before looking to Leo. "I robbed a bank. There's nearly a million dollars in the trunk of a car parked outside. And I'm wanted by the FBI. That's my story."

Leo first showed him a serious expression, then grinned, before starting to snicker. Bill tried not to smile but couldn't help it as they both began to giggle like young school children. Soon, their giggles turned into belly laughs as they leaned into each other and rolled around on the floor.

"Rob. . . rob. . . robbed a bank! That's a good one, Bill!"

They both tried to regain their composure, before hysterically laughing again.

"It feels good, don't it, Leo?"

"I like you, Bill," Leo said, trying to catch his breath between cackles.

"Hand me that bottle." Bill reached for the whiskey and took a big gulp.

"Come on. Tell me your story. What's with the outfit you're wearin'? You don't seem like the bro, mesh-shorts, flip-flop type."

"I lost my luggage. I picked these up at a convenience store. It was the only place open."

"On the bed," Leo pointed. "Take what you want. There's some nice things there. Most of that stuff was left behind here at the motel over the years."

"Thank you, Leo. I'll go through it before I leave, but you have to let me pay for it."

"Shit, Bill. The stuff's free. I didn't pay for it. And don't worry about bed bugs. I washed all those things myself, sometimes twice."

"You're too kind."

"One more bowl?" Leo asked, lifting the whiskey bottle to his lips. "And we'll finish this whiskey. Then I got to turn in. My job is full of surprises. I don't know what's comin' tomorrow."

Leo took a drink of the whiskey and handed the bottle to Bill who finished what was left.

"Any family, Bill?" Leo asked, packing the bowl with fresh weed. Bill didn't initially answer. "I see you have a wife. Where is she?"

"Home."

"Where's home?"

"A long way from here."

"What's a long way?"

"Back east."

"She doesn't know you're here, does she?" Leo handed Bill the freshly loaded pipe and lighter. Bill fired up the bowl and took his longest and hardest hit of the night. "Any kids, Bill?"

"A son and daughter," he said with a grimace, holding the smoke in his lungs.

"What's your daughter do?"

"Boys and cigarettes," Bill answered, releasing the smoke from deep inside and filling the room with the white cloud.

"And your son?" Leo asked, reaching for the pipe and lighter.

"He *is* the flip-flop, bro', mesh-short type. He was a good kid until he went to college and discovered beer, vodka, and fast cars. He doesn't make good decisions."

"Do they know you're here?"

"I better go, Leo," Bill said. "I didn't intend to stay so late."

"Do you want to call her?" Leo asked, reaching for the phone attached to his belt.

"Who?"

"Your wife," Leo said, holding the phone out to Bill. "Here, call her."

"I need to, yes," Bill said after a brief pause, "but not yet."

"Where you sleepin' tonight?" Leo asked, returning the phone to its holder on his belt.

"Probably my car."

"I'd let you stay here, but. . ." Leo said, motioning to the clutter. "I don't think you'd be too comfortable. I barely have enough room for myself."

"I may hit the road."

"Why aren't you stayin' with your young lady friend? I saw you walkin' with her earlier this evening."

"I think she's busy."

"I don't mean to pry, but what's your connection to her?"

"A long story."

"I got time. Unless of course, the urinal in the lobby starts actin' up again."

"I'm certain I'll be leaving Oklahoma without her." Bill tried to push himself up off the floor. "You got to help me up, Leo. I've hurt myself pretty bad the past couple days."

"And you're shit-faced drunk."

"Yes, and I'm shit-faced drunk."

"It feels good, don't it, Bill?"

"It does indeed, Leo. I had a wonderful time with you tonight."

"If you're ever passin' through, you know where to stay."

"Yes. Yes. I hope to see again."

xxx

Day 10. Saturday, May 6. 6:11 AM

Wiping at his nose and shivering, Bill shuffled out of Leo's room with a pronounced limp. He had a bundle of clothes rolled under his arm—a pair of pants, a few shirts, a jacket, socks, and a single pair of shoes. As the new day dawned, he wondered what had happened to the night. His head was light, and his legs were sore and uncertain. He was both drunk and high. It had been decades since he felt that way, and it felt good and seemed right. His evening with Leo was a blast and much needed, but his brief respite was over. As he neared the car, an uneasy feeling overwhelmed him. His mood changed as he suddenly crossed some imaginary threshold to the dark side. He couldn't escape the sense of impending capture that dwelled heavy on his mind. The authorities had to be close, and it was time to leave Norman.

The air was damp and heavy, and the sun was rising. Bill hobbled through the parking lot to the Ford Escort. He opened the trunk and checked to make sure the garment bag was there. He surveyed the parking lot in the early morning haze. He was alone. He grimaced as he gingerly took a seat on the edge of the open trunk to change clothes and scanned the motel property. On the other side of the lot, he noticed a lone figure smoking a cigarette outside one of the ground-floor rooms. It was Kat.

With both arms folded across her chest, she bounced on the sidewalk as if trying to keep warm. After an initial reluctance, Bill slowly approached. More of the sun had risen, rousing the birds into song. A gentle breeze stirred. The early morning light transitioned from hues of gray to an odd and ominous purple and pink. Kat turned to Bill. He stopped, keeping several feet between them. They studied each other. As Kat looked away, Bill spoke up.

"Get your things. We're leaving."

"Have you been up all night?" she asked, still avoiding eye contact.

"We should have left hours ago."

"Don't you think you should get some sleep first?"

"It's time to go, Kat."

She didn't respond, looking back to him and dragging hard on the cigarette. He glanced to the ground as if expecting words he didn't want to hear but knew were coming.

"You know how much I care about you," she said, tossing the cigarette to the ground, "and what a fantastic thing you're doing with the mo—"

"No, Kat," he interrupted. "Don't. . ."

"I've had such an amazing time with you, but—"

"I'm not leaving without you," he said, interrupting her again. "You need to continue what you started."

"No, Kat," he said, shaking his head.

"But on your own," she finished, looking apologetic. "I'm staying here, Bill."

He maintained his distance from her. She was silent. They awkwardly stared.

"See you around, Wild Bill. I'll never forget you."

Devastated, he turned away as she opened the door to her room, but before she could go inside, he quickly spun around and called out, "I love you, Kat."

She quietly closed the door again and stepped towards him. "I love you too, Bill."

"No," he said, shaking his head with a sly smile but keeping his distance. "Not the way I love you."

His comment softened the mood as they both grinned then chuckled. Kat held out her arms and approached him. Her smile grew, brightening the dreary morning.

"Ah, Bill."

They embraced. He desperately latched onto her as if to never let go, engulfing her within his trembling arms. Trying to hold back the tears, he rested his head on top of hers. Never had he been so close to a woman other than his wife. For the last many years of his marriage, he felt alone. He hadn't felt that way since meeting Kat.

"I knew this would be hard," she whispered in his arms.

He pulled her comforting body tighter into his. She audibly sighed. His heart raced.

"Goodbye, Bill." she said, patting his chest as a signal to release her.

He let go as she pulled away. He turned his back. Tears rolled down his cheeks.

"Look at me, Bill."

Wiping at his runny eyes and nose to regain some composure, he slowly turned with a deep breath.

"You changed my life," she confessed. "I've never said that to anyone before. Please be safe. Please."

xxx

Rubbing her misty eyes, Kat cheerlessly entered the motel room. Ken paced the floor of the small space, holding a phone to his ear. He also held a folded newspaper. Kat looked up and smiled to him as she took a seat on the bed. He nodded and started to talk into the phone.

"Yes, Ma'am. Slumberland Motel, room 12, off of 77. A gray Ford Escort."

Puzzled, Kat stood and approached Ken.

"No, Ma'am, he's alone," Ken said, turning away from her. "Yes. Yes. Yes, I believe so."

"Who are you talking to?" Kat loudly asked.

He placed his hand over the phone's receiver and said to her, "He won't turn you in, right?"

He held up the newspaper and showed her Bill's photograph on the front page. The headline read: "Missing banker in area, large reward offered."

"What?"

"Bill. He won't turn you in?"

"Ken! What are you doing?"

"Collecting fifty-thousand dollars. We'll be able to go anywhere we want." He returned his attention returned to the phone. "Yes, Ma'am. Yes. I'm here at the motel now."

xxx

With slumped shoulders, Bill sat behind the steering wheel of the beat-up old car with little desire to continue. Lowering his head, he started to quietly weep. He immediately stopped and pulled himself together, taking several deep and calming breaths. The heaviness of his farewell with Kat had jolted him sober. What was left of his journey and its cause had seemingly lost their importance. He scanned the motel's parking lot one last time. He was on his own. Turning the key, he planned to take the backroads that brought him to the Slumberland.

He put the car in reverse and checked the rearview mirror: someone ran towards him, waving their arms. It was Kat, and she was shouting. Unable to hear through closed windows, he slammed the brakes, shoved the gear shift into park, and jumped out.

"*Bill!*" she called out. "*Bill! Bill!*"

Suddenly, Ken appeared in pursuit of Kat, quickly gaining on her. Bill dashed from the car, sprinted past Kat and intercepted Ken with a wild roundhouse right-hand punch. Ken ducked and lowered his shoulder, spearing Bill in the gut like a hard tackle in football. They hit the asphalt with Ken on top of Bill, who had flopped onto his belly. Kat leaped onto Ken's back and batted at his head and neck with flailing slaps.

"Ken! Stop!" she screamed, scratching at his face and leaving deep red marks across his cheeks and forehead. "Stop it! Leave him alone!"

"Get off me! I thought you'd be on my side!" He swatted at her and flipped her off his back. "Don't fuck this up!"

Kat landed hard on the pavement, her hip taking most of the force. Bill rolled from his stomach onto his back. Ken raised both fists clasped together for a final blow. Grimacing in pain, Kat screamed. But before Ken could strike, Leo appeared through the dust the melee had stirred up and smacked Ken in the face with a quick swing of a shovel. Ken fell to the pavement, like an anvil, his body rigid as a board. He was out cold before he hit the ground, his legs twisted awkwardly underneath him.

"Holy shit, Leo!" Bill yelled, sitting up next to Ken. He lightly pushed at Ken's legs and arms to check if he was conscious.

"I think I killed him, Bill."

"Oh, my God!" Kat shrieked, lifting her boyfriend. "Ken! Ken? Please wake up!"

He didn't respond when she grabbed his shirt and aggressively shook.

"Yep, I fuckin' killed him."

"Quick," Bill whispered, checking the parking lot. "Let's get him in the room."

It was still relatively early in the morning, and the parking lot was quiet. Kat, Bill, and Leo raised Ken's torso off the ground and quickly dragged him into the room. Once inside, they struggled to lift his unresponsive body higher before tossing him onto the bed. Bill opened the door and scanned the parking lot, then closed it. Kat and Leo stared in shock at Ken's bleeding and mangled face, which was swollen and nearly unrecognizable.

"Is he dead?" Kat asked.

"I hope not. Manslaughter don't look so good on a résumé. Shit! I've been thinkin' about lookin' for a new job." He turned to Kat. "I'm Leo Malcolm Jeffries by the way."

"Kat," She nodded and looked at Bill. "He called the cops."

"We need to get out of here," Bill said.

"Is he breathin'?" Leo asked.

She leaned her ear close to Ken's chest. "Barely."

"Leo, you got to help us," Bill said, peeking out the window and checking the parking lot.

"Follow me," Leo said.

"We can't leave him like this," Kat said. She lingered by the beaten body as Bill and Leo headed for the door.

"The fuck we can't," Leo shouted. "I don't believe I have neither the disposition nor the constitution for prison!"

"Let's go, Kat!" Bill ordered.

After one last brief look, Kat stood and joined Bill and Leo at the door. Bill didn't initially move, closely studying Ken's beaten face.

"Hold on," Bill said. "Look at him. Who does he look like?"

Leo and Kat glanced at Ken, then Bill.

"You messed him up pretty good, Leo," Bill said.

They both nodded as Bill pulled his wallet from his back pocket and walked over to Ken. After removing his last paycheck, Bill stuffed his wallet into one of the back pockets of Ken's pants and took Ken's wallet. He took off the filthy Pirates baseball cap and stuck it on Ken's recently buzzed head. The three of them stared at Ken a moment, and Bill checked again to make sure he was still breathing. The three of them left.

Sirens wailed in the distance; the sound of approaching helicopters filled the air. Bill pit-stopped at the still running Ford Escort that was parked sideways in the middle of the lot. He quickly retrieved the garment bag of money, leaving the trunk and driver's side door open. He watched Leo and Kat duck into the motel's laundry room and followed, limping as fast as could with his mangled foot. The cramped room was active; multiple industrial size washers and dryers rocked and rumbled.

"We need to leave the motel." Bill was trying to remain calm.

"No, they're too close," Leo snapped. "They'll chase us down!"

"But they don't know what they're looking for."

"Yeah, Leo," Kat agreed with Bill, "they'll be here any minute and lock this place up. There's no place for us to hide here."

"Findin' Ken will stall them," Leo said. "And distract them. We'll slip away then."

The first police car squealed into the lot with lights flashing.

"Get in there!" Leo said, pointing to a large laundry cart on wheels.

Bill clumsily hopped in, nearly tripping as his bad leg got caught on the edge. Kat followed, tumbling in on top of him. Additional police cars sped into the lot as the sirens roared louder.

"Now, get down and keep quiet," Leo said, covering Bill and Kat with a pile of dirty sheets and towels.

Within minutes, the entire lot was jammed with police and FBI vehicles. Several news helicopters circled overhead. Leo watched from the window as squads of Oklahoma state troopers, SWAT team members, and FBI agents surrounded Bill's car and swarmed the motel, especially focused on room 12. Standing behind his car, Agent Stack barked orders from a megaphone. He instructed teams of officers in pairs to search every room and space at the motel as a SWAT team moved into position outside room 12. He also instructed a group of local cops to secure the parking lot's entry and exits. As Leo watched, two state troopers worked their way towards the laundry, deliberately and thoroughly checking all the guest rooms.

"Shit," Leo mumbled, feeling trapped in the confined room.

"Kat, you smell like, like, ah, sweat," Bill said from the cart under the dirty laundry. "No, like sex."

"What does that even mean?"

"You have a peculiar, yet familiar, odor about you."

"What do you think I was doing all night? You still smell like a dirty pig,"

"Sssh," Leo hissed. "Be quiet."

There was a short silence as Leo again glanced out the window. Scores of media trucks and vans were arriving. Multiple ambulances pulled into the parking lot.

"Why'd it have to be with that asshole?" Bill whispered. "He turned us in."

"He turned you in."

"You know, I was wishing it was me in that room with you."

"You're married, Bill. Remember that."

"Shut the fuck up, you two!" Leo yelled as the pair of cops entered the guest room adjacent to the laundry.

"Get out," Leo hissed, pulling off the blankets and towels in the cart. "*Get out. Get out of there.*"

xxx

A local female field reporter with a microphone stood before a lone cameraman behind the police barricade on the perimeter of the motel's parking lot. Storm clouds formed to the west, so she pulled on a raincoat and flipped the hood over her head, ready for her live report from the scene.

"FBI sources have confirmed to us," she said, staring with the most serious gaze into the camera as it started to lightly rain, "that Mr. William Moreland, the runaway banker from Pennsylvania, is believed to be isolated in a room at this motel, the Slumberland Motel, just outside of Norman, Oklahoma."

The camera panned across the active parking lot, before focusing on the door of room 12.

"SWAT team members have gathered around the room and are prepared to enter," the reporter continued. "It appears to me that they have knocked and called into the room multiple times with no apparent answer from inside."

As it started to rain, the focus of the camera was directed back to the reporter. The cameraman wiped the lens of the camera with a handkerchief.

"Our sources have told us that the FBI received a tip about a possible sighting of Mr. Moreland at the motel early this morning. They also indicated that the sighting was confirmed to be a positive identification of the banker."

xxx

There was a knock on the laundry room door. Leo opened it and warily peeked out. He was greeted by two hulking Oklahoma state troopers. Rainwater beaded on their hats and the shoulders of their uniforms.

"What's happenin' out there, officers?" Leo asked. "I've been afraid to even look out with all the commotion and chaos."

Both officers entered the laundry and scanned the cluttered room.

"Can we look around?" one of the cops asked, walking deeper into the room.

"Sure."

"Anyone one else here?"

"No," Leo said, as the other cop sifted through the towels and sheets in the laundry cart where Kat and Bill had been hiding. "Jus' me and my dirty laundry."

The other cop opened a door that led to the back of the laundry room. A white motel utility van was parked near the door.

"Do you know the owner of the van?" the cop asked, walking outside and checking the van doors. They were unlocked.

"It belongs to the motel," Leo answered. "They use it as a shuttle into Norman and for haulin' and other errands."

"Do you have the keys?"

"No, sir," Leo said. "I do a lot of things around here, but they don't let me drive the van."

The cop slid one of the side doors of the van open, leaned in and examined the inside with a flashlight. He checked the ignition, the glovebox, and under the driver's seat. He found no keys. The van was empty. After thoroughly inspecting the space behind the laundry, he reentered the room and wiped the dripping rainwater from his hat. The other cop stood beside another closed door inside the laundry room.

"What's in here?" he asked, pulling it open to a disorganized and messy storage closet.

"Don't tell my boss," Leo said. "It's such a mess, and boy, does he hate the messes I make around here."

The two cops scanned the room one last time, before walking to the window and peering out. The rain had picked up. Squatting behind a police squad car and holding an umbrella over his head with his left hand, Agent Stack surveyed the parking lot and assessed the positioning of the police and FBI officers. He glanced to the SWAT team leader, Officer Carl Reynolds, huddled with his men next to the entrance of room 12. Stack cautiously stood with his right arm raised. Officer Reynolds nodded as a signal for Stack who dropped his arm. In a flash, the SWAT team members bashed open the door to room 12 with a battering ram and stormed inside with rifles raised.

Within seconds, Officer Reynolds stepped from the room.

"Send the medics!"

A team of paramedics rushed toward room 12, closely followed by Agent Stack and other high-ranking FBI agents. The two state troopers in the laundry room watched from the window as Leo peeked over their shoulders. Rain was coming down harder than ever. For several minutes, scores of police officers, FBI agents, and media members helplessly stood by, waiting for any sign of activity from Ken's motel room. Becoming restless, the two state troopers turned to Leo. and one of them said, "Don't you dare leave this room until instructed."

Leo nodded and the curious troopers joined the group that had gathered outside room 12.

"Now!" Leo called out, unlocking an industrial-sized dryer. Kat pushed the bedcovers and bath towels off her and Bill, who were huddled tightly together inside. Bill took several large gasps of air.

"*Get in,*" Leo said, pointing to a laundry cart. They hopped in the cart, and Leo covered then with the bedcover and towels and took a quick glance out the window. Ken was being wheeled from room 12 on a stretcher, an IV hooked to one arm and an oxygen mask covering his face. His legs and chest were tightly strapped to the stretcher.

Leo locked the front door of the laundry room and pushed the cart with Bill and Kat out the back. He guided the cart through the heavy downpour and stopped next to the motel van. He slung the side van door open and pulled down a metal ramp. He ran the cart up the ramp into the van and slid the side door closed. He pulled the ramp away from the van and jumped into the driver's seat. He smiled as he took a set of keys from his pocket. Nothing gave him more joy than knowing he had lied to the state police. Wiping the rainwater that dripped from his long, stringy hair into his eyes, he calmly drove away from the back of the laundry room unnoticed and out of sight from the distracted crowd in the parking lot. In the rain and suddenly developing fog, he escaped on a side road used by locals as a shortcut through a nearby neighborhood.

As Leo, Bill, and Kat disappeared from the scene, a waiting ambulance with flashing lights and slapping windshield wipers had pulled next to the door of room 12. Ken was loaded into the ambulance and was gone. Agent Stack appeared from the room with a few members of his team. The many police officers and news reporters outside intently watched him. He looked concerned, even puzzled as he stood in the doorway of the room out of the rain. Finally, appreciating the attention on him, he motioned to the local state police sergeant.

"It's all clear."

"All clear!" the sergeant barked out over a microphone.

"Good work, boys," Stack's young FBI partner, Agent Steve Robinson, said.

"Something is not right," Stack said, scanning the motel complex and parking lot.

"You don't think it's him?" Robinson asked.

"Once they get him situated at the hospital and stable," Stack said, "I want him ID'd immediately."

"So, you don't think it's him?"

"Did you all find anything unusual in the motel or rooms?" Stack asked the group of officers who performed the searches.

"No, sir," Officer Reynolds said. "I was told all the occupied rooms were clear. The motel's manager is ready to take the officers through the unoccupied and empty rooms now."

"You don't think the guy we found in the room is him, do you?" Agent Robinson asked Stack again.

"I did not get a real close look at him, but. . ." Stack said, before pausing and turning to his partner. "Did he look like a fifty-year-old man to you? He looked much younger. And I expected him to be dirtier and more weathered from days on the road."

"So, you're telling us, the search is still on?"

"Any sign of the stolen money?" Stack asked Officer Reynolds, who shook his head. "Where is the money? And why was the car still running and parked the way it was? It looks like someone left here in a hurry or after a struggle. Maybe it was the unidentified man who called in the tip."

"We got some info on the car," Agent Robinson spoke up, checking his phone. "It's registered to a twenty-one-year-old male."

"How did the banker get it?" Stack asked.

"We just spoke to the kid on the phone. An officer is on his way to pick him up and bring him to the local police station for further questioning."

"What did the kid say?"

"He sold it."

"Sold it?"

"For four-thousand dollars."

"Four-thousand dollars? For that? That's a desperate man."

"Yeah, said he sold it to a middle-aged man at a convenience store about thirty miles from here, and. . ." said Robinson, before pausing. "The man was muddy, missing a shoe, appeared to be injured, and smelled awful, like a farm or something?"

"Like a motherfucking farm. *And missing a shoe,*" Stack snarled. He opened his umbrella and stepped into the rain, walking towards his car with Agent Robinson trailing him. "Was his alone?"

"The kid said the man was alone."

"The injured man is not the banker," Stack announced to the officers and agents surrounding him. "So, what are we fucking standing around here for? I want this motel turned upside down and every road in and out of Norman blocked. I am not leaving Oklahoma without him."

Stack stood by his car, while many of the FBI agents and police officers of his small entourage had dispersed. He stared at the ground as water puddled on the asphalt around his feet. The rain poured even harder.

"Agent Stack?" the local field reporter said as she walked up. Stack didn't initially acknowledge her.

"Agent Stack, did you get your man?" she asked again. He finally looked up.

"Due the excellent work of my team at the FBI as well as the local Oklahoma authorities," he said, speaking quietly and confidently, "we have apprehended a person of interest."

"Is it Mr. Moreland, the banker?" she asked as camera operators and sound techs joined them with their cameras, microphones, and tape recorders.

"We need to confirm the identity first," Stack said.

"Confirm the identity?"

"The subject has been severely injured and was rushed to the hospital."

"Was he injured during the apprehension?"

"No."

"Do you, sir, believe you have the missing banker?"

"I am not going to comment until we get a definitive identification."

"And what about the missing money?" she asked, pressing Stack. He appeared uncomfortable with this line of questioning as rainwater poured from his umbrella like an open spigot.

"We have secured the premises and have started a full examination of the area," he said. He waved the rain from his hands and kicked it from his shoes. "I cannot comment any further."

Closing the umbrella, Stack turned away and ducked into the driver's seat of his car. Agent Robinson got into the passenger side.

"How did we miss him?" Stack mumbled into the steering wheel, not looking at his partner. "We should have had him by now. I'm starting to wonder if we're dealing with a brilliant genius or a lucky fool."

"He's halfway across the country, and we haven't got him yet," Robinson said. "What's that make us?"

"He is a fool," Stack said, turning the key. "We have just been unlucky so far. I will get him. I always do."

xxx

Continually checking the rearview, Leo pressed on in the heavy

168

rain, keeping to the lesser used backroads and finding himself in an unfamiliar neighborhood. He constantly checked the laundry cart behind him as it skated over the open floor with every turn. Bill and Kat were still huddled under piles of dirty laundry. Neither had said a word, and neither moved.

But with pain in his ribs and cramping in the weary muscles of his legs, Bill began to fidget, to unfold his bent legs. Kat tried to accommodate his need for more space and turned her cramped body sideways to allow him extra room.

"You okay, Bill?" she whispered.

"I'll be fine. Just a little too old and beat up. I feel like I just went fifteen rounds with a pissed-off Mike Tyson."

"I want to apologize," she said. "I shouldn't have snapped at you back in the laundry. I can't imagine what you went through and what it took to make it to the motel after we got separated."

"No. No. I have no excuses. It's me who needs to apologize for what I said. You know you can leave whenever you're ready."

"I never promised you anything, Bill."

"I know. I know. Being on the run isn't any kind of life for either of us. It's my job to get you home safely when you're ready."

"Seeing that my options are limited at the moment, I guess you're stuck with me for a little while, at least for now."

"I don't know how this story will end," he said, "but when it does, I hope you'll still be around."

With his eyes glued to the wet road before him, Leo stretched his right arm back over the driver's seat and reached for the laundry cart, grabbing it.

"I think we got away," he loudly announced, dragging the heavy cart towards him. "We fuckin' got away!"

The cart started to wobble as Bill and Kat shuffled and rearranged their bodies. The soiled bedcovers, towels, and linens on top of the pile began to move like a wave on the ocean. First, Bill popped his head out, then Kat's head quickly followed. They glanced around the inside of the van and out the clouded windshield.

"We're several miles from the motel," Leo said, "and ain't no

169

one chasin' us."

"You did it, Leo!" Kat hollered. "You did it."

"But we don't got much time. They're goin' to find they got the wrong guy."

"What's the plan?" Bill asked.

"I don't got one."

"We'll need to ditch the van," Bill said.

"I planned to return it."

"We'll need a car," Kat said.

"Do you have a car, Leo?" Bill asked.

"Oh, I got a car."

"You saved us, buddy," Bill said, digging into the garment bag of money strapped over one of his shoulders. "Please let me pay you."

Leo glanced back to Bill who offered a stack of hundred-dollar bills bundled together.

"Here. Here."

"Where'd the hell you get that?" Leo asked, looking back to the road.

"I told you. I robbed a bank."

"You were shittin' me, right?" Leo asked, glancing back to Bill and grinning.

"It's all true," Bill said, unable to hold back a laugh.

"I really like you, Bill," Leo said, laughing along. "I really, really like you."

"Let me reimburse you, Leo. Please! You might be in big trouble."

"I can't take your money," Leo said, shaking his head and staring back to the road.

"How can we ever repay you?"

"Let me go with you," Leo said without hesitating.

xxx

Agent Stack silently stood outside a room in the intensive care unit at the University of Oklahoma hospital in wet shoes. He

170

watched through the observation window as a doctor and nurse examined a heavily sedated and unconscious Ken Mercury. Ken was hooked to numerous beeping devices that delivered medications and monitored his heart. An Oklahoma state trooper sat on a chair by the doorway as Agent Robinson quietly appeared behind Stack.

"Who is he?" Stack asked, not turning.

"Ken Mercury. A twenty-five-year-old male from New Orleans."

"New Orleans?"

"We did a background. Nothing too much. Minor teenage stuff."

"The banker was in New Orleans."

"We're pretty sure that Mr. Mercury was the one who called in the tip."

"He must have met the banker in New Orleans," Stack talked to the glass, still watching the doctor and nurse. "Either joined him there or followed him here."

"But there were no eyewitness reports in Texas of a third person. Only the banker and young woman."

"Do we have an ID on the young woman?"

"She is a Katherine McCarthy."

"From the fingerprints in the car?"

Agent Robinson nodded. "Originally from Chicago, currently living in New Orleans."

"Maybe Mr. Mercury followed the banker here because he knew about the money. And a scuffle at the motel likely occurred after the banker found out Mr. Mercury had tried to turn him in."

"So, you think Mr. Moreland assaulted Mr. Mercury?"

"I can't picture the banker causing all that," Stack said, finally turning to his partner and pointing to Ken Mercury's incapacitated body as the doctor finished the examination. "Get someone to New Orleans. Interview Mr. Mercury's and Ms. McCarthy's friends, family, employers, co-workers, roommates, everyone. I want to know everything there is to know about those two and why they left New Orleans."

The doctor appeared from Ken's hospital room.

"Doc?" Stack called out before he could walk away. "How is he?"

"Could be worse."

"Is he going to be all right?"

"I think so. Right now, he has a significant head injury with extensive swelling of his brain. We sedated him, and he's currently in a drug-induced coma."

"When will I be able to question him?"

"He might be this way for a while. It may be days, or even weeks, before the swelling subsides."

"He is a key witness with important information related to a case we're working on," Stack said. He pointed to the state trooper guarding the room. "Can we keep someone here around the clock?"

"Of course."

Agent Robinson held a phone out to Stack.

"Moreland's wife," he whispered.

Stack took a deep breath and took the phone. He greeted her enthusiastically but insincerely.

"Good afternoon, Mrs. Moreland. So glad to hear from you."

"Where is my husband, Mr. Stack?" she sternly asked. "Is he in your custody? Has he been injured?"

"Well, um. . ." he mumbled.

"My phone has been ringing off the hook, Mr. Stack. Not from you, but from my family. From my friends. From my neighbors. From reporters all over the country. I need to know *what in the hell* is going on. I thought out of courtesy you would've called by now. Is my husband, okay?"

"We have not located your husband. We do have a —"

She interrupted. "Who do I contact to request a different agent to lead this case? You seem way over your head, Mr. Stack. Are you unqualified for this particular job or just completely incompetent?"

"We do have a subject, a badly injured male subject, in

172

custody," Stack calmly said. "He was with your husband as recently as this morning. Because of a physical resemblance, this individual was thought to perhaps be your husband."

"And nobody called to tell me!"

"I wanted to be sure, Mrs. Moreland. We just got the ID on the individual a few minutes ago. He is not your husband."

"You have no idea what me and my family are going through right now. We can't leave our home without being attacked by reporters. Film crews are climbing on the roof of my house, trying to get pictures of us. Strangers are camped out in the front lawn. Some of our neighbors and old friends won't talk to us anymore. My children and I are gawked at like lunatics from an insane asylum when we go to the grocery store or fill the car with gas."

"You are right, I cannot begin to imagine what you and your family are experiencing, Mrs. Moreland."

"I can't take it anymore."

"I will find your husband."

"I want more updates, Mr. Stack—from you, *not* the media. Not the neighbors."

"I promise, Mrs. Moreland. From here on out, I will update you regularly."

xxx

After a forty-five-minute ride on assorted backroads, Leo pulled the van onto a muddied hidden dirt road in a secluded wooded area on the outskirts of Norman. After a mile or so, he turned onto a long driveway that ended at a blacked-out, two-story stone house that belonged to his brother. The house was dilapidated, and the top floor sat above a large garage that made up the entire bottom floor. After parking, Leo lifted the windowless fiberglass door and led Bill and Kat inside, exposing a cavernous workshop and garage equipped with what looked like an efficiency apartment. In the back, there was a small kitchenette with refrigerator and electric stove, a

173

bathroom, and an open space that had a small bed and dresser.

"I come out here from time to time to clear my head when I need a break from the motel," Leo said, pulling off a cover of an immaculate and spotless 1968 black Cadillac Eldorado. The vintage car was a two-door hardtop with a unique angular backend, white-striped tires, a red leather interior, concealed headlights, and a 375-horsepower V-8 engine.

"Oh, I got a car," Leo repeated what he said earlier, beaming and admiring the magnificent machine. "It was my brother's. He don't need it now."

"Where is he?" Kat asked.

"He died in a car wreck last Christmas. The car was filled with presents. They had to dig him out of all the ribbons and bows."

"I'm sorry, Leo," Kat said.

"Since I am the last one left in the immediate family, I got it all. This house, the car. He was always workin'. Saved all his money. Never got to enjoy it, you know. He not once left the state. I don't want to end up like that."

"Never?" Bill asked.

"Not one fuckin' time did he make it across the state line."

"I can't believe that," Bill said.

"It's true."

"What about you?" Kat asked.

"I went to Texas once. On a school field trip to Dallas. I saw the spot where Kennedy was shot."

"You've never seen the mountains?" Bill asked.

"Nope."

"You've never seen the ocean?"

"Nope," Leo walked to the kitchen area of the garage, opening the refrigerator. "Anyone hungry?"

He smeared pieces of bread with peanut butter and began cutting slices of cucumber with a pocketknife to put on the bread. Kicking off the shoes he took from Leo's motel room, Bill eased his aching body on the bed. Kat fiddled with an old radio on a shelf in the garage, trying to find a clear signal through the heavy static. Leo started to devour the slices of peanut-cucumber bread.

"I love this shit," he called out.

"That's gross," Kat said, crinkling her nose.

"Bill?"

"I'm good," Bill said. "My stomach isn't right. Too much whiskey and tequila last night."

"I read that women are aroused by the aroma of a mixture of cucumber and peanut butter," Leo said with a mouthful of food, staring at Kat.

"I can smell it from here," Kat said. "It doesn't do anything for me. How 'bout your girlfriends?"

"Girlfriends? Shit! I ain't ever been laid."

"What?" Kat and Bill asked in unison.

"No, I take that back," Leo said with a mouthful of food. "I made love to Kate Upton thirty-five times one month. That was before my *Sports Illustrated* subscription expired."

"A virgin, really?" Bill asked, sitting up in the bed.

"I ain't lyin', dude. That ain't something to brag about."

"How old are you?" Bill asked.

"Twenty-nine years old."

Bill and Leo looked at each other before slowly turning to Kat who still thumbed the knobs on the radio. Leo raised the peanut butter-cucumber sandwich over his head and waved it in the air.

"What?" she asked, before shaking her head. "No, no. No way."

"I wonder what the psychological role the cucumber's shape and size plays," Leo mumbled. He finished the sandwich and reached for another cucumber.

Kat finally dialed in a news station on the radio with a clear signal. The announcer was reporting on the missing banker case.

"FBI Agent Stack has indicated that an unidentified male, who many presume to be William Moreland, the missing Pennsylvania banker, has been admitted to the intensive care unit of an Oklahoma hospital. The individual is listed in critical condition after an apparent beating. When pressed further on the identification of the injured subject, Agent Stack had no further comment."

"Oh, my God," Kat said. "Critical condition."

"At least, he's alive," Leo said. "I ain't no manslaughterer."

"Not yet," Bill said.

"Hey, wait a minute?" Leo wondered aloud, scratching his head. "I thought your last name was Runner, Bill?"

"I need to see him," Kat said.

"What?" Bill asked. "No way!"

"What if he were to die? We can't leave until I see him one last time."

"He's in intensive care," Bill argued. "You won't be able to get close to him!"

"I need to know more about his condition and his long-term prognosis."

"Absolutely not!"

"Come on, Bill," Kat pressed him. "Let's give Stack something to think about. We can make a donation to the hospital."

"This is not a game."

"Stack doesn't know what I look like."

"Going anywhere near that hospital is suicide."

"We're doing it."

"No, we are *not*."

"We *are*.

"We're *not*." Bill looked to Leo.

"I like the idea, Bill," Leo said. "Let's fuck with the police. They been fuckin' with me all my life. You can stay here and rest up. Take a nap. I'll drop Kat off a few blocks from the hospital. No one will see the Cadillac. It's not something you can hide, you know. People take notice of it. Kat will run in, check on the kid, and make the donation."

"But there're likely cameras everywhere," Bill said. "Once they see Kat, they'll be able to. . ."

"Kat, you can wear this," Leo said, reaching for a medical facemask from a counter in the kitchen. "When my Momma was in the hospital dyin' of cancer, we all wore masks."

"I don't know. I don't like it."

"You need the rest, Bill," Kat said. "We'll be back in a couple hours."

"Remember what happened the last time you left me alone, Kat?"

"You're safe here," Leo said, trying to reassure him. "I'm the only one who's got a key to the place."

"What if something happens to you guys?"

"Here's the key to the van. The thing's yours if we don't come back." Leo pointed at an old rotary phone that hung on the wall. "And there's a phone that's still active. We'll call if something unexpected comes up."

"But the hospital will be crawling with cops and the FBI."

"I'm going to see Ken," Kat said defiantly.

Bill tossed her the garment bag. She fished out ten-thousand dollars and stuffed it in a worn leather satchel that Leo handed to her. Before leaving, she spotted a cowboy hat that rested atop a coat rack near the garage door. She glanced to Leo who nodded. She took the hat.

xxx

Stepping off the elevator to intensive care, Kat was immediately greeted by the chatter of numerous men and women, both law enforcement and reporters. She pulled the mask tighter to her face and carried the cowboy hat. The intensive care unit was secured by electronically activated windowless doors located behind an administrative nursing station. Several nurses moved in and out of the station, collecting medical records and other paperwork as well as pouring themselves cups of coffee. Kat stopped at the station.

"Can I help you?" one of the nurses asked Kat.

"I'm looking for the ICU patient waiting room."

"To your left there," the nurse pointed, "where the others are gathered."

"Is it possible for me to see a patient?"

"Patient visits in the ICU are limited and need to be approved. A nurse is regularly available in the waiting area if you have questions about a specific patient."

"Thank you," Kat said, before wandering over to the waiting area where she took a seat and listened closely to the conversations among the reporters.

"My source," one reporter whispered to another reporter.

"What source?" the other reporter asked.

"I have a source in the FBI. I worked with him after the Oklahoma City bombing."

At that moment, a spokeswoman for the hospital entered the waiting area.

"I'm sure most of you here are interested in information about the injured individual brought in by the FBI," she said. "All I can say is that he's in critical but stable condition. His room is under twenty-four-hour police surveillance as he is a subject of interest in the missing banker case."

"Is he the missing banker?"

"I don't have any information other than the statement I just provided."

"Are the injuries life threatening?"

"I'm sorry. I don't know."

Many of the reporters scattered. Some headed for the elevator. Some pulled out laptops and banged at their keyboards. Others hurriedly scribbled notes on pads of paper.

Kat leaned in as she heard the one reporter whisper to another, "According to my FBI source, the subject is not the banker. He has a serious brain injury, but it's not considered life-threatening. He is in an induced coma to allow swelling on his brain to go down. The FBI has been unable to question him about what happened."

"What about the location of the banker? Or the stolen money?"

"I don't know any of that."

With the information she wanted, Kat quickly and inconspicuously joined the reporters waiting for the elevator. She exited with the group on the ground floor and found a map and directory of the entire hospital complex. She was looking for the children's part of the hospital. She walked to another wing and rode a different set of elevators. She got off on a floor where the administrative and billing office for the children's hospital was located. She placed the cowboy hat on her head and again pulled the mask up higher over her face. Without hesitating, she entered briskly through a set of glass double doors and placed the satchel full of money on the receptionist's desk.

"Our group, the Friends of FBI Agent Julius Stack, would like to make a ten-thousand-dollar donation to the children's hospital," she said quickly. The receptionist looked puzzled.

"The friends of who?" the receptionist asked, studying the satchel, then glancing to Kat.

"FBI Agent Julius Stack. The money's all there. In the satchel."

As the receptionist unbuckled the straps, Kat sneaked away from the desk and disappeared out of the office. She found what appeared to be a lightly used stairwell, pulled the cowboy hat low, and raced down six flights of stairs to the ground floor. A short hallway led her to a bustling cafeteria. Without slowing her pace, she rushed through the cafeteria and slipped out through a glass door marked employees only. The rain had lightened some, and she took several side streets around the hospital complex that were different from the ones she used to enter the main building earlier. She found Leo and the Cadillac parked in the lot of a busy fast-food restaurant.

xxx

Under a warm woolen blanket and hypnotized by the soothing rhythm of the pouring rain, Bill instantly fell asleep, reaching a

179

deep catatonic stage of sleep within minutes. His brain needed to regenerate after the stressful and exhausting thirty-six hours. If a stranger would have discovered his unresponsive body, they would have guessed he was paralyzed, or maybe even dead. Every cramped muscle in his battered body relaxed during his hour-long power nap. His heartbeat and breathing slowed. A contented smile creased his face as he tightly clung to the garment bag of stolen money like a sleep-deprived mother clutching a newborn. Nothing could wake him, not even the roar of the idling Eldorado as it pulled next to the garage. Leo and Kat hurriedly exited the car and pounded on the locked garage door. Leo had left the only key to the garage with Bill.

"*Bill! Bill! Bill!*" they both shouted.

Unable to rouse him, Leo rapidly returned to the Cadillac and reached in, punching at the obnoxiously loud car horn multiple times as Kat continued to bang at the garage door with her fists. Finally, Bill, in a state of near delirium, gradually opened his eyes, initially unsure of where he was, or even who he was. With squinting eyes, he scanned the foreign-looking, dark, garage that smelled of oil and grease, trying to figure out what all the noise was about. It wasn't until he glanced down and recognized the garment bag that rested on his chest that he snapped back to reality. He dashed to the garage door and hastily unlocked it.

"The keys," Leo snapped. "To the van? We have hide it in here."

"We need to go, Bill," Kat said.

"Once they figure out the van's gone," Leo said, taking the keys from Bill. "And figure out I'm gone. This will be the first place they check."

"And with the donation," Kat added. "They have to know we're still in the area."

Leo climbed inside the van and drove it into the spacious garage.

"What's the plan?" Bill asked as Leo jumped out of the van.

"My cousin's got a huntin' cabin in Colorado near the state line. I think we go there next."

"We need out of Oklahoma," Kat said.

"Music to my ears, girl," Leo said, grinning. "Music to my ears."

xxx

Agent Stack stood in the corridor outside the intensive care unit, listening to members of his law enforcement team led by his partner Agent Robinson. He appeared frustrated as he jotted notes of the conversation regarding the case. He kept looking up from the note pad and glancing to numerous television and newspaper reporters who were corralled several yards away within a boundary of yellow police tape.

"A van, white in color, owned by the motel is missing," Agent Robinson said.

"Missing?" Stack asked.

"As is one of the motel's employees."

"Do we have a license plate number for the van?"

"Yes."

"And an ID and address for the employee?"

"He lives at the motel. He's the handyman. His name is Leo Malcolm Jeffries."

"The motel manager vouched for him," another agent spoke up. "Said Jeffries is a bit of an oddball, but it wouldn't be in his nature to run off like that. He's a hermit, a hoarder, supposedly never strays too far from the motel."

"He had the keys to the van?" Stack asked.

"He was the van's primary user," Robinson said.

"Do you think Jeffries was kidnapped or held against his will?" one of the other agents asked.

"Nah," Stack said, shaking his head. "Even if he had a gun, I don't think the banker has it in him to force someone to do something against their will. I bet Jeffries is with him."

The elevator dinged loudly and opened, distracting Agent

181

Stack and his colleagues. A young Oklahoma state policeman stepped from the elevator.

"You'll never believe this, sir," he said to Stack.

"I will believe anything at this point."

"A donation has just been made."

"Donation?"

"Ten thousand dollars."

"Where?"

"Here."

"Here? Where?"

"The children's hospital."

"When?"

"Sometime this morning."

"Do they have a description of the person who made the donation?"

"A young woman."

"Our banker's lady friend has returned," Stack said. "Anything else? Did we get her on the security cameras?"

"Yes. Similar physical appearance to the young woman in Texas."

"They are still nearby," Stack said as his grin grew, turning to the others. "This might be the break we need. Put an APB out on the white van and—"

"One other thing," the trooper said, interrupting Stack.

"Yeah?"

"The donation was made in the name of. . ." the trooper paused.

"Well?"

"In the name of The Friends of FBI Agent Julius Stack."

The confident smirk on Agent Stack's face dissipated. His face turned white as if suddenly given terrible news about unexpected death of a loved one. With eyebrows raised, the members of his team glanced at each other but avoided eye contact with Stack. Not only had Bill Moreland outmaneuvered Stack to that point, he openly taunted him.

"Get the hell out of here!" Stack shouted after a moment of

silence. "He cannot be too far away. He's heading west. They all head west. I want his fuckin' picture sent to every motel, hotel, and charity between here and California. We need roadblocks on every highway out Oklahoma. Pull over anything that looks suspicious."

The FBI agents and law enforcement officials scattered. Stack took a deep breath and began to walk away before being ambushed by several reporters.

"Agent Stack?" one called out. "Anything new to report concerning the missing banker?"

"No comment," he grumbled as many other reporters scrambled towards him. "I will have no further comments for the rest of this evening. So go on home. There's no reason to be here any longer. Let the medical staff here do their work."

The gaggle of reporters milled about gathering their belongings and making notes regarding the story. Agent Stack kept his distance until all of them were gone. He wandered into the waiting area and took a seat. He was spent. He hadn't slept much the past several days. A few family members of different ICU patients lingered in the waiting area. One turned up the volume of the television that was anchored to the wall above him. The television was tuned to the cable news channel that was airing the legal talk show, "The Law Today."

"We just received breaking news," announced the host Cassandra Stevens. "It appears, Mr. Moreland, the missing banker, is still on the loose."

"You got to be kidding me," the show's co-host, Milton Shears, said.

"Can you believe that?" Ms. Stevens said, shaking her head. "The runaway banker is not in an Oklahoma hospital as we were initially led to believe!"

"So the beaten man that carried his identification is not Mr. Moreland?" Mr. Shears asked. "Unbelievable. Who's in the hospital?"

"Apparently," Ms. Stevens reported, "FBI sources admitted the identity error after a ten-thousand-dollar donation was made to the children's hospital in Norman right under their noses."

Agent Stack leaned forward in his seat in the waiting room.

One of the family members in the waiting room spoke up: "I hope they never catch him."

"I agree," another family member said. "He's obviously too smart for them. I'm glad he's still free!"

Puzzled, Agent Stack shook his head and studied the two family members.

"He's a crook!" Ms. Stevens screamed from the television screen. "He's a thief!"

"I agree with her," Stack said out loud to the others in the waiting room. "Throw him in jail. The FBI will catch him."

"He's not hurting anyone," a guest on the show said.

"There's a man in a hospital bed!" Ms. Stevens exclaimed. "What about him? And what about all the people who lost money from the bank?"

"Come on, now!" the show's guest said. "The money's insured. He didn't hurt them at all. And no one feels sorry for the insurance companies."

"I still think it's awful what that greedy man did to his family," Ms. Stevens continued.

"It doesn't matter what any of us think," Mr. Shears said. "This is a great story. It keeps getting better. I can't wait to find out what happens next!"

Chapter 6
Colorado Eastern Plains

Day 10. Saturday, May 6. 7:08 PM

Despite the dreary day, the mood had changed. Leo brought a lightness and a different level of energy as he set out on his journey to foreign parts of the country he'd only read or dreamed about. But a feeling of anxiety and dread still hung heavy, especially for Bill and Kat. They both believed that their wild excursion across country could end only one way, and it wouldn't be happy or good. They were on the run without a decided end game. And the longer they ran, and the more Bill's picture was plastered on every cable news channel, the fewer options they had for freedom. They spent every waking hour checking behind them, hoping no one was chasing. They had made it as far as Oklahoma with Kansas in their sights, but they wondered how much further they could go.

"I'm sure there're roadblocks everywhere," Bill said from the passenger seat. He studied the roadway behind them in the sideview mirror of the rambling Cadillac.

"They can't block 'em all," Leo confidently replied from the driver's seat. "They ain't got the resources for that."

Kat leaned forward in the back seat and asked, "Do you know where you're going?"

"My cousin drove these roads on his way to the cabin in Colorado. He gimme a map one time in case I had to do it for 'em. He supplied weed to the college circuit from Norman to Boulder."

"Weed?" Bill asked.

"Yeah, weed," Leo said, nodding. "Grass. Marijuana. Pot. Smoke. He ran weed and made good money doin' it. When the trunk of your car is stuffed with trash bags full of marijuana you want to cross state lines without gettin' too much attention."

There wasn't much to see as the sun was setting on their time in Oklahoma. With Leo's knowledge of the highways and farm roads that zigzagged through northwestern Oklahoma, the Eldorado cruised into the night without a cop in sight. Grinning from ear to ear, Leo bounced in his seat as if he had just won the lottery. The blackness of the overcast sky and the heavy rain provided additional cover from the authorities.

"You seem excited, Leo," Bill said.

"You don't even know what this trip means to me. I needed out Oklahoma. You two saved me."

"You saved us," Kat said.

"I feel like I'm startin' a new life," Leo replied. "And the timin' couldn't be better."

"How so?" Kat asked.

"It's my birthday!"

"Today?" Kat asked.

"Yes, Ma'am! The big three-oh!"

"We'll need to celebrate, have a party," Kat said, glancing to Bill, who slumped down in his seat and shook his head. "Isn't that right, Bill?"

"We need to get to that cabin before we think about anything else," he said. "We still have several hours to go."

"A party sounds fun," Leo said.

"No, not until we're settled and secured."

"Don't be such a party pooper, Bill," Kat said. "A little fun is all we got. What could a little party for our new friend hurt?"

xxx

The Eldorado was parked at the pumps of a random convenience store and gas station near the small town appropriately named Leoti, just off State Highway 25. Leo was inside the store paying for gas. Bill sat down low in the passenger front seat so as not to be seen. Kat fidgeted outside the parked car, scrolling through one of the mobile phones.

"I think I know what we should do for Leo's birthday," she said, talking to Bill through the window but not looking up from the phone.

"Let's first get to the cabin. Please. There'll be plenty of time to celebrate with Leo later."

"We don't know much about Leo," she said, still staring at the phone, "but what's the one thing he really, really needs?"

"We're not getting him anything today."

"Come on, Bill." She looked up from the phone. "What does Leo really need?"

"Forget about it, Kat! I'm serious!"

"Come on. What does he need?"

"I don't know," he said, shaking his head and scanning the busy parking lot. "Tell me. What does he need?"

"Her!" she exclaimed, reaching out the phone, and showing Bill a photograph of an attractive young woman.

"Who?"

"Her, Bill," she said, handing him the phone through the window of the Eldorado.

"What is this?"

"She's available tonight."

"A hooker?" he said, handing her back the phone.

"An escort."

"You want to buy Leo a hooker for his birthday?"

"They can hang out. Like a date. According to her site, she services the area not too far from the cabin."

"You want to buy Leo a hooker?"

"As a matter of fact," she said, looking back at the phone. "She's the only escort in that area. If I'm reading this map right, the cabin is in the middle of nowhere."

"No way, Kat! We are not buying Leo, or anyone else, a hooker!"

"She can keep him company. We'll have a party. The four of

us. He'll never forget this birthday as long as he lives."

"Are you crazy? That would be suicide. We can't let anyone know who we are."

"She wouldn't have to know who we are."

"Well, she can't see me. My goddamn face is all over the news."

"She won't know who you are."

"Bullshit. We can't take that chance."

"I think it's a great idea."

"It's the *worst* idea," he shouted as Leo approached the Cadillac. "This is crazy talk. Insanity."

"We're doing it," she said defiantly.

"No, we're not."

"I'm calling her later," she whispered as Leo got into the driver's seat.

"You will *not*."

"There you two go again," Leo said. "Bickerin' like an old married couple. What is it this time?"

"We're celebrating your birthday after we get to the cabin."

"For real?"

"Yes, for real," Kat said, before glancing to Bill. "Isn't that right, Bill?"

"Whatever," Bill grumbled.

"So, we'll need to stop sometime later for beer, champagne, and cake," she said.

"Cake?" Leo said, grinning.

"And I'll need to make a call to order your gift."

"Gift?" Leo said as his face lighted up, before first glancing to Kat and then to Bill. "This is the best day ever. My thirties will be lit. I know it. Finally!"

xxx

Day 11. Sunday, May 7. 5:15 AM

Bill, Kat, and Leo made it to the cabin sometime before daybreak without incident. They each collapsed in different

188

places in the cabin and slept most of the day away. The four-room hunting cabin was hidden in a wooded area along a stream in the eastern plains of the state far from any main road. It seemed the perfect place to hide for a day or two, at least. On the drive, they had stocked up on plenty of beer, booze, snacks, assorted party favors, and a birthday cake. Kat had called the young escort. She agreed to meet them at the cabin sometime after nightfall. Kat hadn't told Leo about the escort. It was to be a surprise. Leo also didn't know until after arriving that there was an eight-person outdoor hot tub on the deck outside a set of sliding glass doors. Kat fired up its heater and turned the jets to full massaging power, so it would be heated and ready for use later.

xxx

It was early in the morning. Agent Stack and his FBI team had left Norman the day before and were huddled with local law enforcement officials in a conference room of a federal building in Oklahoma City. They reviewed updates concerning their ongoing investigation. Stack pounded his fist numerous times on a white board covered with handwritten notes.

"We should have had him by now," Stack moaned. "What's the word from the roadblocks?"

"Nothing, sir," one of the agents said.

"What do you mean, *nothing*?" Stack asked, throwing a wadded-up piece of paper at him.

The agent ducked and said, "There've been no reports of anyone matching the descriptions of Mr. Moreland, Mr. Jeffries, and Ms. McCarthy."

"Do you think they're still in the state?" Agent Robinson asked.

"I doubt it," Stack said. "They know we are here. They are on the move. I am guessing they took a lesser used road."

"Jeffries is from Oklahoma and may know different ways to get in and out," a state police lieutenant said.

189

"What about motels, hotels in the neighboring states?"

"We've faxed and texted photos of Mr. Moreland and the reward information to hundreds in the Texas and Oklahoma panhandles, New Mexico, Arizona, Colorado, and parts of southern Kansas," one of the agents responded.

"We should do the same for as many campgrounds as we can from here to California," Stack said.

"Are you sure they're headed west and not going back east?" Agent Robinson asked.

"I have been investigating cases like this for over twenty years," Agent Stack answered. "Rarely do they backtrack. Runaways want to go somewhere new where no one knows them. They want to be anonymous and blend in with the surroundings. If they do backtrack, it's to see or pick up a loved one or close acquaintance. And it's been too easy to catch them. Someone they know always turns them in. I think most fugitives understand that."

"What's the latest on the kid in the ICU in Norman?" one of the agents asked. Stack looked to a state policeman to answer that question.

"I just talked with the doc," the state trooper said, as a local state detective quietly slipped into the room. "He's still out cold. Going on eighteen hours now. No change in his condition."

"Agent Stack?" the detective who just entered the room called out. "We found the motel van. It was parked at an unoccupied house that belonged to Mr. Jeffries's deceased brother."

"Any evidence of Moreland or anything of interest?" Stack asked.

"One thing," the detective said, with a nod. "A 1960s model Cadillac Eldorado, black in color, registered to Mr. Jeffries's deceased brother, the only vehicle in his name, was not at the residence. And we couldn't find any record of it being sold."

"Put an APB out for the Cadillac," Stack advised. "Year, make, model, color, license plate and VIN number. Everything.

190

And let's get a picture of that particular model of Cadillac on all the local news stations in the area as soon as possible."

"Are you sure they're in the Cadillac? They have the money to buy any car they want. Moreland's done it before."

"They had to leave his brother's place in something after dropping off the van. It is all we got at this point. If we locate the Cadillac, we may find something that leads us to Moreland."

"Anything else?" Agent Robinson asked Stack.

"Let's also get photographs of Ms. McCarthy and Mr. Jeffries on the news and posted at as many campsites and cheap motels as we can."

xxx

The escort was late. It was near midnight. The frosty spring air smelled fresh, and the sky was clear and full of stars. Bill had insisted to Kat earlier that they keep the garment bag of money locked under the passenger seat in the Cadillac because of the surprise visitor that was scheduled to arrive later. As they waited for the escort, Kat blew up balloons and attached pointed cardboard birthday hats on top of Bill's and Leo's heads, before putting one on herself. She then filled three pint glasses with heavy pours of whiskey sodas and chased Leo outside to the bubbling and steamy hot tub. Leo immediately stripped naked and jumped into the tub, wearing only the birthday hat. Kat undressed to her bra and panties before sliding into the hot churning water. With the whiskey in his hand, Bill lingered on the deck by the open sliding glass doors, the small, pointed cardboard hat awkwardly rested sideways on his head. He had stripped down to his boxer shorts and tee-shirt but was in no mood to party or join them in the hot tub. His foot and ribs hurt, and it was still very painful to breathe.

"Come on, Bill," Kat called from the tub. "The water's great!"

Bill half-smiled and shook his head.

"What's a matter?" she asked as Bill retreated into the cabin

191

without responding.

Suddenly, a car pulled next to the secluded cabin.

"Who can that be way out here?" Leo asked.

"Stay here," Kat said. "I'll check on it."

Kat hopped out of the hot tub and covered her dripping body with a towel before entering the cabin. Bill took a sip of the whiskey and stared at her.

"Our friend's here."

"I'll stay in the bedroom until she's gone. I don't want her to see me."

"Do what you want," she said as he stepped into the cabin's lone bedroom and started to close the door. "But the three of us are going to have some fun tonight. It might do you good to join us."

There was a knock at the front door. Kat quickly opened it. Bill spied from the cracked-open bedroom door. A young woman in her late teens or early twenties entered the cabin. The car she'd been riding in pulled away. She was quite stunning, with an angelic face, blonde curly hair, and curvaceous bombshell of a body. The top she wore was so tight it appeared her breasts were about to pop out of it. But before Kat could welcome her, Bill bolted from his hiding spot in the bedroom.

"Hello, there!" he called out, nearly slobbering, trying to keep his eyes from drifting to her busty chest.

"Welcome," Kat said, reaching her hand out. "I'm Kat. This is Bill."

"Tina," the young woman replied, shaking each of their hands. She glanced to Bill who continued to gawk at her. "Why are you lookin' at me like that?"

"You're so young. I expected an older woman."

"Can I get a drink?" she asked, noticing the bottles of liquor on the table.

"We have whiskey, tequila, and champagne," Kat said.

"I love tequila."

"How old are you?" Bill asked as Kat poured her a shot and reached it to her.

"Old enough for tequila," she said, taking the shot and knocking it back.

"How much?" Bill asked.

"Huh?"

"How much?" he asked again.

"Bill?" Kat scolded him.

"How much for the visit?" he asked.

"I tend to get paid at the end," the young lady replied.

"I want to pay you up front."

"If y'all want to party for a few hours," she said, glancing around the cabin and noticing Leo for the first time outside in the hot tub, "it'll be three hundred."

"Dollars?" Bill asked.

"Three-hundred dollars."

"It's our friend's thirtieth birthday," Kat said, motioning to Leo.

"If you want me to stay the night, I'll take a thousand."

"Here's five-thousand dollars," Bill said, immediately pulling a stack of hundred-dollar bills from his pocket. Tina's face lighted up as she took the money. "I'm sure you have no retirement plan. You should put most of that into a thirty-six-month CD or some type of IRA or money market account. Who knows how much you'll have after ten or fifteen years if you do that?" The girl stared at Bill then the money. "What's wrong with working at Wendy's or Denny's? Or Starbucks? Starbucks even has benefits for someone young like you."

The cork from one of the bottles of champagne that Kat held suddenly exploded in the air and bounced off the kitchen ceiling. Foaming champagne flowed from the top of the bottle, and Kat quickly filled four glasses and handed one each to Bill and Tina. She took the other two glasses of champagne and a bottle of whiskey out the sliding glass door. Tina followed, but Bill stayed behind and watched from inside.

"Happy birthday, Leo!" Kat said, reaching him one of the glasses of champagne. "This is Tina. She's your date tonight."

His face instantaneously turned red. He had trouble looking

Tina in the eyes.

"The water is a soothing ninety-eight degrees," Kat said to Tina as she strapped a birthday hat on top of her head.

Tina kicked off her spiked heels, slipped out of the short skirt she wore, and pulled her top over her head, before joining Leo in the hot tub, wearing only her bra, underwear, and a birthday hat. Kat dropped the towel covering her and joined them in the tub. Not being shy, Tina immediately slid next to Leo and cuddled up to him. He reached for the whiskey bottle and took several large gulps for courage. Tina first played with his hair, which was wet and curled from the steam that rolled off the surface of the hot water. She then reached her other hand under the water. His eyes instantly widened as he popped up straight in his seat, rigid as a board. It wasn't long until Tina was completely naked, just like Leo.

Bill continued to watch through the glass doors. He waved to Kat to come inside and give the two some privacy. If there was a question of whether Bill was going to heaven or hell, it was answered that night. He was certainly bound for hell. He couldn't take his eyes off the young lady's full and wet naked breasts as she frolicked in the hot tub with Leo. Limp tissue in his nether area suddenly stirred. As the teenagers say, he was woke. And sadly, he didn't look away. He couldn't look away. His mouth was open. Both eyes were fixed on the young lady's wet body that shimmered in the tub under the bright shining moon. A drip of drool rolled off his lip. He was pathetic, and he knew it.

Kat lifted herself out of the hot tub. Still, wearing only the bra and panties, she wrapped a towel around herself and entered the cabin, dripping wet. As Bill continued to ogle the young lady's pristine nude body, Kat unexpectedly and forcefully shoved him to the couch with both hands, knocking him off his feet and rousing him from his trance. Dropping the towel, she mischievously crawled on top of him as he sat on the couch, the bottom of her wet underwear pressed into his lap. He winced as she leaned into his wounded ribs. She made eye contact, but he had trouble looking back and averted her probing eyes. Horned up from the spectacle in the hot tub, he was at the height of his arousal and assumed Kat could feel it under her. But he was no mood for fun and games. He wanted to go back to Pennsylvania. He knew it was time. He needed to see Rita and the kids. He had lost all control of everything. The man in that room who wore his clothes was a stranger. A person he no longer knew or understood. He again admitted to himself that taking the money and running away was one colossal mistake. He wished to go home.

"What's wrong, Bill?" Kat asked. "You're not yourself tonight."

"That could be my daughter," he said, watching Leo and the young woman make out in the tub. Kat didn't take her eyes from his. He finally looked back to her. "And you could be my daughter? What have I become? Buying another human being as a birthday gift."

"You made a friend very happy tonight. He'll never forget this or you."

"But, still," he said, glancing away.

"Nobody's holding a gun to her head, Bill."

"How do you know?"

"Look at me," she said, grabbing his chin and turning his face towards her. He wouldn't look her in the eyes. "Look at me, Bill."

Finally, their eyes met. Kat lifted his motionless arms that dangled at his side and wrapped them around her back. He tried to look away, but she wouldn't let him. She placed both hands gently on his cheeks and slowly rocked her bottom deeper into his lap. He immediately froze and lifted his arms away from her, awkwardly holding them out, as if pinned to a cross, and not knowing what to do with them.

"What are you doing?" he whispered, scanning the room as if to check to see if anyone was watching.

"Just relax," she said, softly grinding her body into his. "Is this, okay?"

"Please, Kat, stop," he said.

"I thought this is what you wanted."

"More than ever, but. . ."

"But, what's wrong?"

"If I wasn't married. If I wasn't on the run. If I was younger. . ."

"Sssh. Stop it," she interrupted, leaning forward to kiss him. He turned his face away.

"If I had two wishes," he confessed, not looking at her, "you would never let go of me."

"And?"

"And tomorrow would never come. I'm almost out of tomorrows. What a mess I've caused. For my family. For the bank. For you. For Leo."

"Do you regret taking the money?"

"Every single minute I'm awake I regret taking that money and leaving my family. I want to go home. But I will never regret walking out on the six-in-the-morning alarm clocks, the four lanes of traffic, the two-hour commutes, the bullshit meetings." He paused a moment as they studied each other. "But if I hadn't taken the money, I never would've met you. And I needed to meet you. You brought me back to life."

She smiled as he tried to look away. Before he could turn his head, she eased her face forward and softly touched her lips with his. He accepted the advance and enveloped her curled body in his arms. An electric warmth surged through him as if he'd been electrocuted. His mind raced. A voice in his head pleaded with him to stop and push her away. But a louder voice screamed to not let her go. Listening to the second voice, he rolled her warm body underneath him and pulled his face away from hers. His heart pounded against his chest. He tried to catch his breath. Kat stared back. She looked different. Her long, wet hair was spread out on the couch cushion around her head. She appeared younger. Bill barely recognized her. He pulled his hand from behind her back and slowly crawled it across her naked belly to between her legs. Goosebumps instantly formed on her bare arms and legs.

The front door to the cabin suddenly busted open as an angry young man in his early twenties stormed in.

"Where is she?" the stranger screamed, frantically scanning the small cabin.

Startled, both Bill and Kat fell off the couch onto the floor, their bodies tangled together.

"Where in the fuck is she?"

The stranger glanced out the sliding glass door and spotted Leo kissing and groping Tina in the hot tub. Both of them were completely nude. Bill stepped in front of the angry man but was violently knocked out of the way. The stranger threw open the sliding glass door.

"Hey!"

Leo looked up and separated from Tina. She immediately tried to cover her naked chest with folded arms.

"Get your fuckin' hands off her!"

The young man lunged toward Leo, trying to strangle him as the woman crawled out of the hot tub. With legs and arms flailing, Leo struggled to free himself, splashing water all over the deck as the stranger plunged Leo's head underwater multiple times.

"Bobby! Stop! Stop it! Stop! Please, stop!" Tina pleaded, punching the stranger repeatedly in the shoulders and back as Bill and Kat rushed from the cabin.

Once outside, Bill slipped on the wet deck and fell hard to the ground. As the stranger held Leo's head underwater and the young lady pounded on the stranger's back, Kat suddenly slugged him in the head with the whiskey bottle, causing the young man to fall and release Leo. Kat pulled Leo's head out of the water as he gasped for air and spit out mouthfuls of water. As Kat tended to Leo, Bill slowly stood, holding his back and one of his knees. Shaking his head after the blow to the head, the stranger turned to Bill and slugged him with a solid right cross to the nose. Blood squirting in the air, Bill fell face first into the bubbling hot tub.

"Bill!" Kat screamed.

The stranger gathered himself, threw a towel over Tina who continued to jab and punch at him, grabbed her arms, and dashed into the cabin. He hurriedly dragged her to the door but suddenly stopped. Pulling her with him, he rushed through each room of the small cabin and scooped up all the bags, clothes, shoes, and towels off the floor and took them with him.

The angry stranger's pickup peeled away with squealing tires. Taking deep breaths, Leo sat on the edge of the tub, head bowed, taking deep breaths. In the tub, Kat lifted Bill's head from the water and held a towel across his busted nose. Bill's eyes were red and nearly swollen shut, his expression dazed. A small pool of his blood floated on the surface of the tub's hot water.

"Shit," Leo mumbled. "Story of my life. I can't ever get past second base."

"We have to get out of here," Kat spoke up. "Someone knows we're here."

"Can't let no damn fool enjoy nothin'," Leo complained. "Not even on his birthday."

"Bill, we need to get out of here," Kat warned.

"They don't know who we are," Bill said with a glazed look in his eyes, opening and closing them multiple times and trying to shake the cobwebs from his head.

"It doesn't matter. We need to go, and we need to go now!"

After collecting their senses and attending to their wounds, all three of them reentered the cabin, appearing conquered. Holding a towel over his bleeding nose, Bill wore only boxer shorts and a tee-shirt. Kat followed, wearing just a bra and underwear. Leo wore nothing but a towel. The birthday celebration didn't turn out with the happy ending as he imagined. They all stopped at the same time as they realized most of their possessions were gone.

"What the. . .?" Kat was looking around and around. "Did he take all our clothes?"

"The money!" Leo exclaimed.

"It's locked in the car," Bill said.

"Your phone?"

"In the bag with the money."

"And the car keys?" Kat asked.

"Ah, shit!" Leo exclaimed. "They're in my pants!"

"We need to go!" Kat said. "We're sitting ducks out here!"

"Without keys?" Bill wondered.

"That won't be a problem," Leo reassured them.

"Won't be a problem?" Bill asked. Bill thought they had a *big* problem.

Kat started rummaging through a set of dresser drawers in the bedroom, holding up the only things she could find: a slinky sundress, a lady's one-piece bathing suit, and a small clean towel. "This is all we got, boys." She turned to Bill: "And this is why you never pay until the end."

xxx

Kat and Bill kept their distance from the Cadillac as Leo picked up a brick from the yard. Pressing a towel against his bleeding nose, Bill stood shivering in boxer shorts and tee-shirt. Kat had slipped on the sundress but had nothing underneath. Leo wore the woman's one-piece bathing suit; his plump, hairy testicles hung out from the bottom of it. All three were barefoot.

"I ain't proud," Leo said, raising the brick over his head as he approached the Cadillac. "I know Jonathan Livingston Seagull never acted like this."

Leo hurled the brick through the back window of the Eldorado, driver's side. The window exploded, filling the front and back seats with tiny shards of glass. He stared at the shattered window for a moment, almost not believing what he had done. He reached through the wound in the immaculate antique car and unlocked the driver's side door. Sweeping chips of glass that looked like diamonds off the seat, he slid his barely clothed body underneath the dashboard. Kat shined a flashlight under the steering wheel for Leo to see. She elbowed

Bill and motioned to Leo's exposed testicles as he worked to start the car with only a screwdriver and knife. Bill cringed as Leo cut a set of wires needed to jump-start the car.

"Good thing this is American," Leo grunted, stretching and contorting his skinny and mostly nude body under the steering wheel. "I don't know shit about foreign cars."

Within minutes, the car's powerful engine quietly coughed and started with a thunderous roar. Leo slid from under the dashboard into a sitting position behind the steering wheel. Pieces of shattered glass were stuck in his naked back. He revved the engine a couple times. He smiled and called to Kat and Bill who quickly got in the car. The first thing Bill checked for was the bag of money. It was safe under the passenger seat. He reached in the bag and fished out his last paycheck.

"What's up with the paycheck?" Kat asked. "You have all the money you could ever need in that bag."

"It's my only reminder of home."

xxx

Day 12. Monday, May 8. 1:45 AM

The Cadillac was near the small unincorporated town of Joes on rural U.S. Route 36 in the eastern plains of Colorado, heading west. Still in bare feet and the one-piece woman's bathing suit, Leo drove, humming to the classic rock on the radio. In only boxers and a tee-shirt, Bill sat beside him, looking nauseous and holding his arms against his sore ribs. The nasty cut on his nose oozed blood. He kept checking to see if anyone followed. The sky was black, and the night road behind them was empty. Kat slept in the back.

"Slow down, Leo," Bill cautioned, continually checking the speedometer. He touched at his busted nose and face, which were still numb from the punch.

"I'm tryin', but this baby, she wants to move."

"We need to ditch this car for something not so noticeable."

"We're makin' good time though," Leo grinned.

"Good time?" Bill asked. "Good time to where? We don't even know where the hell we're going."

"I thought we're gonna see the mountains? And the ocean?"

"We are, we are," Bill said. "But we need some clothes first!"

xxx

On the deserted stretch of the highway, a Colorado state policeman was parked mostly hidden in a rolling cornfield. The Cadillac, with its busted window, zoomed by. The highway patrolman popped up in his seat and studied the vintage car. He checked the radar gun, remembering an FBI advisory to be on the lookout for a late model black Eldorado. The Eldorado was traveling fifteen miles an hour over the speed limit. As Leo casually checked the rearview, the state police car rolled into view behind him.

"Oh, shit," Leo mumbled, glancing to Bill in the passenger seat. "I think I just buzzed a cop."

Bill whipped around in his seat as the cop flashed his lights.

"Don't worry," Leo said as Kat sat up and checked out the back window.

"Don't worry?" Bill said. "*Shit*. We're screwed."

"I have a plan."

"A plan?" Bill called out, slumping down in the seat.

Leo eased the Cadillac off the road as the cop parked his cruiser behind him.

"What are you stopping for?" Bill asked.

"I got this," Leo said. "Relax."

The Colorado State trooper reached for his radio and keyed it: "I think I got somethin'. It's a Cadillac that meets the description of the one the FBI is searchin' for."

"Where are you?" the dispatcher asked.

"Highway 36. About fifteen miles west of Joes. I got 'em pulled over."

"Don't let them out of your sight. Stall until I can contact FBI

201

Agent Stack and patch him through to you."

As the cop waited to hear from Agent Stack, he ran a check on the license plate. It was a Colorado plate and not an Oklahoma plate as indicated in the advisory. Kat had swapped plates at a gas station soon after they left the cabin. As the cop lingered in his squad car, Leo watched from the mirror.

"We got to be patient, Bill," Leo said. "Let 'em feel comfortable. Let 'em get out."

"We're toast!" Bill barked, scanning their surroundings in search of an escape.

"Get out, Big Boy," Leo mumbled, still watching the cop. "Come on, Mr. Blue. Get out. We jus' need for you to get out. And we'll be fine."

The state policeman's car radio buzzed. Agent Stack was on the line from his hotel room.

"This is Stack. What do you got?"

"A Cadillac. It might be the one you're after."

"How many people are in the car?"

"Looks to be three."

"And you have them stopped?"

"Yep. I'm parked twenty feet behind 'em."

"The license plate?"

"It's a Colorado plate. It must be stolen. It's registered to a Toyota."

"Listen to me closely. I want you to request backup. Plenty of backup. Do not spook 'em. Make it seem like a regular stop for speeding. Do not do anything until back-up arrives. I'll alert the local FBI offices. Do not fuck this up. You can't let them get away."

"Ten-four, Boss."

After calling for more officers, the portly state patrolman took a deep breath. He checked his watch a few times over the next several minutes. Finally, he couldn't wait any longer and pulled himself out his car without waiting for backup as Stack had ordered. Leo raised his hand to the cop and waved to acknowledge him. Sirens could be heard in the distance.

"And when he least expects it," Leo whispered, closely watching the cop as he approached the Cadillac. "*We gooooo!*"

Leo slammed his foot on the accelerator just as the cop reached the rear end. Kat and Bill were jerked backward in their seats. The policeman stumbled awkwardly, falling hard to the ground. As he struggled to get up, Leo laughed as the car squealed away, leaving a trail of white smoke. The cop scrambled to his squad car and immediately began pursuit.

"Three-hundred-seventy-five horses pullin' us," Leo hollered, "and we'll need every single one of 'em. *Shit!*"

Leo jerked the rumbling tank-of-a-car onto the first exit, wheeling the car under the highway's overpass and parking in its shadow. Within seconds, the cop car screamed by with sirens blaring on the overpass above the parked Cadillac. Other police cruisers soon followed, also speeding by on the overpass above.

"Safe for now but not for long," Leo said, taking a deep breath. "We ain't exactly invisible in this thing."

"We need a place to disappear," Bill said, watching out the back. "Or find a different car. We need clothes and other supplies. Somewhere to hide."

"No." Kat shook her head. "Just the opposite. We need to find a place not to get noticed."

"Dressed like this?" Bill asked.

"I know a place," Leo spoke up. "There's nearly one in every town. They'll have everything we need."

xxx

Two junior FBI agents stood outside a conference room in the federal government building in Oklahoma City where Stack and his team had gathered. Agent Stack was inside the room, preparing several reports. He had just ended an early morning conference call with his superiors. One of the young agents outside the room had finished a phone call with Colorado law enforcement authorities. The news was not good.

"Does he know?" one of the agents asked.

"You gonna tell him?"

"I'm not gonna tell him."

"One of us has to."

"Shit," the agent mumbled, reaching for the door to conference room. "He's gonna lose his mind."

". . . to Colorado as soon as they get me a car," Stack was saying as the agent entered the room, not taking his eyes from the reports he filled out. "Once we get the papers, I am taking Moreland back to Pennsylvania myself." The young agent didn't say word. Stack finally looked up to him. "You need something?"

"There's a problem."

"What problem?" Stack asked, his hand suddenly tightened on the pen he held.

"The banker."

"Don't tell me," Stack said, closing his eyes. "He got away?"

"He got away."

"Jesus Christ!" Stack yelled. The pen snapped in half. "I just called the director to tell him the good news. What I *thought* was good news. Jesus fuckin' Christ! How in the goddamn world did he get away?"

"Once the trooper got out of his car and approached the Cadillac, they left."

"What about his backup?"

"Hadn't got there yet. Guess he rushed it."

"Goddamn it! I specifically told that son-of-a-bitch to stall until backup arrived. Jesus Christ Almighty! Everybody wants to be a goddamn fuckin' hero!"

"The banker and the others had just enough head start to lose the trooper and the several squad cars following."

"And where did the banker go?"

"He disappeared like a ghost."

"And no new sightings of the Cadillac?"

"No one's seen it."

Another agent poked his head in the door. "Agent Stack? The

news lady, Cassandra Stevens, from 'The Law Today' is on the phone. She'd like an interview about the banker's case."

"Now is not the time!" Stack hollered as the agent stared at him, holding out the phone.

"Sir, she's on the line."

"Tell her I'm unavailable.! I do not have time for her nonsense. I am going to Colorado. We're *all* going to Colorado. Round up the boys and get some cars. I will get the banker myself."

xxx

Day 12. Monday, May 8. 10:39 AM

After driving north on State Routes 59 and 61 through the night, Leo pulled the Cadillac behind a deserted gas station on a stretch of the empty plain for some desperately needed rest. He could barely keep his eyes open. Because Bill couldn't sleep, he kept watch, letting Leo and Kat nap for a few hours. Later in the morning, they drove into Sterling and found what they were looking for, a Wal-Mart Superstore. Leo slowly circled the busy parking lot. There didn't appear to be a single parking space available. He drove around the lot multiple times, checking each aisle with no luck. Kat intently watched from the back seat, helping search. Losing patience, Bill slouched down low in the front seat, trying his best to hide.

"We got five minutes to ditch this car," Bill growled. "We'll never pull this off. This is ridiculous."

Leo finally found an open space and carefully parked the bulky car in the spot. Kat slipped on a pair of dark sunglasses and the hat she had taken from the garage at Leo's brother's house.

"They'll never let you in there like that," Bill grumbled. "Tits hanging out. No shoes."

"I've seen worse in Wal-Mart," Leo said.

Kat popped open the driver's side back door and hopped out.

205

Bill and Leo watched her hurry to the front entrance of the store and disappear inside.

"Today, my friend," Bill said with a shake of his head, "is where this whole charade sadly ends."

xxx

Inside the chaotic store, Kat danced from aisle to aisle in her bare feet. She carried in a shopping basket several pairs of shoes and socks, assorted snacks, some toiletries, and a new bottle of champagne. They had left the other bottles along with the beer and liquor at the cabin in their haste to leave. She stood in the men's clothing aisle, flipping through different shirts and slacks that hung on discount racks. Several shoppers stared at her, and a security guard approached.

"Ma'am? Ma'am?"

Kat ignored him.

"Ma'am!"

She finally looked up at him.

"You saw the sign at the entrance. No shirt. No shoes. No service."

They studied each other. She slipped on a pair of flip-flops from the shopping basket. The security guard continued to stare.

"Don't worry," she said, "I'll pay for them on the way out."

He glared at her as she added two pairs of men's slacks and two shirts to the basket. As she walked away, he mumbled under his breath.

"Damn hippies."

Hearing him, she flashed him the middle finger over her shoulder. On her way to the checkout lines, she walked through the electronics department. Every single television on display was tuned to a 24-hour news channel that was reporting on the runaway banker. Kat stopped and watched. Rita's face filled every screen; she desperately pleaded for Bill's safe return home.

"I am the luckiest woman in the world," she said, her voice breaking. "We have everything we could ever want. Bill made it that way, for me and the kids. He is a kind and beautiful man who devoted his life to his family. He always put us before himself." She paused a moment; Kat watched intently as did a dozen other shoppers.

"My husband is not a criminal." Rita's hands trembled. "He is a good and honest and decent man. We have our problems. But who doesn't have problems? All families have problems. I wish I could change the past. I took many things for granted, and so did our kids. But I can't change anything now. I want to start over." She paused to take a deep breath. Several more shoppers had joined Kat and the others.

"Bill, if you're somehow out there watching this. . ." She paused and lowered her eyes to again fight off tears. "Bill, if you're watching this, please come home." She looked directly into the camera. "*Please. We need you. I* need you. *I love you, Bill.* I love you so much! *Please* forgive me."

Rita sobbed as the camera cut away; the network returned to the studio of the popular daily news show, "The Law Today." Kat stared in stunned silence. Tears rolled down her cheeks. Over two dozen people had gathered and watched Rita's soulful plea. Some of them were crying.

"Maybe you were wrong about the banker?" Mr. Shears, the show's co-host, asked Cassandra Stevens. "I certainly feel different about him now."

"Not me," Ms. Stevens replied. "It doesn't excuse him for skipping out on his family. They could have talked it out or enlisted counseling or even gotten a divorce if your life is so bad you had to rob a bank and run away."

"Sounds like it was the wife and not the banker who may have been the problem."

"He ran like a coward," Ms. Stevens said, "instead of being a man and facing his problems."

The news show transitioned to an update on the story about Bill and the missing money. Large photographs of Kat and Leo appeared on all the display television screens in the store. The words in bold red letters below the photos proclaimed, "WANTED: FUGITIVES WITH MISSING BANKER." Kat's heart skipped a beat and a pit formed in her stomach. She pulled the straw hat down over her eyes and lowered her head.

"It seems our banker has friends along with him," Ms. Stevens reported. "One is believed to be the young woman on the screen, a one Katherine McCarthy. The other is a young gentleman named Leo Malcolm Jeffries from Oklahoma. And if you remember, we talked to Katherine on the phone several days ago."

Not wanting to be recognized, Kat nervously wiped at the tears still in her eyes and rushed to the cash register area, checking over her shoulder to see if anyone appeared to be watching her. She needed to get out of the store as soon as possible.

xxx

Agent Stack gathered with a team of ten FBI agents and scores of local law enforcement in the parking lot of a state police barracks near Joes, Colorado, located off U.S. Highway 36 not far from where the fugitives had been pulled over. A fleet of well over forty cars had been assembled. Stack held up copies of a detailed map of the state covered in red and blue lines that looked like blood vessels depicting all the routes and small highways. He handed copies of the map; photographs of Bill, Leo, and Kat; and a picture of the Eldorado they were in to another FBI agent who distributed them to the group.

"The Cadillac that the missing banker may be riding in and those photos of the subjects believed to be with him are the only leads we currently have," he called out. "I want anything, and I mean *anything* that looks suspicious pulled over and investigated. Someone walking or hitchhiking on the side of the road. Someone sleeping where they shouldn't be. Do not be shy. We need a hero. If anyone in this group is responsible for the apprehension of Mr. Moreland, I will personally see to it you are awarded with a raise and/or promotion. You have my word."

xxx

Slumped down low in the front seat, Bill and Leo watched the front entrance of the Wal-Mart for Kat. Finally, she appeared and glanced in each direction before racing to the parked Cadillac. She jerked open the heavy back door of the car and hopped in, tossing a shirt and pair of pants to Bill in front. He and Kat scrambled to change into the new clothes. At one point, Kat was completely naked, sitting in the back seat. She looked up and noticed Leo staring.

"Turn around, Leo," she said as he glanced away. "Focus. There's nothing to see back here."

After pulling on the fresh clothes, she patted Bill and Leo on the back.

"You two ready?"

"Goodbye, my love," Leo said, gently running his hands around the steering wheel of the Eldorado.

Still only wearing the woman's bathing suit as to be a distraction in their plan to change cars, Leo hesitated before getting out. He nodded to Kat and then glanced to Bill who turned away. He had zero faith in the plan they had devised.

Leo staggered through the parking lot in the one-piece until stepping in front of a slow-moving Chevy pickup. The driver slammed the brakes as the truck lightly bumped Leo, knocking him to the ground. The driver, a rough-looking fellow, jumped out and scrambled to Leo, who violently flipped and flopped on the pavement. He looked as if he was having a seizure.

"What in the hell?" the driver hollered. He stood over Leo. "Damn, son! You alright?"

The driver knelt to attend to Leo, and Bill and Kat sprinted to the truck with the garment bag of money and the items she'd just purchased. Bill slipped through the open door on the

209

driver's side. To his surprise, another young fellow sat in the passenger seat. This dude was much bigger and more formidable than the driver.

"Why, hello," Bill said, shocked.

The big dude slugged Bill in the face, busting open the gnarly cut on his nose. Blood poured from Bill's nose as his head dropped forward and rested against the car horn. The horn blared continuously, alarming the driver, who shot a look back to the truck.

At the same time, Kat pulled open the passenger door and, before the big dude could react, slugged him with the unopened champagne bottle. The bottle shattered and he slumped forward. The champagne exploded a geyser, flooding the truck's dashboard. Kat crawled over her dazed victim, pulled Bill back up, which stopped the horn, and slipped into his lap. She put the truck in reverse as the truck's owner reached into the open window, angrily grabbing at Kat's shoulder. The truck wheeled backwards, the passenger door flapping open as the driver held on to Kat, trying to wrestle control of the steering wheel from her. Still in the one-piece bathing suit, Leo hopped up and chased the truck, slamming into the driver's back. As Kat and the driver fought for control of the steering wheel, the truck fishtailed backwards. Kat managed to kick the knocked-out big dude from the passenger seat and out of the truck. Sliding Bill over, she pushed the gear shift into drive. The truck jerked forward, before speeding off.

"Aaahhh!" the driver screamed, struggling to hang on. "Stop! My truck! Stop!"

Kat wheeled the truck around the parking lot with Leo on the owner's back, clawing at his face and eyeballs. With a scream, the truck's owner let go of Kat, threw his arms up, and crashed to the ground. He and Leo both rolled for several feet.

"Leo!" Kat slammed the brakes; Leo and former driver wiped at the scrapes from road burn on their knees and arms. "Come on! Before security gets out here!"

Leo clumsily hopped into the back of the truck, landing hard on the bed's floor, his bare ass exposed and his meaty testicles bouncing. The rusty red truck squealed away. Both woozy, the truck's owner and his passenger scrambled to their feet and briefly gave chase as the truck disappeared from their view. Kat watched in the rear-view as Leo hunkered down in the truck's bed, out of sight.

"They have our pictures and our names," Kat said as the truck sped through the small town of Sterling, Colorado.

"Whose pictures and what names?" Bill looked out truck cab's back window to see if anyone was following.

"Me and Leo's. I saw them on the news while I was in Wal-Mart."

Leo popped his head into the cab's back window. "We need to ditch this truck."

"We need to drive," Bill said.

"I agree with Leo," Kat said.

"I said, *drive*!" Bill yelled.

"We're sittin' ducks out here on these empty roads," Leo said.

"Drive!"

"Bill, we have to get out of this truck," Kat said. "Every cop in the area will be looking for it."

"Drive! Drive!" Bill continued to yell. "Drive, goddammit! We're not stopping until it feels right! Just get the hell out of here! We have some time until we need to ditch the truck!"

xxx

Agent Stack and his partner, Agent Robinson, were cruising U.S. Route 34 near Yuma in a black Lincoln Navigator. It had been a little more than an hour since Stack had dispatched his teams of agents and state troopers in search of Bill and his companions. His phone rang.

"Agent Stack?"

"What is it, Agent Collier?"

"They found the Cadillac in a Wal-Mart parking lot in

211

Sterling."

"The one from Oklahoma that we are looking for?" Stack asked as Agent Robinson scanned a map of the state, searching for Sterling.

"Affirmative," Collier answered. "But no Moreland. Seems he and his two partners jumped a couple kids in their twenties and stole their truck."

"What kind of truck?"

"A1990s model Chevy truck, red in color. It's supposedly beat to hell."

"How close are you to Sterling?" Stack asked, pulling to the side of the road.

"About twenty miles away?"

"I want to you go there and interview the two kids and get me the details on that truck as soon as possible. I want color, make, year, license plate number. Look at security footage of the parking lot. Check for eyewitnesses."

"Roger that. I'm on my way."

"Looks like Sterling is at an interchange of several highways," Stack said over the phone, studying the map. "Let's get teams of agents and state troopers to Routes 138, 113, 14, and 71 as well as I-76 in both directions. I am going to stay on 14 and keep heading west. Looking at this map, I am betting he's headed to the mountains where there will be plenty of places to hide."

xxx

Bill, Kat, and Leo were crammed in the confines of a filthy Texaco men's room near Raymer, Colorado. The stolen truck was parked behind the station, hidden from State Route 14. Sitting on the sink, Kat cut her long brown hair with orange-handled safety scissors they had just purchased at a local convenience store. Nudged up against her with his face inches from the clouded mirror, Bill cleaned the gaping wound across his nose and secured a piece of gauze over the cut with a large

212

strip of first-aid tape. Both of his eyes were black and swollen. He looked like a raccoon. His ribs ached, and he still struggled to breathe because of his fall at the impound yard. Leo winced each time he blotted a cotton ball soaked in rubbing alcohol on a cut or scrape on his legs and arms.

"What about the truck?" Kat asked. "We could try to buy a new one."

"Too risky," Bill said.

Leo howled each time he sterilized one of his cuts with alcohol.

"We can replace it.," Leo picked at the small cinders and pieces of gravel imbedded in the road burns on his legs. "And I know where?"

"Where?" Bill asked.

"Outside motel and hotel lobbies. Most folks leave their cars runnin' or with the keys inside when they stop to check in. Believe me, I know. I seen it every day for years."

"Too risky." Bill shook his head. "Besides, it'd be another stolen vehicle. That's the problem with the truck. They have something to look for."

"We have to ditch the truck," Kat said.

Most of her hair had been chopped off. She looked much younger, not unlike an adolescent boy. She turned to the mirror and ran her fingers through her cropped hair.

"I like it," Leo said.

"Me, too," she said, still staring at herself in the mirror.

"Let's keep the truck," Bill said, "but disguise it."

Kat looked to Leo and held up the scissors. Leo defiantly shook his head.

"Come on, Leo. You're next."

"Bill's next," Leo said, wanting to hold onto his long hair a few minutes longer.

"I don't have anything to cut off," Bill said, rubbing his mostly bald head. "Go on, Leo."

"No way, bro," Leo said, still shaking his head.

"You got to," Bill said. "You know that."

"This hair's all I got." Leo traded places with Bill at the sink. "It's part of my personality. My identity. My charm." He ran his hands through it.

"It hasn't gotten you laid to this point," Kat teased. "Maybe a new look will do you good."

"That's a low blow, girl. I ain't cut my hair for decades."

Kat roughly dragged the dull scissors across the bottom of Leo's greasy, sandy brown hair and snipped, lopping off three inches from the bottom, a jagged, uneven cut.

"I jus' lost a part of my soul," Leo said, staring into the sink at his fallen hair. "Damn, dude."

xxx

The sun shined brightly over the snow-covered peaks of the Rocky Mountains far in the distance to the west. Agent Stack checked over his shoulder and pulled onto Highway 14 and zipped past Sterling with lights flashing and sirens blaring. Two other black SUVs and three Colorado state troopers closely followed. In a matter of seconds, the Navigator had reached over one hundred miles per hour as it roared down the highway. Every other car or truck on the road got out of its way. With a determined look, Stack glanced to his partner in the passenger seat.

"I am not sleeping 'til we get him."

xxx

Stepping out of the grimy Texaco bathroom, Bill studied the freshly sheared heads of his two wearied companions. Leo had also dyed his hair black. He wore a pair of khaki dress slacks and a collared button-down. He looked like a changed man. Following Kat, Bill and Leo limped to the truck. They'd been battered from too many days of daring escapes but had to stay ahead of salivating FBI agents and the fascinated media. Kat opened the driver's side door.

"Leo, you look like you just joined a fraternity," she joked.

"I look like an asshole."

As they prepared to traverse the Rocky Mountains, they'd become more than friends after having met in the most unlikely of places under the most unusual circumstances. They were family—three mismatched fools with little purpose and no plan. Bill knew the most challenging part of their trip was ahead. They needed a leader.

They squeezed into the rusted truck, while the FBI, unknown to them, approached fast, only forty miles away. Kat got into the driver's seat. Bill sat in the middle as Leo crawled in beside him, leaning his arm and shoulder out the passenger side window. He studied his new appearance in the sideview mirror as the truck pulled onto an empty stretch of road, headed west across the plains. Highway 14 split the quiet prairie. Colorful spring wildflowers lined each side of the road. The imposing, yet majestic, Rocky Mountains loomed in the distance before them.

"After we disguise the truck," Bill said. "We need a plan what's next."

"I don't want this to end," Kat said.

"I wanna see the ocean," Leo said.

"We need something more than that," Bill said.

"I agree with Leo," she said. "Let's get to the ocean and worry about the rest later."

"We have to get over those first," Bill said, pointing to the Rockies ahead of them. "Let's hope this old truck can make it."

"Does the radio work?" Kat asked as Bill fiddled with the dashboard knobs, tuning into a local station.

"How 'bout this, folks? The national news has arrived in our little neck of the woods," the radio disc jockey announced. "It seems the missing banker from Pennsylvania is here. Have y'all been following that story? I sure have been. I guess he's made it to Colorado and still hasn't been captured. He's supposedly with two others, a younger man and woman. They're believed to be driving a 1991 red Chevy pickup truck with local plates.

A massive statewide manhunt is ongoing as numerous FBI agents are leading the search in different parts of the state. If you have any information about the missing banker or his whereabouts, you're asked to call 9-1-1. They will direct you to the necessary authorities. I believe a large reward is being offered. I think it's up to a hundred-thousand dollars. I'm not sure. It may be more."

"We need to dump the truck, Bill," Kat said.

"Let's find a hardware store," Bill answered. "I have a plan. I'll get us to the ocean."

Chapter 7
Rocky Mountains — Lost

Day 12. Monday, May 8. 2:24 PM

Rita's hair was a mess. Still in her night gown, she hadn't left the couch and was spending the brightest spring day of the season in the darkened living room. A cigarette smoldered in a dirty ashtray alongside an open bottle of cheap wine and a half-filled glass on the end table. She hadn't eaten much or left the house in days. All the lights were turned off. The curtains were closed tight, blocking out the beautiful afternoon sunlight. The outside world could've ended; she never would've known. She couldn't bear to look outside and see the crowd of media and curious onlookers camped in front of her house. Her home had become a tourist attraction. She and her kids were like caged freaks in a circus sideshow.

She blankly stared at the television with its volume turned low. It was tuned to "The Law Today." Rita pretended not to be listening, but she was. She always did, every day since Bill left. The topic, as it had been for days, was Bill and the missing money.

"The saga of the runaway banker continues," said Cassandra Stevens. "Donations across the southern United States are now believed to be well over a hundred-thousand dollars. The reward for his capture has been raised to a hundred-thousand dollars. Everyone wants to talk about Mr. Moreland."

"Unbelievable," Martin Shears, the show's co-host, said. "I guess nobody wants to turn him in. I can't believe he's still out there, running around. People had to have seen him by now."

"And what about the two who've joined him? Where did

they come from?"

"Let's go to a caller, Cassandra. The phone lines are jammed and blinking."

"Philip from Minneapolis," Ms. Stevens said, looking into the camera. "You're on 'The Law Today.'"

"I think what the banker is doing is fantastic," he said over the line. "Is there anywhere I can donate to his cause?"

"Donate? What cause? He's a wanted man! A thief! He's throwing away someone else's money! The money isn't even his!"

Rita couldn't watch anymore. As she reached for the remote control, her phone rang. She checked the number and saw it was Agent Stack.

"Hello, Agent Stack?"

"Mrs. Moreland, I promised I would call when I had information about your husband."

"Have you found Bill?"

"No, Ma'am. He's still at large, but before you hear any wild stories, especially on the news. A Colorado state policeman had your husband and his companions pulled over yesterday morning on Highway 36 near Joes, Colorado. But—"

"But Bill got away?" she interrupted.

"I don't know how, but yes, he got away. Your husband has been quite the foe, Mrs. Moreland. I did not think he had it in him, the endurance and ingenuity it takes to live on the run. He is proving to be very resourceful."

"Please, Agent Stack, can you make one promise to me?"

"What is it, Mrs. Moreland?"

"Please don't harm him if you catch him. Please."

"It is never our intention to harm a fugitive, but sometimes the circumstances call f—"

"Please. I beg you," she interrupted him again. "Don't harm Bill."

"We will try our best not to. You have my word, Mrs. Moreland."

"Thank you for the update, Agent Stack. I do appreciate the

call."

"I also called because I wanted to apologize about my behavior in your house when we first met. It is part of the job, you know, to—"

"There's never a time to be rude, Agent Stack," she interrupted, "especially when you knew what a hard time I was having."

"I'm sorry, Ms. Moreland."

xxx

Day 12. Monday, May 8. 4:42 PM

The stolen truck was backed deep into a partially hidden bay of a manual car wash in northeastern Colorado. Bill and Kat dipped large paint brushes into buckets of a black sealant that seemed more tar than paint. The car wash was near enough to the interchange of State Highways 14 and 71 that they could get back on the road quickly, but they still had to hurry. They hastily and sloppily slathered the truck in an attempt to camouflage it. The truck's windows and lights were outlined with masking tape to protect them from the thick paint. Pretending to hose off the truck's floor mats, Leo stood guard at the front of the bay on the lookout for cops and nosy strangers. He stared into the stark beauty of the flat prairies that surrounded the southern border of the Pawnee National Grassland.

"I saw Rita." Kat glanced to Bill, who was kneeling at the passenger side.

"Who?" Bill asked as he frantically applied the paint to the side of the truck with short, quick brush strokes.

"Your wife. She was being interviewed on television. I saw her when I was in Wal-Mart."

"What'd she say?" Bill asked, not looking up.

"You need to call home."

Bill briefly stopped painting. He stared at the ground a

moment.

"Call home, Bill. It's all right. The FBI knows we're in the area. You two need to talk."

He lifted himself up and looked to Kat. He studied her without much of an expression as black sealant dripped over his hands and shoes, causing him to glance down.

"I thought you were getting regular house paint?" He started to paint the truck again.

"The guy at the paint counter recommended this instead."

"You talked with someone in the store? That wasn't very smart."

"He was just a kid. Don't worry."

"What is this stuff anyway?"

"Roofing sealant. The kid said it would stick better on metal and wouldn't wash away."

"What else d'you tell him? Your life's story?"

"Just relax. I only asked for help."

"It sure is messy," Bill said as the sealant dripped from the truck.

"It's doing what it's supposed to do."

"Rollers would've worked better than brushes on these big parts. Didn't I tell you to get some rollers as well?"

"Ease up, Bill! All right!"

He noticed Leo was not in front of the bay.

"Where in the hell is Leo?"

Leo had wandered off to a bank of vending machines near the entrance. As he scanned the selection of sodas, from the corner of his eye he saw a posse of cars fast approaching from the east. Two unmarked Lincoln Navigators were in the lead with three Colorado state troopers following close behind. Not panicking, Leo continued to study the soda selections and calmly called out to Bill and Kat.

"Guys! You two! Be quiet! Get down!"

Bill joined Kat at the back of the truck. They both squatted, hiding behind it. Within the blink of an eye, Agent Stack and his team roared to a stop near the car wash. The truck was out of view of Stack and his team. Spotting Leo at the vending machine, Stack rolled down the driver's side window and called out, not knowing he was about to speak to one of the men he was searching for. Leo's new look had obviously fooled him.

"Hey, buddy? Did a red truck pass through here?"

"Red truck?" Leo asked, trying not to make eye contact as he reached for a bottle of Mountain Dew.

"An older truck. A little beat up. Red."

"A truck sped by here," Leo said. "I don't know, maybe ten, fifteen minutes ago. I think it was red."

"You are not sure?"

"I'm mostly sure. I didn't really notice the color of it. The only reason I noticed was that it was loud, real loud. I suppose it needs a new exhaust."

"Which way did it go?"

"It went that way," Leo said, pointing to the highway west.

Agent Stack nodded, before squealing away with his squad of police cars close behind. After they were out of sight, Leo hustled to the bay as Bill and Kat hurriedly finished the paint job. They quickly peeled the masking tape off from around the windows and lights. Leo scrambled around the truck, collecting the dirty brushes, the partially emptied sealant buckets, and the stained balls of tape. Bill handed Leo a fistful of fives and ones.

"Get us some drinks and snacks for the road."

Bill and Kat hopped into the truck. Leo first tossed the spent paint supplies in a nearby dumpster and dashed to the vending machines. Black paint dripped from the bottom of the truck as it circled the lot and parked by Leo, who'd loaded his arms with several bottles of Mountain Dew and numerous bags of chips, cookies, and crackers. He squeezed into the truck beside Bill, and Kat pulled out of the parking lot. She started to turn east and head in the opposite direction that Agent Stack and his team took, but Bill stopped her.

He pointed west and said, "We're going west."

"West?" Kat and Leo said at the same time.

"Yeah, west. I want know what Stack is up to."

"You can't be serious?" Kat said. "We're no match for them in this beat-up old thing. We'll be sitting ducks if they see us."

"Trust me," Bill said confidently. "It'll work out. I've learned after thirty years in finance and banking it's best to keep your enemies close."

Shaking her head, Kat reluctantly pulled the truck into the roadway, its fresh coat of paint still wet. She drove west. Bill looked to Leo, who cradled the assortment of drinks and snacks.

"No water?" Bill asked him. "Only Mountain Dew?"

"Who doesn't do the Dew, Bill? Everyone does the Dew."

xxx

Staying on Highway 14, Kat raced the rattling truck west through the flat grasslands, passing the small towns of Briggsdale and Ault. They soon found themselves at the Rocky Mountain foothills of the northern Front Range on the outskirts of Fort Collins. It was a clear spring evening. The picturesque snow-capped summit of Horsetooth Mountain could be seen to the west. Longs Peak was clearly visible to the southwest. They briefly stopped in Fort Collins to top off the gas tank and let Leo drive as they started their ascent into the mountains. Because the gas station was quite busy, Bill didn't allow Kat or Leo to leave the truck to get more food and drinks. He was too worried about being recognized after hearing the radio report earlier.

After filling up, they motored on, following Highway 14 into the Arapaho and Roosevelt National Forest. As Leo drove, Kat was in the middle, and Bill sat beside the open passenger side window. They didn't say much during the drive. They were exhausted and more worried than they had ever been before. They each studied the stunning scenery in silence. The highway ran alongside the rapid white waters of the rocky Cache Le Poudre River and through the pristine woodlands of the rugged Poudre Canyon. Interspersed among the mountains of the hilly highway were stretches of alpine meadows and open

222

pastures. The thinner air was noticeable, especially to Bill, as they had climbed nearly three-thousand feet in elevation since their last stop. Feeling winded and light-headed, Bill stuck his head out the passenger side window of the hot stuffy truck. The fresh mountain air had cooled considerably since earlier in the day. Peering up to the rocky hills at the higher elevations, Bill watched bighorn sheep grazing on the steep mountain bluffs.

At the small town of Rustic, they took Colorado Highway 69 north deeper into the national forest to the Red Feather Lakes area. They drove over a surprisingly busy dirt road near of the village of Red Feather Lakes named Gnome Road. Scores of hikers and campers stood on each side of it, taking pictures. The busy scenic road was lined with ceramic elves and fairy doors placed among the trees and rocks. To avoid other campers, they pushed on into the night and entered the highest ridges of the Front Range of the Rockies in northern Colorado.

Darkness fell fast, as did the temperature of the thin, crisp air. The heavy cover of clouds reduced visibility. A light coating of snow covered the ground. Bill and the gang were not prepared for a frosty night at elevation. None of them had a coat. Kat was wearing shorts. They had no hats or gloves or even blankets. Other than the vending machine snacks and drinks Leo had purchased earlier, they had few supplies. Fortunately, the truck's heater worked as Leo had its blower cranked as high as it would go. To make matters even worse, they didn't have a map, and Bill's last remaining cell phone was without service. Leo squinted into the thick fog that covered them. He slowed to a crawl as he tried his best to navigate the dark, winding roads. He glanced to Bill for guidance. They were lost.

Bill noticed a back road marked only by a set of dirt tire tracks that cut deep into the thick forest of tall pines that covered the mountainside. Leo turned onto the rough, bumpy road and followed it for several miles as they again steadily rose in elevation. He finally parked at a clearing that appeared to have been used for camping. Bill got out and surveyed the area. Because they had no flashlight, the dense fog made it impractical to go into the woods to collect firewood.

"What's that smell?" Bill asked as Leo and Kat got out of the truck. "Smells like burnt rubber."

"Probably the brakes," Leo answered. "With all the hills and turns we took."

"We're staying here for the night," Bill announced as they hopped up and down, trying to keep warm. "We'll have to sleep together in the front seat."

"What?" Kat said.

"We'll have to huddle together to keep warm."

"But there's not enough room in there. We barely fit as it is."

"It's all we can do. At least, we'll have some shelter."

Leo leaned into the truck's bed. He pulled out a stained and wrinkled blue tarp.

"This could work as a blanket," he said, holding it up.

"Let's try to get a few hours of sleep and get out of here early in the morning," Bill said.

"We'll need gas," Leo said.

"I'm sure we'll find something once we get out of these mountains," Bill said but he didn't sound too confident. He pointed to Kat. "You're in the middle."

"I'm not in middle. I'm not sleeping between you two. No way. I'll take the window on the passenger's side."

"I'll take the middle then," Bill said. "Leo, you okay with the driver's side?"

"Yep."

Bill crawled into the middle of the front seat. Kat and Leo slid into the cab on each side of him. Leo and Bill stretched the tarp over their quivering bodies. Kat turned away from Bill. Leo leaned back against the seat cushion opposite the steering wheel. Bill searched for a place to put his arms. He rolled his sore and cramped body towards Kat and rested his arms over her before closing his eyes. Leo was the first to fall asleep, loudly snoring within minutes after getting into the truck. Kat backed her trembling body into Bill.

"You okay?" he whispered, their breaths filling the air inside the cab, causing the windows to fog over.

"I'm hungry, Bill. I'm filthy. I need to shower. I'm cold."

"Here," he said, dragging more of the tarp over her. She tucked the edges of it on one side under her and pulled more of it over the exposed skin of her body, shaking from the cold.

"We're not going to freeze to death, are we?" she asked.

"No. No. We'll be all right. If it gets too cold, we'll start the truck and turn on the heat for a moment."

"Hold me, Bill."

After an initial hesitation, he bear-hugged her and tightly engulfed most of her chilled, tarp-covered body within his.

"This isn't the end of the road, is it?" she asked. "It sure feels like it."

"Ssssh. Try to sleep," he said as Leo's loud snoring competed with the sound of their growling bellies.

"Don't listen to that, Kat," he said, referring to the painful hunger pangs that gnawed at their empty stomachs. "Just imagine how wonderful that next pizza will taste or how great a warm bed or hot shower will feel. This is as bad it will ever be. It can only get better. Trust me. It's not the end of the road. I promise."

xxx

Day 13. Tuesday, May 9. 1:47 AM

True to his word, Agent Stack hadn't slept much except for an occasional afternoon catnap during his pursuit of Bill through the plains and mountains of Colorado. He was surviving on a diet of coffee and sugary pastries during the day and liquor and protein bars at night. As Bill, Kat, and Leo froze in the truck in the mountains north of Red Feather Lakes, Stack shared gin and tonics with an attractive lady FBI agent, Marie Stevens. They'd worked together many times and went to a cushy resort in the lush foothills of the Rockies at the mouth of Rist Canyon. Little did he know, he was only fifty miles away from where Bill and the others were camping.

The resort was covered in fog. Stack and Agent Stevens soaked in the hot healing waters of an outdoor spa not far from their room. She snacked on a room service charcuterie plate of exotic cheeses and meats as he nursed his gin and tonic. Obviously distracted, Stack hardly paid attention to his longtime companion. She sipped red wine and snuggled close to him in the spa, but through the steam that rose off the hot tube, he watched the news coverage of Bill's cross-country journey on an outdoor television.

"Cold night," Agent Stevens commented.

"We wouldn't know anything about that, would we?" he said, not looking away from the television screen. "This water must be a hundred degrees."

"Where's the rest of your team?"

"They had dinner and turned in. It has been a long stretch. They are all tired."

"How 'bout you?"

"There will be plenty of time to rest when this is all over."

Agent Stevens stood up out of the tub. Water dripped off her curvy, bikini-covered body, which was partially shrouded by steam. Stack finally looked away from the television news and stared at her.

"Julius, come to bed," she said, pulling a towel over her wet body, shining under the spa lights. "You look exhausted."

"I will be there in a minute," he said, looking back to the television. "Let me soak here a while longer."

xxx

Leo started to rustle around in the seat of the truck, waking Bill and Kat who lightly slept. His bladder was full, and he desperately needed to heed nature's call. The windows inside and outside the truck were covered in a heavy coating of frost. It was still dark. Much of the fog had lifted. The three of them were jumbled together, trying to stay warm. Arm and legs, knees and elbows, all still stained with black sealant, were entangled under the flimsy blue tarp. Leo was uncomfortably wedged between the steering wheel and gear shift. Bill was mostly underneath Leo. Kat shivered in the fetal position, having pulled her arms and legs tightly into her chest. Nearly all her body was under both Bill and Leo. One of Leo's knees was in her lower back. Bill's elbows were stuck in her shoulder and the back of her head. Leo awkwardly pulled his cramped body away from the others and opened the truck door.

"Leo?" Bill whispered. "What are you doing?"

"I need to piss."

"You're letting the cold air in."

"I don't think it can get much colder in here, Bill," Kat mumbled as Leo crawled out and immediately started to urinate by the front of the truck.

"This tarp smells like dirty feet," Bill said.

"That's us, Bill," Kat said, her teeth chattering. "Not the tarp."

"Did you sleep?"

"Not really."

"Me, either."

"What time is it?" she asked.

"Almost four. We still have a couple hours until daylight. We need to get more sleep."

"It's too cold."

"Start the truck," Bill said as Leo climbed back into the cab, his breath a thick cloud of mist. "Let's warm up a bit."

Leo turned the keys that hung from the ignition. It took a moment, but the frozen engine briefly rumbled to life before shutting off. Leo tried again. The truck started but quickly stalled out.

"We're not out of gas, are we?" Bill whined.

"I don't think so," Leo said, checking the gas gauge. "Looks like we have about a quarter of a tank."

"Don't tell me, the battery's dead?" Bill asked with panic in his voice.

On the next attempt, Leo clicked on the headlights, before turning the key in the ignition. The engine roared to life. Leo pressed the gas pedal several times, revving the wounded engine. The headlights briefly shined before dimming as the truck stalled out again.

"It ain't the battery, Bill," Leo said. "It's the alternator. We ain't goin' nowhere."

"Shit!" Bill groaned.

xxx

With only a bottle of Mountain Dew and a package of Lance peanut butter crackers, Leo left Bill and Kat sometime after daybreak. They knew the plan was a desperate Hail Mary pass at the end of a football game. Leo was to hike a trail down the mountainside and hopefully reach a roadway that would lead into a nearby village. Bill and Kat would stay with the truck. Bill convinced Leo not to take the winding, two-lane road they drove in on in case it was patrolled by the authorities or the local forest rangers. The trail through the woods would be a great deal shorter, but much steeper, as it descended straight down the mountainside. No time to waste. Once out of the woods, Leo would look for a service station or find someone who could provide him with information about the nearest auto parts store. He planned to buy a new alternator and a set of tools. He took a little over four-thousand dollars with him. It wasn't much of a plan, but they had few other options.

It was a slow and treacherous hike through a forest thick with blue spruce and Douglas firs. The morning temperatures hovered just above twenty degrees. Leo's breath hung heavy in the frosty morning air. He struggled to traverse the rugged trail lined with willow, maple, and small juniper trees, gasping for air. The low oxygen levels at the high elevation left him winded and caused his head to ache. He stopped several times for short breaks to catch his breath. It took him more than two hours and a drop over a thousand feet of elevation until he finally reached a paved road five miles from the campsite. By the time he got to the road, he was dirty. One of the souls of his shoes was broken in half and flopped with each step. He had fallen several times in his rush to get help. Fresh morning dew blanketed the ground and was frozen in shaded parts of the trail, making the hike slippery and dangerous. The knees of his khaki pants were torn. Fresh cuts and scrapes covered his arms, wrists, and hands. He jammed his elbow on one fall. Initially, his arm went numb, and later, sharp stabs of pain radiated to his shoulder.

xxx

After Leo had gone, Bill and Kat built a roaring fire. They wanted it to last through the day and into the evening. It would be a long time before they'd again see Leo, if ever. They spent a good portion of the morning gathering armloads of fallen tree branches that were plentiful throughout the surrounding woods. The physically straining activity provided plenty of fuel, but also warmed their chilled muscles.

Bill found a piece of rotted garden hose in the back of the truck and used it to siphon a mouthful of gasoline that helped to start a fire. The fire turned out to be bigger than planned. Although they'd solved their problem of warmth, they were hungry and extremely thirsty. Bill and Kat sat together on a downed tree trunk next to the impressive fire, sharing the last bag of potato chips and the last bottle of Mountain Dew.

"Your eyes look better," she said. "How're the ribs and nose?"

"They hurt if I think about it," he answered, softly touching at the swollen red gash on his nose. "So, I don't think about it. I got other things to worry about."

"Do you think we'll see Leo again?"

"We'll see him again. We got to have faith."

"Even if he makes it off this mountain, finds an auto parts store in a reasonable amount of time, and gets the needed parts, he'll still need to make it back up here. That's a helluva hike and a lot to ask. He may be gone for days."

"I know. I shouldn't have sent him alone."

"And we're out of food and water. And we'll need to keep this fire going."

"Maybe we should've all gone. Just left the truck behind."

"It's too late now," she said. They studied the orange glow of the raging fire.

"I need to get you home. This is no way for a young woman to live."

"I'm not ready to go home yet. I'll let you know when I am," she said, staring into the fire. "I've been meaning to say this for the past day or so, but I didn't know how to say it."

"What's that?"

"I didn't mean to come on so strong back at the cabin on the couch."

"It's all right."

"It was never my intention to have any kind of physical relationship—"

"I know," he interrupted.

"I was caught up in the moment," she said, not taking her eyes from the fire. "The alcohol. Leo and the young escort in the hot tub. I was feeling lonely. I don't want to do anything against Rita or cause you any trouble."

"It's okay."

"But I was a little turned on, Bill."

"A little?" he asked, glancing to her.

"Well, maybe more than a little," she said. "Were you?"

"I was mostly scared."

"Scared?"

"Every night since I met you, I fall asleep with you in my dreams," he confessed, looking away from her. "And everything there is perfect. I need to keep it that way. I don't want to do anything that will mess that up. It's just about all I got."

"You always know what to say to me."

"I mean it."

"I know you do."

"Hold me, Kat," he said, looking back to her as she slid closer and wrapped her arms around him. "I don't know what will happen next. Tell me everything will be all right."

"Oh, Bill," she said, tightly holding onto him.

"I love you, Kat."

"I love you, too, Bill."

"No, not the way I love you."

She smiled and pulled his body closer to hers. He took a deep breath as they both studied the fire.

"Everything will be all right," she whispered. "You told me that last night, and I believe it. And I know you believe it, too."

xxx

Coming upon a paved two-lane road at the bottom of a steep hill near one of the twelve lakes of the Red Feather Lakes area, Leo fell, practically somersaulting into a thicket of heavy mountain sagebrush. Nauseous and lightheaded, he struggled from the thin air, gasping to catch his breath. His legs were like jelly. They were nearly too sore to go on. He leaned back into the cold, wet brush. He was weak from not having eaten anything substantial in days and exhausted to the point of delirium, but he was too cold to nap. After about fifteen minutes, a 1970s Ford Bronco appeared out of the light morning fog. It had a freshly painted baby blue body with a white rooftop. With his last bit of energy, Leo hopped out to the road like a jack-in-the-box and desperately waved his arms as it slowly approached. The truck stopped.

"What you doin' way out here alone, son?" the driver of the Bronco asked through the window. "Where's your coat? What happened to your pants? Your shoes?"

"I'm campin' with my dad and sister," Leo said. "Our truck broke down. Is there an auto parts store in the area?"

"What'd you need?"

"I think the alternator is bad. I can't get it started."

"There's no auto parts store for miles. Closest one is probably back in Fort Collins," the man said. "But I do know a guy not too far from here who fixes cars and trucks for the locals. He may have what you need."

"How do I get there from here?"

"You want me to call a tow truck or something? Or get a hold of the park ranger up near where you're campin'?"

"No tow trucks. No rangers. I just need a couple parts and a few tools. I can fix it myself."

"I think a tow truck is your bes—"

"*No tow trucks!*" Leo snapped. "How do I get to the mechanic's place?"

"You want a ride?"

"Can I walk there?"

"I wouldn't. Especially in those things." The man pointed at Leo's worn-out shoes. "It's about seven, eight miles from here. Get in. I can take you there."

Leo stared at the man a moment then glanced in each direction of the empty roadway. He climbed into the Bronco.

"My name's Richard Kelly," the man said, extending out his right hand as he pulled the Bronco back onto the roadway. "My wife calls me Richie. My friends call me Dick."

Leo shook his hand. The man stared at him, obviously waiting for Leo to introduce himself.

"Jonathan," Leo finally mumbled.

"Nice to meet you, Jonathan."

"Thanks for the ride."

"Jonathan what?"

"Jonathan L. Seagull," Leo said.

"What?"

"Jonathan Livingston Seagull.

"That's an odd name, for sure."

"I can't help that," Leo said, pulling his arms in tight against his shivering body.

The inside of the Bronco was cold and sparse. Except for the windows and seat cushions, the inside was entirely metal, including the stripped-away dashboard and interior of the doors. And it didn't seem the heater worked. The windows were frosty, and Leo could see their breath when he and the old man talked.

"Where's your coat, boy?"

"Where I'm headed, I won't need it."

"Where's that?"

"The ocean. I may settle there."

"Where at the ocean?"

"Who are we going to meet?" Leo asked.

"Chico Wen."

"Chico Wen?"

"He's one of them Mexican Chinamen. He's a genius with cars. Engines and body work both. Everything. Rumor has it he escaped up here from Los Angeles. Can you believe that? Los Angeles? Was the mechanic to the gangs there, I hear. I guess he made them lowrider cars. You know those fancy hot rods that hop up and down. I seen a whole special about them on the Discovery Channel. You ever watch that channel? That's my wife's favorite."

"Nah, I live in a motel. I don't get that one."

It wasn't long before the old man pulled into the parking lot of Chico Wen's garage. The shop was a large aluminum building with three enormous garage doors located on a secluded side road about fifteen miles west of the village of Red Feather Lakes. Assorted cars and trucks in different stages of disrepair were parked in the lot. Leo dug a hundred-dollar bill from his pocket and held it out to the old man.

"Thanks for the ride, Dick," Leo said as the old man stared at the money. "A little something for your trouble."

"No, no," he shook his head, not taking the money. "I'm jus' tryin' to help. Like any decent person would."

"Please, Dick."

"I can't take your money." The old man continued to shake his head.

"Then I'll just lean it here on the seat," Leo said, before

getting out of the Bronco. "Thank you again."

"Good luck. Chico will set you up. He's the man."

Leo watched the Bronco pull away. He stepped to the entrance door of the garage and knocked. He didn't know what to expect when the door opened.

"Hey, man," Chico said in soft, deliberate voice with a strong Chicano accent. "How can I help you?"

Chico presented an imposing figure: long and lean and over six feet, six inches tall. A single gold front tooth stood out and a collage of elaborate tattoos ran from the top of his neck, across his bare back and chest, over his arms, and down to his hands. The tattoos on one arm depicted religious images of crosses, bibles, praying hands, and several portraits of Jesus Christ and the Mother Mary. The other arm was covered in violent images, like bleeding knives, smoking guns, exploding cars, and flying bullets with angel wings. Chico's hair was silky black and hung in a ponytail that reached his lower back. He sported a long, skinny string mustache and a goatee that hung off his chin.

As Leo described the truck's problem, he couldn't help but notice the gnarly scars on Chico's enormous hands and across one of his cheeks. Chico agreed with Leo's diagnosis of the truck's issues and was sure he had all the parts needed to fix the problem. Chico led Leo into the garage. They were greeted by upbeat mariachi music playing from a Mexican radio station. Chico and Leo immediately hit it off based on their shared love and knowledge of all things motorized.

"You don't look like you're from around here?" Leo called out as Chico searched through a variety of car parts stored in cardboard boxes on metal shelving units throughout the garage.

"I'm from Los Angeles. How 'bout you?"

"Oklahoma."

"You on your way back there?"

"Nah, just the opposite. I'm going to see the ocean. I've never been before."

"I used to own a motorcycle repair shop that overlooked

Venice Beach. It was my dream job. I had it made, man."

"What happened?"

"A dude who I thought was important offered me a suitcase full of cash to convert some expensive cars for him."

"Convert?"

"Disguise."

"And you did it?"

"I wanted to impress him. What a mistake."

"Was he impressed?"

"He hired me. I was makin' over six figures a year, man. Trickin' out stolen or repossessed cars."

"Repossessed?"

"Debt payments for unpaid loans."

"The mob?"

"The cartel. I tried to keep myself clean, but I got caught up in the life, you know. Once you get hooked in that crowd, there's no way out. They have you. Your family. Your friends. Everyone, man."

"Shit, dude. I ain't even left Oklahoma 'til now."

"I've been beaten, shot at, stabbed, arrested. My life threatened."

"Jesus. The worst I've done is steal 40s of Mickey Big Mouths from the store and sneak into Iron Maiden concerts."

"I had to run away. They all think I'm dead."

"Have you had any trouble with the locals here?"

"Some folks weren't too friendly at first. Especially the town leaders. They were suspicious. I guess my look can be a little scary. Then I started fixin' their cars and trucks. They all love me now."

"It's beautiful here. Like the ocean, I'd never been to the mountains."

"But the folks 'round here are like everywhere else. Half the people are great. The other half not so much. I quickly learned who the assholes were, man. I don't mean to, but I make them pay a little bit more for their repairs, if you can dig that."

"If only people could be nice and acceptin' of others."

"The problem is most assholes don't know they're assholes."

"Ain't that right," Leo said with a chuckle and a nod. "What do you do up here for fun?"

"This is it," he said, opening his arms and motioning to the garage floor. "I work on cars. That's all I do. That's all I want to do. I send most of the money I make to my daughter back in LA."

"LA? She safe there?"

"Nobody knows she's my daughter, man. Her mother and I kept it a secret. And when she was old enough to understand, we told her about my past. I think it scared her. She's never talked about it again."

"It must be hard not seein' her."

"She comes to visit. We go hikin' and campin'. She loves to fish. I taught her how to drive a car up here. I give her advice."

"Advice?"

"I tell her all the things not to do like I did. No tattoos. Never date a drug dealer. All of 'em I know are either dead, in jail or witness protection."

"How old is she?"

"Nineteen. An honor student. I'm so proud of her, man. She starts nursin' school in the fall. She's gonna take care of her old man when I'm too old and weak to work on cars."

"Are any of these cars for sale?"

"Everything's for sale at the right price, my friend."

"What can I buy for four-thousand dollars?"

"The cheapest thing I got that'll get you to the ocean is that custom yellow Nova over there. I'd like to get six thousand for it. I put a lot into her."

"Can I pay you four thousand now and promise to get the rest to you later?"

"Ah, man. I'm tryin' to put my daughter through college."

"There's a good chance I can get you the rest today."

"I don't know, man."

"Buyin' this car would save me from an all-day hike back up the mountain to my campsite. And it would save me from fixin' the truck. That's if I can fix it at all. And I haven't eaten, and we're out of water."

"I'd like to help you, but. . ."

"And it may keep me and my friends out of trouble."

"Who you runnin' from?"

"Everyone."

"Ah, Jesus," Chico mumbled, before a long pause as he thought about the offer. "I guess so. All right. I'll take the four-thousand dollars."

"Shit, Chico! You're a lifesaver!" Leo howled as he rushed over to check out the car. "I promise to get you the rest of the money."

"No worries, man, if it don't happen."

"Does this run?"

"Like a dream. I drive it all the time," he said, walking to a desk, opening a drawer, and pulling out a set of keys. "I ain't got a title for it."

"1971?" Leo asked as he walked around the car, before popping open the hood and briefly checking the engine.

"Yep. 1971 Chevy Nova sedan."

"V8? Two-hundred-seventy horsepower?"

"Newly rebuilt less than two years ago," Chico said with a nod, tossing Leo the keys. "It'll get you over the mountains and out of here."

"You may have saved my life and my friends' lives," Leo said, getting behind the steering wheel and firing up the engine. "If I can find my friends, I'll be back with the rest of your money," he yelled over the loud rumbling engine. "You gonna be here?"

"I don't go nowhere else, my friend," he said, grinning as Leo revved the engine several times before pulling out of the garage.

xxx

At a convenience store gas station, Agent Stack leaned against the front of the Lincoln Navigator he'd been driving. A stiff

237

breeze blew across the open plain just northwest of Fort Collins, cutting the humidity of the warm afternoon. He stared at his phone, checking numerous email messages as Agent Robinson filled the Lincoln with gas. The other members of his team also were stopped there, fueling their vehicles and stretching their legs. A young FBI agent approached Stack, holding a phone out to him.

"You better take this, Boss," he said as Stack reached for the phone. "The guy on here called the hotline. Seems he picked up a hitchhiker this morning not too far from here. Says the hitchhiker was in need of truck parts. The truck he'd been driving had broken down."

"Agent Stack speaking," he said, talking into the phone.

"My wife thought I should call," the man on the line said.

"Your wife is a smart lady," Stack responded. "Can I get your name, sir?"

"Richard Kelly."

"You have some information for me, Mr. Kelly?"

"I think I do. I picked up a hitchhiker this mornin'. The whole situation seemed odd."

"Odd?"

"Said he was campin' with his father and sister in the mountains, and their truck broke down. Said he needed parts to fix it."

"Why did this seem odd?"

"He didn't even have a coat. His arms were cut up. He was filthy and looked to be freezin'. His lips were blue as a robin's egg. If he was campin', he'd been more prepared, I would think. And I asked him if he wanted me to call a tow truck or get some help. He refused, even got a little testy about it, you know."

"Where did you take him?"

"I told him there was a local guy who may be able to help. Chico Wen."

"Chico Wen?"

"I figured he might have the truck parts the fellow needed."

"And?"

238

"I dropped him off at Chico's place. He gave me a hundred-dollar bill for my trouble. I refused it, of course, but he insisted. That was the last I saw of him."

"Did he tell you a name?"

"Jonathan somethin'. I can't remember the last name. It was a strange name. A bird or somethin'."

"Bird?"

"Jonathan L., um. Jonathan L. Eagle or somethin' like that."

"Jonathan Livingston Seagull?"

"Yep! That's it! You know him?"

"Can you tell me where Chico Wen lives?"

"Do I get the reward money if you catch him? My wife wanted me to ask."

"If the information you have provided me leads to his arrest. Of course."

"He ain't the banker, though," Mr. Kelly said. "I seen his picture on TV. The guy I picked up was younger."

"Did the guy you picked up say anything unusual?"

"I asked him why he didn't have a coat."

"What did he say?"

"Said he didn't need one where he was headed."

"Where is he headed?"

"The ocean. Jus' needed to get over the mountains first."

"Thank you, Mr. Kelly. You've been extremely helpful."

"And he told me he lived in a motel. That's something unusual, right?'

"It is, Mr. Kelly. It is, and especially important in this case. I may have one of my agents pay you a visit to show you some photos later to see if you can identify one of the guys we are looking for. If that is all right with you and your wife?"

"Sure, sure. Anything I can do to help."

xxx

Leo raced back to the dirt road in the mountains that led to the spot where he had camped with Bill and Kat the night before.

He'd been gone all morning and some of the afternoon. He returned much sooner than he and the others had predicted. He expected it would be at least a day to find what he needed and another day to hike the steep mountain trail back to the campsite. The Chevy Nova bounced and rattled as it drove over the rough, wooded backroad. Bill and Kat nervously fidgeted by the fire, which was substantially smaller than when it was started. Hearing something, Bill glanced over his shoulder.

"What is it?" Kat asked.

"What was that?"

"What?"

"That sound. Do you hear it?"

They both held as still as possible and tilted their heads towards the dirt road that led into the campsite. They could hear what sounded like a motorized vehicle approaching.

"Quick," Bill hissed. "Let's hide."

They dashed into the woods and climbed onto a large rock outcropping, scaling it to the top to get a better view of the arriving vehicle. The Chevy Nova roared to stop by the campfire as Bill and Kat squinted, trying to see who was driving.

"What the. . ." Bill mumbled. "Who in the world is. . ."

"Is that Leo?"

"I can't tell."

"It has to be Leo."

"It is! It is Leo!"

"*Leo!*" Bill and Kat called out in unison, waving from the peak of the rock formation overlooking the fire.

"*Leo!*" they called out again, before climbing down and enthusiastically sprinting to the rumbling car. They jumped and danced around, hugging Leo as if they had just won the car from a game show.

"*Leo!* You did it. *You did it, Leo!* You crazy son of a bitch. You did it!"

"Where'd you get this thing?" Bill asked, running his hand over the hood of the Nova. "Please don't tell me you stole it."

"We need to get out of here," Leo said, not in the mood to celebrate or discuss his morning adventure.

"Where'd you get the car?" Bill asked again.

"I bought it."

"Bought it? From a dealer?"

"From a nice fellow at a garage."

"Can we trust him?"

"Yes," Leo said.

"Are you sure?"

"We can trust *him* but probably not the guy who dropped me off at the garage."

"What guy?"

"I hitched a ride with some older dude."

"I thought I said no rides."

"What other choice did I have, Bill?"

"You don't trust him?"

"He seemed suspicious. I wasn't wearin' a coat or in campin' gear or hikin' boots. My arms and legs were scraped and cut up. My pants were torn. He had a lot of questions."

"What'd you tell him?"

"I didn't tell him anything, but we need to get out of here."

"Let's first put out the fire," Bill said.

"What about the truck?" Kat asked.

"We'll leave it. I'll siphon the rest of the gas out of it. You and Leo take care of the fire. We don't have time to find some water. Bury it with dirt."

In between brief coughing fits, Bill sloppily sucked the last of the gasoline out of the stalled truck with the piece of hose. He swallowed some and spilled a lot as he tried to fill several empty 20-ounce plastic Mountain Dew bottles. At the same time, Kat and Leo hurriedly shoveled handfuls of warm dirt onto the fire, smothering the flames. Reeking of gasoline, Bill poured several soda bottles filled with gas into the tank of the Nova.

"We need to make one stop," Leo said as they crammed into the Nova.

"Stop?" Bill asked.

"Yeah, and I need two-thousand-five-hundred dollars."

"Twenty-five-hundred dollars? For what?"

"It's what I still owe on the car. We need to go back to the garage."

"Are you sure we can trust this guy?"

"Yes."

"How are you so sure?" Bill asked.

"He trusted me when I promised I'd be back with the rest of the money."

"I don't like it," Bill said, shaking his head.

"And there in the back," Leo said, pointing behind him. "There's some peanut butter, a half of loaf of bread, and a gallon of water he gave me."

xxx

So as not to spook Chico, Agent Stack showed up at the garage with only his partner, Agent Robinson. The others in the team had stayed behind. Stack parked the Lincoln and got out with Robinson, who followed him to the front door of the shop. Stack pounded on the door. Chico peeked out a side window before opening the door a crack.

"Can I help you?" he asked.

"We are from the FBI. I would like to ask you a few questions about a case we are working on, if that is all right?" Chico was reluctant to open the door. "I will only be a minute."

Chico finally pushed the door open, allowing Agent Stack to enter. His partner stayed outside.

"Chico Wen?" Stack asked, studying the tall mechanic. "I'm Agent Julius Stack of the FBI. My goodness, big fellow. I imagined a smaller man."

"Most are."

"I am searching for someone who may have visited your garage earlier today," Stack said, holding out a photo of Leo. "Did this guy stop here this morning?"

242

Chico studied the photo, before shaking his head and handing it back to Stack.

"Nah, nah. I never seen this dude."

Stack stepped closer within a few inches of Chico.

"I did a little research about you, buddy," Stack snarled. "Who you hidin' from? Awful strange a fellow like yourself all the way from sunny southern California with a rap sheet as long as the Colorado River has settled up here alone. Think harder, Chico. Have you seen this man?"

Stack again held up the photo of Leo. Chico glanced at it and shook his head.

"I ain't seen him. I'm tellin' you the truth."

"This guy didn't visit you this morning?"

"Someone did. But not that dude," Chico answered, pointing to the photo. "The dude that stopped here had more of a buzz cut. No beard. He was young, though. Jus' like the dude in that picture."

"What did he want?" Stack asked as Chico stared back without answering. "Come on, Chico! What did he want? I know a little about you. Your ties with different gangs in LA and the cartels over the border. What did the guy who visited here this morning want?"

Chico was again hesitant.

"And I heard about your father's popular restaurant back in California. I know how very, very successful it is. What is the name? Lavender Garden?" Stack asked as Chico cringed, unable to maintain his stone-cold poker stare after the comment about his father.

"I have also dug around a little bit and heard about his on-and off-again relationship with the IRS," Stack paused. "Come on, Chico. What did the fellow who visited here this morning want? Tell me, and I will get out of your hair and leave you alone."

"He was lookin' for specific parts for a truck and some tools."

"An older truck?" Stack asked, stepping back from Chico.

"All he told me was, it was American. A Chevy, I believe."

"And?"

"When I went to look for what he needed, he noticed all the cars in here," Chico said, motioning to the assortment of vehicles parked throughout the spacious garage. "He asked if any of them were for sale."

"What did you say?"

"What I always say. For the right price, everything's for sale."

"And?"

"He then asked what four-thousand dollars would get him. I pointed to an old car in the corner. I'd jus' rebuilt the engine. The dude walked around the car several times. Looked underneath it. Checked the engine. And asked how it ran."

"What did you tell him?"

"I said, like new."

"And?"

"He handed me four thousand dollars in hundred-dollar bills, and I gave him the keys."

"What was the make and model?" Stack asked. "What kind of car was it, Chico?"

"It's a Chevy Nova.

"What year?"

"1971."

"What color?"

"Primer."

"Primer? What the hell is 'primer'?"

"It needs to be painted," Chico answered. "Call it, gray."

"You better not be puttin' me on. If I find out you lied to me, I am making two stops. The first, here. The second one, in LA. And I love fine Chinese cuisine."

"I ain't lyin', man."

"This better not be some fuckin' fairy tale the two of you concocted to slow me down. I know he has unlimited amounts of cash to keep you quiet."

"He didn't tell me nuthin' about who he was. How would I know the FBI was after him? That's not somethin' you'd tell a stranger."

"Is there a registered license for the car?"

"Nah, nah."

"Was it stolen?" Stack asked as Chico blankly stared back, not answering. "I'll take that stupid look on you face as a yes."

"I can't remember how I got it."

"Did he say anything else or act unusual while he was here?"

"Nah, not really."

"Think, Chico. Did he say his name or where he was going or who he was with?"

"Nah, man. He acted a little nervous, desperate. He was in a hurry."

"I know he said something. I hear he likes to talk."

"I really don't know, man. He knew a lot about cars."

"You better not be lying to me, Chico."

"Nah, man."

"Now, can I see that four thousand he paid you for the car?"

"What?"

"I need that four-thousand dollars. It is evidence."

"What evidence?"

"It is likely stolen money. We may be able to trace it back to the bank in Pennsylvania where it probably came from."

"You're serious? You want my four-thousand dollars?"

"It was used to purchase a stolen car. Am I correct?"

"Shit, man! You are serious."

"Give me the four-thousand dollars, Chico."

"Come on, dude! Give me a break."

xxx

Leo counted out the rest of the cash he needed to pay Chico. Kat kept checking out the back window to see if anyone else was around. The parking lot was quiet. Agent Stack had been there less than an hour earlier. The road they drove in on was dark and empty. Bill nervously fidgeted in the front passenger seat.

"Make it quick, Leo," Bill said. "Pay the man, and let's go."

245

Leo hopped out of the Nova and hurried to the front door of Chico's garage. He re-counted the money and then pounded on the door. Chico peeked out a window.

"I got the rest of your money," Leo said as Chico scanned the parking lot outside his garage. "Jus' like I promised."

"Thank you, brother," Chico said, taking the money, "but you better get movin'. The FBI paid me a visit a little while ago. They know you're in a Nova."

"What else?"

"But not a yellow one. They pressed me hard. I told 'em it was gray."

"There's an extra five-hundred dollars there," Leo said, pointing to the money in Chico's hand. "We were wonderin' if you had any gas to sell us."

"Sure, sure," Chico said with a nod, backing into his garage. "There's two five-gallon cans over by the wall there. Take 'em. They're yours." Leo followed Chico deeper into the garage and towards the cans of gasoline. "They took the four thousand, man."

"What?" Leo asked, stopping as he approached Chico with a gas can in each hand.

"They took the four-thousand dollars you paid me for the car."

"The FBI?" Leo asked. "For what?"

"They said *evidence*."

"Evidence? They're probably ass deep in a roomful of whores right now. Evidence, shit." Leo glanced outside to the Nova. Bill waved for him to hurry up. "Hold on, Chico. I'll be right back."

Leo sprinted out of the garage to the Nova with the full cans of gasoline. He opened the trunk and placed them inside before walking to the passenger side window.

"Let's *go*, Leo," Bill called. "Come *on*."

"I need more money."

"What for?"

"He gave us a bunch of gas."

"I thought we already paid for it," Bill said as he dug into the garment bag and pulled out a ten-thousand-dollar stack of cash. Before he could peel off a couple hundred-dollar bills, Leo grabbed the entire stack.

"That's ten thousand, right?" Leo dashed back to the garage.

"For gas?" Bill called out. "Shit, Leo!"

Chico's long lean frame appeared in the darkened doorway. Leo reached the stack of money to him. Chico wouldn't take it.

"Come on, Chico. You saved us. Take the money. It'll help your daughter get through school."

"I can't take your money, dude."

"It ain't our money. You need it more than we do."

Chico reluctantly took the stack of cash and handed Leo a slip of paper.

"That's a list of some local roads. They're not well traveled. They'll get you outta here."

"Thank you, man," Leo said and rushed back to the car.

"Good luck, brother!" Chico yelled. "Take good care of the Nova! I love that car!"

Leo hopped in the driver's side, handed Bill the list of the roads that Chico had given him, and started the Nova, revving the engine a few times. He put the car in gear and started to pull out of the lot.

"Wait," Bill said, intently studying the names and directions of backroads on the list. "Let me check this out first."

"Wait?" Kat moaned. "We need to get back on the road."

"The FBI was here earlier, Bill," Leo warned him.

"FBI?" Bill asked, glancing up and looking to Leo.

"They know we're in a Chevy Nova. We need to go."

"Wait a minute," Bill said again, looking back to the list of roads. "Let's pick a route out of here."

"We need food and supplies," Kat called from the back seat. "We can't spend another night in the mountains like we did last night. We have to be careful where we stop, especially if the FBI knows what we're driving."

"I have a plan," Bill said calmly, still studying the list of roads. "According to Chico's list of back roads here, we'll start on Highway 73, then switch to 80, and take 87 to the Wyoming state line. It may take us a few hours to get there."

"Wyoming?" Kat questioned him.

"Indian country," Bill said, tapping the list. "Chico wrote 'Indian country' in capitals and circled it with stars."

"Indian country?" Kat asked again.

"It must be a safe place," Leo said. "He wants us to go there. I trust him."

"We won't stop until we get there," Bill said. "We should have enough gas," Bill said, finally looking up from the list. "It's time to make a donation."

"We'll still need supplies," Kat said, "at least for the night."

"We'll trade a donation for supplies," he said.

"Won't that be risky?" she asked.

"Not if we can trust Chico," Bill said confidently as he pointed to Leo, who slammed the gas pedal and peeled out of the parking lot.

xxx

Day 13. Tuesday, May 9. 7:58 PM

The day was fading when they crossed into Wyoming about three hours after leaving the Red Feather Lakes area. After a two-hour drive to the northwest, Leo pulled onto what looked like the main road that led into a small Indian village. It was nearly eight o'clock. Kat had slept the entire time, her body curled in a ball in the back seat under the blue tarp. Although exhausted, Bill was too stressed to sleep. He anxiously watched the road for any sign of the FBI or local law enforcement patrols. His head pounded. His stomach burned. He was a disaster. Despite a lack of sleep and food, Leo motored on, remaining laser-focused for the whole drive. He drove at a steady pace and maintained a calming presence behind the wheel. He only stopped the car on a secluded scenic overlook

248

not far from Green Mountain to refuel with the gasoline Chico had given them.

The dusty road they drove into the village was filled with crater-sized potholes. Kat finally sat up in the back seat, rubbing her sleepy eyes. Simple, and sometimes dilapidated, one-story houses lined each side of the dark road, the windows and doors covered in a thick layer of red dirt. Most of the streetlamps along the road were burned out. The houses appeared empty as they neared the center of town. The place felt eerie and forgotten, like a ghost town in an old western.

Leo followed the road until it ended at a brightly lighted two-story community center. An elderly tribesman stood at the entrance seeming to collect an admission fee for what appeared to be a youth basketball game taking place inside. A sign was taped on the wall next to him with "$1.00" painted on it. A cheering and whistling crowd and the repetitive sound of a bouncing ball could be heard from inside.

"I don't like this, Bill," Kat said from the back seat.

"Get the money," he said as Kat dug into the garment bag.

"How much?" she asked.

"Better give me a lot. I don't want to have much left when we get caught."

"*When* we get caught?" She pulled out thirty-thousand dollars and reached it to him. "Don't you mean, *if* we get caught?"

"We ain't gettin' caught," Leo said confidently.

"I need more than that," Bill said to Kat.

"More?"

"Give me sixty-thousand dollars."

"I don't like this," she said again, handing him the rest of the money.

"I trust Chico," Leo said, getting out of the car. "These folks will help us."

The elderly man at the entrance leaned forward from the wall as Bill slowly limped towards him, still smelling of gasoline. The man appeared to be over eighty, with long white hair and a suntanned and deeply wrinkled face. His pressed white shirt was immaculate. It was buttoned to the top and held tight to his neck by an elegant turquoise and silver bolo tie. He studied Bill suspiciously. Kat and Leo got out of the car and watched. A buzzer sounded from inside as one final loud cheer rang out. The basketball game had ended.

"We need your help."

"How can I help?"

"We're lost and without supplies," Bill said as a few people started to file out of the building. The elderly man nodded to each of them. "I would like to make a donation to your community."

"Donation?"

"To your school. Your homes. The town. This community center," Bill said. "For your help."

"My help?" the old man again asked.

Bill held up the thick stacks of hundred-dollar bills. More people exited the building, including several young kids in tattered basketball uniforms. Some watched the exchange between Bill and the elderly man.

"Me and my friends," Bill said, "want to donate this sixty-thousand dollars to you. In return, we were wondering if you had any old blankets to spare, some gas for our car, some simple food to get us through a couple nights." The old man didn't respond. "Please, sir."

"We can help," the elderly man finally answered, taking the money. "Return to your car. I will have these kids gather the items you seek."

Bill motioned to Kat and Leo. They both got back into the car, and Bill joined them.

"I don't like this, Bill. I don't like it at all," Kat said. "Start the car in case we need to rush out of here."

"Don't, Leo," Bill said. "He'll help us. Don't worry."

They waited for over twenty minutes. A small crowd of the locals lingered in front of the darkened community center. They stared at the Nova.

"Let's go, Bill," Kat said, glancing back to the road they drove in on. "We made the donation. Let's get out of here. What if they called the cops? By the looks of things around here, they certainly could use the reward money as well."

Before Bill could answer, the elderly man appeared with a phone to his ear. He slowly walked towards the car.

"Come on, Bill!" Kat insisted. "Let's get out of here!"

Bill ignored her as the old man stepped towards the passenger window. Bill rolled it down. The elderly man leaned in.

"Open your trunk," he said.

Leo hopped out to open it, and Bill noticed a parade of young kids in their basketball uniforms coming toward them from a side street. Each carried a cardboard box or a five-gallon can of gas. The elderly man directed them to the trunk. Bill and Kat got out, joined Leo at the trunk.

Leo took the gas cans and filled the tank of the Nova until it overflowed down its side. He wasn't paying attention as he watched the others load a bundle of firewood and boxes that contained old wool blankets, loaves of homemade bread, jars of honey, several small plastic bags of elk and buffalo jerky, and three bottles of homemade dandelion wine. Some of the other kids and their families snapped photos with their phones. Bill hugged the elderly man and motioned for Kat and Leo to get back into the car.

"We need a safe place to camp," Bill said to the old man. He pointed to a grouping of hills to the west.

"You will be safe up there, forty-five miles away. Build a fire. It will keep the coyotes and bears away."

xxx

It was a crisp, clear spring night. The mountain air hovered just above freezing. Leo pushed the Nova up the steep hills of Medicine Bow-Routt National Forest, chasing after a crescent moon that slowly rose over the valley in the distance. The group no longer felt tired. As they searched for a comfortable spot to camp, they were excited about the coming days. A new hope filled the car. Even though Stack and his posse were still in the backs of their minds, they seemed far away that night.

At a plateau some 9,000 feet above sea level, Leo pulled the Nova into a clearing and parked. Bill got out of the car first. The thin mountain air was still. The surroundings were eerily but pleasantly quiet. The repetitive coo of an owl hidden in the trees interrupted the stillness. The night sky was bright with stars. Bill, Kat, and Leo silently stared, as if hypnotized by the spectacular view before them.

Bill couldn't help but think of his last night at home in his backyard, staring into the same sky and feeling small and so far away. But after nearly two weeks and fifteen-hundred miles, he stood tall on the mountain. He was in the stars. He was one of them. They shined as if they belonged to him. He was no longer insignificant or forgettable but as big as the sky. He was no longer tethered to a world that had robbed him of his soul. Instead, he had nearly crossed the whole country as a wanted man, still ahead of the FBI's most infamous agent. If these were his last days of freedom, he no longer cared. He had done it. He was on top of the world.

Leo dashed off and climbed to the top of a nearby rock formation that overlooked the sleepy valley below.

"We're gonna live forever!" he screamed into the darkness, believing every word, his voice echoing off the Wyoming hills. And for one night, Bill and Kat believed him.

xxx

They'd quickly set up camp on a high bluff not far from where they parked. The site overlooked a grassy plain split in half by a quick-moving stream. They had a good vantage point to keep watch for uninvited visitors who approached, whether by car or on four legs. A small campfire cracked and popped. They sat closely up against it, trying to keep warm. Kat had draped one of the wool Indian blankets over her. All three were tipsy. They passed the last bottle of the overly sweet and boozy homemade wine and stared above, still awed by the night sky blurred with stars. Their bellies, shrunk from hunger, were full from thick slices of honey bread and pieces of peppery elk jerky. The distant howl of a coyote could be heard from across the valley.

"This may be the best night of my life," Leo said with a grin after swigging from the bottle of wine, his face glowing from the dancing orange flames. "And I ain't shittin' you, dude. I'm serious."

"To think we've come all this way," Bill observed, glancing to the valley below. "And we ended up here. A place so incredibly breathtaking, far from everything I grew to despise."

"Look out there," Leo said, motioning to the quiet plain below. "It sure feels like we're in the middle of a cowboy movie, don't it? You know, the scene where the cowboys are gathered 'round the fire after a long day of ridin' horses and herdin' cattle."

"It certainly does," Bill answered. "It certainly does. But it also feels like the scene right before the cowboys are attacked by a group of crazed Indians that come racing out of the hills."

"You two got quite the imaginations," Kat said.

"I always rooted for the Indians," Leo said. "I'm from Oklahoma. Indian country."

"We're all from Indian country, Leo," Bill said, pointing to himself. "Pennsylvania." He then pointed to Kat and said, "Illinois."

"Why'd the cowboys in the movies always have to win?" Leo asked.

"Because all the directors and most of the audiences were white."

"And that's a shame," Leo said.

"I always wanted me a cowboy," Kat said with a grin, staring into the fire. "He wouldn't have to be bright or even pretty. I'd want him to be tall and fit. Get things done. Be good with his hands. I'd want him to work hard and come home to me sweaty and dusty. After dinner, I'd bathe him and massage his sore muscles."

"I've been known to work pretty hard and get awful dirty." Leo winked at Kat. "And Lord knows that I'm neither bright nor pretty."

"You're smarter than you think, Leo," Kat said. "And even a little cute, especially with that new haircut."

"Come on."

"She's right, Leo," Bill said. "We probably wouldn't be here if it wasn't for you."

"I'd want my cowboy to be honest and faithful, loving and humble," she went on. "And he wouldn't even have to say much."

"Sorry to break it to you, Kat," Bill added, "but that man doesn't exist."

"You know who ain't that?" Leo asked. "Ken Mercury."

"Believe me," Kat said, "I know that better than anyone."

"You're right, Bill," Leo said, peering out over the valley below them. "It's so beautiful here. Unspoiled. One of the few places I bet not much has changed from the cowboy days."

"Let's stay another night," Kat said enthusiastically, taking the homemade wine from Leo. "We could use the rest. And we have plenty of supplies. We could go on a hike and bathe in the stream. We could pick berr—"

"We can't," Bill interrupted. "We need to get out of these mountains and start heading west again. It'd be too easy to get trapped here. There aren't many ways in and out. We need to get back on the open highway."

"Come on, Bill," she pleaded, taking a drink from the wine bottle. "One more night."

"The people from the Indian village know we're up here."

"They won't say anything," Leo said.

"We can't take that risk," Bill said, reaching for the bottle. "We're packing up at daybreak."

"When we get to the coast, can we all live together?" Leo said. "Maybe buy a big house that overlooks the ocean."

"I'd be into that," Kat said.

"I didn't have much family growin' up," Leo said. "You guys feel like family."

"Aw, Leo, you're the brother I never had," Kat said. "And Bill, you're the father I wished I had."

"I don't think that's up to us," Bill said. He finished what was left of the wine. "We're wanted by the FBI. They'll be the ones who decide our fate."

"They're never goin' catch us, Bill," Leo said. "We're too clever and slippery for 'em."

"Maybe not, but they'll never stop searching. And because of that, we'll never be totally free. We'll always be looking over our shoulders."

xxx

In the now dust-covered Lincoln Navigator, Stack and Agent Robinson cruised the early morning roads high in the Colorado mountains north of the Red Feather Lakes area. Stack was in constant radio contact with his team, which was spread out in the high plains and small mountain towns. Agent Robinson suddenly jolted forward in his seat as he studied his phone.

"Check this out, Boss," he said, extending the phone towards Stack who glanced back and forth from it to the road. "Isn't that Moreland and the others? Looks like his two friends cut their hair."

"Where is that?" Stack asked.

"Wyoming. Seems to be a small town, maybe an Indian community. It's near the Medicine Bow National Forest."

"Where did you find that?"

"I've been using search terms, like 'missing banker', 'runaway banker' on social media sites. This picture is from a post on some kid's Facebook page."

"When was it taken?"

"It was posted last night."

"Get me the location. Notify the others. We do not have a

minute to waste. Good work, Robinson."

xxx

Day 14. Wednesday, May 10. 4:45 PM

Most of the day was spent on small, unmarked mountain roads and switchbacks in the high hills near Medicine Bow-Routt National Forest in southeastern Wyoming. Bill drove the Nova for miles without getting too far. Kat sat in the passenger seat, and Leo slept in the back. He'd stayed awake all night, keeping guard over the campsite. Bill wouldn't admit that they were lost, but they were. Because it was dark when they entered the mountains the night before, they were unable to make note of any prominent landmarks or the names of the roads they crossed. The scenery along the roads didn't change as the car wound back and forth down the mountainside; several times it appeared as if they backtracked past the same stretch of trees multiple times. Fortunately, the roads were mostly quiet except for an occasional sightseeing family or lost RV camper. There was no evidence that Agent Stack and his team were in the area.

"We're not getting anywhere, Bill," Kat groaned. "You're just going around in circles."

"There has to be another road out of here."

"We can't do this. We're wasting time and gas. We need to get off this mountain."

"What do you want me to do, Kat?" Bill snapped. "Running from the FBI is all new to me. What else am I supposed to do?"

"You need to find a main road and get us the hell out of here. It feels like we're trapped up here."

"There's got to be a way out," Bill mumbled to himself as they approached an access road.

"What's that sign say?" Kat asked about a large sign that was erected at the access road entrance.

Bill read the sign aloud: "Evergreen Ranger Station number three access road."

"Let's take it. Maybe there's a map of the area that could help us get of here."

"Are you crazy? Every park ranger in the state has been alerted about us."

"Take the road, Bill."

"No."

"Yes."

"*Absolutely not.*"

"I can't take this. Stop the car."

"What?"

"*Stop the car,*" Kat ordered, reaching for the door handle.

Bill slammed the brakes, waking Leo in the back and causing Kat's body to lunge forward and strike the dashboard.

"I'm going home," Kat announced, opening the door.

"You can't go home."

"You promised I could go home whenever I was ready. I'm ready."

"What are you talkin' about?" Bill asked.

"Don't go yet, Kat," Leo said from the back seat. "We haven't seen the ocean."

Kat stared at Leo a moment then glanced to Bill, before getting out of the car. She briskly walked the access road that led to the ranger's station. Bill hit the gas and squealed away in the opposite direction, recklessly driving for a couple miles.

"You can't leave her behind, Bill."

"*I know that, Leo,*" Bill snapped, before stomping on the brake pedal and wildly turning the Nova around on the narrow mountain road.

Within minutes, Bill had returned to the entrance of the access road where Kat had gotten out. He turned down the road and soon spotted Kat marching toward the ranger station. Instead of stopping to pick her up, he zoomed by and drove to the station, a small log cabin with an office to greet visitors. An eighty-foot wooden observation tower stood next to it. A sign in the window of the cabin indicated the station was closed.

Bill parked in front of a large bulletin board near the entrance of the station, leaving the Nova running. As Kat had predicted, several different maps were available in boxes that hung from the bulletin board. As Bill grabbed each of the maps, he noticed a large 'FBI Wanted' sign on yellow paper with bright red letters that displayed a picture of Bill, Kat, and Leo. A picture of the model of the Nova in which they were driving also was included on the sign. Bill ripped the poster from the bulletin board. He hurried back to the car, turned it around and drove towards Kat. He stopped next to her.

"Get in the car."

"I'm going home," she said, walking by the car and not looking at him.

"Come on, Kat. Get in the car."

"It's over, Bill!"

"You were right," he said, holding up the maps as she stopped. "They had maps, but. . ."

"But, what?"

"Our pictures are everywhere." He showed her the 'Wanted' sign. "We'll only get out of here if we stick together. Please get in."

xxx

Bill turned the steering wheel over to Leo and moved to the passenger seat. From the back seat, Kat navigated by using the maps to get them off the mountain. Finally, Leo pulled the Nova onto Wyoming Highway 130 not far from Saratoga. As they headed west, he checked the fuel gauge. The car was nearly out of gas as they approached an isolated but busy truck stop.

"We better stop here," Leo said, pointing to the bustling complex. "We're drivin' on fumes."

"Looks busy. We can't risk it," Bill said with concern in his voice. He pointed to a row of parked semi-trucks, their drivers taking a break from the road. "Look at them all. We're too easy to spot in this old yellow car. You know they're on the lookout

258

for us, wanting that big payday. No, we can't stop here."

"If we need gas," Kat spoke up, "we need gas. We have to stop."

"Let's find a quieter place."

"This might be the only place for miles!"

"I say we continue on," Bill said, shook his head. "We look for something else."

"I say we don't," Kat snapped.

"Am I stoppin' or not?" Leo asked. "We really do need to fill up."

"No, Leo," Bill said. "Keep going."

"Stop, Leo. We need gas."

"No, Kat. Let's see what's up the road."

"There may be nothing up the road. We're stopping here. Running out of gas would be the worst thing that could happen right now. And we've already gone through that once before. Remember Oklahoma?"

"It's too risky."

"We wouldn't be out of gas if we didn't get lost this morning."

"Sorry, Bill," Leo said. "I agree with Kat. We need to keep the tank full."

Against Bill's wishes, Leo pulled the Chevy Nova into the truck stop and found an available gas pump in a far corner of the complex, out of sight from the main road. Bill hunched low in the passenger seat so as not to be seen. Kat provided lookout from the back seat as Leo pumped the gas. But unlike previous stops, that one felt different. It felt like all the eyes at the truck stop were on them and the Nova. Leo continually checked over each shoulder, spying the many folks entering and exiting the convenience store and restaurant. Kat studied the truckers sitting in the cabs of their semis, sipping coffee as they chatted on their phones. It appeared as if they all were watching the Nova.

The car was half-filled with gas when Kat suddenly popped up in her seat and called out to Leo through the open back seat window.

"Leo! Get in the car!"

"It's not full yet."

"Get in the car!" she yelled. "Let's go!"

"What is it?" Bill asked, sitting up. He glanced out the front and back windows and surveyed the parking lot.

"Come on, Leo!" Kat again ordered. "Let's go!"

"I have to pay," he said, hanging the gas nozzle and hose back on to the pump. "And I want to get some food."

"There isn't time. We need to go. *Now*."

"We have to pay," Bill exclaimed. "There's cameras all over this place."

"The FBI's here!" Kat hollered with more urgency, pointing to two unmarked, black Lincoln Navigators at the other side of the truck stop complex. "And plenty of state troopers are headed this way. Look!"

Several Wyoming state police cars sped towards the truck stop. Leo hopped into the driver's seat of the Nova and peeled out of the lot onto an adjoining side road with his car door flapping open and dirt kicking up behind them. He stomped the gas pedal to the floor and slammed the door shut. Bill and Kat repeatedly checked behind them, searching for Stack and his team as Leo pushed the Nova as fast as it could go. Leo glanced first to Bill, then to Kat, and smiled.

"I think we got out of there without 'em seein' us," Leo boasted. "And if they did see us, we got a good head start on 'em. We should be fine."

"Look." Kat hollered as she stared out the back window. "*Look*."

The two Navigators appeared over the crest of a hill behind them, their lights flashing and sirens blaring, and quickly gained on the Nova.

"*Shit*." Bill saw the group of state troopers join the Navigators. "Come *on*, Leo."

"I'm tryin', dammit! I'm pushin' her as hard I can. They got a whole lot more under the hood than we do!"

"Lose them," Bill ordered.

"It ain't so easy with so many. If it was only one of 'em, *maybe*."

"What are we going to do?" Kat asked.

"Nothing we can do but try to outrun 'em."

With the gas pedal still pressed to the floor, Leo raced the FBI and Wyoming state police for another mile, but they slowly closed the distance. Finally, the lead Navigator pulled alongside the Nova.

"*Pull over!*" Agent Stack ordered from a loudspeaker. "*In the name of the law, pull over! There is no escape!*"

Leo punched the brakes as he made a wild right hand turn on an unexpectedly busy side road. The Nova swung wide into traffic on the road, which cut through the center of a small mountain village. Leo aggressively wrestled the stiff steering wheel to the right to avoid a head-on collision. The Nova roughly bounced off a sidewalk, and Leo hit the gas as they zoomed away, briefly losing the Lincoln that Stack was driving.

"I don't see them." Kat spoke from the back seat as Leo pushed the Nova to over a hundred miles per hour on a straightaway.

"Did we lose 'em?" Leo asked.

"I think you did, Leo." Kat watched from the back seat.

Something in the corner of Leo's eye caught his attention, causing him to slow the car. They passed a large sign that advertised the largest flea market in the state of Wyoming.

"What are you doing?" Bill asked, glancing to the roadway behind the Nova.

"Holy moly," Leo mumbled.

"What is it?"

"We jus' passed a flea market. *Holy Christ*. It's a big one, the biggest I've ever seen!"

"What?"

"You know how much I love yard sales."

"Jesus, Leo, let's get out of here"

"They may have some great stuff, you know. I've never been

this far west before."

"*Shit*," Kat hissed as the two Lincolns appeared. "They're back."

As Leo drove towards a bridge that spanned a section of the North Platte River, one of the Navigators rumbled by, speeding past the Nova.

"Oh, God!" Bill cried out, checking the sideview mirror as the other in pursuit gained on them. "*Turn around.*"

The Lincoln that had passed them squealed sideways to block one end of the bridge. Easing up on the gas pedal, Leo checked the rearview mirror to search for an escape. One of the state police cars behind them slid sideways and blocked the other side of the bridge.

"*Shit.*" Leo gasped, slamming the brakes. The car skidded to a stop. "They got us pickled."

FBI agents, including Stack, poured out of the Lincoln that blocked the bridge in front of the Nova. Bill and Kat looked out the back window.

"Out!" Bill ordered, reaching for the garment bag of money. "Out! Out! Let's go!"

They hurried out of the Nova, scrambled to the railing of the bridge and glanced down. Nearly forty feet below, the North Platte River rushed underneath them.

"*Stop or we'll shoot!*" Stack warned as he and his agents approached in a sprint.

Bill and Kat each immediately slipped one of their legs over the railing.

"I can't swim," Leo said, staring to the whitecapped river.

A gunshot rang out. Stack had fired his gun in the air as a warning.

"Come on, Leo!" Bill hollered as Kat lifted her other leg over the railing and jumped feet first, plunging to the river below.

Stack fired another shot. It was aimed over Leo's and Bill's heads in an obvious attempt to scare them. Without hesitating, Leo flipped both legs over the railing and tumbled awkwardly in the air. His body continuously flipped like a cartwheel, before violently belly-smacking the river below. As Stack, his agents, and the police got closer, Bill whipped his other leg over the railing. Stack again fired his gun. The bullet ricocheted off the railing a few feet from Bill.

As Bill released his grip, the strap of the garment bag got caught on the bridge's railing. The bag violently ripped apart and hundreds of thousands of dollars floated into the wind. Bill's flailing body plummeted toward the river below. His last cell phone also tumbled with him into the water. Stack and his team reached the railing and peppered the rushing river with gunshots. The swift current pulled them, and Bill, Kat, and Leo bobbed quickly away from the bridge like apples in a bucket of water. A trail of floating hundred-dollar bills followed them.

Stack and his team moved across the road to the other side of the bridge and continued to fire their guns into the river. With binoculars, Agent Stack scanned the river for the three fugitives as they were swept away. He lowered the binoculars and tuned to one of the local detectives working the investigation.

"Detective, get some dogs and your teams down there. I want all three. I do not care if they're alive or you bring me their dead fuckin' bodies. And send some sheriffs further ahead downstream. Go! Now! Who knows where that river will push them?"

"Yessir, Boss!"

"And you need to get on the river! Collect as much money as you can!"

Bill, Kat, and Leo separated in the fast-flowing river as they struggled to keep their heads above water. Leo was pushed the furthest ahead, occasionally disappearing under the water's surface for short periods of time. Bill battled the strong current when he noticed Kat up ahead of him swimming to the bank of the river about a mile and half from the bridge. After swallowing several large gulps of the dirty river water, he finally reached the river's edge and crawled like a wounded snake across the muddy bank to a grassy area next to Kat. She gasped for breath and tried to wring the water from the dripping clothes still on her body. Bill sat in the mud for several minutes, coughing and gasping for air.

xxx

The air temperature was quickly falling as the sun set. Bill and Kat scoured the riverbank, searching for Leo. They had walked well over two miles. There was no sign of him.

"Leo!" they called over and over. "Leo! Leo! Leo!"

Bill suddenly stopped and scanned the river in each direction in the diminishing light.

"Leo! Leo!" Kat continued to call.

"We need to get off the river, Kat."

"We can't leave without him."

"We're wet. We're cold. It'll be completely dark soon. The FBI has to be near."

"I'm not leaving without Leo."

"We need to move on."

"I'm staying here. I'm not leaving him behind."

"Come on, Kat. He made it out. I know it. But he's probably miles downstream. You felt how fast that river was moving. We'll never reach him at this pace. We need to find shelter or some form of transportation. We need water and food. We've hardly eaten in days."

"We can't leave without him."

"We're sitting ducks out here. Come on, there's a path. Let's follow it."

Bill turned for the path that trekked south and led directly through the heavily wooded forest along the river. Kat didn't follow. She still called out for Leo. Bill stopped and turned to her.

"Come on, Kat! Please!"

She took one last desperate look at the river before reluctantly chasing after Bill. After about twenty minutes, Bill suddenly stopped.

"Do you smell that?" he asked Kat, who raised her head

towards the sky and deeply inhaled.

xxx

Day 14. Wednesday, May 10. 8:12 PM

White wood smoke billowed from a crumbling chimney as Bill and Kat approached the secluded house. It wasn't much more than a shack. In the middle of the woods, there were no neighbors or other structures for miles. Bill noted a 1980s Ford pickup in the gravel driveway as they cautiously crept to the front door. Bill pounded on the door. An old man, tall with thin arms and legs but a round belly, answered. His head was covered with wisps of gray hair. Several of his front teeth were either missing or rotten. He seemed to be alone.

"I hate to bother you," Bill said, "but—"

"Then don't!" the old man snapped and slammed the door.

"A nasty disposition," Bill said to Kat. He pounded on the door and called out. "Sir? *Sir!*"

The door slowly opened, but only a crack.

"Can we please use your phone?" Bill politely asked. "We had a little accident. We desperately need help."

The old man studied Bill then Kat a moment before responding.

"I ain't got no fuckin' phone!" He started to pull the door closed.

Bill grabbed the doorknob, not allowing the man to close the door and said, "We need to get to town."

"Like I jus' told the last one, take the goddamn bus if you need a ride!" he growled, yanking the door from Bill's hand and slamming it.

Kat turned to Bill. "Last one?"

"Leo must've been here."

"Look," Kat said, pointing to drops of blood that led from the front door around behind the house.

"Follow it," Bill ordered. "I'm going in."

"What?"

"I'm going in."

"What are you talking about?"

"We're getting a ride to town. Even if I have to steal that truck."

"I don't think that's a good. . ."

"Follow the blood trail. Look for Leo. The FBI will be all over us any minute."

Kat didn't move. He checked the front door. It was locked.

"Bill, you can't just barge in?"

"*Check for Leo.*"

The old man yelled from inside. "Hey! Get the fuck out of here!"

"Bill, *stop.*" Kat insisted.

"Get Leo."

Kat disappeared around the house. Bill took a few steps back and threw his whole body against the door, splintering it. The old man turned around from a wood stove where he had been stabbing the fire with an iron poker.

"Get the hell out of here!" he yelled. He left the sharp end of the poker in the fire as he grabbed for a gun on a nearby coffee table. "You're payin' for that door, asshole!"

xxx

Following the drops of blood, Kat walked around to the back of the shack. At a crudely built woodshed the trail of blood stopped. She pulled open the door. Leo was huddled in a corner partially covered by a dusty blanket. He was soaking wet and shivering on the sawdust floor, clutching his bleeding right shoulder.

"Leo! *Oh my god.* We searched up and down the river for you."

"I've been shot."

Kat joined him on the floor, tightly embracing him.

"We need to get you to a doctor," she said, wiping at the

266

dirty, clotted wound.

"Where's Bill?"

xxx

Seeing the gun, Bill vaulted through the air, knocking the old man off his feet. The two landed awkwardly on the floor. The old man fumbled the gun once he hit the ground. The two of them wrestled, rolling around on the stained shag carpet for several minutes. The whole time they scanned for the gun on the floor as they scratched and gouged at each other's nose, mouth, and eyes. Bill began to punch at the old man's back and sides as the old man kicked at Bill.

Finally spotting the gun, Bill reached for it. The old man noticed and chomped down on Bill's shoulder with the few rotted teeth he had left. Bill instantly raised his body up and screamed. With his jaw still locked on Bill, the old man violently shook his head from side to side like a rabid dog trying to rip meat off a bone. Bill instantly loosened his grip, and the old man crawled across the carpet and snatched the gun. Bill slid away from the old man towards the wood stove. Disheveled and panting, he grinned and pointed the gun at Bill's face.

"No one breaks into my fuckin' home and lives to talk about it," the old man snarled, "Say your prayers, boy!"

The old man was about to pull the trigger when Bill yanked the iron poker from the fire. The sharp pointed end glowed orange. Bill stabbed the old man between the legs, searing the skin of his groin. The gun went off, deafening them both as the old man fell to the ground with an ear-piercing, blood-curdling howl. The old man's skin was sizzling as a puff of white smoke lifted from between his legs. The noxious smell of burning hair and flesh filled the room.

Kat was helping Leo walk to the front of the shack when the gunshot exploded from inside the man's shack.

"*Shit*," she screamed and shouted, "Bill?"

267

She eased Leo to a spot in the driveway and dashed into the shack. Bill stood over the old man with the gun pointed at his head. The old man writhed on the floor, gasping for air.

"*The keys!*" Bill yelled. "For the truck! Where are they?"

"Bill! Thank God!" Kat exclaimed. "You're alive!"

"Oh, *Jesus*! Please help me!" the old man cried. "Please!

"*The keys!*" Bill screamed louder.

"Help me! Help me! You can't leave me like this!"

"Bill, put the gun down."

Bill ignored Kat and pressed the barrel of the gun into the old man's cheek. His face turned white, sweat pouring from his head.

"*The keys, motherfucker!*"

"Above the counter," the old man whispered. "In the kitchen. On a nail. Please don't leave me like this."

Bill quickly backed into the kitchen, still aiming the gun at the old man. He found the keys and tossed them to Kat. He also grabbed a cell phone from the kitchen counter, stuffing it in his pocket.

"I thought you said you didn't have a phone!"

"Leo's been shot," Kat informed Bill. "We need to get him to a hospital."

"Get him in the truck and start it up."

"Come on, Bill! Let's go!"

"Not yet. I have unfinished business here." He stared at the old man, who whimpered on the floor.

"Bill, *don't*. It's not worth it! You'd regret it for as long as you live."

"*Get Leo. Get in the truck.*"

"I'm not leaving without you."

"Go! Get out of here. *Go.*"

She looked angry, disappointed. "I should leave your ass here," she said, but she slipped through the shattered front door.

Bill stepped closer to the old man. He still pointed the gun at him. The gun violently shook in his hand. He clenched his teeth and wiped at the sweat that beaded on his forehead.

"You goin' shoot me? A helpless man."

Bill wailed, "*Aaaaaahhhhh*!" and a single gunshot echoed through the valley.

Kat froze, then loaded Leo into the truck wrapped in the filthy blanket.

"Shit, Bill." She raced back to the shack. "You son of a bitch! You better not have!"

As Kat entered, Bill stood with the gun raised over his head and emptied the rest of the cylinder into the ceiling. The wounded old man who tried to cover himself from the shards of plaster and fiberglass that rained on him.

"Come on, Bill. Leo needs help."

Bill stared at the man for several moments. Smoke poured from the end of gun's barrel.

"Please help me," the old man pleaded. "Please. . . You can't leave me like this. How will I get to a hospital?"

"Like you told us," Bill said coldly. "Take the bus."

Bill grabbed a box of bullets and a full bottle of Irish whiskey before leaving.

"*Wait*!" The old man hollered, unable to lift himself off the floor. "Wait! Don't leave! Please! I need help! *I'm goin' die*!"

Chapter 8
Oregon

Day 14. Wednesday, May 10. 11:51 PM

In the old man's truck, Bill raced through the evening on I-80 through western Wyoming, rubbing at the sore spot on his shoulder where the old man had bitten him. He didn't stop until he reached Utah near Echo Park. Kat sat beside him, staring ahead in a daze at the dark road rushing under them. In obvious pain, Leo tossed and turned, sleeping lightly, his head against the passenger window and a torn towel across the gunshot wound on his shoulder. The truck was out of gas, and Bill needed to make a phone call.

"Is there a charge left on that phone?" Bill asked Kat, motioning to the stolen phone on the dashboard.

She looked at it. "It's at about twenty percent."

"I want to make a call," he said. He pulled the truck off one of the first exits in Utah. "And we need gas."

"Who you calling?"

"I'm worried about the old man. Is there an insurance card or truck registration in the glovebox? I don't want him dying alone."

Kat opened the glove compartment and pulled out a registration card. "His name is Arthur Popp," she read from the card as Bill parked at a gas pump in a large truck stop complex.

"You better pump the gas. This place looks busy," Bill said. "I'll call 9-1-1 and get an ambulance to the old man's cabin."

"Won't that be risky?"

"I'm guessing it'll take them some time before they connect us to this truck. We'll be at the coast by then. No one knows about it but the old man, and he doesn't know who we are."

"That's if the old dude is still alive to tell 'em what happened."

"We'll ditch the truck once we get to the ocean. I'll toss this phone in the trash here after the call."

"How's Leo?" she asked, after getting out of the truck. She glanced back inside.

"Still sleeping," Bill said. "Get yourself something to eat when you pay for the gas."

"I'm okay. I'm not hungry. You need anything?"

"Nah, I'm good."

"What about Leo?"

"Better get some water. He'll need it. And some alcohol wipes and bandages if they have them."

"We have to get him a doctor, Bill. You know that."

"Just make it fast," he said. "We need to get back on the road."

"Are we staying on the interstate or finding a smaller route?" she asked through the truck's window as she pumped the gas.

"We're staying on the interstate. We don't have time to waste. We'll be all right if we don't get pulled over."

"I'm really worried about Leo."

"Hurry, go pay for the gas and get the other things. Let's go."

xxx

Day 15. Thursday, May 11. 6:15 AM

It was near daybreak. A frustrated Agent Stack paced the floor of a small hotel room near Saratoga, Wyoming. He was alone in the makeshift office he had set up in the hotel. He'd dispatched teams of FBI agents and local law enforcement to canvass sections of the river below the bridge where Bill, Kat, and Leo had escaped. He was shocked that at least one of them hadn't been apprehended. He also wondered if they had drowned in the rapidly moving river. As he continued to pace,

271

Agent Robinson entered.

"Any sign of them?" Stack asked.

"We searched the river and surrounding woods all night," he said. "Each side, maybe six, seven miles from the bridge. No sign of any of 'em."

"Nothing?"

"Nothing at all."

"Did you recover any of the money?"

"Maybe a few thousand. Not much," he said. "I guess word leaked out about Moreland's escape. We ran into ten or so people along the river who also were looking for money. They slowed us down."

"Slowed you down?"

"Yeah, we had to check each of 'em to make sure they weren't Moreland and his friends or helping 'em in some way."

"Do you think they may have drowned?"

"Possible. I can't imagine all three drowning. If they did, we may not see their bodies for days. You saw how fast the current was. Who knows how far downstream they'd end up."

"Keep searching," an exasperated Stack said. "Get some roadblocks set up. Check everything coming in and out of this county. *Jesus Christ*. This should not be that hard."

xxx

Day 15. Thursday, May 11. 6:22 AM

Squinting into the grayness of the dreary morning, Bill pushed the rattling truck across the deserted Oregon highway near Weatherby. They'd been driving all night. At Echo Park, Utah, they had merged onto I-84 and drove northwest around the Great Salt Lake. They gradually ascended Weber Canyon, passing an unusual rock formation known as Devil's Slide.

They pressed on through the rest of Utah, driving through Ogden, Snowville, and Rattlesnake Pass, before crossing into Idaho. They couldn't see much of the changing landscape due

272

the dark overcast skies. They stopped once near Twin Falls for gas, some more water, and a few snacks. After the stop, they sprinted northwest through the remainder of Idaho to the state line, passing through the foothills of the Danskin Mountains and Boise before crossing into Oregon at Ontario along the Snake River. They were about six hours from Portland.

Bill had never seen a sky as black. Dense, churning clouds hung low over them. Visibility was poor. A storm was quickly sweeping in from the northwest. Kat sat beside him in the middle of the truck's cab, the gear shift between her long legs. Grimacing in constant pain, Leo leaned against the passenger door, resting his sweat-drenched head against the cool window. Kat pressed a blood-soaked towel against the oozing gunshot wound between his neck and shoulder.

"We need to get him to a hospital," Kat said.

"*No hospitals*," Leo barked through gritted teeth.

"*Bill*," Kat pleaded. "We need to stop."

"*No*," Leo groaned.

Still squinting through the nicked windshield into the dark morning, Bill didn't initially respond.

"He's lost a lot of blood. I think he has a fever."

Bill finally glanced to Leo, then looked Kat.

"Bill, you *have* to stop. Please."

"I can't see shit," Bill shouted at the windshield.

"I don't need a doctor," Leo moaned.

Bill leaned closer to the windshield and stared to the dark empty road before him.

"I don't know where the hell we are," he said.

"What does it matter?" Kat asked.

"Where are we, goddammit?"

"In Oregon, somewhere in the middle, I think," Kat said. "I haven't been paying attention."

Bill continued to stare at the road before him. An occasional flash of lighting in the distance illuminated the stormy sky.

"Bill, you have to stop."

"Let's wait until we get to the coast. That was the plan! We'll figure it out then."

"We can't wait," Kat exclaimed, reaching for the steering wheel. "This is serious. We have to stop."

"We need to keep moving!" he said, batting her hand away.

"Bill!" She slapped at his shoulder. "We need to find a hospital or doctor. Pull off the next exit. *Please!*"

"We can't. We'll get arrested."

"He needs medical help!"

Bill sighed and looked to Leo.

"How you doing, Buddy?"

"How close are we to the coast?" Leo asked.

"I don't know," Bill answered. "Six or seven hours, maybe more."

"I want to see the ocean," Leo said.

Bill looked to Kat. She glared back and shook her head.

xxx

Day 15. Thursday, May 11. 1:04 PM

With a loud explosion of thunder, the sky opened. A heavy downpour followed, quickly flooding the empty highway. For several miles, Bill white-knuckled the shaking steering wheel as the old pickup skated on worn tires over the slick roadway. Concerned, Kat sat up straight and pressed both hands against the dashboard to brace herself. They stared into the driving raindrops that smashed against the windshield. The compromised wiper blades couldn't keep pace with the deluge, making it difficult to see. A green highway sign on the side of the road flashed by them, indicating that Portland was twenty-five miles away. Bill frantically glanced to Leo who labored to breathe, restlessly thrashing back and forth. As the storm raged, Bill eased the truck off the interstate under an overpass and shut off the lights.

"You can't stop, Bill."

"I can't see a damn thing."

274

"We need to get to Portland."

"He wants to see the ocean."

"He needs a doctor. Look at him. He can barely breathe."

Bill glanced out the driver-side window. Thunder cracked followed by repetitive flashes of lightning.

"We aren't going anywhere 'til this storm passes."

"It might be too late by then!"

"He wants to see the ocean. Once we get there, I'll find a doctor. I promise."

Kat shook her head. Leo had finally drifted into sleep, his breath still labored. Bill and Kat didn't say a word for several minutes. They stared out the windshield. A heavy stream of rainwater poured off the overpass and dumped on the hood of the truck.

"I'm sorry, Bill," she said, breaking the silence. "I'm tired. I'm hungry. I need a shower. I'm just worried about Leo."

"I know. I'll take care of him."

"I've been wondering this whole trip," she said, changing the subject as they waited out the storm. "Why'd you really do it?"

"Huh?"

"Take the money."

He looked away and talked into the driver's side window: "I've been trying to figure that out myself."

She snuggled her body closer and rested her head on his chest. He winced in pain as she pressed against the sensitive area where he'd been bitten. He wrapped his right arm around her and pulled her closer. The pouring rain had lightened.

"I don't know," he continued. "I guess, maybe I just wanted to be loved."

"We all want to be loved, Bill. There's something more than that."

"And I wanted to be important."

"You weren't important before?"

"I've always felt invisible before this."

"And now. . ."

He interrupted her. "And now I have to hide to stay out of

prison because everyone knows who the hell I am. Ain't that a something? A real bitch."

Breaks in the clouds appeared in the sky. The rain had slowed. Bill checked the rearview mirror. The lightning had moved on. The thunder was but a muted rumble in the distance. Bill and Kat studied Leo. He seemed to be sleeping more peacefully. Kat then glanced to Bill.

"Do you need a nap?" she asked. "I can drive. You've been awake for days."

"Nah. I'm good for now. We need to get Leo to the coast and find some help."

He lifted his arm away from her and hit the headlights before putting the truck in gear. He pulled it back onto the unusually quiet highway. They were alone on the interstate as if they were the last people on earth.

xxx

Yawning and wiping at his eyes, Bill drove west over U.S. Route 26 before turning north onto U.S. 101. He guided the sputtering truck towards the town of Seaside on the Oregon coast. Kat was asleep beside him, her head resting on his shoulder. Sweating profusely, Leo struggled to keep his eyes open. Most of the color had gone from his skin. A partially hidden sun hung high in the sky over the Pacific before them. Bill glanced to Leo who smacked his chapped, dry lips.

"You want some water?"

"I need somethin' stronger."

Bill reached under the driver's seat and grabbed the bottle of Irish whiskey he took from the old man at the cabin.

"Me, my friends," Leo started to ramble, "we were too young and stupid to know that there was somethin' outside of Oklahoma. Norman and OU were our universe, man. It didn't fuckin' matter what the rest of the world did."

Bill reached the bottle to Leo.

"Here you go, buddy."

276

Leo took the bottle with shaking hands and struggled to take a drink, wiping at the whiskey that spilled down his chin.

"Our lives were Friday nights. Except in the fall. It was OU football on Saturdays. Bob Stoops was *God!*"

"Did you go to OU?"

"Sure, I did, but I never got too far. I was a freshman for three and half years. I could never pass calculus. All I remember was countin' the hours 'til Friday night, wastin' our lives at nowhere jobs, and dreamin' about one thing."

"What was that?"

"Pussy. Somethin' none of us ever got."

Bill smiled and grabbed the bottle, taking several large gulps of whiskey. He lowered the bottle and wiped his lips. He took another big drink, before resting it in his lap.

"We had cheap beer and shitty weed and AC/DC," Leo said, before starting to sing, "*For those about to rock, we salute you!*"

Bill grinned. Leo smiled, nodding his head and flashing the devil-horns sign with both hands.

"Shit, I saw them once in Oklahoma City," he continued. "Changed my life."

"You know, Leo, you had it made."

"Fuckin'-A, I did. Fuckin'-A."

Bill suddenly pulled the truck off the highway to an overlook with a spectacular view of the Pacific Ocean. Mist lingered over the rocky beach below as the waves pounded the surf. Leo struggled to keep his eyes open. Bill rolled down his window. The truck immediately filled with the fresh scent of salty sea air. Neither said a word for a few minutes. The caw of hungry seagulls soaring the coastline echoed in the cab of the truck. Bill nudged Kat awake with his elbow. She yawned and rubbed at her sleepy eyes. Bill put a finger to his lips to signal for her not to say anything. She peered into the light of the afternoon.

"Bill?" Leo said, his eyes fixated on the waves of the ocean roughly slapping at the jagged rocks below.

"Yeah, Leo."

"If you're ever at a yard sale and see a reasonably priced

robot. . ." He paused.

"Yeah."

Kat looked to Bill. She tried to hold back her tears.

"Can you pick him up for me? I'll gladly pay you later."

"Sure, Leo. Anything for you."

"I love yard sales. And robots."

"I know, Leo."

Leo struggled even harder to keep his eyes open. Both of his arms started to gently shake as he wiped at both eyes. Bill reached the whiskey bottle to him. Leo took a small drink, spilling some on the front of his shirt. As he squinted at the ocean, a small smile creased his colorless face.

"I'm glad my brother could be here with me to see this," he said, dropping the whiskey bottle is his lap. "I never thought humans could be so fragile."

His head slowly nodded forward.

"Leo!" Kat screamed, grabbing the front of his shirt and shaking him. "No! No!"

"Leo!" Bill yelled. "Leo!"

Leo didn't respond. His head limply slumped against the passenger side door.

xxx

Day 15. Thursday, May 11. 8:12 PM

Still idling, the truck was parked on a bridge off a densely wooded backroad not far from Fort Stevens State Park. The bridge spanned a waterfall twenty feet below that fed a quickly moving creek that dumped into Youngs Bay between the Oregon and Washington state lines. Kat stayed in the passenger seat and sobbed as Bill pulled a cover off the truck's bed, exposing Leo's body. It had been wrapped in a thick canvas tarp. Under the cloak of darkness, Bill opened the bed's tailgate and pulled the body towards him. He pounded on the back of the truck a few times to get Kat's attention. Wiping her eyes and

278

nose, she eventually joined Bill at the back of the truck and helped him lift Leo's limp body out of the bed. She kept her eyes closed the entire time. She refused to accept that Leo had passed away. Bill checked the roadway in each direction before they carried the body to the side of the bridge and hoisted it up onto the railing. They let it rest there a moment.

"Jesus, Kat, no one was supposed to die."

Bill placed both of his hands on the body and bowed his head. Kat turned away and lowered her head, covering her face in her hands. Tears poured from their eyes. Bill spoke quietly, choking through quotes from Jonathan Livingston Seagull he remembered from reading to his kids.

"We're free to go where we wish and to be what we are. We can be free. We can learn to fly," Bill said, lightly shoving the lifeless body. "You deserve better than this, my friend."

As Leo's body slid on the railing and plummeted to the rushing river below like a torpedo dropped from a bomber plane, Kat wailed.

"Fly on, buddy. Soar."

They both cried uncontrollably as Bill watched the body pierce the water without much of a splash and disappear a moment. Kat didn't watch. Wrapped tightly in the tarp, the body resurfaced several yards from where it had entered the river and was quickly whisked away with the strong current. Once the body was out of sight, Bill dropped to his knees. He started to gag, then violently vomited on the asphalt. Kat moved next to him as he tried to catch his breath in between heaves and rubbed his back. He turned to her. They hugged. Pulling away, she studied the defeated look on Bill's face, knowing their cross-country adventure was nearing its end.

xxx

Agent Stack was in the hotel room in Wyoming. The bed in the room was still made and appeared to have never been slept in. Half-full disposable cups of cold coffee littered the room.

Multiple mobile phones and piles of papers and folders were scattered everywhere. A pistol and holster hung from the top of a closet door. A fax machine hummed, spitting out page after page of possible leads or reported sightings of Bill and the others. Most led nowhere. The broadcast of a twenty-four-hour cable news network blared from the television. Stack stared blankly out the lone window of the room at the mostly empty parking lot. Never had he felt so helpless during an investigation. Agent Robinson knocked on the door, before entering the room.

"We may have something," he said as Stack continued to stare out the window. "An older gentleman from the area not far from the bridge is in a local hospital. He had been assaulted and his truck stolen sometime yesterday."

"Assaulted?"

"He was violently stabbed between the legs with a sharp iron rod."

"Is he okay?"

"He's going to make it, but they had to lope off his Mr. Goodbar, if you know what I mean."

"Jesus!"

"The doc said he'll be pissing through a straw into a plastic bag for the rest of his life."

"Can we ask him some questions? Is he conscious?"

"He was sitting in a wheelchair in the parking lot of the hospital, smoking cigarettes this morning. We have an agent talking with him right now. Tough old geezer, I hear."

"Do you think it was Moreland who assaulted him?"

"It's possible."

"It is Moreland. I know it. Get the specs on that truck as soon as possible and send the info to the local authorities and media."

"If it is them, they got at least a twelve-hour head start on us."

"I am leaving then as soon as I can. I will take the next flight to Portland."

"But they could be anywhere."

"Nah. They are going to the ocean. That is their plan. We will set up in Portland and fan out from there."

xxx

Day 16. Friday, May 12. 8:57 AM

Out of gas, low on money, and losing hope, Bill and Kat spent a restless night in the truck at a secluded campground. Neither said much the entire night. They finished the bottle of Irish whiskey, trying to soothe their waning spirits after the devasting loss of Leo. They had hoped to get some sleep to recharge themselves before traveling on. Instead, they both cried most of the night.

With the hood of a dirty sweatshirt pulled over his head, Bill filled the truck with gas at a quiet, nondescript convenience store off the Oregon shoreline near the Washington state line. Kat intently watched from inside the truck, worried that Bill would be recognized. After the truck was filled, he hopped back in. They both were starved, sleep deprived, and grubby. Kat stared at Bill. He couldn't look at her.

"That was our last thirty dollars," he said, talking into the windshield.

"What are we going to do?"

"I need to get you home."

"Let's go to Canada."

"It's over, Kat."

"Don't say that."

He pulled out the weathered six-thousand-dollar paycheck he had kept with him the entire trip and showed it to her.

"I need to get this cashed."

"You still have that?"

"I knew we may need it one day."

"No one will cash that!"

"Probably not. But I'm going to try."

281

"See that bank across the street?" he said, pointing.

"They'll call the cops once they realize who you are." Bill grabbed the handgun from under the driver's seat. "Don't, Bill. This is crazy!"

"If I'm not out in fifteen minutes, you're on your own."

"Bill!" she called out. He wouldn't look at her as he reached for the truck door. She grabbed his arm. "*Wait*. What if this is goodbye?" He still wouldn't look at her. "Bill, look at me." He finally turned, and she said, "We haven't said goodbye."

"Just be ready to go when I come out."

He opened the truck door. Looking concerned, Kat slid into the driver's seat, started the truck, and nervously watched as he hurried across the street to the bank. He hesitated at the bank's entrance and took a deep breath before pushing the door open. Scanning the inside a moment, he spotted a receptionist who sat at an information desk and quickly approached her. With both hands in his sweatshirt pocket, he looked desperate, pacing in front of her and continually checking over her shoulder.

"Can I help you?" the receptionist asked, studying him closely.

"I need to see the bank president."

"Is there a problem?"

He shook his head, constantly glancing around. Others in the bank stared, seeming to recognize him, as the manager approached.

"I really need to see the bank president."

"He's unavailable right now."

"Can you please get him? I need to talk with him immediately."

"He's in a meeting."

"Can I help you, sir?" the young bank manager asked.

"Can we talk in private?"

Hesitant at first, the manager motioned Bill to an office. Bill followed him in and took a seat at a desk as the manager closed the door.

"I know who you are," the manager said, sitting behind the desk.

He picked up the phone as Bill suddenly pulled out the gun and motioned for him to hang it up.

"I'm not here to cause anyone any harm. I just need you to cash this check," he said, setting the check on the desk. "It's good. It's a payroll check."

"I'll likely lose my job or even go to jail if I cash that check."

Bill placed the gun on the desk next to the check as the manager stared at him.

"Take the gun, call the cops, and I'll surrender quietly. You'll be a hero." Openly perspiring, the manager glanced to Bill who held the check out. "Or cash this check. It might keep an innocent girl out of jail."

The manager stared at Bill.

"How old are you?" Bill asked.

"Twenty-eight."

"Twenty-eight years old?" Bill said. "Hmm. After everything that has happened, maybe I'm here, in a bank of all places, for a reason. It feels I'm staring into a mirror twenty years ago. I see a young man, full of life, dreams."

Bill paused as the manager glared at him, then glanced to the gun.

"Can I give you some advice?" Bill said as the manager looked out the inside window of the office as several bank employees watched. "Don't let the young man die. Don't end up like me. I gave away a lifetime. Now I'm trying to bring that young man back. But he died, he died a long time ago."

The manager looked back at Bill, leaned forward, took the check, and studied it a moment.

"You can tell them I held a gun to your head."

"I'll be right back," the bank manager said, standing.

He stepped out of the office as Bill stuffed the gun into his pocket. He checked the clock on the wall and scanned the office. Within minutes, the manager returned. Bill stood as he entered. The manager reached an envelope out to Bill, who looked surprised.

"Now get the hell out of here."

Bill grabbed the envelope, stuck it in the front of his pants, and turned for the office door.

"My wife supports what you are doing."

Bill first looked puzzled, then amused, and paused before opening the door. Many of the bank employees waited outside. They applauded as Bill stepped out of the office. He looked back at the manager and nodded. The bank workers had formed a gauntlet that led to the exit. They loudly cheered and hollered for Bill as he dashed between the two rows of workers and disappeared outside.

xxx

Not having slept much in days, Bill pulled the truck into a parking area off Washington State Highway 103. The rest area overlooked a quiet, mostly deserted beach between Ocean Park and Long Beach. He and Kat opened the truck's windows. A cool but comfortable salty breeze blew off the gentle surf rolling across the sand and the black rocks in the mist below. Unable to keep her eyes open, Kat quickly dozed off. Bill, far from sleep, stared at her, knowing this likely would be the last day the two of them would spend together.

As she slept, he tried his best to be quiet. The Beethoven Symphony No. 7 softly played from a public broadcast station on the radio. The intermittent sound of the crashing waves provided a quiet background. As he studied Kat, visions of Rita filled his head. He was reminded of their first trip out of town together. Soon after meeting in college, they spontaneously left Pittsburgh for the coast of North Carolina for a long weekend. They drove through the night, arriving around daybreak near Kill Devil Hills.

With it being too early to check into a motel, they parked along the ocean to nap. Rita fell asleep first. Bill stared at her for nearly an hour. He was overcome with a sensation he'd never felt in his young life. His heart raced. He didn't feel like eating. He struggled to find the right words when they spoke, which never had been a problem before that weekend. He was more hopeful than ever. All the things he cared about no longer mattered at that moment and for many years after they got married. He was in love for the first time in his life. He promised Rita then that he'd never leave her side. But after all those years together, he'd finally broken that promise — sixteen days ago with the entire country following him.

Kat awoke and glanced at Bill. He stared at her with a troubling look she'd never seen from him before. His eyes were glazed over. He didn't blink or even move. His breathing was barely noticeable. He studied her in a deep trance as if he were trapped in another place from another time. Near delirious from a lack of sleep and little food, he imagined he saw Rita sitting beside him in the truck. It was as if thirty years had instantly dissolved before his eyes, and they were starting over.

"Bill?"

"Rita?"

"No, it's me, Bill."

"Rita, is that you?"

Kat didn't look away from his bewildered, gaze. She hoped she hadn't lost him. She also wondered if he'd just had a stroke. It had been a strenuous and stressful couple of weeks for him. He was exhausted, both mentally and physically. He looked ill.

"Bill? You okay?" she asked again, but he didn't respond. "Bill? Wake up."

The mournful moan of a foghorn from a lone fishing boat brought him back to reality. He closed his eyes and held them shut for a few moments. After opening them, he took several deep but painful breaths. He hands shook. He desperately wished the vision of Rita to be true. He glanced to the choppy Pacific Ocean. The lights from the boat flickered well off in the distance as it bobbed on the heavy sea like a helpless toy. He looked back to Kat. They stared at each other as he tried to regain his senses.

"Bill. It's me, Kat. Are you okay?"

"I need a drink."

"You need something to eat."

"We passed a small pub a mile or so back."

"But the folks at the bank. And this truck. We should keep moving."

"I need a drink."

"Are you sure?"

"Yeah, I'm sure," he said. "You don't have to go with me. You can take the truck. . ."

"I'm going wherever you're going."

Bill wheeled the truck around and drove south a few minutes before driving into the crowded parking lot of a local pub named The Driftwood. Kat was worried he was about to turn himself in. He was oddly quiet and becoming more distant with each passing minute. He took the last available parking spot and pulled the hood of the sweatshirt he was wearing tightly over his bald, sunburnt head.

"You sure about this?" she asked. "It looks busy."

"It's better this way," he mumbled.

Not looking at her, he hopped out and hurried towards the entrance of the pub, leaving the keys in the ignition with the truck running. She shut off the engine and grabbed the keys before hustling after him. He no longer limped but strutted across the parking lot like a man on a mission. She had trouble keeping up. He seemed strangely taller and bigger to her. He walked with more presence and purpose. She caught up with him at the front door.

"Bill?" she called, reaching out the keys. "You left the truck running."

"Hold onto them for me," he said, stepping into the pub like he owned the place.

It was a festive little bar, obviously popular with the sunbaked local fishermen who filled the place. Fishing rods and bait buckets overflowing with seawater were leaned against the wall near the entrance. The place had an unusual but not

286

unpleasant odor that mixed the sweet, nutty, and exotic scent of coconut sunscreen with the hunger-inducing smell of French fries and frying fish. All the seats at the tables and most of the stools at the bar were occupied. The jukebox played classic songs from the 1970s that the regulars were singing along with.

Bill walked directly to two open stools at the bar like he'd been there before. He hesitated before taking a seat, allowing Kat to choose the one she wanted. The bartender, a young busty blonde, cheerfully greeted them.

"What can I get you?" she asked as Bill scanned the place, noticing the many tall red and white cans of the same beer scattered on the bar and tabletops.

"We'll take two of those," he pointed.

"Rainier tallboys?"

"Yes, two cans of Rainier and two shots of your finest tequila."

"Wonderful," she said with a grin, before walking away.

"Wait," Bill called, throwing two hundred-dollar bills on the bar. "And I'd like to buy a round for everyone here."

"Yessir!" Her grin grew as she happily rang a large bell that hung behind the bar and shouting over the loud chatter and jukebox music to a rousing cheer, "Y'all got one comin'!"

"Don't tell 'em it's from me," Bill whispered as she placed the icy cans of Rainier and shots of tequila in front of them.

Bill stared out the sliding glass doors behind the bar that opened to a deck that extended out to the beach. A warm breeze lightly blew in their faces. Kat sipped at her tall can of beer as Bill watched the calm ocean waves, lost in thought. The petrified remains of a long wooden pier jutted out from a mound of wet sand not far from the back of the pub. A few determined fishermen fished the surf that followed the outgoing tide. Kat pushed Bill's can of beer next to his hand.

"You okay?"

"I'm tired of running," he said, not looking at her. "I want everything to slow down. I need to catch my breath."

"You haven't been yourself this morning."

"I need to call Rita. I miss her."

"Call her, please."

"And I've never needed a beer more than I do right now."

She reached for his cold 16-ounce can of Rainier and held it up to him. He took it with a smile and pressed it first against his cheek, then rested it on his swollen nose.

"It's Mother's Day this Sunday," he said, holding the cold can against his nose. "It'll be the first time I'm not there."

She studied him, concerned that she indeed was losing him. She reached for the tequila shot and motioned to his. They raised the shots, before throwing them back. Bill grimaced and quickly reached for the can of beer, nearly draining half of it in one long, satisfying chug. He wiped away the beer that dripped from his chin and smiled, before putting the can back to his lips and finishing the rest of it in one last drink. He set the can back on the bar and crushed it in his right hand.

"I wish we could stay here all day." His eyes were glassy after the shot and sixteen ounces of beer. "I feel like getting drunk."

Before Kat could respond, the bartender returned, holding menus, and asked, "Lunch?"

"Yes!" Kat said immediately.

"No!" Bill responded at the same time.

With a puzzled look, the bartender glanced to Bill, then to Kat.

"We'll take a basket of fries," she said.

"Great! I'll put that in for you."

Before the bartender could walk away, Bill held up his crushed can.

"Let's stay," Kat said as the bartender slid Bill another Rainier tallboy. "Let's get drunk. I'll do whatever you want."

"I think back to where I started and where I'm at now," he said, cracking open the beer. "I never got to enjoy any of this. Never appreciated where we've been or what we saw."

"You did steal a million dollars, Bill. There is that."

"I know, but. . ." he said, pausing to take a big swig of beer from the can. "I should've gone on this trip before taking the money."

"You had to have some favorite places along the way."

"New Orleans. The first day I got there. The seafood boil," he said, before pausing. "And when I met you."

"Where else?"

"The night in Norman with Leo. We got so shitfaced. I hadn't had that much fun in decades."

"Oh, poor Leo. I will always miss him. That kid was the best."

"If I never would've taken this stupid trip, he'd still be alive."

"You can't think like that. You don't know that."

"I should've listened to you and gotten him to a hospital, but I didn't want you to go to jail. I didn't care about myself, and I didn't think of Leo. I'm such an asshole."

"What a good soul and sweet spirit."

"But my favorite place may have been the mountains of Wyoming. I naively thought that we'd won. We were free. But I quickly realized we'd never be free until I turned myself in."

"Oh, Bill."

"I should've done it before Leo got shot. I killed him. I will never forgive myself for that. I can't stop thinking about him."

"Ssshh, Bill. We couldn't have known what would happened."

The bartender appeared with the basket of fries as the jukebox was silent for the moment. Bill grabbed his beer and wandered over to it. Kat picked at the fries and ordered a couple more shots of tequila. She thought she'd be hungrier but could only eat about a quarter of the basket. Her stomach didn't feel right. Bill returned to his stool after selecting a few songs. The bartender approached holding the two shots and one for herself. Before they knocked back the shots, the Elton John song "Rocket Man" started to play on the jukebox.

"I played that," Bill said proudly, before they all swallowed the tequila.

"Y'all from around here?" the bartender asked, cringing from the shot.

"No," Bill said, shaking his head.

"Where you from?"

Bill paused. "We're not from anywhere." He glanced at Kat. "We're not from anywhere anymore."

"Who are you then?" the bartender asked with a sneaky, inquisitive grin as if she suddenly recognized him. "You sure you haven't been here before? You look awfully familiar."

He studied the bartender with a lost look but didn't answer. After a moment, he placed several hundred-dollar bills on the bar, "Buy another round for everyone here and keep the rest for yourself."

The bartender's grin again widened as she walked to the bell behind the bar and enthusiastically rang it several times, and then turned up the volume on the jukebox. A very loud and vocal cheer followed. Bill grabbed Kat's hand.

"We have to go," he said, pulling her off the stool.

"I think she knows who you are."

"Not yet," he said, dragging her to the door, "but she'll figure it out."

Before leaving, they hesitated at the front door. Kat glanced up to Bill. He stared back until she smiled. The final verse of "Rocket Man" blared from the bar's speakers: "I'm a rocket man, burning out his fuse up here alone, and I think it's gonna be a long, long time. . ."

"Thanks for coming all this way with me," he said to her over the loud music as the bar patrons sang along. "I don't have much now. Your shining smile is all I have left."

"I love you, Bill," she said, squeezing his hand tightly.

"No, no. Not the way I love you."

"Maybe," she said with a chuckle. "Maybe not. I don't know. I will surely miss you."

She tightly squeezed his hand again as they pushed open the door together. They dashed to the truck in a full-out sprint, giggling the entire way. She handed him the keys as he quickly fired it up and started to pull out of the lot. They scanned each side of the road, looking for the authorities. The road was empty in both directions. As he pulled the truck onto Highway 103 and headed north, they could still hear the regulars loudly singing along to the final chorus of "Rocket Man,": ". . . it's gonna be a long, long time. . ."

Chapter 9
Washington

Day 16. Friday, May 12. 12:21 PM

With a nearly flat tire, a pair of dead headlights, and a busted muffler, the old truck was parked in the corner of an empty parking lot at the Seattle-Tacoma International Airport. A light sprinkle of rain fell from the gray sky. Bill stared out the truck's cracked windshield. Kat leaned against him. He wouldn't look at her. She fumbled and played with a stack of hundred-dollar bills he had given her.

"I never jumped out of airplanes or danced on any bar," he said. "I never swam with sharks. But I did this trip with the entire world watching the whole way. And we never got caught. Hell Kat, we could sit here for days, and they still would never find us."

"You were my outlaw."

"And you were my co-pilot. I couldn't have made it this far without you."

"What are you going to do?"

"I don't know yet, but it's the first time in my life that I'm not worried about what's next."

An awkward silence followed as he finally glanced over.

"I love you, Kat."

"I love you too, Bill."

"No, not the way I lo—"

"I know," she interrupted. "I know."

He looked away as she smiled and wiped away her tears.

"Bill, look at me."

He hesitated before turning. They stared a moment before

she leaned more of her body into him. Their lips touched. He quickly pulled away. She smiled.

"You better go," he said. "And do what I told you. Buy a red-eye flight to Florida tonight with cash."

"They're not going to let me get on a plane. We have to be on the top of every no fly-list at every airport."

"Don't book the flight until tonight. I'll take care of it."

"But I want to stay with you."

"You can't. My time has run out." He reached for a slip of paper, jotted an address on it, and handed it her. "I don't have anything to give you but my old Buick in Florida."

"You gave me the time of my life. I don't need anything else."

"It's parked in a garage in Jacksonville. There are some personal things in the trunk. Take whatever you want. I won't need them where I'm going."

They stared until she eventually slipped the piece of paper into her pocket.

"See you around, Wild Bill," she said, opening the truck door. "I will always be thinking of you."

He nodded and smiled as she hopped out of the truck.

"You saved me, Kat. This trip saved me."

"I can't leave you, Bill."

"Go. Please."

"But I want to stay."

"I'll be all right," he said, as an airport terminal shuttle bus suddenly pulled up. "There's your ride." They studied each other. "Go. It's okay."

She again wiped at the tears in her eyes and slightly nodded without much of an expression—then slammed the truck's door. Without luggage and only a handful of cash, she sprinted in the softly falling cold rain towards the bus. Tightly squeezing the steering wheel, Bill watched. Reaching the bus, she took one last look, pausing before getting on. He dropped his head and hung onto the steering wheel as if it anchored him to the inside of the truck, preventing him from chasing after her. He knew he had to let her go. He finally looked up. She was gone. The bus pulled away and disappeared through a tunnel near the airport terminal. He never felt more alone.

xxx

Bill stood in the parking lot of an isolated convenience store not far from the airport. He talked into perhaps one of the world's last public pay phones. The rain poured. He huddled against the brick wall at the building's front, trying to stay dry. He was spent and cold. His clothes were stained and frayed. He hadn't changed out of them in days. It had been just as long since he had bathed.

"Rita. It's me. I can't talk long."

"Bill! Oh my God! Is that really you? Are you okay?"

"I'm okay."

"Please come home!"

"I can't come home. You know that."

"I miss you."

"I miss you, too."

"I'm so sorry. If I did any—"

"No, no, this had nothing to do with you." He paused, "Or the kids. I waited too long. I should've taken you on this trip with me many years ago. And then done it again and again."

"Bill, come home. I need you. The kids need you. We all need you."

"Where did the time go, Rita? When did we drift apart? I let us get stale. I didn't do anything about it. I focused on the wrong things. It's all my fault. Please forgive me."

"Oh no, Bill. It was me, too."

"The thing with the bank, this trip, and giving the money away—none of it was planned. It just happened. I guess I wanted to do something more than who I was and to be bigger than what I had become. I don't know what I was thinking. Maybe I just got tired of being of good."

"Please come home! We'll get the best lawyer!"

"I never meant to hurt you or the kids."

"You can't go to prison!"

294

"I just called to tell you that I love you. I will always love you."

"Bill?"

"And Happy Mother's Day. I know it's a couple days early."

"Bill?"

"Remember those Mother's Day breakfasts we used to make? Remember?"

"Please come home," she pleaded, starting to cry. "*Please.*"

"Give my love to the kids. I have to go."

"Bill, please! Don't hang up! Bill!"

"I tried my best, Rita."

"No, Bill, please!"

Still leaning against the red brick wall of the convenience store, Bill gently hung up the phone. He turned to the rain, watching the bustling parking lot. He still found it hard to take full breaths because of his likely broken ribs. The passing storm raged on. Pickups and assorted delivery trucks hustled in and out of the lot. The heavy sheets of rain provided him perfect cover. Most everyone who entered and exited the store hid their faces in jackets and hoods or under umbrellas. For the first time in what seemed like a lifetime, he felt at ease in an open public space. He reveled in his new-found sense of freedom. He lingered for a short time, enjoying the storm and pondering his next move. His choices were limited, and he was smart enough to know that his time as a free man was nearly over.

After ditching the truck, Bill caught a commuter bus that dropped him off in the middle of downtown Seattle. He hid himself on the bus ride, slumping low in the back seat and hiding his face behind a soggy newspaper. Still without a plan, Bill stood in front of a men's fine clothing store after getting off the bus. Grungy, he entered the store. One of the store salesmen turned to approach Bill but abruptly stopped and smirked with a shake of his head, upon noting Bill's ragged appearance. Bill slowly perused the store, walking the aisles and specifically checking out the suits. From what Bill could tell, the cheapest suit in the place was not less than a thousand dollars. A second salesmen noticed Bill and studied him a moment, before retreating to the back of the store without offering help. Eventually, Bill stopped and glanced around the store, searching for assistance. Both salesmen pretended to be busy: one dusted a shelf with a feather duster and the other rearranged a variety of suits on a discount rack. Bill finally approached the sales counter and started tapping a bell for service. A young cashier appeared.

"Yes, can I help you?"

"I need a suit," Bill said.

The two salesmen turned and watched from different areas of the store as the cashier studied Bill's natty appearance.

"These are top of the line, designer--"

"I know. I plan to pay with cash."

Bill reached into his pocket and pulled out a thick bundle of hundred-dollar bills. Before the cashier could respond, one of the salesmen stepped in front of Bill, handing the cashier the feather duster.

"I'll be happy to assist you, sir."

xxx

Not far from the clothing store, Bill found a swanky boutique hotel and reserved a suite on the top floor for the night. A perfectly pressed shimmering gray suit was carefully displayed on the bed. On the floor was a pair of black Versace derby shoes. A bottle of a top shelf bourbon rested on the nightstand. The ripped and soiled clothes Bill had been wearing were balled up in a corner. Bill was in the shower, singing the Rolling Stones' tune "100 Years Ago" at the top of his lungs. He sipped at a glass of bourbon he brought into the shower with him. His entire body was soaped up, from the top of his sunbaked bald head to his dirty feet as he tried to wash away the layers of filth and grime that had collected on him the past several days. Unable to drag his road-weary body from the hot water that rained on him, he continued to sip at the bourbon and remained in the shower for nearly an hour, filling the bathroom with a thick cloud of dense steam.

Once the bourbon was gone, Bill stepped out of the shower, wrapped his dripping body with a towel, and walked into the bedroom of the suite to refill the glass. He peered out the room's window high above the downtown streets of Seattle. It was a clear bright sky. The morning rain had passed on. He could clearly see the snowy peaks of Mt. Rainier to the south. To the west, the crystal blue waters of Puget Sound shimmered under the afternoon's golden sunshine. He hesitated at the window a moment and enjoyed the view, something he hadn't been able to do as much as he would've liked during his wild ride across the country.

With the fresh bourbon, he returned to the bathroom and lathered his face with shaving cream. He wiped at the fogged-over mirror and caught a glimpse of his distorted reflection. He leaned in closer to the dampened mirror, wiping at it as it continued to fog. He no longer recognized himself. His nose was swollen and badly cut. His eyes were slightly black. His face was leaner and tanned from too many days on the road. He looked younger. He glanced down to his mostly naked body. He'd lost more than twenty pounds over the course of the trip. The large bruise on his left side had yellowed. His hands and feet were blistered and scarred.

He sipped at the bourbon and stared at his reflection for many minutes. He finally set down the glass. A dollop of shaving cream remained on its rim. Reaching for a razor, he slowly and methodically shaved off the scraggly beard he'd grown during his time on the run. He continued to stare at himself. He was a new man but with few places to go and little hope for a future. But he didn't care. He was going out on his own terms.

xxx

Day 16. Friday, May 12. 5:11 PM

Wearing his immaculate new suit and looking fresh after a much-needed scrub and shave, Bill stepped out of the hotel

297

lobby with a new-found confidence in his stride. He no longer cared if he was recognized. In the back of his mind, he knew it would be his last day of freedom. With a growl as loud a lion's roar in his hungry belly, he entered a fine-dining seafood spot near the hotel that was highly recommended by the concierge. The place was packed with a happy-hour business crowd. The hostess at the entrance greeted Bill, who scanned the bar area and noticed a few empty seats. She smiled and nodded as he motioned to the bar.

Bill studied the many folks who'd gathered around the large circular bar — the pathetic smiles, the perfect hair, the expensive clothes, the insincerity and unoriginality of it all. He saw his former self in the faces of the strangers attached to the bar as if their beers and cocktails provided life support. The scene was all too familiar, having spent many lunches and dinners at swanky joints just like this one to entertain boorish and entitled bank investors and board members. He often wanted to shower after those meetings so as to cleanse the soul he'd sold off to his employer years before.

"That used to be me. You remind me of where I don't want to be," he said under his breath, knowing he was headed to prison, likely for a long time. "I wouldn't trade places with any of you, not even now."

The busy but attentive bartender nodded to Bill to let him know he'd be over to take his order in a moment. The television was tuned to a twenty-four-hour news channel. It was broadcasting "The Law Today." Of course, the topic was The Runaway Banker. A map of the United States showing the route Bill had taken was displayed on the screen along with a phone number and caption that read "FBI Agent Stack on the line, Seattle."

"There are eyewitness reports that the missing banker is in the Seattle metropolitan area," Ms. Stevens said from the studio. "We have FBI Agent Julius Stack, who is currently in Seattle on the line. . ."

As Bill watched, the bartender appeared and asked, "Dinner

298

or just a drink?"

"I'll take the Copper River salmon special and a double of your finest bourbon, neat."

"Excellent choices," the bartender said and turned to walk away.

"Hey, buddy," Bill called out, pointing to a random, unattended cell phone near a cash register behind the bar. "Can I use that phone there?"

The bartender studied Bill a moment.

"It'll be a very short call. I seem to have misplaced mine somewhere today."

The bartender reached for the phone and handed it to Bill. Before the bartender could walk away, Bill pointed to the television.

"And can you put on a ballgame or something? I don't care for that woman."

The bartender poured Bill a bourbon and changed the television channel. Bill took a small sip of his drink and studied the phone in front of him for several minutes. Finally, he grabbed the phone and dialed a number. He calmly and quietly talked into the phone for just a few seconds, covering the receiver and his mouth with his cupped hand. After turning off the phone, he drained the double bourbon in one large gulp.

"I'll take another," he called to the bartender, holding out his empty glass with a twenty-dollar bill underneath it as a tip. "Thanks for letting me use your phone."

Within minutes, a significant police and media presence began to build outside the restaurant. Surrounding streets were cordoned off by yellow police tape and barriers. Bystanders and curious onlookers were immediately herded across the street behind rows of arriving police sport utility vehicles and assault trucks. Numerous television vans and trucks sped to the scene. News reporters and camera crews were scrambling into place. Helicopters filled the sky. Bill focused on the drink in front of him, not allowing himself to look outside. The curious patrons in the crowded restaurant suddenly surveyed the inside of the place, concerned about what was unfolding around them. The chatter in the place quickly grew. Soon, all eyes were directed at Bill, who now sat alone at the bar. The servers and hostess looked first to the bartender and then a manager for direction. They both shrugged. The bartender turned to Bill.

"It can't be."

"It is," Bill said.

"What are you doing here?" the bartender asked.

"This is the end of the road. I went as far north and west as I could go."

The cell phone at the bar started to ring. The bartender glanced to Bill.

"That'll be for me," Bill said, before draining his second bourbon.

Several of the restaurant patrons got up from their tables and tried to leave. The manager stood in front of them and waved her arms. "Please! Please!" she implored them. "Stay seated until we get more direction! It'll be all right! Please!"

Other patrons began to enthusiastically cheer, realizing that the infamous runaway banker sat before them. A lady yelled out, "We love you, Bill!" Someone else hollered, "Don't stop now!" Soon the restaurant patrons began to chant together, "Bill! Bill! Bill!" Others tried to force their way out, but the manager wouldn't allow it, physically pushing them back.

"Please! Go back to your tables! Please! I don't want anyone getting hurt!"

Bill let the phone ring a few more times before answering. Agent Stack suddenly appeared outside the front glass door of the restaurant, holding a phone to his ear. Bill motioned to the bartender to fill his glass.

"No monkey business, Moreland," Stack said into the phone. "I got three sharpshooters here who have your head in their crosshairs."

Bill glanced out the window. Scores of heavily armed policemen had gathered outside. The restaurant's chef appeared behind the bar, holding Bill's dinner. He looked to Bill who nodded and directed the chef to put the plate of food in front of him.

"I want you to slowly and calmly raise your hands above your head and walk out of there," Stack directed. "And no one gets hurt."

The patrons at the restaurant continued to chant Bill's name in unison but much louder: "Bill! Bill! Bill!"

"No," Bill confidently replied into the phone. "I'm not coming out."

"What?"

"I'm not coming out until I finish my dinner. And. . ."

The crowd in the restaurant loudly cheered. The chants of Bill's name were almost deafening.

"And what, Moreland?"

"And I want you to promise me," Bill said, before pausing, "that you won't go after the girl. I'll plead guilty to everything. You'll be a hero."

Stack didn't initially respond.

"I can make this a real shitshow," Bill said. "There's more people on my side than yours. This could go sideways real fast. Don't go after the girl. She's flying from Seattle to Florida tonight. Make sure she gets on that flight with no issues. Got it?"

After another brief hesitation, Agent Stack nodded and said, "You have my word. I will leave the girl alone. I will contact the airport."

"Thank you."

"But I am coming in now, Moreland. And when I walk through that door, you better have both hands in the air."

Stack shut off the phone and stared at the door a moment, before glancing behind him to the crowd of police officers who covered his back. He then cautiously stepped towards the door. Unexpectedly, the hostess, who obviously was one of Bill's fans, slipped away from the wooden stand that she was partially hiding behind and locked the dead bolt on front door as Stack reached for it. The restaurant patrons wildly cheered as Stack violently pulled and rattled the locked door, trying to open it.

Watching from the bar, Bill shook his head in frustration and set down the fork he was using to enjoy his final dinner as a free man. He stood up from his stool and calmly walked to the front door. Stack immediately raised his arm and glanced back to the police force behind him as Bill approached. Several of the officers raised their rifles to the shoulders and aimed. The crowd in the restaurant cheered louder. But Bill stopped before he got to the door and turned to the crowd, motioning for them to quiet down.

"No, Bill!" a man yelled.

"Don't give up yet!" a woman called out.

With his arms at his side, Bill stood at the door and stared at Stack. Again glancing back to his men, Stack kept his arm raised over his head. Perspiring, Stack looked to Bill, then to the news reporters and cameramen filming the scene. His hand above his head started to shake. Stack again glanced to the officers and agents behind him, then to back Bill who slowly began to lift his arm. Stack's eyes widened, his hand and arm shaking more violently.

"You will not make a fool of me again, Moreland."

Bill unlocked the door and hesitated as he stared at Stack, before turning and returning to his seat at the bar. Stack briefly sighed, slowly dropping his arm. The officers cautiously lowered their rifles. After a short pause, Stack finally entered the restaurant. He was greeted by a loud round of boos and jeers. Bill calmly ate his dinner as Stack approached and took a seat next to him at the bar.

"What are you drinking, Stack?" Bill asked, not looking up from his food.

"It is time to go, Moreland."

Bill reached for his glass of bourbon and finished it, before pulling some cash from his pocket.

"How much do I owe you?" he asked the bartender.

302

"Nah, man, this is on us."

"Come on, how much do I owe you?"

"$105.75," the bartender answered after a brief pause to calculate the bill in his head.

"Some last meal," Stack said.

"The Copper River salmon are running this time of year. They're quite delicious. Have you ever had a Copper River salmon?"

Stack shook his head as Bill placed the last of his money on the bar—eight hundred-dollar bills. The bartender scooped up the money, looking surprised.

"Take your co-workers out for drinks later."

"Let's go, Moreland," Stack said, glancing to the all the police and media waiting outside.

"You know, Stack, these salmon travel hundreds of miles through the swiftest, most rugged river in the world to spawn. Don't you think it's amazing they remember from where they came from and when it's time to go home?"

They studied each other a moment, before Bill finally put his arms behind his back.

"I feel like going home."

Stack slapped a set of handcuffs over Bill's wrist to the groans and disappointment of those in the restaurant.

"You ain't going home, Moreland."

"You know," Bill said as Stack directed him to the door, "you never would've caught me."

"But here we are."

"You didn't stop me. The ocean did."

"They don't know that," Stack said, pointing to the crowd gathered outside.

"But I do. And you do, too."

Before they could leave, the restaurant patrons stood and applauded. As Bill stepped outside, the cheers echoed even louder as members of the media and thousands of bystanders had suddenly filled the downtown Seattle streets. With helicopters and planes buzzing overhead, Bill and Stack quickly and quietly, without incident, disappeared into an armored FBI van. It immediately sped away.

"Whatever happened to the Jeffries character?" Stack asked Bill from inside the armored van. "We have a warrant for his arrest. He is wanted for theft of a motel van and assault and battery of Ken Mercury."

"We dropped him off at the Oregon coast. He wanted to see the ocean."

"So, you don't know where is he's at?"

"Not now," Bill said with a straight face and a shake of his head. "And whatever happened with Mercury?"

"He is better. Doesn't remember a thing though."

xxx

Day 17. Saturday, May 13. 7:16 AM

A taxicab pulled into the lot next to a six-story parking garage in downtown Jacksonville, Florida. Kat got out of the cab and glanced up to the garage framed by a cloudless blue sky. It was a ridiculously hot and humid day. She studied the imposing parking structure a moment, before glancing at the piece of paper Bill had given her. The only information she had was the lot's address, a floor, and a parking space identification number. She slipped inside the building and found an elevator that took her to the fourth floor. The shaded garage was cool and drafty. Shortly, she stood before an unremarkable silver Buick sedan. She wiped at a layer of dust that had collected on the hood and blew more dust off the handle on the driver's side door.

Following Bill's instruction, she moved to the rear of the car and glanced in each direction to check if anyone else was around. Alone on the garage's fourth floor, she squatted behind the car and reached under the back bumper. As Bill had instructed, there she found the hidden key.

Before starting the car, she opened the trunk to see what Bill

304

had left. She pulled out a box of Cuban cigars, opened it, and smelled them, grinning—an obvious reminder of Bill. She put one of the cigars in her shirt pocket. She picked up the framed photograph of his family and studied it a minute, before smiling and setting it back into the trunk. She next found a Pittsburgh Pirates baseball hat and put it on her head backwards, like a catcher. Noticing a garment bag, she pulled it out and unzipped it. To her surprise, it was filled with hundreds of thousands of dollars. Bill never said anything about the extra money in the trunk of the car.

"Holy. . ." she whispered. "Wild Bill, what have you done?"

xxx

With the windows rolled down, Kat drove Bill's Buick among the swampy marshes on a quiet Louisiana backroad not far from Lake Pontchartrain. It was a muggy afternoon. The air was damp and heavy as storm clouds formed to the west. To pass the time on the long drive, she switched back and forth between different local AM radio stations. She still wore the Pirates ball cap on backwards and draped her right arm over the bag of money that had rested against her for the entire time since leaving Jacksonville. She had decided to go back to New Orleans. But she was undecided on what she would do once she got there. She was ready for a new start. Her trip with Bill had changed her life. She promised Bill and herself she would never settle again. She turned up the volume of the radio as a news story came on.

"In national news," the reporter announced over the air, "charitable donations across the United States are up nearly one hundred percent just in the last two weeks. Experts believe the increase in giving throughout the country has been inspired by the case of the runaway banker."

Kat grinned and tightened her hold on the garment bag of money. As the news story ended, she changed the station, searching for music. She quickly found a classic country music station. After a couple of songs, the Patsy Cline song, "Crazy," came on through the static of the station. Smiling and singing along with the song, she pulled the car off the roadway into a small residential area of trailers and ranch-style homes. Mailboxes lined one side of the neighborhood. She reached into the bag of money and slowed the car at the first mailbox.

The End

About the Author

Jim Antonini is an award-winning author from West Virginia. He has written two novels published by Pump Fake Press.

The first, BULLETS FOR SILVERWARE, is a gritty, murder-mystery thriller set in the backwoods of West Virginia. It was a finalist for the Appodlachia 2020 Best Appalachian Book of the Year. What others have said:

"...the characters were real... like I knew them personally... the prose itself was the real prize- gritty, sympathetic... READ THIS BOOK!" - Amazon review - 07/07/2020

"...chills, titillates, and above all entertains...the scenes roll out smoothly, and it is easy to imagine this story as film noir...has a Hitchcockian flavor..." - Independent Book Review - 07/28/2020

"...feels fast-paced, hard-boiled, and edgy..." - BookTrib - 05/05/2021

The second, LIKE FALLING FROM AN AIRPLANE, is a romantic, urban drama set on the downtown streets and back alleys of San Francisco. What others have said:

"...A fast-paced novel of family, betrayal, and undeniable attraction... If you love a bad boy, a shot of tequila, or a forbidden love story, you'll be more than pleased... ... a swirling storm of events in this quick literary fiction..." - Independent Book Review, April 8, 2022

"...vivid, detailed, nuanced scenes and dialogue... sympathetic treatment of the "down & out" as well as the "well-to-do"... a great story with a kind of wide-open ending... Highly recommend!" Amazon Review - 06/15/2022

"…Fast-paced… break-neck story telling centering around unstable dreamers… Set in a dreamy version of San Francisco… it's a chaotic and rollicking trip that is unsettling, and at the same time wildly satisfying… Full of bad decisions and good fun…" Amazon Review – 08/11/2022

Both books and other Pump Fake Press merchandise available at https://jimantonini.com

Printed in the USA
CPSIA information can be obtained
at www.ICGtesting.com
LVHW092321280124
770187LV00030B/328

9 798218 240554